Time is Relative for a Knight of Time

Written by

Brett Matthew Williams

Edited by Jessica Grogan & Kathryn Dennis

Copyright © 2012 Brett Matthew Williams

All rights reserved.

ISBN-10: 1470029456

EAN-13: 9781470029456

Library of Congress Control Number: 2012902451

CreateSpace, North Charleston, SC

To Gretchen Leigh

– You are my Sunshine

Time is Relative
for a Knight of Time

Table of Contents

Act I:

Act II:

Act III:

Warning

Ignorance is bliss – should you decide to read further you might learn something truly shocking.

All dates and events are true. The participants… maybe not.

Historian's Message — Part I

Keeper of Records

We are all of us unique, born with innate talents given to us through means beyond our control. To some, this is simply genetics, while others find comfort in putting their faith in a higher power. Regardless of your beliefs, the irrefutable fact remains that as human beings we are far more different than we are alike. The explanation for this lies slightly beyond our reach along with the answers to many of life's questions – just past reality, in something greater and more mysterious. Faith.

Faith is a tricky thing. It incites both the best and worst actions of mankind, and in our eternal quest to solve life's mysteries we often find ourselves looking inward, tapping our own faith and determination in order to persevere. This is the story of one family's faith in its ability to preserve not just itself…but mankind as a whole.

Specifically, it is a story about a boy; a boy who grows into a man who becomes something beyond legend.

This is the story of Father Time and the world he called home – Earth.

Allow me to introduce myself. I am the Historian, keeper of Earth's recorded history. I'm not merely some sort of strange hoarder; I keep only important things, like the tales recorded within these pages. I've kept them hidden away for many years, waiting for the right opportunity to tell the world the truth of humanity's journey into the light, waiting for the right opportunity to reveal mankind's true past, present, and future.

These accounts, like all historical records, have been compiled from personal logs, records, and authorized edits collected throughout Earth's adolescence. They reveal a story, a 'Tale of Time'; if you will.

What is the Tale of Time you ask? It is the story of human development from ditch-digging Neanderthal to modern man, the unabridged, absolute, and unequivocal truth of mankind's trials and tribulations on planet Earth.

Not all is as it seems...

A secret is known to a select few individuals on Earth, one that, if revealed, could rock the very core of human belief and give credence to those skeptical enough to believe in conspiracies.

The widely held belief that aliens are real and walk among us is a half-truth, for what we perceive to be 'aliens' from another planet are actually human beings like us... from another dimension. They are from a paradise that exists outside what we understand as time and space.

Outside of our world exists a land where time has no meaning, and the illusion that it represents is given the form of a stream of white water jettisoning into the never-ending tide of tomorrow. The gateways to this paradise lie all over Earth, and have existed there since the dawn of creation. This Promised Land has gone by many names, El Dorado, Atlantis...but for those who call it home, it is simply known as Eden.

To understand the reasoning of these 'aliens,' or as they prefer to be called 'Travelers of Light,' one need look no further than our own past. Human ingenuity has set a precedent for conceiving and implementing the greatest innovations ever seen by mortal eyes, from the wheel, to democracy, to the internet; mankind has bettered itself by recognizing what it needed to successfully accomplish its immediate goals. In learning from the past, we learn from our mistakes.

In order to truly know the past, we must first look within ourselves, for therein lies the joy, sorrow, anger, and imagination that has inspired the human condition.

Human beings are defined by 46 chromosomes that dictate the patterns of our DNA and make us who we are. The Travelers of Light, while human beings, possess two extra pairs of chromosomes; a grouping of which results in extra genes and extraordinary abilities that defy our common perception of reality. A dangerous prospect, given that they are not confined to Eden.

The Travelers of Light exist among their fellow man as individuals born with distinctly different traits. These traits can be as simple as being double jointed or especially beautiful, but for others it is a more complex and perilous gift — like speaking to the beasts of the field or hearing voices that claim to be the Almighty. Some, three or four throughout known history, have even been able to control the very fabric of time and space that gives context to our existence.

To think of time is to think of a river, flowing one way with a current that takes everything and everyone with it into a new horizon. While the future is not yet written, the past acts as the river's banks, buffering and guiding the flow of events onward. Time travel is only possible by tapping into this, diverting its momentum, and becoming one with the natural balance of the universe. Some fight it, some encourage it, yet they all accept it as the natural progression of things happening in their own time, free will aside.

Then there are those personal milestones in all of our lives; moments when the planets seem to align and your destiny is set before you with clear understanding, just waiting for you to walk down its now illuminated path. These moments of clarity are rare, but inevitable. Without them life would be a constant drive into the abyss without proper direction.

Some call these moments fate; others call them coincidence.

Today I have the great pleasure of informing you that these moments are neither happenstance, nor scripts to be followed. Life as we know it is a mixture of both. Now you might be asking yourself, how can this be? How can these seemingly opposite ideas co-exist and explain the great mysteries of the universe? The answer lies within each of us.

Human beings are said to exist in their Almighty Maker's image. This allows them to use their natural abilities to enrich their lives. Thumbs allowed us to advance past primitive dwellings, logic allowed us to survive the tribulations of nature, and our five senses gave us a better understanding of ourselves and our place in the universe.

These same senses are the key to unlocking our individual destinies. Because most humans are content in the knowledge that we possess only five senses, we no longer explore the possibility of further senses... further abilities.

When one displays these abilities in an otherwise normal setting on Earth, an elite group of Travelers of Light, The Knights of Time, are called in to safely extract the gifted individual from the time stream. In addition, the Knights also stand steadfast against those who might attempt to warp and manipulate the time stream for their own personal gain. The Knights serve all mankind, and are ready at a moment's notice to lay down their lives to protect the time stream from harm.

The Knights of Time are led by the empathic Marcus L. Turtle-dove – the sworn Protector of Eden. His valor is only matched by his wisdom, a trait displayed early in his career by drafting Scott Wright: the only known natural born time traveler in the last two millennia. Together with his fellow Knights, Scott uses his abilities to help his team travel through time to defend the helpless and preserve history at all costs.

But our story does not begin here. No. Just as with life, our story begins with the death of one star and the birth of another. With the end of Scott Wright's life begins a journey that will change mankind forever.

It is with great pleasure that I present to you the first part in the Tale of Time –

Time is Relative for a Knight of Time

Chapter 1:
The Face of Evil

August 24, 1812 - Washington D.C

The White House – 9:43PM EST

"If you don't leave now, you will die."

The statement was devoid of compassion or consideration for its target, for at that moment the speaker was addressing an audience he was totally unaccustomed to. Few indeed dared to speak so bluntly to Dolley Madison, the First Lady of the United States of America, much less a common enlisted man.

Dolley Madison was a confident and headstrong woman who had been acting as caretaker of 1600 Pennsylvania Avenue for over a decade. Her tireless efforts to preserve the grounds and its most precious treasures had taken her to the ends of the Earth in pursuit of the finest extravagances, all in the name of keeping up appearances for her husband and leader of the States United, James.

A woman of conviction, patriotism, and tireless dedication to her home, Dolley wished above all else that her fellow countrymen would follow her example and devote their lives to the service of their shared nation. Living, loving, and sacrificing, all in the name of her homeland was the price she and many of her friends had paid to ensure the prosperity of the American people.

Before her husband, James Madison, had accepted the great honor and responsibility that came with the title of president, that burden had fallen upon the capable shoulders of the Madison's good family friend, Thomas Jefferson. As Jefferson was a widower, James had lent his wife to the charitable cause of maintaining a feminine presence around the nation's highest office. Though Dolley's husband had lent his wife somewhat begrudgingly, his generosity had met with great reward, as James took over the office of the Presidency some years later.

Now everyone had left, save for her and her African handmaiden, Hannah, who had been with Mrs. Madison since the girl was no more than five years old. A maternal bond had been created, overcoming the traditional roles and stereotypes of the time, and Dolley had very much come to think of the girl as one of her own children.

The slaves had been the first to flee, citing a cold chill and the presence of impending death in the air. It was not long after that that the regiment of guards her husband had left behind to protect her had followed suit. They had abandoned their posts when their country, and First Lady, needed them most. Soon, all that had been left was a single conscripted man whose parting words had run down Dolley's spine like ice, leaving her speechless as he too made his escape.

A sad, hollow feeling sat in the pit of Dolley's stomach as she took stock of all she was about to lose to the British, from the fine china she had collected on holiday in France, to the large, professionally painted portrait of George Washington, commissioned the day he had taken office as the first President of the United States. Stepping forward, she used all her strength to pry the portrait off of the wall, placing it under her arm and turning back to Hannah.

A sudden volley of cannon fire poured through the dining room windows that filled the space between Dolley and Hannah, knocking both of the women off of their feet. Though neither was hurt, the shock of finding themselves in the middle of a combat zone was enough to finally convince the First Lady to abandon the residence.

"Take my hand, quickly!" Hannah shouted to Dolley, reaching for her. The frightened First Lady clung desperately to the lifeline the girl offered, and the two of them fled the house.

Fire quickly engulfed the limestone building that locals had come to call the White House, forcing the frantic women out the large front doors and into the wide open marshland beyond the carefully manicured grounds. The night air hit Dolley's skin with a damp unevenness that made every hair on the back of her neck stand on end. Looking over to Hannah, she saw her own terrified expression mirrored on her handmaiden's face. While she watched, Hannah's terror surpassed even her own, as the girl gazed out into the darkness towards the tree line. There, in the light of the blazing White House, stood a man so still the trees themselves surpassed him for movement.

The dark figure walked towards them, seemingly impervious to the chaos that surrounded the nation's capital, the shadows and light from the inferno behind them dancing across him. As he neared, they saw that he was an older man with bits of silver streaking through the black mass of hair sitting atop his slim yet polished frame. He was dressed in a dark crimson sweater vest over a pressed long-sleeved button down shirt, and what looked to be crisp and freshly tailored pantaloons.

"Good evening, Lady Madison," said the man in the sweater vest, pausing for a moment to bow to her before continuing in their direction. His face was expressionless, eyes mimicking the darkness of the night around him.

"Wh-who calls?" Mrs. Madison asked, her throat dry as a bone. Without realizing it, her left hand had begun fidgeting nervously behind her- a bad habit she had managed to hold on to since she was a child and a quiet insult to years of etiquette training.

The man was not especially scary looking, especially in his elegant dressings. Still, there was an aura to him that spoke to the survival instincts within the two women, evoking impressions of jackals — sharp teeth, claws, and minds.

Despite her terror, Dolley was unexpectedly struck with the comical image of the tugging winds sweeping his thin frame off and away into the night. Of course, her capacity for rational thought was not what it usually was at that moment, evidenced by the fact that Hannah had been the one to insist that they flee the blaze now consuming her home.

"Allow me to introduce myself" the man said, pulling Dolley from her reverie and now standing within twenty feet of them. "My name is Edward Vilthe. I am an associate of your husband."

Fear and mistrust clutched at Dolley Madison's heart as she listened to the man's unpleasant voice. Desperately she searched his eyes, looking for a soul, some flicker of humanity she could relate to. Instead she found only darkness and despair. Surely just a trick of the light, she thought, stunned. She struggled to compose herself, and unconsciously her fidgeting hand found Hannah's, lending her the strength to speak once more.

"What business have you here?" Dolley demanded, her grip on Hannah's hand becoming tighter each moment. "Can you not see that there is a war going on, sir?"

"My dear lady, I need but a moment of your time," the man said, his face splitting into a hideous grin. "Just a moment of your time, and, at the risk of sounding tediously cliché, your souls!"

Dolley looked on in horror as his eyes rolled back into his head, going from black to the brightest yellow. Tilting his head slightly, he raised his hand toward them. Without warning a bolt of lightning leapt from the madman's palm, straight toward the spot where the two terrified women were standing. With a swift jerk, Hannah grabbed her mistress' arm, knocking them both sideways and narrowly out of harm's way.

Laughter filled the air as another bolt of blue lightning shot over their heads, hitting the limestone foundation of the giant house, leaving a large black stain.[1] Scrambling to their feet, Dolley and Hannah turned and ran. Heading into the surrounding forest, neither woman ever let go of the other's hand.

"Run if you like!" Vilthe shouted maniacally after the two women.

As they fled, there was no doubt in their minds that they were still running for their lives. Only the number of threats had changed.

Looking down upon fledgling DC, one could have seen the British troops gathered in large groups near the harbor. With their ships resting brazenly in the American docks and their commanding officers ordering them to march on, the British regulars focused intently on reclaiming the helpless American capitol for His Majesty. Their orders were simple enough; invade from the East at the Chesapeake and burn everything to the ground, merciless and efficient. Even after crossing the marshlands and pillaging the villages dotting the countryside between the bay and the patriot's

---

1   The stain remains, at 1600 Pennsylvania Avenue, two hundred years later.

capitol, the redcoats were untouched by fatigue, so inspired were they to finish the job their grandfathers had started decades before.

Less than half a mile away, in a field speckled with tall grass and vegetable patches, Dolley thought back to her childhood. She had been Dolley Payne, little girl extraordinaire, a nickname her many misadventures around the school yard on those sunny afternoons had earned her. But those days were gone now – replaced with a different kind of running.

This moment of self-pity cost her footing on the uneven terrain, causing an embarrassing fall to the wet ground below. Luckily, Hannah was there to encourage her.

"Come on, Miss," Hannah said, staring back behind them into the darkness, now barely visible by the glow of the burning capital. "We got to keep on movin'."

Spirits flagging, Dolley suddenly spied lights in the distance. Small, bright white orbs seemed to be hovering at eye level just over a hedge nearly a quarter of a mile away. Dolley smiled as she took the lead, pulling Hannah towards what she dearly hoped was safety.

The sky weighed dark and unforgiving, its folds and creases of steely cover resting comfortably on the shoulders of those who knew the secrets of bending the night to their will. The sorrow that blanketed the swampland known as Washington D.C. called out to its victims in a high-pitched howl that reverberated through the hearts and minds under her watch. It was a sound that touched places where voices were never meant to reach.

A natural energy foretold the coming storm. An overcast sky gave way to two bolts of lightning that plummeted through the Washington skyline and streaked over the swamplands like shooting stars. Upon a nearly two-hundred-foot-tall overlook that sat behind a tall, ivy-choked limestone curve in the rock, two figures landed unnoticed - one man, one woman. The rock curve stood as a barrier between the overhang and the steep drop off overlooking the presidential residence, sheltering those behind it in a veil of secrecy. A few drops of rain fell from the clouds looming high above the city, traveling the immeasurable distance between the heavens and the Earth in mere moments to land sporadically on the shoulders of a man who already felt as if he was carrying the world upon his shoulders.

This Earth felt no less cruel than any other to him as he took stock of his surroundings. Winds swept across his long, chiseled face, forcing him to squint beneath his worn, wispy brown hair. He wore black from head to toe -- a long sleeved, button down shirt disappeared into pants as dark as the night that pressed in around him. Attached to his belt was a long, Bowie-style hunting knife that had been given to him by his father a lifetime ago, a simple weapon for a complicated man. A black leather jacket was the one variation to his uniform that he refused to part with, half because it had been his late wife's favorite, and half because he honestly thought it made him look cool. Though he appeared disheveled and unkempt, he carried an air of masculine elegance, not unlike the gladiators of ancient Rome. His name was Scott Wright, and he was senior member of the Knights of Time.

A stoic man, Scott had been a member of the team for two decades, training diligently under the renowned Marcus L. Turtledove. A daring sort, Scott thought nothing of risking everything, even his life, on a single chance to exact revenge and end a long standing rivalry. His piercing gray eyes looked up at the sky, searching for something unspoken, something that could only be granted from the heavens themselves. Walking over toward the ledge that overlooked the White House, he saw no sign of the fire he knew was sure to come.

What he did see, however, was an odd, white bolt of lightning that extended well beyond its normal life span. Before his eyes the aberrant streak darted sideways and grew exponentially before bending onto itself and forming a wide, swirling, white opening. It lasted only seconds before reversing its cycle, and disappearing completely, replaced by a massive rumble of thunder that rocked the entire city in its wake.

Though the act of nature would appear random to the untrained eye, any individual equipped with the knowledge of Eden and the Travelers of Light would easily identify the source as the brunette teen standing upon the hillside next to Scott. The young woman to his right was nothing short of a picture of grace and perfection. Her long flowing brunette hair rested gently on her strong yet delicate shoulders. She wore the same black team uniform as her companion, with her boots coming up to her knees over pants Scott could swear were a size too small. She personified everything he wanted to keep away from his son.

Scott looked at her out of the corner of his eye. Sephanie reminded him so much of his late wife, Taylor. Her silhouette glowed in the moonlight and made her instantly identifiable, even through the alcoholic haze that rocked his mind to momentary serenity. Scott had known her since she was only nine years old, and he held a special place for her in his heart. The poor girl had been an orphan he had found in the basement of an old abandoned barn. She was the treasure he had found that day – this girl who became a woman before his very eyes. They had been working together now for years, forming a sort of father-daughter relationship instead of mentor/mentee. Watching her from the shadows, the Earth's foremost time traveler stood in a quiet awe.

Moments ticked away from Scott as he sat locked in his reverie, the sounds of the second hand mocking his existence with every beat. Sweat formed a band around his hairline as he took another swig from his flask and slid it effortlessly back into his coat pocket.

Time travelers like Scott were extremely rare. Because of this, he never had too much in the way of formal education beyond the basic requirements at The Academy of Light where he had learned how to hone and control his abilities. He recalled the months he spent studying under his tutor, a cognitive time traveler[2] by the name of Captain Bradford Nareau. A rough, older man, Captain Nareau never shied away from beating a point into his students, an approach Scott had refused to implement with his pupil, Sephanie.

Sephanie stood silently at Scott's side, both of her feet rooted to the ground, her back straight as an arrow, her mind focused on her task. She looked like any normal teenage girl lost in thought, provided the phrase "normal teenage girl lost in thought" could be applied to anyone with glowing white eyes.

"Soon as old lady Madison gets here we ride, got it, Natch'?" Scott said to Sephanie, careful to keep his hands from wandering into his pockets. Even in her current state this small gesture did not go unnoticed by the girl. Scott watched her eyes move as he spoke to her. A small cascade of white rippled through Sephanie's eyes once, twice, three times; each sweep removing more and more of the corneas that opened a gateway into her mortal soul. She was more than that now, more than flesh and blood, more than any of the soldiers consumed by their battle plans below could ever have guessed. She was what her team name had implied; she was Mother Nature incarnate.

"I know what you're thinking" Sephanie said, with only the barest movement of her lips. She rose above him now as she floated in perfect suspended animation nearly two feet off the ground. "Alcohol isn't going to help. If anything it just makes things worse. You know that."

"I...I don't know what you're talking about" Scott mumbled, now too frazzled to resist the instinct to stuff his left hand into his pocket to nervously touch the smooth, cold surface of his flask.

---

2   Cognitive time traveler – similar to astral projection; one who is able to mentally project themselves to certain time periods throughout the time stream; does not physically time travel.

Crash

Their awkward moment was interrupted by the sounds of trumpet song, cannon fire, and the lightning Sephanie had summoned only moments before.

Peering over the ledge of the overhang, Scott saw two figures emerge from the White House, now fully engulfed in flames. As he watched, a third person stalked out from the shadows in front of them and unleashed a blinding bolt of blue electricity, narrowly missing the two panicked figures. Scott's heart skipped a beat; it was him. After two years of searching, he had found him, and Scott would finally have his revenge.

"You're up kiddo!" Scott shouted back to Sephanie, his voice finding nothing but thin air. She was gone, off to coax Mother Nature into action. Scott glanced at his watch. It was ten minutes till ten, and history was running right on schedule.

With his privacy momentarily secured, the weary widower walked briskly to a nearby tree, and opened the dark green sack tucked away beside it. Retrieving the M16 rifle he had brought for the occasion, Scott hesitated for a moment. This weapon broke every rule in the book. Then again, so did murder.

Crash

Scott reached his flask again, this time draining it of its remaining contents. Staring down the empty canister, Scott returned it to his coat pocket and prepared to intercept the three figures running towards him. A quick glance at his surroundings confirmed that his traps were ready, should he need them. All that was left to do was wait.

Crash

Their invasion orders given, droves of British regulars flooded the square at the heart of the young city of Washington. Beneath their boots, the grounds and courtyards were littered with papers and pamphlets condemning the arrival of foreign troops on American shores. With a vengeful spirit, many of the soldiers began pillaging and setting fire to the few businesses and homes in the surrounding area, taking what they could and destroying the rest.

The sounds of British war drums echoing in his ears, Scott watched the madness unfolding below him. Without thinking, he again brought the flask to his lips, expecting another sweet, momentary escape from reality. When none came he remembered that it was empty, drained.

"Useless piece!" Scott cursed, knowing full well that it was his own fault for indulging too much early on. Turning it over in his sweaty palm, Scott eyed it with disdain. It was an odd trinket, given to him by an old friend what felt like lifetimes ago. He slid it, not into his right front pocket like before, but his left, pulling out a photograph in its stead.

It was a faded portrait of a teenage boy, around sixteen years old. He had Scott's big brown eyes and his mother's unruly blonde hair. It was a picture of his son, Rolland- a child that no one, not Sephanie, nor his commanding officer Marcus L. Turtledove, knew existed.

While both Taylor and Scott believed unfailingly in the knightly creed and swore allegiance to Eden, they had each yearned to raise a family away from the extraordinary influences that were so much a part of life there. It was for these reasons that they chose to give birth to and raise their son in the present time stream on Earth, their belief being that if Rolland had no knowledge of Eden he would not be subject to any of the limitations imposed by his homeland or any of the bureaucracy that came with being a traveler of light until he was of an age to decide for himself. After Taylor's murder two months ago, however, Scott had done little else but plot against and pursue his wife's killer. His goal consumed him, forcing every other concern out of his conscious thoughts. Small things like taking care of himself, his family, or even contacting his son faded under the white-hot blaze of his rage. With the silencing of one heartbeat Scott had become a tangled mess of revenge and regret, crying out for an outlet for his frustrations. His near madness and his time traveling abilities made for a deadly combination, and just the one he felt he would need to bring Vilthe, his wife's murderer, to justice.

Centuries of worry and strife weighed heavily upon his forty-five-year-old frame. Perhaps if he had not been otherwise preoccupied by his own thoughts and distracted from his duties, he would have heard the woman's cries for help echoing through the forest. Instead, his self-pity gripped him like all vices do, tighter and tighter with each passing moment.

Hear them he eventually did, softly at first and then more clearly as he left the safety of the overhang and approached the outlying part of the woods. The trees grew tall, weaving their branches into one another and blocking out what little light the moon could have provided. The voices certainly seemed female, but Scott refused to rule out some sort of trick. He had seen enough in his day to suspect even the most innocent creatures.

Unsheathing the hunting knife that hung from his belt, Scott walked toward the forest entrance with silent apprehension, his drunken mind unable to recall who was scheduled to arrive first, Madison or Vilthe. Preferring to be safe, rather than sorry, and with a total disregard for any fear a nearly nine-inch-long, three-inch-wide curved piece of steel could instill in an otherwise defenseless person, he positioned himself closer to the edge of the woods.

Luckily, Scott saw Hannah first, followed closely by Dolley, an unreadable reaction washing over her as she saw Scott standing before them, knife in hand.

"Who goes there?" Dolley asked, swinging her lantern wildly into the unyielding dark.

"A friend, my lady," came the response, accompanied by a cough. Scott lowered his knife and holstered it at his side before stepping forward into the light from their lamp. "But one can never be too careful, eh?"

Dolley and Hannah both squinted as he came into view. With his calming and charismatic demeanor, Scott seemed to personify the assistance the two women most desired.

"You have to help us, please," Dolley pleaded, swinging around again to verify they were not being followed.

"Bad man behind us. He shot lightning from his hands," Hannah explained, genuine terror filling her face and causing her eyes to water.

Realizing at once that the girl must be referring to Vilthe, Scott walked past them, preparing to retrace their path.

"Well hot damn, right on schedule," Scott murmured drunkenly.

"What?" Dolley asked, holding up her lantern a little higher to examine Scott's face carefully.

"Never mind. Here's what I want you to do -- run as fast as you can that way until you come to an older guy. He will remind you of your granddad, real nice fella'. He'll protect you until your husband comes. Got it?" Scott said, pointing southeast.

Though neither of the women was exactly sure what he was talking about, they both nodded their heads and began running in the direction Scott had indicated.

"Thank you!" Dolley shouted back at him as Scott reached for his flask one last time, remembering it was empty as soon as he touched it.

Frustrated, Scott took the flask out of his pocket and threw it to the ground, along with the remaining contents of his pockets --

his wallet, a box of matches, and the single photograph of his son. He then unsheathed the hunting knife at his side and planted his feet, standing ready against the forest.

For a few minutes, everything else faded away, leaving Scott alone with the darkness. It was a nice metaphor for his life he thought, impatiently wishing to begin the endgame and get past the pain in his chest that was going on without his wife. He had no delusions of grandeur in winning against Vilthe. This was most likely a suicide mission, even if he succeeded. He would risk it all for this one shot, one try at revenge. The wait was not long.

Some small sound pulled Scott from his reverie. There in the shadows stood a deceptively unimpressive five feet, five inches of evil, a man known without exaggeration as a reaper of souls and bringer of chaos. Though Vilthe saw Scott, he paid him little attention until they were within a few feet of one another.

"My stars… it's a genuine oddity," Vilthe said, smiling kindly, referring to Scott by his ability only.

"Vilthe," Scott said, gripping the handle of his knife a little tighter.

Scott had dreamt of this moment all of his adult life, but never more so than in the past two months, ever since the day that Vilthe had taken his bride, his wife, the mother of his child out of this world and changed his life forever. Scott had sworn he would make the madman pay.

At the base of the overlook stood the doe-eyed teenager who controlled the elements of nature, Sephanie Kelly.

Both hands raised to the sky, Sephanie closed her eyes and breathed deeply for a long moment, careful to concentrate on exactly what it was she wanted the atmosphere to do down to the very finest detail. Like a maestro conducting a symphony, her hands moved with a rehearsed ease and precision as they danced through the night air, each flick of the wrist winding itself further and further into the gravity surrounding it.

While Sephanie stood rooted to the spot, her surroundings began to take on a very different tone. The line of advancing British regulars was halted by winds strong enough to stop the dragging of their cannons and encourage the spooking of their horses. Then it whirled and spiraled in a circular motion, creating a cone that tied the river to the clouds above, spawning a massive tornado the likes of which the swamplands of Washington DC had never seen before and would never see again.

With a counter clockwise flick of her wrist, Sephanie sent the twister across the Potomac, collecting more water to fuel the cyclone's rage before directing it due west, straight for the White House. Along with it came a raging thunderstorm, blowing stinging rains directly at the invading British forces, halting any advancement by the brave souls still attempting to fight on against Nature's might.

Overhead, birds panicked in mid-flight, dodging the elements and taking shelter wherever possible. Men on the ground acted much the same way, many of them jumping at the sound of thunder and fleeing at the sight of the monstrous tornado. Officers and enlisted men alike scurried and scattered like rats abandoning a ship.

Within a matter of minutes the entire city of Washington had been drenched by Sephanie's wrath, and the British momentum had been effectively reversed, bringing their invasion to a grinding halt. Their retreat and return to their ships was a gratifying sight, no doubt, and one that cost not a single life.

As they headed west against the British advancement, Dolley and Hannah both agreed that they were happy to have met the stranger who had directed them away from the lightning shooting madman, but they also agreed that they would feel better if he had stayed with them instead of staying behind. This sentiment was only exaggerated by the freak rainstorm and strong winds that they experienced, turning most of their planned trail to mud and slowing their progress significantly.

Reaching the end of a wheat field, the two women came to a flat clearing near a water crossing that Dolley recognized as the Potomac River. Standing in front of the wooden boardwalk that stood between them and the docks was an older man with a graying beard, wily blue eyes, and a gentle smile, just as the stranger had said.

"Madam First Lady?" inquired the kindly looking man, holding his hands up high over his head to show he was unarmed.

"Who calls?" Dolley asked, with her free hand discreetly making its way behind her to Hannah's.

"My name is Marcus Turtledove and I am here to help you," the stranger said to Dolley, taking another step toward her but never breaking eye contact.

There was something in his voice that gave her a sense of trustworthiness and understanding. Maybe it was because he reminded her of her own grandfather, but something within him was paternal and warm. It was strange, but she thought that if anyone would believe her that a man shooting lightning out of his hands was chasing after them, this man would.

"Thank goodness," Dolley said, reaching out to greet the stranger in a formal way before proceeding further. She was a lady after all. "Dolley Madison, First Lady of these states united."

"A pleasure," Turtledove returned, bowing his head as he took her hand. Then he turned to Hannah. "And you are?"

16

The shock of Turtledove, a white man, directly addressing Hannah, someone traditionally below his station, rocked both of the women a bit, but it quickly became apparent that the conversation could not go on without Hannah introducing herself.

"My name is Hannah, sir," the girl said, still cowering behind Mrs. Madison.

"Very nice to meet you, Hannah," Turtledove said, extending his hand to her. To Dolley's great surprise, Hannah let go of her hand and accepted his greeting without hesitation.

This affirmation of the man's character from her most loyal servant gave her reason to smile for the first time in hours, and provided a sense of renewed hope for their survival.

"Now then, have you seen any of my people?" Turtledove asked them, drawing a look of dread from the two women.

"Yes, a man of yours," Hannah said, with mild trepidation. "He was going to fight the man who was chasing us, the one called Vilthe."

Vilthe wasted little time as he lunged toward Scott, left palm forward to send a bolt of blue lightning hurling towards his adversary. Prepared for this, Scott moved into position to release the first of his traps, and Vilthe's attack missed him by feet, not inches.

From Vilthe's left came three arrows. He dropped to his knees and avoided them all easily, but their purpose was to only to distract as Scott gained the upper hand and launched an attack from the air. Poised to stab his opponent through the heart, Scott came down on him from above. With uncanny strength and speed, Vilthe reached for a nearby log and brought it up between them, deflecting the knife.

Without warning, Scott was gone, leaving Vilthe off balance from the log's momentum. As he struggled to get out of the mud and regain his bearings, Scott reappeared, landing a solid kick squarely to the prone man's jaw, sending him sprawling back into the mire.

Bruised but not defeated, Vilthe reached for the M16 lying nearby. Seemingly unaware of its true function, he used it to brace himself as he got unsteadily to his feet, vulnerable for only a second. Only a second to Vilthe, but something decidedly more to a man with the ability to bend time to his will.

Before he had even a moment to recover, Scott appeared again, grabbing his arm and twisting it behind him, driving his full weight into Vilthe's back. There was a sickening pop as he pulled the smaller man's arm from its socket, and with a brutal grin he used the man's injured arm to whirl him back around. This was his moment, and he wanted to witness the same agony on Vilthe's face that he saw on Taylor's every time he closed his eyes. Blow after blow rained down on the older man, driving him mercilessly back down to the sludgy ground, gasping for air.

Then there was silence.

In a transitory moment that could have held a lifetime, he became aware of a building agony unlike any he had experienced in the centuries he'd been walking the Earth.

The pain began in Vilthe's left hand, a mild annoyance that quickly grew into a searing agony spreading through every one of his fingers. Frantically wiping the mud from his eyes with his sleeve, he stared at his hands, seeing only blood. He scrambled to wipe it off, revealing small, precise cuts bisecting the webbing between each digit. As he stared at his hands in horror and disbelief the pain jumped to his left ear like a spark between wires. Then to his right ear. The backs of his knees, and inside of both of elbows. His eyelids.

The cuts were not deep, just enough to set every nerve ending possible torturously ablaze across carefully practiced points on the man's body. Scott looked down at Vilthe, his face unreadable, and saw countless hours of obsessive planning brought to reality. All but one final stroke, meant to be deep, clean, and precise, across Vilthe's jugular.

Fantasies are dangerous things, and if you let them take you, they will try to keep you. Scott savored the moment, and it was a moment too long. The paradigm shifted, and his fate came crashing back down from where he'd held it at bay.

"Sugan ditto titikmadr!" Vilthe screamed, his eyes blazing with a sick yellow fire. With a flick of his functioning arm he sent Scott flying through the air and into a nearby tree with devastating percussive force, sending splinters flying. His limp form fell unceremoniously onto a small pile of rocks and broken tree limbs below.

Winded and more than a little broken, the Knight of Time willed himself to his knees. A few drops of blood fell across his vision. This is it then, he thought, making his way laboriously to his feet. Finding his balance, he snapped his fingers and slapped his left palm to his right hand- a comforting and familiar gesture that allowed him to wrap the moment around himself like a blanket. With his strength waning, it occurred to him that it might be the last time he ever did, and he most likely couldn't hold it for long. His hands moved under his coat to the small of his back, each hand retrieving its own dagger. He forced his breathing to steady. And then, he let the moment go.

Scott Wright faced Edward Vilthe then, as the man he truly was. Gone from his face was any trace of the grief-stricken madness that had driven him here, leaving behind a steely determination that was entirely his own.

"How is this possible?!" Vilthe bellowed as he climbed to his feet, his fury a living, palpable thing. He lunged wildly at Scott like something from a nightmare, covered in his own blood. At the last second Scott dropped into a crouch, bringing both daggers from behind his back and driving them up into Vilthe's abdomen as his body bowed, arching over Scott. With his daggers buried deep, he ducked forward, bracing his wrists against Vilthe's shoulders, and used the villains own momentum to throw the man over him. Rising, Scott turned to face his opponent.

"Who are you?" Vilthe asked quietly, coughing blood onto the damp leaves.

"You don't recognize me?" Scott asked with a mild annoyance. "You killed my father, and my wife, and you have the nerve to *forget*?"

"You would be surprised how often people say that to me," Vilthe said as he rose, the hilts of the twin daggers protruding obscenely from his sides. Without warning he leapt, his good arm outstretched, claw-like fingers reaching for Scott's throat. Scott deflected the attack instinctively, crossing both arms in front of his face. With both arms occupied, all he could do was watch as Vilthe drove a glistening crimson blade up under his ribcage with his other hand, the bones in his dislocated shoulder protruding at impossible angles.

"You took everything from me," Scott whispered, forcing Vilthe to the ground with him as he fell to his knees. "I hear that every time you kill someone, you take a piece of their soul."

Vilthe laughed, an ugly, grating sound.

"You believe you can get her back, don't you?" he cackled, his own blood dripping from the corners of his mouth. Vilthe shoved him onto his back. Seconds after the weapon left his hand, Scott watched in horror as the blade reduced to so much black liquid in the moonlight, the majority remaining in his own body.

Befuddled and heartbroken, Scott attempted to collect his thoughts. He could feel his body shutting down, unable to even process the amount of damage it had taken. He missed Taylor, and he missed their life together. He missed his son. Even in his own mind, he couldn't seem to find any words of comfort.

Vilthe stood over him, something moving in his upturned palms. Seconds passed like eons, and Scott came to realize that the cuts he'd inflicted were bubbling over-- fountains of blood from each tiny wound. The viscous liquid rose with a life of its own, and Scott's stomach heaved as he realized the extent to which he had been violated.

"Come... I tire of these games," Vilthe said, now holding two blades, wicked in every sense of the word. Choking on bile and blood, Scott could only watch as he was impaled through the meat of his body, just below each collar bone, literally speared to the ground by his enemy.

Vilthe released the blades, and the blood he'd driven into Scott collapsed, washing over him, back over his shoulders, down either side of his chest.

Long, slender middle fingers inched their way to either side of Scott's cranium, Vilthe's face filling his vision, which had mercifully begun to fade around the edges. Jets of red light shot into Scott's temples, ricocheting off. A momentary oddity flashed in the periphery of Vilthe's awareness, but when he turned nothing was there. Dismissing the phenomenon, he returned to the task at hand.

"First, I take the soul" Vilthe said, resting the palm of his hand in the middle of Scott's forehead. Curving his hand, he began to pull out a thin stream of white light. The grayish green of Scott's eyes faded to white, and then nothing as his eyes vanished into his head. On the heels of the stream of white light came another, this one turquoise. Finally Vilthe began to wrench the eternal spark of life itself from Scott's lifeless body – his soul.

Peeking out from between Scott's eye sockets, it spiraled and twirled above its previous host for a few seconds before reluctantly hovering slowly toward Vilthe.

Resembling a light bulb being screwed into a lamp, the inside of Scott's head flashed red, blue, and green as Vilthe extracted his soul, the very essence of what made him a father, husband, teammate, and master of time and space.

"I may even take your visage..." Vilthe said, tracing his hand over Scott's ruined chest for a moment. Using his razor sharp nails, he dug deep into the time traveler's flesh, up through the fatal wound he'd inflicted only minutes before. He reached elbow deep into Scott's chest and with the utmost joy, he wrenched out Scott's heart to wave in front of his lifeless eyes.

"I like to do this part last. Looks like I've broken your heart twice now" Vilthe said, cackling at his own joke. He bit into the slowly dying organ spitefully, bursting it like an overly ripe piece of fruit.

Suddenly the lights stopped, leaving nothing but darkness around them both. Holes marked either side of Scott's head, his forehead, and his chest and left him resembling something like a jack-o-lantern after All Hallows Eve.

"Now let us see what your little tricks can do, shall we?" Vilthe said, dropping Scott's body carelessly to the ground. With a wave of his arm the scene before him jumped sixty seconds into the past. He watched himself finish off Scott Wright. With another wave of his arm he returned himself to the present, smiling mercilessly.

"This shall do..." Vilthe said to himself, his eyes dancing with pleasure. He turned to the discarded shell on the ground beside him -- all that was left of the most formidable human Vilthe had faced in centuries. "Thank you for –"

Vilthe stopped short as something strange caught his eye. Scattered on the ground was what looked to be the contents of the dead man's pockets, but what captured Vilthe's attention was a small photograph, jumping frenetically in the wind and attempting to escape from beneath a worn leather wallet. As he scooped it up carelessly, it tore, half of it whisked away by the wind. Vilthe looked down at the remaining half of Scott's picture of Rolland.

"He looks a lot like you" Vilthe murmured thoughtfully.

"...Retreating! The British are retreating!" The shouts and hollers echoed through the air like nails on a chalkboard inside of Vilthe's ears, and a rustling nearby told him that it was time to go.

It seemed that just a few moments ago the idea of heading back toward the decimated White House would have been absurd, but now, at Turtledove's insistence, Dolley found herself doing just that. Turtledove had accompanied the two weary women as they walked roughly half a mile back toward the site where a kind stranger, now identified as Scott Wright, one of Turtledove's men, had directed them to safety.

Though the two women traveled in silence, Hannah continued to cling to Dolley's hand. As they made their way through the early dawn twilight they happened upon Sephanie who, with her eyes returned to their normal shade of green, they found to be quite a charming young lady. After brief introductions they continued their journey back to the overlook.

The sight was not for the faint of heart.

All around were stains of blood, sprayed and spilt in a savage killing that left far more questions than answers.

As her eyes wandered uncomprehendingly over the carnage before her, it occurred to Dolley that a place that had seemed if not safe, then at least normal as they'd fled for their lives in the dark of night, had been transformed into a nightmare by the light of day. She felt that the last few hours had destroyed everything she knew of the world. It was too much. Clinging to Hannah's arm, Dolley found just enough strength to support herself and the ridiculous painting of General Washington that had tagged along under her arm all evening.

Sephanie made a small, strangled sound, her eyes coming to rest on what could only be a human body. She didn't have to see its face to know who – and what – she would find. A hole gaped at her from the side of the skull she could see. Vilthe's involvement couldn't have been clearer if he'd left a calling card.

"Oh Scott..." Sephanie said. Turtledove stopped her as she moved a few steps toward what was left of her friend.

"Don't" Turtledove said softly, moving in front of her to crouch down beside Scott's corpse. Turtledove gently untangled his teammate's limbs and laid him on his back, crossing his arms over his chest. This was indeed a great loss. He clasped the dead man's hand in solidarity, closing his eyes for a moment. As he opened them again, a small movement from a nearby tree caught his attention. Carefully replacing Scott's hand, he rose to retrieve one half of a photograph, tangled amongst the roots.

Turtledove was quiet for a moment as he examined the half of Rolland's face in his hand. He saw Scott, and he saw Taylor. He saw a fresh tear across a 16 year old secret. What he did not see was the other half.

"I think we have a situation" Turtledove said aloud, his voice full of an authority rarely heard outside of addressing the Council of Light.

Before anyone could reply, the ground beneath them began to shake, the sounds of horses and a carriage master added to the din, rousing Dolley from her swoon. Before long lantern lights could be seen through the morning fog, and a carriage could be seen coming toward them.

The carriage was as extravagant as it was large, and must have gone through incredible lengths to reach the overlook. Four heavily armed men poured out before it even had time to roll to a stop. The horses looked exhausted and the driver haggard, yet it took only a matter of moments for the short, extremely well dressed man inside to step out and search for his wife, his face a picture of panic and concern.

"Dolley, Dolley!" President James Madison called, gloved hand to his mouth.

"I'm right here James" Dolley said, rushing over to his side, dragging Hannah along with her. Their embrace brought both of them such great comfort that Dolley temporarily forgot that Hannah still clung to her left hand.

A curious thing Hannah was indeed, Turtledove thought as he watched the handmaiden untangle herself from the presidential couple and retrieve the previously discarded painting of George Washington from the ground below.

"Mr. President," Turtledove said, bowing his head and shaking the president's proffered hand firmly. "It is truly an honor, sir."

"Thank you for saving my wife, Mister...?" President Madison trailed off.

"Turtledove, sir. Marcus Turtledove" Turtledove said grinning broadly and attempting to not loom over the unexpectedly short commander-in-chief.

"Well Mr. Turtledove, I thank you again. I am truly sorry if there was any... trouble" President Madison continued, motioning to Scott's corpse still lying in the mud.

All of them, from the President of the United States to the lowly carriage driver stared at Scott's lifeless form for a moment, though none of them particularly knew why.

A sudden rustling from the trees heralded the arrival of a large, well-built African man, his manner of dress similar to Turtledove's and Scott's. He emerged from the foliage aloof and unarmed, but the four soldiers surrounding Mr. and Mrs. Madison quickly drew their weapons regardless.

"That's Victor. He's one of ours," Turtledove explained. Madison set his guards at ease, leaving the newcomer to advance further into the camp and closer to Scott's body.

"Oh no," Victor said, crouching beside his friend's body. The holes in his forehead, eye sockets, and sides of his head left no doubt that he had suffered greatly before he died.

Taking off his shirt, Victor lay it on the ground and wrapped Scott's body in it with room to spare. With a teary look to Turtledove, he signaled his readiness to leave. Sephanie's eyes filled with tears, and a light rain began to fall.

"You'll be going then?" Dolley asked Turtledove, the loss of their comrade moving her to tears as well.

"Yes, it's time that we returned home. Time that we returned Scott to his…" Turtledove stopped, seemingly at a loss for words.

"Well, we will be on our way then as well," President Madison said gently, motioning for his wife and servant.

"I'm afraid, Mr. President, that I must insist on the girl coming with us," Turtledove said respectfully, turning his attention to Hannah and taking both the President and First Lady by surprise.

"Why must she go with you?" Dolley exclaimed, recent events having worn her nerves to shreds.

26

Looking over at Mrs. Madison, Turtledove could see the tears in her eyes were for more than the man she believed had lost his life protecting her. Dolley stood as one of the few people throughout history who had lived to tell the tale of Vilthe's merciless wrath. With this in mind, Turtledove decided to go a different route in his explanation as to why he must take the girl.

"Hannah, you can stop protecting her now. She's safe. Her husband is right here, as are his guards," Turtledove turned to the young woman, his voice calm and soothing.

Abruptly Hannah turned her face to the sky. Raising her hand, she began tracing counter clockwise circles in the air, around and around. At first nothing happened, causing the carriage driver to snicker. His gloating was short-lived, however, when a thin, barely visible pink bubble began to appear around Dolley, growing more defined every second.

"What is it?" President Madison asked, holding his guards at bay.

"Protection projection [3] would be my best guess, but I just met the girl." Turtledove spoke matter-of-factly, making both his own confidence and President Madison's ignorance plain. Though the president recognized the older man's words, he could assign no contextual meaning to them nor could he ask for clarification, the societal norm requiring that the President appear omnipotent in public.

"*She* is responsible for my wife's safety?" President Madison asked Turtledove, looking from him to the servant girl and attempting to piece together what little information he had to account for what was happening.

"Oh yes, no doubt she saved her life at least once this evening," Turtledove said, looking over at Hannah with a smile.

---

3   Protection projection – A psychic shield of safety upon one or multiple living souls

The soft, pink bubble raised itself off of Dolley's head and wafted above the crowd, floating high into the air. Every one of them looked on in amazement.

"Then it is you to whom I owe my gratitude, Hannah," President Madison said, wholly overwhelmed. He approached his wife's handmaiden and placed his hand on her shoulder, of an equal height to his own. "You may do as you wish."

As one, those present turned to Hannah, gazing at her in wonder. For the President and First Lady it was one more surreal experience in the strangest night of their lives.

"If I go with you, will I be able to help people like you do?" Hannah asked Turtledove, her voice a little braver.

"You will," Turtledove said, smiling down at her. "This I promise you."

"Then I'll go," Hannah said with a nod, looking him in the eyes.

Mrs. Madison, perhaps realizing that soon her surrogate daughter would be leaving her, decided to buck the societal trend and began clapping for her handmaiden, the woman who had saved her life. Soon President Madison, Turtledove, the carriage driver, Sephanie, Victor, and finally the guards joined in their praise for the young girl's bravery.

Not a single eye remained on Hannah, only her work in this world. For the first time in her life, she was more than a slave; she was the center of attention.

With more in her eyes than she could ever hope to put into words, Hannah handed Dolley the portrait of George Washington that had seemed so terribly important only hours before.

"Thank you, my dear," Dolley smiled at Hannah moments before a bright white light appeared in the sky and the handmaiden, along with the rest of Mrs. Madison's extraordinary new allies disappeared from their lives forever.

Chapter 2:
A Knight's Tale

Woodland Hills, California – Present Day

5:34AM

It had been an unusually quiet Friday night in Woodland Hills, California – especially for football season. The breeze from the Santa Ana winds filled the air with a quiet chill that blanketed the entire valley and brought with it an eerie sense of calm. From the outset, it appeared that not a soul was around to marvel in this event, this break in the hustle and bustle that was an integral part of living one's life but a stone's throw away from Los Angeles. This was an illusion however, as there was someone awake. Someone who relished in the lack of excitement. Someone on patrol.

The town had but one major road, Pecan Street, which stretched from one end of the county line to the other. The two lights radiating from the black and white Dodge Charger pierced the darkness in search of lawbreakers, and behind the wheel sat the man who defined justice for the sleepy little town.

Lt. David Rowley was a twelve-year veteran of the Woodland Hills police department. His knack for always being in the 'right place at the right time' had gotten him promoted once or twice within the ranks of his fellow officers. Tonight, he believed, was no exception. A strange, uneasy feeling had settled into the pit of his stomach the moment he had clocked in for duty at midnight and had remained there stubbornly.

"One more sweep through town couldn't hurt," Officer Rowley said to himself, taking another sip of his lukewarm coffee. Though he was not usually one to talk to himself, his partner, Deputy Dunn, had taken the night off for his sister's wedding. The quiet scared Rowley a bit, reminding him of home.

The local entrance sign reading 'Woodland Hills, California' sat covered in toilet paper and streamers from the evening before, when Woodland Hills High School had won its first playoff game in nearly ten years. With a relatively low crime rate in the city, it was this kind of vandalism that had caused Officer Rowley to be dispatched as the extra officer on duty that night.

He now sat comfortably behind the wheel of the department's newest Dodge Charger, a vain purchase justified to the affluent city council with the excuse that 'bad guys drive really fast'. Whatever the hell that meant.

Pulling into the high school parking lot, Rowley noticed two things. First, that the vehicle illegally parked overnight on public property had a person in it, then that the person was unconscious. Nothing made Rowley more uncomfortable than waking up sleeping perps, regardless of the circumstances. As he put the cruiser into park, he readied himself by unbuttoning the holster for his stun gun. It was now ready at a moment's notice.

Rowley got out and approached the vehicle cautiously. Using standard protocol he inspected the vehicle, keeping one hand on his flashlight, and the other firmly on his nightstick. He was always careful, and tonight was no exception. Usually Rowley would simply call a tow truck to come and get the irresponsibly parked vehicle, but the figure inside was a bit of a complication.

Taking the nightstick from his belt, Rowley tapped on the glass, holding the light steady on the boy's eyes. Inside he could see what appeared to be an older teenage male, probably old enough to be graduating soon. He was passed out, his head resting between the window and the headrest of the beat-up, old El Dorado.

'It was strange though', Rowley thought to himself. 'The boy looks almost like he is glowing, like there was a fine layer of white light surrounding him only visible because of the dark of night.'

Rowley again tapped the end of his nightstick against the glass, this time with more ferocity and vigor.

The noise was deafening, yet the boy would not wake up. Officer Rowley continued to pound on the glass, until the boy inside finally began to stir. His eyes opened, seeing the officer through tiny slits before turning his head away and continuing to sleep.

'Good, not a suicide,' Rowley thought to himself, remembering a particularly difficult time early in his career in Los Angeles. Dismissing the long-suppressed thought, he pounded on the glass again.

Inside the vehicle, the teenager moved slightly, though still unconscious. Rowley suspected that he was a local high school student, probably passed out drunk from the night before. His eyes opened slightly as he raised his hand to shield them from the officer's maglight.

"Good morning, sir," Rowley said, with a pronounced display of pleasantry. "Mind rolling down your window?"

31

The teenager inside did as he was told, and rolled down the El Dorado's window. It was obvious by the lad's disposition that he had not expected to wake up in such a manner, but there he was.

"Identification please," Officer Rowley demanded, keeping the business end of his flashlight pointed toward the boy's hands. Rowley's free hand was cemented firmly on his sidearm, a precaution he had learned to take ages ago when out alone on patrol.

The blonde teenager looked dazed for a moment before reaching for an old brown wallet lying on the dashboard. He was broad shouldered but slim, and very good looking with a strong chin.

Rowley moved closer to the window. With his keen, hound-dog like sense of smell he could sniff out a drug runner in seconds flat. Sadly, neither his instincts nor his nose gave him any cause for concern. A shame really, since his monthly quota was nearly due.

"It seems to be in the glove compartment. Do you mind?" the wavy haired blonde teenager asked cautiously after shuffling through the contents of his wallet. Obviously he had been warned by an officer before to proceed with a respectful apprehension.

In a post Patriot Act world, the boy's last statement sounded like probable cause to Officer Rowley, causing him to shine his flashlight into the back seat of the young man's Cadillac El Dorado, looking for any excuse to search the teenager's vehicle for possible narcotics, weapons, or other illegal goods.

What he saw in the back seat had nothing to do with the illicit drug subculture, however. Instead, he saw signs that the boy had been living out of his car. He could clearly make out crates of food, laundry, and toiletries scattered amongst newspapers, blankets, and various sorts of trash. Looking further back he saw textbooks featuring such words as 'Biology' and 'Trigonometry'.

Rowley had seen this before. Back when he worked in Los Angeles. Back before he got the sweet gig in the suburbs. There was a time in his career where he might have let this kid go about his day, letting him off with just a friendly reminder to watch his back. But it was the end of the month, and he did have a quota to meet. In this town, he would take what he could get.

"Is this your vehicle, Mr..?" Officer Rowley asked the young man sitting behind the wheel, his composure coming back to him.

"Wright, Scott Wright," said the teenager. Opening up the glove compartment slowly, the young man who called himself Scott Wright pulled out a California driver's license and a piece of paper. He next handed them to Rowley, who disappeared behind the El Dorado and surveyed the top of the trunk and rear light with a raised brow before returning to the driver's side window.

The teenager, who called himself Scott Wright, was obviously not the real Scott Wright. The real Scott Wright had, unbeknownst to Officer Rowley, been missing for some time now. Nearly twenty months to be exact. The young man sitting in Scott Wright's 1979 Cadillac El Dorado hardtop convertible was none other than his only son – Rolland Alan Wright.

"Well Mr. Wright, may I ask what you're doing here at 4:30 in the morning?" Rowley looked Rolland dead in the eye, unable to find any sign of dishonesty.

"Just very early for class," Rolland said to the officer, giving a half smile.

"Please wait in the vehicle, sir," Officer Rowley said to Rolland before walking back to his vehicle and climbing inside.

Watching the portly police officer struggle to get back into his cruiser from his rear view mirror, Rolland Wright knew that his long journey had come to an end. What began nearly two years ago with the death of his mother and disappearance of his father leaving him evicted from his childhood home, would finally end with him being arrested for sleeping in the high school parking lot.

Pushing a few strands of his wavy blonde hair away from his eyes, Rolland contemplated the idea of making a run for it. He'd have to change his license plates again, but it was worth it to stay out of jail. Worth it to not to have to wait for parents who would never come to bail him out. Worth it to not be humiliated.

Rolland snapped and clasped his hands nervously together, a bad habit he had picked up from his father years ago. He did it again and again, creating a clicking noise as he braced himself to the most reckless thing he could imagine. Checking the rearview mirror again, the bright lights of the police car looked almost like they were moving in slow motion with their seemingly endless flashing of blue and red.

A cold rush of excitement washed over Rolland as he allowed his instincts to take over. Closing his eyes, Rolland turned the keys in the ignition and gripped the leather steering wheel cover until his knuckles turned white. He knew that things were about to either get much better, or much worse.

Putting the car into gear, he opened his eyes and pushed the gas pedal flush to the floor, and sped out of the parking lot. His heart pounded as he moved the driver's side mirror to check behind him, but the road was empty.

"Good," he said, reassuring himself. Rolland had long since given up on the idea of NOT talking to himself. After all, these days he kept very little company. He snapped his fingers and hands together again in an attempt to relieve some of the tension, the knot in his stomach refusing to relent. Deciding that 4:30 in the morning was as good of a time to start the day as any, Rolland set course for the only store in town open twenty four hours - the Sack & Save grocery store.

As he drove, Rolland could not help but ponder the circumstances that had brought him to this point. As he pulled up to the stop light at the intersection of Pecan and 2nd Street, suppressed memories of life before homelessness shoved their way back to the surface.

He had been living out of his car for almost two years, though even the El Dorado was not Rolland's. It legally belonged to his missing, presumably inebriated, father.

The Wright's busy working schedules (both Taylor's and Scott's) demanded a lot from their family when Rolland was young. While he was never exactly sure what his parents did, he knew that they worked for the federal government. His mother had never been what one would consider the typical mom, but with her gentle touch and warm embrace, she had been there to guide Rolland through the early days of his childhood. Throughout much of elementary school he would come home to find her waiting there for him, usually with an after school snack and a genuine interest in his day.

That was before September 11, 2001. Before the world as he knew it changed.

After the terrorist attacks, time became a commodity, and the Wrights began to spend more time at work and less time with their son. By the age of nine, Rolland came home from school to be greeted by an empty house. Because of his forced solitude, Rolland developed an active fantasy life, and dove enthusiastically into books and movies – primarily of the historical and adventurous variety.

This process continued through most of his childhood and early teen years, his marks in school remaining moderately high. Since he had no behavioral problems, his parent's complete lack of involvement in his life went quite unnoticed by public school faculty. Most individuals would look upon Rolland's arrangement as neglectful at best, but in an age where most parents were as versatile as a public pantomime, his were missing in action.

Rolland looked back at that golden era of his life and missed sleeping indoors the most; a rather harsh realization when considering the fact that both of Rolland's parents were still alive at the time. Back before he carried a large knife around for protection.

Pulling into the Sack' & Save grocery parking lot, Rolland put the car in park and popped the reclining lever on his seat. Looking up at the grey, fuzzy ceiling above him, Rolland was reminded of the snow that covered Beaver Creek, Colorado the night his mother died.

Two years ago, Scott had surprised his family over the holiday break with a skiing trip to Colorado. Having never gone skiing before, Rolland took the good-natured gesture by his father in stride and agreed to make the best out of their time together.

The skiing itself had proven to be easy enough that Rolland mastered it on the first day. He had looked forward to reporting his accomplishment to his mother, but it had been too late.

Two holes graced either side of her otherwise beautiful, albeit pale, face. Her chest cavity had been ripped in two, a large chunk missing from the left side. They had taken her heart.

Scott Wright was beyond devastated by his wife's death. That night Rolland, still in shock from discovering his mother's body, attempted to approach his father after they gave their statements to the police. Scott would have none of him. Instead, he sent the boy away, never breathing another word to him until the day he disappeared. A curt "Be right back," and Scott was gone, never to be seen again.

Rolland took the keys out of the ignition, retrieved his toothbrush, deodorant and soap, and got out of the car. He locked the door behind him, leaving the memories of his past inside.

Upon entering the Sack & Save grocery store, Rolland immediately came face to face with Charlie, the lovable greeter who worked there in the mornings. The two of them shared a special relationship. Charlie was one of the only individuals privy to Rolland's living arrangements.

This breach in secrecy was due to necessity, as Rolland had to remind himself every morning when passed by Charlie on the way to use the facilities.

"Good morning, Charlie," Rolland said, extending his hand and greeting Charlie with the enthusiasm of someone who'd had far more caffeine.

"Mornin', Rolland," Charlie said meekly, giving a kind hearted smile to the homeless teenager he had taken pity on in exchange for a dinner companion once a week. He, like Rolland, was lonely, but for completely different reasons. Unlike Officer Rowley however, Charlie the greeter had no monthly quota to meet, and cut Rolland a break on using the bathroom every morning. "You're early."

"Got caught sleeping up at the high school," Rolland said, walking past him and entering the restroom.

"Oh, that's not good," Charlie said, feigning mild interest as he went back to watching the door. He liked Rolland, but not enough to bail the lad out of jail.

What felt to him like twenty minutes later the transformation from pauper to prince was complete, and Rolland emerged from the men's restroom looking polished, groomed, and clean. Slipping his toothbrush into his back pocket, Rolland thanked Charlie again and wished him a good day as he walked through the automatic doors.

A quick glance at the clock told him it was nearly 6:30AM, giving Rolland less than an hour to drive to school, find a parking space, and get to class if he wanted to be on time. He put the car in gear and headed for the school.

Memories of how he had gotten to this point bombarded him as he drove. It's a strange feeling to know that all hope is lost. There is no more angst... no more uncertainty. All that's left inside you is a void that you know, deep down, can never be filled. He remembered that moment, too.

Suicide was an option, sure, but not any more so now than it had been nearly two years ago. Besides... it's not like it was going anywhere. There it could sit, like an obedient little dog, waiting for its master to make a decision. No... if Rolland was going out then he planned on taking out all the enemies he had made first.

It wasn't in Rolland's nature to go about making enemies, mind you; it's just that life on the streets has a certain way of hardening people. It wasn't as if Rolland's life living in the backseat of an old Cadillac had dissuaded him from living it to the fullest. On the contrary, as it was his general impression that only those who had nothing left to lose were truly alive.

The yearning to make a difference was still living within him; it was just bogged down by the everyday worries of the world. He saw it all on the streets; the suffering, the inhumanity, the horrible conditions for children. The children... there were dozens of them. Dozens upon dozens, travelling with their poor, homeless families visiting the camps other vagabond travelers had already established around the greater Los Angeles area.

Rolland had seen them all. On the weekends he would drive to them, get the lay of the land, and crash for the evening. During the night he would keep tabs on all the comings and goings. He would learn who it was best to avoid and whose eye you should catch if you wanted a free meal. The types were the same everywhere he went, and one by one he picked them off of the map that Charlie had given him.

Slab City was the name given to the worst Rolland had come across since moving into his car. Known as the 'last free place in America,' the old decommissioned Navy Seals training camp was now host to hundreds, if not thousands, of souls living on the fringes of society. It was a far drive, one hundred and fifty miles southeast of Los Angeles. There was no electricity or law enforcement, only an abundance of victims and people down on their luck.

But they were still people.

They were human, all of them, and American to boot. Why then were they allowed to go on with their lives like they were second rate citizens? Why wasn't the government doing something?

Rolland posed this exact question to his American History teacher, Joseph Paladino, that day at school. Mr. Paladino was a strict but good natured man in his own special way. At first glance, one could assume correctly that he had a military background. Not content with 'getting more done before noon than most people get done all day', he went into public education as a means of serving his community, a decision he had come to regret after interacting with most of the students. Most.

Joseph's training and keen sense of observation told him at the beginning of the school year that something about the young Mr. Wright was a little off. Perhaps it was the boy's odd sense of curiosity about specific details about history. Or maybe it was the long periods of time when the boy wouldn't say anything at all, no matter how hard he attempted to provoke him.

To Joseph, it was like the Wright boy was living a double life. But that would be impossible for a seventeen year old. After all, his parents would be keeping at least some amount of supervision over him. They had a legal obligation, after all.

"Big government is bad for free enterprise," he told the boy, almost mimicking the voice of Bill O'Reilly as he rapped his pen on the desk with his free hand.

Mr. Paladino was pleased to have an audience for his nonsensical ramblings, even if he sensed an alternative motive behind the boy's sudden interest in national politics. He wasn't surprised when he saw Rolland's eyes drift toward the doorway after a minute or two. He was obviously avoiding someone. Thinking he would find a young girl, Paladino faked a cough and stole a quick glance at the door.

To Joseph's surprise however, it was a not girl standing there, but a tall, very skinny, Brazilian teenager with black, greasy hair and a rather unpleasant expression, attempting to open a locker. His name was Richard, and he was Rolland's only remaining friend.

Richard, Rick, Rich, (and sometimes the 'Brazilian Bronco' whenever they spray-painted buildings) had met Rolland in elementary school, sharing a passion for toy cars and battling little girls. For nearly ten years they had run together, discovering girls, automobiles, and the inevitable downsides of friendship.

Without a word, Rolland stood up from his desk, the cheap wooden door creaking as he shut it hard behind him. Upon later reflection, it occurred to Rolland that perhaps the noise he had heard was not the door, but his instructor's indignation. At that moment however, he didn't care. All Rolland cared about was talking to his friend Rick and securing a place to sleep that evening.

"Hey man, I just wanted to make sure that we were cool," Rolland said with a somewhat genuine tone to his voice. "Not sure why your mom threw me out of your house last night, but…"

"She threw you out because it was like the 50th time you've slept over without her permission," said Richard, attempting the combination to his locker again.

"Yeah, but it's not like it's a big deal, right? I mean I'm not hurting anyone and…" Rolland said, but was interrupted again by his visibly upset friend.

"What's wrong with you man? Can't you see that you aren't wanted at my house? I mean, geez," Rick said while stuffing his backpack with binders and textbooks.

"You don't have to be a dick about it, Rick," Rolland said, thinking to himself that he sounded a bit like Doctor Seuss for adults.

"And you're lame, dude," Richard said, closing his locker and shouldering his bag. "Nobody likes a mooch."

"Dude, I let you copy off of me on the trig test last week. I got you that job at the grocery store. You kind of owe me," Rolland said, laying down the gauntlet.

"I don't owe you anything, Rolland," Richard said, stuffing the rest of his books into his tan knapsack. "Look how many friends you have. There's a reason for that."

"Alright…" Rolland said, pulling on the strap of his own backpack a bit, making the shoulder strap it was connected to tighter. "Well then what about…"

But it was too late. Richard was half way down the hall and by the time Rolland realized it, he was out of sight. The sad part was that Richard didn't know how right he was. There was a reason, a perfectly valid reason, why Rolland was using his friend's houses as a hotel and going through acquaintances like disposable napkins. He had no other choice.

Sure, the guilt of losing Richard as a friend was sad to Rolland, but so was being woken up by yet another police officer at four in the morning. His belief in humanity was dwindling along with the number of places he could sleep indoors. It was a scary thought for the teenager and one that he wasn't quite ready to accept. So, swallowing everything BUT his pride, Rolland took what titles his former friends gave him.

The prospect of being that 'rude' guy was still better to Rolland than being that 'homeless' guy – a title he wasn't ready to accept at

the age of seventeen. Deciding to skip out on the rest of his class-
es, Rolland put the combination lock into his pocket and walked
out of Woodland Hills High. He found his El Dorado waiting for
him, right where he had left her.

Deciding to find some moderately priced entertainment for the
day, Rolland drove down the road to the local Books Half Price,
finding a parking spot near the middle with relative ease. He put the
car into park, and felt around the backseat until he found his brown
bomber jacket pulling the journal he had kept for the past twenty
months out from under it.

It wasn't that Rolland fancied himself a writer -- quite the contrary. More often than not, when he brought his pen to paper the
words of greater and more famous men sprang to life instead of
his own. He picked up the Pilot pen that sat next to the journal.
The weight of this tool, this tube filled with ink, was almost nothing, yet it held such immense power.

After securing his father's old hunting knife, a somewhat
chipped and jaded relic he had been given by his old man on his
thirteenth birthday, which he kept in a well-placed pizza box in
the back seat, Rolland decided to set the tone of his day. Putting
the pen to the notepad, he wrote down the first quote that came
to mind.

"Perhaps the art of life is the art of avoiding pain."

Thinking it too melodramatic, Rolland shut the spiral notebook, placed it on the seat next to him, got out of the El Dorado,
and locked the door behind him. It being only ten o'clock in the
morning, there still weren't many people out and about.

The mid-morning sun was bright, and barely hid behind the
brick structure he faced. A quick glance directly into its glowing

magnificence and the inside of his eyelids glowed for a long moment. It wasn't until Rolland pried his eyes back open that he saw her. A beautiful, almost angelic woman elegantly marched toward him dressed in white, her long flowing hair cascading down her slender shoulders. She glided past him, turning to smile at him as she passed by. Rolland's heart stopped as he watched the hourglass figure walk away. The sun was too bright, causing him to blink.

'Was she a vision?' Rolland thought to himself aloud. 'I have to know!'

Running back to the parking lot to find the pretty girl in white proved to be futile. Rolland turned around, glad to be free of the sun's blinding persistence. The brunette beauty was long gone now; along with Rolland's first and only smile of the day.

Believing her to be a momentary lapse of his senses, Rolland turned his attention back to the bookstore. Walking back to the front of the store, he noticed the bins of clearance priced books. It had been his experience that the bargain bin was always the fullest first thing in the morning.

Lines of carts were out in front of the store, overflowing with books on sale for a dollar each. Rolland picked through them looking for his favorite authors. With no Michener, King, or Crighton to be found, the best he could come up with was what looked like an old library copy of a Robert Stone novel. No sooner had Rolland flipped the book than he was interrupted by what appeared to be a police officer.

"You. What's your name?" the officer asked gruffly, grabbing the teenager's wrist and twisting it painfully.

"Salt-Tina. It's Yiddish," Rolland said sarcastically, as he attempted to break free of the shady officer's grip.

Rolland let his impulsive nature take over, fighting back against the ugly policeman.

"Let go of me!" Rolland shouted as he kicked the standing cart of bargain books into the officer's hip, sending the man toppling over. The momentary distraction allowed Rolland to free himself from the officer's grip and he took several steps backward.

Turning to run, Rolland didn't make it far before his feet were pulled out from under him, and he fell face first onto the pavement.

"Got you now little bass-turd." The officer laughed, revealing a mouth full of cracked and decaying teeth.

The officer drew his firearm and aimed it squarely at Rolland, as he lay defenseless on the sidewalk. His nose was bleeding and throbbing profusely, a slow stream of blood trickling onto his shirt and the sidewalk below.

"Please, I don't know what you're talking about." Rolland pleaded. "I haven't done anything!"

"Quiet you," the officer said, cocking the gun clenched between his stumpy fingers. "Dey told me all bout you, dey did. Won't be trickin' me wit your... ew..."

From out of nowhere what looked like a flaming baseball flew at the police officer, hitting him squarely in the chest, sending him flying backward into the side of the building.

"Are you alright?" said a deep, booming voice from above Rolland, who looked over to see a very large, very dark African gentleman offering him his hand.

"Thanks," Rolland said, accepting the man's gesture, and climbing to his feet. "Uh, not to be rude, but who are you?"

"I am Victor. My friends also call me Flint. I'm here to help you," he replied, letting go of Rolland's arm.

"Thanks, I guess. Uh, why do they call you Flint exactly?" Rolland asked, looking at the man's overly large arms, each covered in cracked, scaly dark skin.

"Because of this…" Victor said, taking a knee and placing his fist on the cement. He then ran it in a quick, striking motion across the pavement, and small bits of flame quickly spread over his skin, completely engulfing his arm.

"Don't worry, I'm alright," Victor said, smiling at Rolland as he stood up and shook his arm, expelling the flames. "Are there any more, or was it just him?"

Before Rolland could reply, a long electric-blue whip lashed around the cart full of books next to them, flinging it onto its side. At the other end of the whip stood a very tall red-headed woman, smiling at them wickedly.

"The boy is mine!" she shouted, as she readied her electric whip for another attack, sprinting toward them.

In the blink of an eye, the whip slapped against the ground and whizzed back through the air at them with such a force that Rolland barely had time to consider dodging. To his great surprise, Victor stood there defiantly as debris from her fury flew all around them. Raising one arm above his head, Victor caught the glowing, electric whip as it cracked and coiled itself against his charcoal skin.

"Nice try," Victor said, using the whip to pull the red-headed woman to him and throwing both woman and weapon aside. He turned his attention back to Rolland. "Come on, follow me."

Together they ran past the carts of clearance books and over the two would-be assailants, through the double doors that led to the air-conditioned safety within the bookstore. Oddly, no one inside the store seemed to take any notice at what was going on outside, nor had anyone tried to leave.

"Come on, we'll sneak out the back," Victor said, attracting the same attention any six-foot-five inch muscular black man running through the store naturally would.

They had barely crossed half of the distance to the emergency exit when a man wearing a bowler hat and necktie walked in through the side door wielding a Maschinengewehr machine gun, firing at anything that moved. Right behind him was the officer that had first stopped Rolland, opening fire as well.

"Watch out for the..." Victor shouted to Rolland, but was cut off as a giant, catlike paw the size of a Volkswagen came crashing through the front window, taking a swipe at Victor and knocking him to the floor, unconscious.

Whatever creature owned the paw was large, with a strange bellowing roar; a noise that drowned out the screams of panic that echoed out throughout the bookstore.

Rolland felt nothing but responsibility. Though he did not know why, he knew that the beast was there for him alone. He knew he had to get out of the store and lure the beast away from the innocent patrons inside.

Having never been stung by a bee as a child, Rolland had no idea what being shot might feel like. Had he not turned toward the exit of the Books Half Price at that moment, he might have found out firsthand as a blaze of bullets rained down upon the spot where Rolland's heel had been a breath earlier.

The shooter was a tall man, dressed in a crisp black military uniform, complete with shiny boots, honors, and bars of rank. Rolland also spotted something unusual on his uniform. Something that Rolland could just make out as he spun around to take cover from the deluge spewing from the automatic weapon aimed at him.

There was a band on the man's right arm branded with a large X. Only it wasn't an X.

Then, as quickly as the gunfire had started, it stopped, leaving a startling silence in its wake.

"Give up now, kinder," The man said, removing the empty clip from his weapon and reaching for a new one. "Zhere is no need to get hurt."

Confused, afraid, and out of ideas, Rolland hunched over, his back leaning against two fallen bookshelves filled with National Geographic magazines from the 1980s. Stretching nervously, Rolland wracked his brain in search of another plan.

Rolland never heard footsteps, only the labored breathing of the trained gunman who stood a mere three feet away, the barrel of his Type 81 assault rifle pointed directly at the side of the teenage boy's head.

"Howdy," Rolland said nervously, his throat dry and his palms sweaty. This had to be the end.

His assailant sneered, and Rolland took a closer look at the man's uniform. The nametag on the man's left breast read 'HESS' in big white letters, and the X on his sleeve was not an X at all, but a swastika, the insignia of fascist Nazi Germany.

"Kind of insensitive of you to sport that armband, don't you think?" Rolland said nervously, as he put more and more weight into the slow backward retreat he was mulling over.

"You got far'therzen I zhought you would," The man in black known as Hess said, not moving another muscle in his body. "But here you ztop."

"Thanks – I guess?" Rolland replied, staring at the stoic Hess and his Type 81, which still held steady, seemingly eager to finish its assignment.

Without warning, the sun suddenly peeked through the side window of the bookstore, temporarily blinding Hess, and giving Rolland the seconds he needed to make a break for it.

Avoiding the man's blind fire, Rolland dragged Victor by his hands across the tile floor to the far side of the wall where a group of people, the store's cashier and about ten patrons, were cowering. Rolland reached them just as a fresh wave of bullets was shot in their direction.

Hess was on the move.

"Is everyone alright?" Rolland asked the huddled masses all at once. There were about a dozen of them all together, four children, five women, and three men. All of them looked terrified, angry, and confused.

"What the hell is going on out there?" one of the men asked, stepping forward and peeking his head out from around the corner. Bullets came within millimeters of the man's nose as Rolland pulled him back behind the shelf.

"Stay here and watch him!" Rolland shouted as he dropped Victor's arms and ran from the group, drawing the gunman's fire upon himself as he went.

It wasn't more than a few steps before Rolland ran into the redheaded woman again, apparently recovered from their altercation in front of the store.

"Going somewhere, doll face?" the crazed woman asked, cracking her blue whip in midair and sending a bolt of electricity through its coarse wiring.

Rolland thought it would have looked rather cool if it weren't about to play a part in the end of his life. He jumped, dodging behind another overturned bookshelf and the redheaded woman miscalculated Rolland's position, catching her whip on something he couldn't see.

Utilizing this distraction, Rolland crawled away and ran towards a group of people who had gathered in the 'Arts' section. Seeing them unharmed gave him a jolt of hope and a second wind as he ran to them.

"I'm going to get help," Rolland told them, scanning their faces for any sign of smoke inhalation. He looked down at Victor, who still lay on the ground motionless, the two scratch marks deep across his chest and bubbling oddly through his white t-shirt.

"Please hurry," said an older, Hispanic woman who had two little boys sitting behind her.

With a rush of adrenaline, Rolland nervously clasped his hands together and made a mad dash for the emergency exit. Heart pounding in his chest, he sped through the storm of bullets the two mad gunmen rained down on him.

Opening the door, Rolland immediately knew something was wrong. It was pretty obvious, since there was a 90 foot shadow looming over him and blocking out the sun. He looked up, craning his neck to see the most grotesque, misshapen thing he had ever laid eyes upon. Purple veins stood taller than him, and his eyes followed them over the hunched shoulders to the front of the beast.

The horned creature towered over Rolland, with a long, curved tail that easily doubled the creature's size. Its head was shaped like a flattened football, with two massive, ten-foot-long tusks protruding from either side of a mouth filled with razor sharp teeth.. Two large, copper colored eyes sat on opposite sides of the beast's head, blinding it to Rolland's immediate presence.

"At the door – get um!'" shouted the man wearing the tattered uniform as he ran toward Rolland and the open emergency exit. The beast stirred at the sound, and as it shifted, it saw Rolland.

The man reached the door just in time to take the full brunt of the fireball the beast spewed at the source of the noise, completely engulfing him in flames.

Running back into the bookstore, the flaming man hurled himself into bookcases left and right, flailing his arms frantically. The redhead suddenly lost all interest in Rolland and ran to her friend's side, beating at the flames on his neck and shoulders. Unfortunately for her the sum of her efforts was the spreading of the fire to a nearby pile of books, along the carpeted floor, and finally to the store's interior walls surrounding them.

To Rolland's amazement, there were no police, nor any sign of rescue workers to assist the injured. The surroundings of the Books Half Price appeared perfectly normal, as if it were still a typical morning in the sleepy little town of Woodland Hills; that is, besides the ninety foot tall monster that was trying to kill him.

Skidding to a stop as he maneuvered around the side of the Books Half Price, Rolland made impressive time, keeping at least twenty-five feet in front of the beast. Making it to the parking lot, Rolland pulled at the lanyard in his pocket and grabbed his car key, lunging for the lock before he was even to the car door. He turned the rickety old lock left, and got inside of the car with a practiced ease.

Digging around the backseat, Rolland found what he was looking for. There, inside the old pizza box, was the twelve-inch-long Bowie knife that Scott had given to him on his thirteenth birthday. He grabbed it and wheeled around just in time to see the beast bearing down on him.

Both massive ivory tusks pierced the roof of the El Dorado, pushing themselves past the upholstery and clear through to the undercarriage, lifting the car off of the ground. Rolland jumped out, tucked into a ball, and rolled away as the El Dorado stuck to the monster's tusks, agitating the creature and making it paw at the large chunk of metal with its front paws.

"Dick!" Rolland hollered at the beast as it tore through the only home he had come to know for the past two years. Unsheathing the knife, he ran as fast as he could to the beast's massive webbed paw. Rolland raised his father's knife over his head, and brought it down into the creatures flesh with reckless abandonment. It landed square and deep into the middle of the limb, sinking clear to the handle, and making it impossible for the beast to dislodge the knife.

The enormous fanged beast thrashed and snarled, enraged by the vehicle lodged in its mouth and the knife lodged in its paw. It let out a loud growl before breathing another fiery breath and popping out of existence as quickly as it had arrived, leaving only a trail of chaos and destruction behind.

With the creature gone, Rolland turned and tried to find a way back into the bookstore to help the dozen or so individuals still trapped inside. He looked over at the double glass doors and saw smoke slowly billowing out from underneath. Running over to them, he was careful not to touch the door handles. The plastic safety rings on the edges had already melted and re-hardened into a shapeless mass.

Cupping his hand, Rolland leaned as close as possible to the glass without touching it to peer inside. He saw flames everywhere, and he feared that he might be too late to save anyone, much less everyone.

"Think, Wright!" Rolland shouted to himself, again clasping his hands nervously together, a mirror of his father's nervous gesture. Scott had called it his 'key to success', but Rolland merely thought of it as stress relief for middle-aged middle management. Still, he did it, again and again, snapping his fingers, clasping his hand to his palm, over and over.

That's when it caught his eye. Like a diamond catches the light no matter what room it's in, or a beautiful woman turns heads when she walks by, it made itself known to him for reasons beyond his understanding. There, through the glass, Rolland could see a soft, yet incredibly bright white orb of light hovering just on the other side of the door. It was comforting, and called to him with a purity that he hadn't felt since he was young.

"What?" Rolland asked himself out loud as he walked over to the door and leaned in to the door handle before jumping back. But to his surprise it was not red hot like before, but cool to the touch, allowing him to get a closer look at the treasure within.

Looking into the swirly bright light of the orb, Rolland was filled with the confidence that he needed to not only find a way into the building, but to save all of the people inside as well. Somehow he knew he would be safe doing it, though he couldn't have explained why.

Deciding not to look a gift horse in the mouth, Rolland looked around and found a nearby rock he could use to shatter the glass door's lower pane. He stepped inside and came face to face with the shining white orb.

It was beautiful, simple, and amazing.

All around Rolland the flames still raged, but softly, slowly. It was almost as if someone had pressed the slow motion button on the entire world, allowing Rolland to control the action.

Thankful for the blessing, Rolland followed the white orb through different patches of floor and around flaming shelves through what would otherwise surely have been a mad dash to find his way in a house of death. Eventually the orb led him back to Victor and the 'Arts Section' crowd before disappearing entirely.

"Spooky," Rolland said, a band of sweat forming on his forehead from the heat of the fire surrounding him. Time was of the essence, and he intended to make the most of it.

Deciding to take the children first, Rolland threw one of the little boys over his shoulder and picked up another other, turning to find the white swirly orb waiting and ready to guide him back outside. He did this nine more times for the cashier, Hispanic woman, two more children, and other remaining patrons.

Though the orb had a set course, Rolland did get a chance to look around at the surreal scene before him. Only one body – the fake cop who initially attacked him outside of the bookstore was plain to see, adding credence to his theory that the redheaded woman and the guy in the Nazi uniform must have found a way to escape.

Victor was the last to be pulled from the burning bookstore, as he took the longest to drag out. Stopping only long enough to check on each patron's vital signs, Rolland continued dragging Victor past them, out across the bookstore's parking lot where the upside down shell of his Cadillac El Dorado lay, flames still burning slowly as she melted away to nothing more than steel.

He dragged Victor up the small hill behind the bookstore and away from prying eyes. It proved to be quite a task, but as they arrived at the top, Rolland was grateful he had chosen to get away from the scene as fast as possible. He turned around to examine the building from which he and a dozen other people had only barely escaped certain death because of a strange glowing ball. Just thinking it seemed strange, even after living through it.

With the first problem of escaping the bookstore out of the way, Rolland was at a loss as to what to do. With nothing but the singed clothes on his back, an unconscious man named Victor at his side, and a serious fear that he might be going crazy, all Rolland really wanted to do was go home.

Home…

The beast that attacked him in front of the store had not only destroyed his only means of transport, but had taken his home as well.

Rolland had always had his trusty Cadillac to fall back on, and a meaningless, destructive void now filled his heart in her absence. How strange it was to become so attached to an inanimate object, but then again, if there had been only one lesson he had learned over the course of the last twenty one months, it was that getting attached now only lead to being separated later on.

Loss... it is inevitable.

Silently, Rolland bowed his head and said a little prayer of remembrance for his fallen shelter.

Chapter 3:
Fate = Fight or Flight

"Is he alright?"

The voice came from everywhere and nowhere all at once, interrupting Rolland's morose moment. Again it rang out above the chirping of nearby crickets, apparently distorted along with the flow of time. Their song fell upon Rolland's ears in a calm, study beat that reverberated all around him, only underscored by the raspy voice.

"Is he alright?" it asked again, echoing through Rolland's head like it was the dome of a concert hall during a rock and roll show. Rolland looked around, but saw no one.

A pair of pale green eyes came into focus first, followed by a head, a torso, and finally the full body of an older man wearing what appeared to be little more than the tattered remnants of clothing. His short, well-kempt beard was a patterned mixture of brown and gray, with white whiskers sporadically peeking through. His face was kind and wise.

Rolland thought that this man too might be homeless, and allowed his free hand to drift toward his car keys, interlacing them between his knuckles for defense.

"That will not be necessary," the man said in a calm, collected voice. "I mean you no harm."

"...Okay..." Rolland said, at a genuine loss for words.

"How long has he been like this?" the older man asked, moving closer to Victor and attempting to prop him upright against the tree Rolland had left him under.

"Uh..." Rolland began, confused by the man's complete disregard for the fact that they seemed to be frozen in time.

"Quickly! You saved his life for the time being, but without my help he will die. Please, how long has he been like this?" he asked again, pale green eyes darting back and forth, before focusing intently on Rolland.

"I dragged him up the hill," Rolland said, managing more than one word for the first time since the gray stranger had appeared. "So maybe six or seven minutes."

"Good, good," The man said, taking one of Victor's hands and holding it between his. "Now when the bubble begins to crack, you must pop it. Understand?"

Rolland did not understand at all, but he nodded anyway. He watched as the older man took Victor's other hand and closed his eyes, humming to himself. From inside their conjoined hands emerged a large, white, translucent bubble that surrounded the two of them like a protective barrier.

Rolland could see both men encased within the bubble, neither one moving a muscle.

The bubbles' crust began to crack and peel like sun-burnt skin, creating a chalky, white outer layer that flaked off at Rolland's touch.

Remembering his promise to pop the bubble, Rolland searched his pockets for something that might do the trick. Pulling out one of his favorite ball point pens, he proceeded to pop the large, flaky bubble, taking out a great deal of frustration on it as he did.

"Thank you," the man said, appearing exhausted and considerably weaker.

"Don't mention it," Rolland said "Now if you'll excuse me, I think I left the oven on... or something."

"Wait," the older man held his hand out as if to prevent the boy from leaving. "I've saved his life for now, but neither of us will survive without your help."

"Why should I help you?" Rolland asked, trying desperately to figure out what possible use he could be to a man who could appear out of thin air and wrap people in weird, peeling bubbles.

"Because both of your parents would have helped, even if I was a perfect stranger," the man said, clutching his chest and falling slowly against the tree beside him.

"But you're not, are you?" Rolland asked.

"No, you're right. I was a friend of theirs," the old man replied, checking his own pulse.

"Was, or are?" Rolland asked, suddenly assaulted by a strange mix of emotions. "Do you know where my father is?"

"Oh, dear child. Yes, I do know where he is," the man said. The weight on his shoulders suddenly seeming much heavier. "He is dead, my son."

"He's dead?" Rolland repeated. The strange finality of his father's fate rang through his mind. It was a strange thought to him, knowing that Scott Wright no longer walked the Earth, a fate that he had wished on his drunken dad many times since he'd left Rolland to fend for himself. The reality though, was a much different story.

"Thanks for telling me," he said over his shoulder as he turned to leave.

"Your father was a hard man to get along with, I'll admit," the gentleman called after him, his head still wobbling a bit from the healing bubble trick a few moments prior. "But he was a dear friend of mine, as was your mother."

This statement caught Rolland's attention, and he paused midstride, turning around to address the strange traveler.

"What do you know about my mother?" Rolland asked with a mixture of curiosity and indignation, his face filled with conflicting emotions. He saw the man's eyes grow wider, his head drooping, and Rolland knew that the offense in his voice had not gone unnoticed.

"I know that she was murdered by the same man as your father. I know that she was a kind and generous soul, with exceptional abilities and a true sense of what it took to be a Knight of Time," the man said, coughing into his free hand, sending gold and purple sparks out of his mouth and onto his shirt. "Excuse me."

"A what?" Rolland asked, his brain having apparently given up trying to process all the strange things being thrown at it.

"The Knights of Time, a group to which your mother – and your father -- belonged. A group that I happen to be the leader of," the man managed, obviously in pain. "A group for those with extraordinary abilities to help humanity."

"Well that's nice and all," Rolland said, regaining some semblance of logical thought, "But I've got to find a way to fix..." he paused, searching for words and finding none. "...all of this, before it gets dark."

"Yes," said the old man, coughing again. "About that…"

Eyeing the stranger suspiciously, Rolland caught sight of the burning shell of what was once his beloved El Dorado sitting in the parking lot beyond.

"Damn," he cursed quietly.

"You must have done something to cause this. Think. What were you doing when this first started?" the stranger interrupted impatiently.

"Me?" Rolland asked with startled indignation. "You're trying to tell me you think this is *my* fault?"

Rolland's heart felt like it was trying to tie itself in knots as he looked at the old man's face. His demeanor had a certain character to it – like an old house that had weathered many storms but never caved in on itself. It felt like hours since the man had made his presence known in Rolland's life, and years since he'd not been keenly aware of the fact that he was a freak, and an orphan.

"I honestly don't know," Rolland said throwing both of his hands up in the air and shaking his head vehemently.

"Think!" the man encouraged, his face eager.

"There was a lot going on at the time, the store was on fire!" Rolland stammered. "We were under attack!"

"Who attacked you?" the man asked Rolland, struggling to stand.

"I don't know who they were," Rolland snapped. "A red headed woman, some ugly dude with bad skin. A guy named Hess, you know, like the Nazi. Oh, and this big ass monster…"

As Rolland threw both of his arms into the air to emphasize the immense scale of the fire-breathing beast, he became very much aware of the fact that he was not getting the reaction he would have expected from the stranger. In fact, he got no reaction at all, almost as if the man had strange creature attacks interrupting his own shopping excursions on a regular basis.

"I'm sorry, really I am," Rolland mumbled sheepishly, hoping to recapture some good will and feeling extremely guilty that he was unable to offer any more useful information.

Rolland began nervously snapping the fingers on both hands before forming a fist with his right hand, and bringing it down hard upon his open left palm, creating a smacking sound.

"Wait, what was that?" the old man asked Rolland, craning his neck to peer at Rolland's hands.

"What was what?" Rolland asked him, helplessly confused.

"That thing you just did. The snapping and clasping of your hands," the man said, pointing at Rolland. "Do it again."

Rolland watched the man's green eyes narrow as he did as he was told. Their silver gray centers never lost their gleam. Though try as he might, he could not figure out what he was looking for. The chirping of the crickets seemed to stream together into one constant barrage against Rolland's nerves.

"Do you hear that?" the man asked Rolland, urgency filling his voice.

"Hear what?" Rolland asked him, looking around.

"The crickets; listen to what you've done to the crickets!" the older man said, out of breath from his excitement.

"They're chirping. So what?" Rolland asked, snapping and clapping his hands and fingers together once more.

"Not just chirping, Mr. Wright. Not at random," he said triumphantly. "You're controlling them."

"What, me? How?" Rolland asked, unable to keep frustration from filling his voice.

"Your hand gesture, I believe," the man said, pointing to Rolland's hands. "As I recall, it was one of your father's favorite ways of controlling time and space."

In that moment, everything in Rolland's life changed.

"Wait, did you say time and space? What are you talking about?" Rolland asked, forcing himself to stop mid-gesture.

"Your father," the man managed, struggling to catch his breath, "was a very important part of my team. The most important, you could say."

"Sorry mister, but we're obviously not talking about the same guy," Rolland said, stealing another glance at his flaming vehicle. The flames had moved slightly from where they were a few minutes ago. Against his better judgment, Rolland admitted the flames' motion could support the man's snapping theory.

"Scott Wright had his faults," the man snapped, losing his patience for a moment. "But he had a good soul, much like you do."

"How do you quantify the soul?" Rolland asked solemnly, his frustration turning again into a silent, painful despair.

"By its actions on Earth, of course," the man explained. With great effort he lifted his right hand and pointed at Rolland. "You are the sum of your actions, Rolland Alan Wright."

"You think so, huh?" Rolland asked, offering a small smile to the supposed friend of his late parents.

"Oh, I have very little doubt that you are your parents' child," the man said to Rolland with a smile that reached from ear to ear. "You have your mother's brains and your father's tenacity. And like both of them, you rush head-first into danger instead of running away. Not a wise choice for someone as smart as you."

"Yeah, well," Rolland said, putting both hands back into the pocket of his blue jeans. "There's a difference between being smart and being capable."

"Lucky for you, you appear to be both," The man said, clinging to the tree just to support his own weight.

"Hey, you alright?" Rolland said, shuffling his feet nervously. He wanted nothing more than to help the old man up and on his way, but since he was the only other human being not moving in slow motion, Rolland's curiosity got the better of him. So many questions though, better to start with something small. "What's your name?"

"My name is Marcus L. Turtledove, and I assure you that I'll be just fine, though I appreciate the somewhat belated concern," the man smiled, extending one hand to Rolland.

"Rolland Wright," Rolland said to him rather redundantly, returning the gesture.

"Look Rolland, I can provide somewhere safe for you to think," Turtledove said. "Please let me help you that much."

"Alright," Rolland agreed. "But I should warn you there are some pretty bad people after me."

"I know," said Turtledove, pulling what appeared to be a white pillow case from the inside of his shirt pocket. "Take this, say your name into it, and lay it flat on the ground."

Confused, Rolland did as he was asked before laying the white pillow case on the grass between them. It puffed up, filling the space inside.

The top of a wavy blonde head appeared out of the bag, followed by a face. Rolland's face.

"What...?" Rolland stammered, shocked and unprepared for his own appearance.

"This will throw them off of our trail. It's all very organic, I assure you," Turtledove said sarcastically.

"Weird," Rolland said under his breath, shaking his head in disbelief. "Then again, I did just stop time."

"No, you didn't," Turtledove said rather sternly. "You merely slowed it down."

"Oh well in that case..." Rolland trailed off, turning from Turtledove back to his carbon copy, which was steadily emerging from the oversized pillowcase like toothpaste being squeezed through a tube. When it had ejected an entire boy out onto the grass the it flattened, a normal sack once again.

"The first time you see yourself being copied can be surreal, yes. I remember my first time with... less than fond memories," Turtledove said, trying to regain Rolland's attention. "It's best to remember that it's just a copy and has never truly lived, not like you have."

Comforting words to a simpler minded fellow, these had no effect on Rolland as he watched his own carbon copy being made. He wished he had spare clothes to dress it.

"Please, if you would be so kind as to humor me, do it again," Turtledove said, squinting at Rolland.

"Uh, do what, exactly?" Rolland asked, swinging his arms nervously. For the Wright men it had never been about hand tricks, only nerves.

"That snap-clap movement you did a moment ago, with your hands. The thing we've been talking about for the last ten minutes," Turtledove said, a hint of annoyance creeping into his voice.

Rolland looked at the old man as if he were crazy, but began snapping the fingers of both of his hands before forming a fist with his right hand, and bringing it down hard upon his open left palm.

Suddenly, the air was filled with the screams of sirens as time returned itself to normal around the three men on the hill and fire trucks rushed toward the Books Half Price.

"Right as rain," Turtledove said, over the sound of sirens. "Come along then."

With a final glance over at the parking lot, Rolland saw the dozen people he had pulled out of the building sitting upright and looking dazed. It was amazing how close they had all come to death, and none of them would ever know it.

Jogging over to Victor's side, Rolland wrapped the large African man's arm around his shoulder and helped Turtledove carry him down the small hill that led back to Pecan Street.

They only walked three blocks east before they came to a stop in a rather familiar part of the downtown district. The red brick building in front of them was older than the others, giving it a sense of no longer belonging as it sat wedged between coffee houses and cellular telephone stores.

"The public library?" Rolland asked with distaste as he came to a stop on the pink marble steps. "You have got to be kidding me."

The man who called himself Turtledove was again one step ahead of him, and without saying a word, he brought his index finger to his lips before resting it upon Rolland's forehead. Turtledove's strangeness, it seemed, knew no bounds.

Rolland, who felt that he had tolerated a great deal from this strange man, did not take kindly to people touching him. Nor did he enjoy being made a fool of. But before he could open his mouth to protest, Turtledove had picked up one half of Victor's overly large frame and was flopping him about in an attempt to move him inside.

"Really?" Rolland said to himself shaking his head before catching to the other side of Victor and correcting the weight distribution.

"Your cynicism is well-founded, my young friend, and I'm sure it has served you well in the past. But for this experience, I'm afraid you'll have to rely on other instincts," Turtledove said, his free hand moving to the brass knob on the library door.

It was an older library, built just after the Second World War. Purists hell bent on avoiding change from the so called 'glory days' had even petitioned the city council ensure that no electronic locks or security systems were ever installed. Who, they argued, would ever want to break into a library?

"You're wasting your time," Rolland said matter-of-factly. "The library doesn't open until noon on Fridays. And even then..."

Rolland stopped short when a small golden flap appeared just above the doorknob.

"This, my young friend, is step one," Turtledove said, pulling down the golden flap to reveal a plain yellow post-it note. Two words were written there – June Lin.

"Oh, no, not her," Rolland moaned, taking a few steps backward and causing Victor to slump between the two other men.

"You know Ms. Lin?" Turtledove asked, pulling a ballpoint pen from an unseen pocket and scribbling the words 'Marcus L. Turtledove to see June Lin' and placing the post-it sticky side down on the golden flap. He folded the small door back into the wall and waited.

"I guess you could say that," Rolland said, slightly embarrassed that his past misdeeds were coming back to haunt him. "Don't you?"

"Not at all," Turtledove said, taking a step back and taking back his half of Victor's weight. "But something tells me that she knows me."

Perplexed, Rolland watched as the golden flap on the door simply hung there for a few moments. He reached out to feel it with his free hand, finding its surface smooth and cool to the touch, like silk cloth.

Then it vanished.

Of its own volition, the large oak door to the library opened, granting them access.

They walked in still carrying Victor, his feet dragging across the floor behind them. Standing in a large hallway connecting the entrance to the main library itself, Rolland eyed the glass display cases on both sides as they passed. A large globe the size of a small automobile stood to their side, Eastern Florida and the Gulf region facing them as they walked past and through the glass entrance door.

It was but a moment following their entry that a small Chinese woman wearing horn rimmed glasses appeared from behind the counter and came running toward them at a frantic pace.

"Mr. Wright, how many times have I warned you about breaking in when this library is closed! I have half a mind to... oh... what's this?" The librarian's tirade ground to a halt as she spied infamous Knights of Time, Victor and Turtledove, accompanying the rambunctious minor. "Marcus Turtledove...?"

"Hello, Ms. Lin, isn't it?" Turtledove said amiably, lifting Victor's arm and slipping the large man into a nearby chair. "We need your help."

The librarian looked from Turtledove and back to Rolland again, as if to verify both of them were real. "But you're with him...?"

"Mr. Wright found out this morning that his father, Scott Wright, has been killed, leaving him an orphan. Because of this, I have decided to take him back to Eden with me," Turtledove said, oblivious to the naked surprise on Ms. Lin's face. "Would you be so kind as to help us with Victor?"

"But... well... oh my. Of course, Mr. Turtledove," June said, walking backwards and never taking an eye off of Rolland as she moved along the familiar path back to her office.

"Marcus will be fine, Ms. Lin," Turtledove called after the woman as she scurried away.

"We aren't on the best of terms," Rolland said, feeling an odd need to defend himself.

"You must have done a number on her," Turtledove said, with a smile and a wink.

Rolland returned the smile, but was unsure how to respond. The public library was his first attempt at 'living off of the radar', back when he was still learning the basics of life on the street. He had been kicked out almost a year ago for 'unruly behavior' and had not been back since.

Ms. Lin returned a few minutes later with what looked like a long, metal book cart. With her help, Rolland and Turtledove lifted Victor off of the chair and on to the cart.

"Do the honors?" Turtledove asked Rolland, following June Lin to a room in the back. Feeling as if he had no choice, Rolland pushed the cart carrying the large African man and hoped that they weren't going far.

Three people walked and one rolled to Ms. Lin's office. Once inside she closed the door and shut the blinds behind them.

"We will have to be quick. There isn't much time before we open for the day," June said as she walked behind her desk and turned on a small lamp. Using both of her hands to feel underneath the desk, she pressed a small button and stepped back quickly.

It felt like an earthquake as the ground moved beneath them. Rolland looked over at Turtledove who smiled again, winking at him like a grandfather about to pull a quarter from behind his ear. This trick was much more complex however, and June Lin's desk slid slowly to one side of the room, revealing a six foot hole and a staircase leading down into the darkness.

"Leave Victor here for the moment, we will come back for him soon," Turtledove said, motioning to June and Rolland. "After you."

"Wait a second," Rolland said, as he eyed the stairs nervously. "There are no basements in L.A."

Turtledove and June looked at one another and started laughing. Turtledove even stopped to wipe a tear from his eye, shaking his head as he headed into the bowels of the library. "Come along then."

There were only two small flights of stairs beneath the floor of Ms. Lin's office. Though they seemed very old, it appeared they had been used often, and the path was clean and well lit. They came to a nondescript room. It was small, no bigger than a standard ten by twelve, nothing in it besides a door at the far end.

"So what now?" Rolland asked, impatiently, the novelty of the library's secrets wearing thin.

"Now... you tell us if you notice anything strange about this place," Turtledove said, offering no clarification.

Dismissing about half a dozen possible smart-ass answers, Rolland simply played along, and began looking around the room. There was nothing special about the dingy walls. The door wasn't particularly distinct either, with its off-white paint. The faintly glowing doorknob on the other hand, got his attention.

"Whoa…" Rolland said, walking over to the door. "There's something weird going on with the door handle."

"What do you see, Rolland?" Turtledove asked, careful not to offer any hints.

"The doorknob over here, it's glowing, just like that orb that guided me to save everybody from the bookstore," Rolland said, curious, but overwhelmed with feelings of claustrophobia, helplessness, and disaster echoing back from the earlier trauma.

"It worked out well for you last time you approached the light, did it not?" Turtledove asked, hoping to goad his new charge into repeating himself. "Why not go to it again, hmm?"

Rolland considered this for a moment. "Where does it go?"

"Paradise," Turtledove said. "But there is only one way to find out. So…"

"That's alright, I'm good," Rolland said in a flat tone. "Do all libraries, all over the world, house gateways to some mythical paradise?"

"Yes," Turtledove said, clasping his hands behind his back. "Why else would they still be around?"

"Place for homeless people to bathe…?" Rolland guessed, more serious than his tone revealed.

The librarian, June Lin, merely shook her head sternly, muttering something about how irresponsible Rolland was.

"It is alright, Mr. Wright, nothing bad will happen if you touch it," Turtledove assured Rolland, though he still would not move so much as a finger. "Trust me, this is what I do."

"Lure kids into a basement and lock them in closets? Yeah, I bet." Rolland smirked.

"I extract people, Rolland. That's what I do," Turtledove answered sincerely.

"Kidnap them, you mean?" Rolland retorted, defensively.

Turtledove was undaunted. He took a deep breath, and explained.

"Certain people have abilities that could be too complex, or even dangerous for the regular population. People like you and me. So WE have been tasked with finding others like us and helping them cope with their unique situation. More often than not, that includes taking them back with us and teaching them how to control themselves, yes," Turtledove finished.

"Still sounds like kidnapping to me, making people leave their lives behind to join you," Rolland said, keeping eye contact with the kind, yet adamant Turtledove.

"We agree to disagree," Turtledove said flatly.

"Please, just open the door Mr. Wright," June demanded, clearly annoyed at Rolland's teenage cynicism.

"I have an idea, why don't you do it?" Rolland snapped. Living on the streets had left him undeniably defensive, and extremely intolerant of anyone questioning his resolve under duress. "What's going to happen if I do, anyway? Some beast will pop out and I won't be able to tell if it's real or not?"

"I firmly believe in science, Mr. Wright," Turtledove said firmly, taking a step towards the boy and nudging him a little closer to the doorway. "You stand here questioning things you do not yet fully understand. One hundred years ago, mankind believed that the human mind could never be understood at all due to its complexity. Yet with the right tools, and methodical investigation, with hypotheses, evidence, and experimental proofs, we have gradually made progress."

Rolland stood with no further argument against Turtledove's sound reasoning. He looked over at Ms. Lin, who was cleaning her glasses with a spare tissue she had retrieved from her pocket.

"Quantum flux extends to the subatomic level. Yours is asynchronous with normal matter," she said, putting her glasses back on. "In other words, you do not belong in this universe."

"What?" Rolland asked, his eyes darting back to Turtledove for confirmation.

"All matter in the universe resonates on a quantum level with a unique signature. That signature is constant. It cannot be changed through any known process," June Lin said, crossing her arms.

"It is, essentially, the basic foundation of your own physical existence," said Turtledove, reminding Rolland of what he thought a grandfather would sound like when lecturing on some important topic, like religion or politics.

"So you're saying that my quantum signature is, uh, different from everyone else's? That's what allowed me stop time?" Rolland asked, desperately hoping this simple explanation would satisfy the claustrophobic feeling building inside of him.

"That's impossible. You didn't stop time. He didn't stop time, did he, Turtledove?" June Lin demanded, looking panicky and mildly horrified.

Rolland was unsure if he should take offense considering her previous disdain of him and his habits of the previous twenty months.

"No, no, Ms. Lin. He simply slowed it down. It was quite impressive though. You should have seen it," Turtledove stated proudly, nearly beaming with delight.

"Oh, I've seen the boy do enough, Marcus," June said, her already narrow eyes squinting in the dim, lamp-lit room.

Thoughts of the previous winter, when Rolland had broken the library's men's room toilet, came crashing into his head. He also suddenly recalled the numerous overdue books that had just recently gone up in flames inside his Cadillac. The look of utter contempt that shot from June Lin was enough to send shivers down his spine.

"Are you two different? I mean, do you have those quantum, uh..." Rolland trailed off, hoping to both change the subject and get some questions answered.

"Quantum signatures?" June Lin asked sarcastically. "Yes, of course we have them. Just like everyone else on Earth. It's like an imprint, a stamp that identifies you as human. In fact, now that I think about it, the fact that yours is a little off is hardly surprising."

Her pretentiousness had always rubbed Rolland the wrong way, but he doubted very much that the librarian was human either, especially if she was in league with Turtledove.

"But why? Why do we have them?" Rolland asked with the impatience of a child.

"Why do we have arms? There is no simple explanation, if there even is an explanation at all. But I can tell you with certainty that you... You, kid, don't come from this planet," June Lin said, her impatience as alienating as it was harsh.

"Nor do you belong here. So Rolland, if you please," Turtledove said, indicating the door prompting Rolland to lead the way.

Rolland suddenly was faced with the realization that they were not merely trying to educate him; they were trying to recruit him, and he immediately imagined the worst case scenario. Visions of lab tables and restraints ran through his head until his palms began to sweat profusely.

"Listen man, I don't know if I..." Rolland started, but was interrupted almost immediately by Turtledove.

"Rolland, please don't think that I'm going to harm you in any way," Turtledove said, his face a picture of sincerity. "I merely want to provide answers and a safe place for you to regroup and think about your future."

"All I have to do is open the door?" Rolland asked, taking a deep breath.

"Yes," Turtledove said, nodding his head slightly.

Without another word Rolland placed a hand on the doorknob, but found it locked. Using both hands, he tried jiggling it a little in both directions, but it was no use. Opening his mouth to tell Turtledove this, Rolland felt something strange and unpleasant on his fingertips.

To Rolland's great surprise the glowing door knob seemed to melt away at his touch, much the same way as the bubble did in the field outside of the bookstore, yielding to a beam of light that filled the room.

Mouth agape, Rolland leaned down to stare at the baseball sized hole. "Well would you look at that..."

"That's impossible!" June Lin exclaimed, rushing over to the door. With every step she took, an inch of the door began to melt away, leaving nothing but a brilliant light.

Shielding his eyes, Rolland gazed at the bright vortex beginning to take shape in the middle of the doorway, bringing a soft buzzing sound with it.

"How did you do that?" June demanded in a low, resolute voice.

"Do what exactly?" Rolland asked, watching little gray lines run wild through the bright white backdrop of the spinning vortex before shooting out like bottle rockets behind the seemingly unfazed librarian.

"Ohhhh!" June said, her cheeks turning red. "I hate it when you kids play your tricks!"

"This is no trick, June," Turtledove said, above the buzzing sound that filled the room. He turned to Rolland. "Will you go?"

Rolland made his decision, and approached the vortex, stretching his left arm forward into the abyss. It was cool and slippery to the touch, like the fog from dry ice.

He found it to be rather pleasant compared to the cramped basement, almost inviting.

Deciding to take the leap, he closed his eyes and stepped through the doorway.

It felt just like falling asleep.

Chapter 4:
Eden

It felt like waking up from anesthesia.

There are moments in everyone's journey when the path seems crystal clear, when the slings and arrows of everyday life strike out in perfect unison, placing you at the right place in the right time. Walking through the doorway of bright, white light, Rolland believed that this was his moment.

Since he was a baby, Rolland had always woken up the same way. With the haze of the subconscious wafting away from his mind like the morning dew on a field, Rolland could always recall wiggling his toes first. This small gesture kept him tethered to reality and always guaranteed his safety when he was having a nightmare.

Bad dreams had become the norm in the past couple of years, and that small gesture had grown into a full blown personality trait. He was understandably shocked to find that upon waking this particular morning he was unable to wiggle his toes as normal – they wouldn't move. Nothing would.

Then he remembered the fire, Turtledove, and the vortex. Rolland's thoughts suddenly become clear and sharp as tacks.

'What was going on?' Rolland wondered silently as he attempted to open his eyelids, a feat now comparable to lifting a pickup truck by hand.

Dark shapes began to take form above Rolland's head as he attempted to open his eyes a second time. Two large shapes loomed above him, too dark to see in any definition, yet he couldn't take his eyes off them.

"Mmmmmmpphhff," Rolland managed through gritted teeth.

"Glad to see that you made it across in one piece," Turtledove said, apparently one of the shapes. He smiled broadly and placed one hand on Rolland's chest. "Unfortunately, Ms. Lin's responsibilities to the library have kept her from joining us on this side of the doorway."

The sudden appearance of this strange man coupled with his inability to move convinced the frightened teen that he had somehow been drugged, and was probably in great danger.

"Wha, what izzz.." Rolland mumbled, the syllables cart wheeling out of his mouth with the grace of a tap dancing giraffe. "What is this place?"

Turtledove couldn't help but chuckle at the young man. His reaction was the exact opposite of what his father's had been when he first gazed upon Eden's wondrous gates. Some things, it seemed, were not hereditary.

"There are many names by which the golden city is called. Some claim it to be the lost city of El Dorado, others say it's Atlantis, but I, and everyone else who lives here, simply call it Eden," Turtledove said in a low, resonant voice that reminded Rolland of church services.

"Eden... right. But uh, wasn't Eden just a garden?" Rolland asked, almost wishing he hadn't. The look of admiration quickly disappeared from Turtledove's face as he turned to face the impudent teen sprawled out on the table.

"Your father asked me the same thing when he first arrived," Turtledove said, intentionally lying to the boy. "So I'll tell you the same thing I told him. Disregard what mortal man has written as historical fact, for the record tells only one side of each story. Disregard it, Rolland, but do not forget it, for history is full of missing pieces."

The words seemed wise, almost too wise for a man dressed as oddly as Marcus Turtledove was. Rolland was only half listening to what he considered little more than the sanctimonious ramblings of the lunatic who had drugged him, planning on doing who knows what to his unconscious body.

"All of us here were given something extra. Something special and unique, an extra sense or ability that you will never see duplicated the same way in another human being," Turtledove continued, so deep into his train of thought that he did not notice the fact that Rolland had regained the feeling in both of his legs and his left arm.

"I suppose you're wondering why you were unable to move. Well, you see my boy, Eden doesn't exactly exist in what you would call traditional time and space," Turtledove finished, turning back to Rolland.

"What do you mean?" Rolland asked, beginning to feel the now familiar cooling sensation in his right arm as well. Based on the reaction time of his other limbs, he guessed it would take another couple of minutes or so before he could it would function fully. There seemed little choice but to keep the crazy old man talking.

"We have left Earth as you know it, Rolland. The gateway that I took you to underneath the library has transported us here to

Eden, a land that exists outside of time and space," Turtledove restated calmly. "I can repeat it again if you wish."

Growing impatient with his host's wild fables, Rolland decided that it was time to go.

"No thanks, I'm kind of attached to my kidneys," Rolland said, rolling off of the table clumsily, barely catching himself on one knee. Making full use of every newly mobile limb, he sprang to his feet and ran from the bewildered Turtledove.

It didn't take Rolland long to realize that he was running in circles. A long, dimly lit hallway awaited him as Rolland made his way farther away from his assumed captor and the ornate room he woke up in. The halls he ran through were near pitch black, and appeared to be made out of a flat, gray stone. Along with the lack of windows and natural light, Rolland began to notice a more pronounced incline the longer he ran. A mounting heat upon his brow told his mind what his eyes would confirm a moment later as impossible.

Beneath him lay a series of old rope bridges forming a labyrinth of synchronized complexity over two giant, circular, black cauldrons the size of dining room tables that served as lights to guide the way through the chamber. Inside of them bubbled an immensely hot concoction of an orange, soupy substance with a hard shell on its surface. If it wasn't for the tepid temperature in the looping chamber, Rolland would have sworn the substance was lava. A fork in the corridor broke his train of thought, and forced him to choose left, away from the entrance to the magma cauldrons. He pushed on, hoping to have chosen correctly and not end up on a rickety rope bridge.

Coming to the end of the now steep corridor, Rolland found himself face to face with a large, wooden door. Trying it, it opened much easier than he had anticipated. A lucky break, as he had yet to shake the tingling feeling that came with 'waking up in Eden' as his crazed abductor had called it, a phrase Rolland could only assume was a euphemism for some as yet unknown street drug.

The early afternoon sun hit Rolland full on, blinding his un-prepared eyes just as it had in front of the bookstore. He rubbed them with his palms as they adjusted to the light, but no amount of rubbing could have prepared his eyes for the scene that slowly emerged from his dotted vision.

Everywhere he looked there were people of different races, each displaying what Turtledove had referred to as an 'extra sense'. From what Rolland could see, these senses ranged from the comi-cal to the downright scary.

Examples of both extremes were on display as Rolland walked further into the bizarre courtyard, and the midday shadows lift-ed, letting the sunshine beat down and bathe the patrons in its warmth. Looking up, Rolland saw not just the sun, but also the moon. Two moons, actually – an identical moon hung right beside the first.

"Two moons?" Rolland muttered to himself, looking around to see if anyone was around to ask about the strange phenomenon. The market place was filled with life as patrons crowded the space with typical midday hustle and bustle.

To Rolland's left a little girl with bright pink hair was sitting on the sidewalk making her dolls waltz with one another. This scene wouldn't normally be odd, but this little girl was clapping happily to an unheard rhythm and cheering for her toys as the male doll dipped the female to the floor.

On Rolland's right, a portly, middle-aged man was leaning against a cottage sleeping. Also fairly normal, except he wasn't standing on the ground, he was hovering above it. Rolland leaned in closer to verify the impossible feat. The man was literally defying the laws of gravity. In his sleep. As if it were nothing.

Merchants tended their booths all along the alley, their wares on display for customers to peruse at their leisure. Various odd objects graced the tables: gadgets, fruits, and cuts of meat. There didn't seem to be any prices on any of the items, however, replaced by what Rolland could only assume was bartering and free exchange.

Rolland watched as a kindly old woman bought a hunk of meat the size of a small car hood from another woman who was dressed as a butcher. Oddly enough, four large culinary knives continued to chop vegetables and various meats behind her. With one eye on the knives, she completed the exchange, accepting what looked like a large bushel of apples in return.

Never in his wildest dreams would Rolland ever have conjured the absurdity that seemed every day here. It was a walking, talking affront to what he knew as reason and logic. It was… paradise.

Smiling to himself, Rolland took a deep breath and exhaled a mixture of panic and amusement in no less than a hundred directions. Fearing that he looked exactly like the tourist he felt he was, he decided to stick to the shadows and keep a low profile, at least for now.

Turning the corner at the end of the street, Rolland came face to face with a small, fenced off area brimming with tables. A large banner hanging between the two apartment buildings on either side read 'Purple Martin Bazaar'. It had obviously been hung there by two short, mustached gentlemen who were standing nearby, both sporting a set of wings sprouting from the smalls of their backs. They both seemed to be enjoying their lunches, their wings fluttering happily though both men were firmly on the ground.

Nearby, a man Rolland guessed was the owner of the Bazaar stood against the wall behind the tables with his arms crossed and his jaw squared. His dark, unforgiving eyes were fixed on Rolland..

"Buy something or move on!" he shouted at a group of children who had approached his table and were playing with his trinkets. A gruff, middle-aged man, he didn't seem particularly personable. Picking up a large wooden stick, the man began swinging wildly at the children as if they were pigeons or some other sort of unwanted rodents. The portly bazaar owner managed to catch one of the boys, tripping him before he could run off. He waddled a few steps and grabbed the boy's arm, yanking him forcefully to his feet.

Almost unconsciously, Rolland stepped toward the man.

"Why don't you leave them alone?" Rolland hollered, grabbing the man's wrist just as the man had done to the child moments before.

The bazaar owner looked at Rolland indignantly for a quick moment before his eyes wandered past the teenager, spying a bigger problem.

Rolland glared at him, but saw no recognition. Turning slightly, Rolland saw what had distracted the bazaar owner.

Walking past the alley were two green-skinned individuals with giant, catlike faces and whiskers extending from above their eyes and lips. Their ears sat prominently on top of their heads, with lines of spots running in stripes down their skin, covering their entire bodies in random patterns that reminded Rolland of leopards.

They stood on two legs and wore clothing in the same manner as the humans that surrounded them, but as they got closer, Rolland could clearly see that what he had assumed was skin was actually a fine fur covering them from head to toe. Though neither had any lips to read they appeared to Rolland to be speaking to one another in plain English.

"Wha... what are they?" Rolland stammered, letting go of the bazaar owner's wrist.

The man let out a sharp snort and took several steps back, away from the stranger that had challenged his authority.

"What are ya', stupid?" the man asked, a small smile peeking out for the first time in years. The cracked and yellow teeth filling his mouth were seeing light for the first time in years, if the smell was any indication. "Dis is an elemeno. Dis guy don't know what an elemeno is, eh? Tough guy? Come on…"

Before Rolland could question the man any further, a series of small crashes drew him back to his booth where the children were once again causing mischief with his wares.

"Hey, you cut it out you mashugana kids!" the bazaar owner yelled, flailing his arms about it an accidently comical way.

"Why are you so mean to kids?" Rolland asked him, wondering if there was something that this man could do to make him regret asking.

"That is sprocket, sprocket!" the fat, hairy bazaar owner continued before going back to nursing his wrist.

The children ran off, away from the bazaar and further down the alleyway into the darkness. Deciding that he had enjoyed the man's company long enough, Rolland followed them in search of more answers.

Walking past the bazaar and through the apartment buildings, Rolland was presented with a scene less paradise and more east L.A. Dirty buildings crowded him from every direction as the corridor he walked narrowed. The street it led to was old and littered with broken bottles and trash.

Rolland could not help but wonder why the man who brought him here, Turtledove, had called this place Eden. A memory from far away came rushing into Rolland's mind, of Sunday school, and the re-telling of the story of the Garden of Eden. As he recalled, it was described as a paradise where fruit and vegetation grew abundantly. This was not that place.

To Rolland's right was a billboard featuring the face of one of the green cat people he had seen walking by the bazaar. The caption beneath it said 'Vote NO on Prop 10 – because our children deserve an education too.'

Not knowing anything about Proposition 10, and not really caring to at this particular moment, Rolland turned and walked away from the advertisement, continuing his search for a familiar sign or even a phone he could use to find his way back to Woodland Hills. Back home.

The farther Rolland walked, the more he began to realize that this wasn't home at all. In fact, it wasn't Los Angeles, or California, or even Earth.

The fear of being trapped in such a foreign place set in, setting Rolland even further off guard as he came to an intersection and saw a group of the green cat people turn and start walking in his direction.

Panic-stricken, Rolland stopped dead in his tracks and began speed walking away from them, back toward the marketplace. That was when Rolland saw her. There, a mere ten feet away from him, standing in the middle of the road, was a sad little girl who appeared no older than ten. With her eyes cast down toward the pavement, Rolland could only see the top of her blonde head, her hair sitting on her shoulders like fields of wheat. He approached her without the slightest apprehension. Being that she was the first identifiable human he had seen in the past half an hour, he was grateful for her presence and wanted to help her in any way he could.

Kneeling down to her eye level, Rolland placed one hand gently on her shoulder just as his mother used to do to him.

"Hey, are you lost?" Rolland asked, taking his hand off of her shoulder and clasping them in front of him so she didn't feel threatened.

The little girl looked up at him, her baby blue eyes meeting Rolland's and forming an immediate connection. Within seconds, her melancholy demeanor had vanished and was replaced by one of urgency.

"Mister, you have to help me!" the little blonde girl said to Rolland, taking him by the hand. "I've lost my mommy and I need to find her!"

"Sure. Uh, where is she, exactly?" Rolland asked the girl, startled by her sudden change in attitude.

"This way, this way!" the little girl said, tugging on Rolland's hand as she pulled him further into the dark alley.

Every bone in Rolland's body screamed that allowing the little girl to lead him there was a bad idea. Still, she was rather adorable, and the idea that she was telling the truth and her mother might actually be in trouble was worth investigating. They dove further into the covered alley, leaving the sun and all reason behind as they went.

Garbage bags and cardboard boxes lined the walls on either side of them, making the narrow pathway even less bearable to the claustrophobic teenager. Ahead of them the debris became so dense that nothing was visible save the outline of a person standing perfectly still in the middle of the walkway. Rolland stopped.

"Hello…?" Rolland shouted to the figure, cupping his hand to his mouth to amplify the sound. With no response, he tried again, but the little girl tugged on his hand impatiently.

"Come on, come on, that's my Mommy. Can't you see, that's her!" the little girl whined, shifting her feet.

"It is?" Rolland asked, looking from the little girl to her supposed mother standing a mere fifteen feet away but not acknowledging their presence.

"Yes, she's just shy!" the little girl whined, tugging at Rolland's hand with all of her might.

"Ma'am?" Rolland asked, taking a couple of steps toward the figure. He could clearly see that it was a woman. She wore a simple maroon dress and had long black hair, though it became obvious to Rolland that she was facing away from him, the lights playing shadows off the side of her face. "Miss, I think I have your daughter."

The words prompted the woman to turn around, revealing a flat, faceless surface with   large fleshy flaps of skin stitched together from her chin to the middle of her forehead. She titled her head slightly, extending her arms outward and bending her knees. A bright beam of crimson light split her face down the middle, temporarily blinding Rolland and forcing him to avert his eyes.

From deep within the folds of the open face, three long, jagged splinters of dark brown shrapnel shot out, flying through the air towards Rolland and the little girl.

With only seconds to react, Rolland began snapping his fingers and clapping his hands wildly in an attempt to stop the coming onslaught, but he could not summon the same urgency he had in the bookstore. He glanced at the girl, but she was gone.

Rolland had just enough time to turn and see three furry green missiles, each rounded at the end with an opening for a mouth filled with rows of razor blades, headed for his torso, and knew that he was helpless to stop them. Whatever mojo he had had going on Earth was not happening here in Eden.

A sudden explosion to his left startled Rolland and caused him to trip, bringing him face to face with death.

Then, just as the three green minions of certain dismemberment were crossing the threshold into Rolland's personal space, three shots rang out, filling the alleyway.

Rolland watched as each of the furry monsters exploded in mid-air, their cries echoing through the dark alley as they were reduced to green goo. The faceless 'woman' was gone as well. Rolland was covered in a healthy amount of leftover monster goo, and he barely had time to wipe his eyes before he heard the strong, graceful voice of his savior.

"You must have a soft spot for blondes," said a woman who, as Rolland turned to look at her, appeared very heavily armed. "Sprockets usually pray on the weak. And the dumb. Wonder which one you are."

"Uh," Rolland stammered, noticing that cluelessness and confusion seemed to be the flavors of the day. "What?"

"They're called sprockets," the woman said, removing her goggles to reveal a pair of beautiful green eyes. "Nasty little bastards like to take the form of children and lure idiots into alleyways. They'll kill you if they get the chance."

"Thanks," Rolland said, the shock beginning to wear off as his eyes came to rest on a very large gun. "Is that… a grenade launcher?"

The green eyed woman smiled and picked up the business end of her weapon, showing it off. "Yep."

"Huh," Rolland said, green goo still falling off of him and hitting the ground in big clumps as he stood up. "I've always wanted to see one of those. Guess I thought it would be bigger."

"Well, after all, seeing is believing," the woman said, wiping a bit of the green goop off of her weapon with her glove.

"Who are you exactly?" Rolland asked, hoping for a straight answer for once.

The green-eyed woman smiled, taking off her helmet to reveal a mess of braided blonde hair, the two braids falling off of her head and down her back. She shook a bit, causing some of the goo on her brown jacket to fly off. She removed her glove and reached out to shake Rolland's hand.

"Joan Rothouse. Er, Raines. Joan Raines. Sorry," the woman said, her left hand clasping Rolland's and squeezing slightly. A large glistening diamond sat upon her left ring finger, practically screaming that she was married.

"Rolland Wright," Rolland said, squeezing her hand in return.

"Rolland Wright?" Joan said, stopping their handshake and tilting her head slightly. "Did you come here with Turtledove and Victor?"

"Oh. Uh, kind of," Rolland said, caught off guard.

"You came from Earth, right? The present?" Joan asked, wiping the goo off of her rifle using the bottom part of her shirt.

"Yeah," Rolland said, growing increasingly wary of Joan's familiarity with him.

"You're probably freaking out right about now, huh?" Joan said, chuckling slightly as she put her glove back on and continued to wipe the mess off her arms, chest, and stomach.

"Maybe a little bit," Rolland said reluctantly. Perhaps it was because she saved his life, or because he felt unbearably lost at the moment, but something told him that he could trust her. "It's nothing I can't handle."

"Oh I bet," Joan said, straightening out her uniform. "Your parents would be proud."

"You knew my mom?" Rolland asked, his curiosity piqued by yet another person with more knowledge of his life than he had.

"Yep," Joan said, picking her rifle back up and throwing it over her shoulder. "Wanna come home with me? I'll tell you about her."

This proposal, though probably not sexual in nature, sounded too good to be true. Had Rolland gotten to spend any time with his father as a teenager, Scott probably would have told his son not to accept offers from much older women to accompany them home. Probably.

But as it was, he hadn't, and Rolland followed Joan as she walked away from the scene of a very messy crime.

Chapter 5: Grapples

Much to Rolland's chagrin, it didn't take Joan long to find Turtle-dove. The older man stood whistling to himself just outside of a large gate near the center of town. Although Rolland felt a bit of a fool seeing him again, the wiser of the two men didn't seem to harbor any animosity. Patience, it seemed, was a virtue that came with age.

Turtledove's muttered comments about 'what they were going to do with him' left Rolland less than excited to see the giant oak and brass door that stood before them. Kerosene torches lit either side of the massive doorway, which Rolland guessed stood at least fifty feet high. He thought it odd that the torches were lit in the middle of the day, but decided against asking.

"Open the gate, please!" Turtledove shouted to no one in particular.

Looking over to Joan, Rolland assumed that she might think the old man mad as well, but she didn't seem to notice that anything was out of the ordinary.

"Is that you, Turtledove?" said a man's voice from the other side of the painfully large oak door.

"It is," Turtledove stated with an air of haughtiness.

"Oy, one moment, sir," the man's voice said, this time in a more submissive and controlled tone. The great wooden door began to creak, and a seam appeared directly down the middle of its impenetrable surface.

Rolland barely had time to stare before a little man appeared, dressed as a squire, armor and all.

"Michael!" Turtledove greeted the man warmly, extending his right hand in a sign of friendship and brotherhood. "It is good to see you."

"Morning, Marcus," said the ornately armored guard, apparently called Michael, returning the gesture. "Morning, Joan. Who's your friend? A new recruit?"

Turtledove and Joan exchanged a look of quiet understanding before they both turned back to Michael with a curt "Yes."

Eyeing them all suspiciously, Michael simply nodded his head.

"Say, that reminds me…" Michael said, as he thrust his left hand into the one pocket in his armor. "This came about an hour ago. Doesn't look good."

Michael leaned forward and produced a piece of parchment from his pocket, seal already broken. He handed it to Turtledove hastily.

"Oh hell…" Joan exclaimed, her eyes glued to the parchment in Turtledove's hands.

Rolland felt as if he were the only person not in on a particularly bad joke as he watched Joan and Turtledove read the short document over and over.

"Pardon us for a moment, would you, Michael?" Turtledove said to the guard rather politely before turning away.

"Sure thing, sir," Michael said, turning his back toward them and focusing on Rolland for the first time. "Hello."

"Hi," Rolland said, both fascinated and amused by the man's ability to switch gears back to soldier so quickly. "How's it going?"

"Alright I suppose. Nothing interesting to report today," the guard Michael replied, looking out over the gorgeous hills that lay before them.

"Is there ever?" Rolland asked.

"Not so much. We do live in paradise after all," Michael offered, smiling and shifting his tall spear slightly.

"Listen, may I ask you a question?" Rolland asked.

"You just did. But I wouldn't be offended if you asked me another," Michael said to Rolland with a large, toothy smile that reminded him of Chiclet candies.

"Those people that I'm with…" Rolland began, but was cut off before he could get the chance to finish his sentence.

"Oh, yeah, don't think I didn't notice neither. It must be a big deal for a young pup like you to be riding along with a couple of the Knights of Time like you are," Michael said, child-like wonderment peeking out from behind his slightly worn face.

"Knights of… what?" Rolland asked innocently enough to pass for genuine ignorance.

"You new around here or something?" Michael asked, raising an eyebrow.

"Something like that, yeah," Rolland mumbled, his eyes pleading for compassion, if not outright mercy.

"Alright kid," said Michael, relaxing a bit and transferring his golden spear from his left to his right hand. "Quickly, before they come back. What do you want to know?"

Taken aback by the man's sudden change of heart, Rolland's mind bombarded him with questions. Where was he? Who were these people?

"Who are they?" Rolland asked Michael, pointing to Turtledove and Joan.

Michael gave a loud chuckle, placing his free hand on his rotund belly and saying. "That's Marcus Turtledove and Joan Raines. They're the numbers one and two for the Knights of Time, they are. Run the whole show."

"Well, yeah," Rolland said, taking a moment to muster some patience before continuing on. "But who ARE they? Like, are they dangerous, or criminals, or…what?"

Michael tossed his head back and gave another, more audacious bark of laughter. "You really aren't from here, huh, kiddo."

Deciding that the term 'kiddo' is where he would draw the line, Rolland tightened both fists and readied himself for the tirade he was about to unleash on the unsuspecting gatekeeper, but before he could say a word, Rolland felt the touch of Marcus Turtledove's hand on his shoulder.

"Thank you for your help, Michael. We'll be on our way now," Turtledove said, giving the guard a nod and a half-hearted smile.

"Alright, Turtledove," Michael said, clearing the path to the gate and the bridge beyond. "Good luck, kid!"

The couple hundred yards of hiking past the bridge came and went without a single word between the three travelers. Any feelings of attraction to Joan were quelled, putting her on par in Rolland's mind with dozens of other women who had turned him down in his short adolescent life.

"You mustn't let your emotions get the best of you," Turtle-dove said, patting Rolland on the back as they walked. "Your anger boils over too quickly, clouding your good judgment."

Taken aback by such bluntness from someone he hardly knew, Rolland stopped walking and stared at the older man in sullen confusion. "Just what the hell do you know about me?"

"You're forgetting, Mr. Wright, that I'm an empath, I can sense your emotions," Turtledove said with a smile. The two shared a silent, complicated look before continuing on. "Best to keep moving, eh?"

"Yeah, well, it's not that hard to forget stuff that isn't explained very well," Rolland muttered grumpily.

They walked for nearly ten minutes before Rolland spotted an odd glow in the distance. The closer they got to it, the brighter it became, nearly blinding Rolland as they approached the outer banks of a river running through the picturesque grassland.

"What is it?" Rolland asked, eyeing what he assumed must be rushing water.

"See for yourself," Joan said, nudging Rolland slightly toward the glowing unknown.

Approaching it cautiously, Rolland bent down enough to get within a few feet of the glowing material inside the riverbed. To his immediate surprise, he discovered that it was not water that was rushing through the embankment, but a dense fog that illuminated everything it touched. With less trepidation than he should have had, Rolland reached down and submerged his hand in the flowing white fog, watching it disappear under the thick blanket of mist. Panicking, Rolland lifted his hand out of the substance and shook it madly, grateful that it was still there.

Not only was Rolland's hand still in one piece, it was completely dry. He heard Joan laughing at him as he turned and saw his two traveling mates standing close now, both entertained by his obvious inexperience with their homeland.

"This, this isn't water," Rolland said in disbelief. "What is it?"

Turtledove knew that not only was this awkward boy completely unaccustomed to this world, he was in possession of a unique ability that made this particular discovery all the more important. He walked to the side of the riverbed and, looking from Rolland to the river and back again, said one word. "Time."

The word made sense but, having little knowledge of Eden geography, Rolland found himself once again unable to appropriately place it in context. He didn't find it unreasonable that he was having difficulty with the concept that this river of illuminated fog was the embodiment of time on Earth, or wherever they were exactly.

"Wait, so you're saying that..." Rolland began, but was interrupted by Joan, who had obviously been through this many times before.

"That this river is the living embodiment of the time stream itself, yes," Joan stated, as if she were reciting airline safety instructions without believing them to be effective. "But you should know. This *is* your thing after all."

"Huh?" Rolland asked, completely confused. "What happens if you fall in?"

"Perhaps it's best if we keep on moving," Turtledove suggested, meeting Joan's annoyed glance with a more patient one of his own. "But to answer your question my boy, you disappear."

"Yep," Joan said, nodding her head and crossing her arms "One way ticket to getting lost in time."

Not sure what to say to this, Rolland offered a meek "Oh... maybe there should be a fence or something..."as Turtledove led them across the bridge and over the glowing river of time.

"Joan, my dear, how long until sundown?" Turtledove asked.

"Roughly four hours," Joan said, gazing up in the sky at one of the moons.

"Excellent," Turtledove said with a smile, "There will be plenty of time to look around."

Beyond the gates of Eden Town proper was a paradise that puts even the great redwood forests of California to shame. Hundreds of thousands of great oak trees married with vast fields of grass, laying complement to the clear blue afternoon sky.

Rolland, not sure what to call this place except paradise, turned to Turtledove and was met with a laugh.

"Your mouth is open, kid," Joan observed good-naturedly, punching Rolland in the arm.

"Oh, uh, whoops," Rolland said, his hands nervously finding their way back into his pockets.

"Do not trouble yourself," said Turtledove, motioning for the two of them to follow his lead as he made his way to the stone pathway and the grasslands beyond.

Forcing his mind to wander away from the breathtaking view, Rolland zoned back in just in time to follow Turtledove and Joan up a steep, grassy hill. He picked up a large stick that lay among an assortment of smaller ones and used it to brace himself as they made their way, step by step, to the top.

"So, if I can stop time, what can you two do? Out of the ordinary, I mean," Rolland asked, sounding, he thought, like a complete idiot. Joan only embarrassed him further when she stopped dead in her tracks to address not him, but Turtledove.

"Wait, he stopped time?" Joan asked, staring daggers at her mentor.

"No, he didn't," Turtledove said flatly before turning to Rolland, answering his question while taking back possession of the walking stick again. "I am an empath, Mr. Wright, which means I can detect the wants and emotions of those around me."

"Oh," Rolland said, expecting a more interesting explanation. "Cool."

With only a quick glance from the top of the hill, Rolland Wright suddenly saw Eden in a whole new way. All around him, the land was covered in a vast assortment of trees and oddly constructed buildings and farms as far as the eye could see. To his right was what looked to be a large, industrial complex with a single light shining parallel to the hillside. On his left sat a small, round coliseum, open to the sky.

"Come along now, we must not dawdle," Turtledove said, taking a step down the hill and quickening his pace considerably. Tossing aside his walking stick the self-proclaimed empath flung himself forward in the most improbable way. In other words, the old man did cartwheels down the hillside.

Rolland watched in awe, not so much for the sight of what appeared to be nearly perfect somersaults, but for the herd of elegant white stallions moving across the valley below.

Moving as one, the creatures seemed to flow in a pattern similar to the time stream Rolland had seen a short time ago, although the flock was heading east, and the river of time had flowed west. Never the less, the two seemed linked somehow in Rolland's mind, goading him to get closer to the majestic beasts. But there was only one way to do that, by following the old man down the hill.

"Show off!" Joan said aloud, choosing to walk gingerly down the hill herself.

Using Turtledove's discarded walking stick, Rolland made his way down the treacherous terrain and thought to himself that as nice as these people were, their penchant for getting him into trouble was beginning to take a toll on his nerves. This, plus the green slime that was still caked on his favorite and only remaining shirt sent his mood spiraling from mildly annoyed to downright sour.

"The 'corns haven't gotten to this hill yet," Turtledove observed, getting to his feet with the speed of a man half his age.

"They'll get it. Don't you worry," Joan retorted, rolling her eyes and attempting to keep up with her colleague.

Rolling down the hill not far behind the two came Rolland, whose loose footing caused him to fall on his backside before sliding the last quarter of the way down toward his new traveling companions. Still, their topic of conversation piqued his interest.

"Excuse me, but uh, what are… corns?" Rolland asked, landing at the bottom of the hill with a thump.

"Take your time, Mr. Wright," Turtledove said to him "There is no rush. All of your questions will be answered, I assure you."

Assurances were worth as much as I.O.U.s in Rolland's mind, but the thought was quickly forgotten as the beasts galloped past them.

"What is that? What are those?" Rolland asked, his curiosity getting the better of him.

"Those, Mr. Wright, are unicorns," Turtledove said, his eyes glistening with a hidden wisdom.

Rolland could only stare in amazement as the animals grazed in the open field, completely uninterested in the three travelers. They looked like horses with their white coats and shaggy manes. The creatures were as elegant as they were beautiful, with the obvious nearly foot long horns adorning the top of each head like the crowns of royalty.

"Unicorns? No way!" Rolland said out loud, realizing what Joan had meant by 'corns'.

Rolland's overzealousness in seeing the unicorns left him blind to the large, ornate, castle-like structure that stood just a few hundred feet away.

"That's us over there, by the way, but you just go on ahead," Joan hollered after Rolland as he approached the herd of magnificent beasts. Once Rolland was out of ear shot, she turned back toward her boss and asked "So what do you think?"

"About the child?" Turtledove asked his second in command, eyeing Rolland as he made friends with a young mare and began petting her head and neck. "He's full of life."

The doors to the Halls of Time were made out of pure reinforced steel. This was important to note, as once Rolland did finally reach the doors he found no knob, bell, knocker, or really any traditional door hardware at all. Out of options, he began banging with both fists on the smooth steel surface that had the letters 'K.o.T.' engraved into the dark wood panel. It took three rounds of this before the doors opened slightly to reveal a tall, quite pissed-off-looking man with a cigarette behind his ear.

"Would you please..?" said the man, who had a British accent and short, spiky blonde hair, as he opened the door just enough to poke his head out to see what was causing the commotion.

"Oh hello," Rolland said, unsure as to who the man was. "I'm just here with Turtledove and Joan and they told me to…"

"Joan is with you?" the blond man asked, opening the door up a little more.

"Well, yeah," Rolland said, eyeing the man suspiciously.

"Right then," the man said, removing the cigarette from behind his ear and pocketing it before looking around and focusing again on Rolland. "Name is Raines, Doctor Judah Jacob Raines, smartest man alive. Who the bloody hell might you be?"

"Rolland Wright," Rolland said, shaking Raines' hand firmly. He in turn gave Rolland a moderately firm shake, a true sign of respect amongst gentleman – no matter what era in time.

"You're Scott and Taylor's secret kid, yeah? So I've bet you've heard all about me," the blonde man said to Rolland. "Judah Jacob Raines -- Master of the atom, inventor of the Dream Phoenix, all that hoopla. You smoke?"

"Uh, no, actually," Rolland said, wondering what else the blonde man could do to make him more uncomfortable. Unsure if it was a British thing or just the way he came across, Rolland decided not to mention the rude first impression.

"Ah, I see you've met our resident scientist," Turtledove said, entering the building followed closely by Joan as they approached the reinforced steel doors guarding the Halls of Time.

"Would you like the tour?" Joan asked Rolland, motioning for him to follow her through the entryway and into the dining area beyond.

"So this is where it all happens, huh?" Rolland asked, with very little idea what "it" actually was. He stepped inside and looked beyond the entryway into a dining area next to a very wide, open space with lots of sunlight. As if by instinct, he walked to it, and found himself standing underneath a skylight, the sun shining directly on top of him, as if singling him out. "This is where my folks spent all of their time."

A bit perplexed by the teenager's odd attraction to the sunlight, Turtledove watched as Joan and Judah exchanged a stifled laugh at

Rolland's expense. Perhaps they too felt the generation gap in the room. "Do you have any specific questions yet, Rolland?"

"Yes, actually," Rolland said, stepping out of the sunlight. "What gives? Is this heaven, or... I mean. Where's... you know?"

"Elvis?" Judah said, laughing at his own joke. He was the only one to do so.

"The grand architect of the universe?" Turtledove asked, venturing a guess that Rolland was assuming that the travelers of light possessed some sort of ancient knowledge on matters of religion and theology.

"Yeah, yeah where is he in all of this?" Rolland asked naively.

"The simple answer, Rolland, is that we don't know any more than you do," Turtledove said to him patiently and with a kind smile. "Though we possess extraordinary abilities, we are still limited by the answers given to us in nature and science. There is no hidden knowledge here."

"Nor do we know anything about Eden before humans got here," Joan added.

"When was that?" Rolland asked without skipping a beat.

"Oh, about 10,000 years ago now," Turtledove said. "Give or take a century."

Contemplating this for a moment, Rolland thought of all the possible answers to life-altering questions a place called Eden could offer, and then imagined them all falling away into the ocean. Just out of his reach.

"Alright, I get that," Rolland said furrowing his brow in concentration. "But if we are currently outside of time and space, then how do we still exist?"

"Well..." Turtledove began, but was cut off by the blonde man.

"Allow me, Turtledove," Judah said, brimming with enthusiasm. "What you say is true. We, you, me and Ol' Man River here, along with the rest of Eden, DO exist outside of the space-time continuum as we know it."

This validation of Rolland's suspicions oddly did nothing to ease the anxiety that still welled up within his chest. Perhaps it was the stress of facing an unknown future in a strange place without the slightest bit of anything familiar. Or maybe it was the fact that he hadn't eaten all day.

"BUT we are still here, yeah? That is to say, we still exist. We exist and, perhaps more importantly, we continue to perceive our own movement through time. Ergo, we must be moving in a forward motion universe in which time does progress. Though naturally my use of the word 'forward' is completely arbitrary and was intended solely to make the concept more digestible to the layman, "Judah said, motioning wildly with his hands.

"Oh, that's, uh, good news. I think," Rolland agreed, genuinely at a loss for words, choosing instead to suppress the blonde man's infuriating assumption and his branding as a layman. He watched as Turtledove and Judah exchanged a look of exasperated disbelief.

Suddenly feeling very stupid and embarrassed, Rolland decided to say something, anything that might make himself sound smarter. "So – um, what's the conversion rate, in time?"

"That's a very good question, Rolland," Turtledove quipped.

Feeling a bit patronized, Rolland decided against responding to Turtledove and instead decided to press the brainy blonde for an answer. Looking over at Judah, Rolland caught his eye again and persisted. "Well?"

"As far as we can tell…" Judah said in a slow, condescending voice. "It's about an hour and a half, or 90 minutes here for every year in Earth time."

"Out of curiosity," Rolland asked, hoping to catch the self-proclaimed 'smartest man in the world' off his guard. "Is that set to Pacific Standard Time as Earth time?"

This sarcastic comment drew a surprised bark of laughter from Turtledove.

"It's set to the Queen's Greenwich Mean, actually," Judah said, ready for the question. "That's the third most asked question I get. Work on your material, Junior."

"Will do, mate. Oh wow…" Rolland said dismissively as he noticed a giant telescope in the middle of the room, facing a large bay window. "So that's what the future looks like."

"This isn't the future Mr. Wright, it's the present," Turtledove chimed in. "The world has gone on without you, as it does for all of us. The fact is, no single human being can make a difference in the grand scheme of things. Together, we can."

A sudden chill ran through the room, every one of them silently remembering the lives that they had had, back in the so-called 'real' world. Each one of them, like Rolland, had faked their deaths and joined up with the travelers of light and later the Knights of Time. While the level of dedication each knight held to their cause and the pride they felt in each other was obvious, not a single one would have passed up the opportunity to go back to their old lives, even for a day. With this in mind, Turtledove spoke again.

"There is something you should know, Rolland my boy," Turtledove said, his face taking on the gravity of a parent informing a child that a pet has passed on.

"As we discussed, your parents hid you away, concealing any knowledge of you from us or the Council of Light," Turtledove said, retrieving a file and laying it on the table next to him.

"Council of Light?" Rolland asked, looking from Turtledove to Joan.

"Bureaucrats," Joan offered in clarification.

"Yes, well, they are quite specific on regulations for copulating. For both humans and Elemenos, I'm afraid," Turtledove stammered a bit, losing the cool, collected edge to his voice for the first time.

"What are you trying to say?" Rolland asked with a quizzical look of trepidation.

"Your parents broke the law in having you," Judah said bluntly. "When the council finds out, it's you they'll be after."

"Me?" Rolland asked looking at Turtledove with concern. The graying man before him suddenly looked his true age, all signs of the spry, versatile senior that Rolland had come to know in the last few hours had vanished. Had it been only hours? Or was it days now...

The intensity of the situation quickly escalating, Rolland decided that it was still within his control to halt this line of conversation for the evening and move onto another topic.

"So, what do you guys do for food around here?" Rolland asked in an awkward attempt to lighten the suffocating atmosphere. As it turned out, his comments did not have the desired effect.

"Accompany me on a walk, Rolland?" Turtledove asked a short time later, a twinkle appearing in the old man's eye as the sun began to fade outside the window behind them.

"Sure," Rolland said curtly. He wasn't keen on forgiving Turtledove, his parents, or anyone else involved in placing him in his current predicament just yet, and he failed to see how the old man planned on establishing an open dialogue between them.

Never-the-less, he decided to humor the old man, and he followed him down the curving staircase and out into the yard.

The sun was fading fast from her perch, and though it was beautiful, with its cascades of purple and red, it seemed to frame structures and buildings all around them that Rolland had not noticed when they arrived. As they walked, he began to realize that the round, coliseum-like building he had seen from the hilltop was their intended destination. Seeing this, he looked around and picked the next most interesting looking structure, the one with the large glowing light on top.

"What's that?" Rolland asked, pointing to the large industrial complex off to their left.

"That would be the Academy of Light," Turtledove said, pointing to the row of lights off in the distance beside it. "That is where you will be going tomorrow to begin your training."

"Training for what?" Rolland prodded.

"Well," Turtledove began, coming to a complete stand still and looking up at Rolland with his large, wild green eyes. "You will be trained to fight, to extract, and to live your life with these abilities that have been bestowed upon you."

Catching a glimpse of the light golden hue of the time stream to his left, Rolland imagined that he could almost feel the warmth it radiated with its glowing white hot surface interlaced with streaks of golden ripples at the surface. Distracted, he only belatedly realized that Turtledove had been answering his question.

"Sorry," Rolland said, embarrassed of his teenage imprudence and lack of social skills. "I was distracted by the, uh, time stream, I guess you call it."

The words fell out of Rolland's mouth with an awkward ineptitude that spoke volumes about his thought process.

Once again, Marcus Turtledove forced himself to close his eyes, open them again, and smile whole heartedly at a less fortunate soul than himself. He had known all of his life that circumstances only dictate the players, not the actions themselves. "Come – we're almost there."

Without another word, Marcus Turtledove fell back into his vigorous pace, forcing Rolland to keep up as they approached the coliseum.

An old wooden sign that read 'Blackard Family Orchard' greeted them as they passed through the wrought iron gate and into the grounds. Though the sun was setting nearby, the crimson light fell brightly upon the orchard as apples of various shades and colors lined the trees resting against the walls in rows on all sides.

"It's beautiful," Rolland said, looking around at the different varieties of fruit growing around him. It appeared that apples were just the beginning, as green, orange, yellow, and even purple fruits lined the twenty-foot walls that spanned outward, circling in on themselves and making the entire grounds smell like fresh produce.

A clipping noise, followed by a slight movement near the purple fruit gave Rolland reason to pause, as he suddenly realized that the two of them were not alone. "Who is that?"

"That man's name is Sherman," Turtledove said in a low, raspy voice. "He is the caretaker of this orchard."

"What's he doing?" Rolland asked, squinting his eyes to get a better look at the man.

"Watering, planting seeds, you know – all the things a blind farmer does," Turtledove said without a hint of sarcasm.

"He's blind?" Rolland asked.

"Oh, yes," Turtledove responded in a low, serious tone.

"Why is he working then?" Rolland wondered aloud. Then he cringed, expecting another long-winded story.

"A long time ago, he was a king among men," Turtledove said, his wild eyes settling on the blind man watering the vines of apples and assorted fruits. "Quite literally, actually. He, like you and I, was not born in Eden. But unlike you my friend, he is not from what we would consider the present on Earth."

Out of the corner of his eye, Turtledove saw a look of quiet comprehension on Rolland's face, and he felt confident enough in the boy's attention span to continue with his tale.

"He is from a point in Eden's history when we did not recruit those with extra genes in their DNA, they came here instead," Turtledove finished, finally turning to face Rolland for the first time since they arrived at the orchard.

"Wait, what?" Rolland asked, his voice losing its somber tone. "You mean people like... us...founded Eden on their own and came here without help?"

"Precisely," Turtledove said, giving Rolland an approving nudge.

"Well, that kind of puts things in perspective, huh?" said Rolland, picking up a spade and walking toward the blind gardener.

There were so many questions he wanted to ask this man who had apparently been around Eden longer than Turtledove, or anyone else for that matter, questions about the moons, or any of the million other little things bothering him. But the closer he got, the more Rolland realized that Sherman was probably just a regular guy who had once upon a time fallen from grace and now found himself here at dusk, tending his garden.

"What are those that you're growing there?" Rolland asked, forming a fist and knocking on the wood plank that stood next to the strange purplish-red fruit growing there on a tree limb.

Sherman smiled and nodded his head appreciatively before giving a polite response of "Grapples. They're half grape, half apple. Take one if you'd like."

Picking up the piece of fruit and turning it over in the palm of his hand, it was clear for the first time in his life that he was where he belonged. He knew this because, well, in this place no one really belonged. No one was a native. They were all transplants, taken from their lives on Earth and placed here. That's what made Sherman unique, what made everyone in Eden so special. Rolland, just like Sherman and Turtledove, was a grapple, and damned proud of it.

Chapter 6:
This Magic Moment

After chatting with Sherman for a bit, Turtledove interrupted politely, and he and Rolland excused themselves. Leaving the Blackard Family Orchard, Rolland could not help but wonder how Sherman, a supposed former king, could make his way to Eden with such a disability. This puzzle only confounded him further when he thought of all the other possible extraordinary abilities the citizens of Eden possessed. Based solely on the people he had encountered during his brief foray into Eden town proper earlier that day, Rolland guessed that there must be at least one healer amongst them who could fix Sherman's eyes.

"Why would anyone want to be blind in paradise?" Rolland asked Turtledove, following the man closely as they approached the cathedral that served as the meeting place of the Knights of Time.

"Atonement, perhaps. I'm not sure. It really isn't my place to ask. A man's reasoning is his own, Rolland. Heaven is what you choose to make of it," Turtledove said, as he opened the doors to the Hall of Time.

"You're telling me," Rolland said, staring up at the seventy-five-foot vaulted ceiling.

"Now if you will excuse me, I'm going to go wash up for dinner," Turtledove said, bowing slightly and leaving Rolland to his thoughts.

Alone, Rolland was free to browse the many knickknacks and books that openly graced the shelves of the Halls of Time. Medieval paintings, various sculptures indefinable to the naked eye, and for some odd reason, old license plates from around the world covered the walls. The largest of these assorted oddities was a tapestry in the form of a banner, which proudly displayed what looked to Rolland like the group's creed.

"I am a Knight of Time itself. I pledge to uphold the standards, practices, and fraternity that come from holding my title, and to defend the time stream from all those who wish to do her harm. Furthermore, I swear to lay down my life in the defense of Eden, her citizens, and any whose heart strives for the betterment of humanity."

A sculpture of what Rolland thought was a Minotaur piqued his curiosity enough to wander from the tapestry for a closer look. Look was about all he could do though, as it was fixed to the wall about nine inches above his head.

"Messing with the antiques?" said a familiar voice, as Victor sauntered into the room followed closely by another man. With a toothy white grin, Victor greeted the teenager who had saved his life a few hours before with a large bear hug, completely enveloping him.

"Yep, about to rob all of you blind," Rolland said, attempting to look the larger man in the eye but seeing only sternum. "Good to see you up and about."

Squeezing his little blonde friend, Victor let him go and took a step back before remembering why he had come down in the first place. "You meet everybody yet?"

"Yeah, yeah I think so," Rolland said, looking around for signs of others.

"Geoffrey," the man behind Victor said, extending his hand enough for Rolland to realize that something was very wrong with the man's arm. He was a gangly sort, skinny, with a sullen face and a nose that took up the majority of his face. Though his raised eyebrows and pleasant disposition were disarming enough, granting a good first impression.

"Oh, uh, hi, nice to meet you," Rolland said, examining the man's hand before taking it in his own, and looking up at his face again. Though this time it was not the face he had seen moments before, but that of Rolland himself. "Woah!"

"Geoff, cut that shit out!" Victor hollered. He slapped Geoffrey on the back with a baseball-glove-sized hand, causing the shape shifter's face to contort and change back to its original shape.

"Sorry, kind of a tradition to screw with the new guy. So, you meet the ladies yet?" Geoffrey asked excitedly.

"I met Joan," Rolland said enthusiastically.

"Joan's cool," Victor said nodding, "But she's married. Off the market, man."

"How about Sephanie and Tina? Seen them yet? Huh?" Geoffrey asked eagerly, morphing into a cartoon version of what Rolland remembered his grandmother once referring to as a 'lady of the night'.

"Uh, no, not yet," Rolland stuttered, attempting to block the large-breasted Jessica Rabbit from bumping into him awkwardly.

"They're gorgeous, man," Victor said, referring to the absent women and pointedly ignoring Geoffrey.

"Yeah, so hot," Geoffrey reiterated, apparently intent on convincing Rolland of this fact.

"I don't know. I saw this one chick this morning," Rolland began, allowing his mind to wonder back to the brunette girl who had lifted his spirits without saying a word earlier that day.

"At the bookstore?" Victor asked, trying to figure out which one Rolland might be referring to.

"Yeah, only no. It was before you got there," said Rolland, clarifying that she was not one of the people he pulled out from the fire. "She was just so... perfect."

"Well, what did she look like?" Geoffrey asked, far too interested in the entire conversation for Rolland's tastes.

"Well, let's see, um, she had brown hair, skinny, great body," Rolland said, pausing for a moment to reflect on the young woman's curves. "I don't know fellas, I only saw her for a moment but she was just so... perfect. It was almost like I dreamed her into being."

"That sounds like Sephanie," Victor said, flashing his big toothy grin.

"Oh, really?" came a musical soprano voice from somewhere beyond Rolland's line of sight.

Turning around at the sound of her voice, Rolland came face to face with the same angelic beauty from that morning in front of the bookstore. The instant that their eyes met, a strange sensation crept into Rolland's mind. Dull, hazy feelings covered every possible thought like a soft blanket of freshly fallen snow. It crept into every corner of Rolland's head, and made everything better just by association. It was love, it just had to be.

"Do I look like someone that you would just make up out of thin air?" the young woman asked Rolland, placing both hands on her curvy hips.

"Why, yes, ma'am, you do," Rolland said without thinking.

"Cute *and* funny," the brunette girl said "Definitely your father's son."

"Yeah, I guess that biologically speaking, Scott Wright is my father," Rolland said, attempting to use big words while still lost in the girl's stunning beauty.

"...We'll be going now," Geoffrey said, punching the much larger Victor playfully before running off toward the entryway and staircase near it. Victor followed him at a somewhat slower pace, a knowing smile resting upon his lips as he shot a wink to Rolland as he left the room.

This left Rolland completely alone with the gorgeous, intelligent brunette woman who had suddenly entered the fray as if from nowhere. He guessed her to be roughly his age, maybe a year or two older, but still within the window he considered necessary to make a move.

"I've been watching you for a while now, you know" said the brunette young woman, twirling a long strand of her hair and biting her lip. "Security and surveillance are a big part of my job."

"Wait, what? You've been watching me?" Rolland asked, pronouncing each syllable very carefully, trying to focus around the sensual thoughts racing through his head.

His cheeks turned bright red as she accidently grazed her hand over his right arm. It was soft, gentle, and only barely touched him. Yet he could feel her warmth and grace pass to him, filling every pore with unbridled joy and excitement. She made it look so effortless, carrying her beauty around, like some great secret that everyone knew, but no one had ever told her.

"Yeah," the brunette young woman said, biting her bottom lip again and casting her eyes upward playfully. "Everything for the past couple of days."

Rolland could not help but grip tighter to the arm of the chair he'd unconsciously been leaning on, and it supported more and more of his weight as the conversation went on. One thing did bother him though, and that was the subtle but distinct impression that something was lingering in the air between them. Something unsaid that breached the cultural divide they had already come to in their few short minutes together.

"Did I do anything… embarrassing?" Rolland asked tentatively, slouching a bit in preparation for a litany of his most embarrassing moments of the past ninety or so hours. Still, he could not pry his eyes away from her.

A coy smile graced her perfectly rounded cheeks, and Rolland couldn't help but stare as she lifted her head to meet his gaze.

"You mean aside from your grocery store shower?" She said mischievously, playfully punching him in the arm. Multiple strands of her shiny brown hair followed her tiny fist, cascading over his arm and causing goose bumps to rise to the surface.

Oh, what a beautiful marigold of color and joy. She was the one bright beam of light in Rolland's otherwise dreary world. Where there was only shadow and darkness before, there was now a gleam of pleasantness beyond words. For words were failing Rolland at that moment.

'Her skin was like… Her legs were… Her breasts are… Nice,' Rolland thought to himself decidedly. Poetry never was his strong suit.

"Nice," Rolland said aloud without meaning to.

A smile was the brunette's only response. It was enough. It was magical.

"I'm Sephanie," she said, extending her hand to him in greeting.

Crossing the short distance between them, Rolland casually wiped his sweaty hand on his pants before offering it to her.

Hers was softer than he imagined.

"We met before. Well I mean, we didn't exactly meet, but I saw you. You were blocked by the sun, but I saw you clear as day," Rolland trailed off as he got lost in Sephanie's emerald-green eyes. Their sparkle swallowed him in a sea of majestic beauty.

"Wait, what are you talking about?" Sephanie snapped, her tone changing from flirtatious to annoyed in the blink of an eye.

"In front of the bookstore; you know, just before the fire." Rolland said, his normal trepidation around girls becoming agonizingly apparent in front of the object of his desire.

"I don't think so. No, I would have remembered that," Sephanie retorted, her expression souring as her lips pursed.

"Oh. Sorry, then," Rolland said, blushing awkwardly. "My mistake."

The silence that fell between them for several long moments was only broken by the unexpected entry of someone else. It was a teenage girl, a bit shorter than Sephanie, with beautiful fair hair. She was carrying a stack of volumes so large that it completely dwarfed her five-foot, three-inch frame, making all but the top of her little blonde head mostly invisible behind the books.

"Oh, I didn't know that anyone was in here," said the girl with the books, dropping the large pile at her feet as she entered the room.

"No, no. I was just leaving," Sephanie said, flashing another look of forced flirtation to Rolland before leaving him and the new girl alone.

"Here, let me help you with those," Rolland offered, walking to the girl's side and helping her to pick up the books at her feet.

"Thanks so much," she said, reaching for a thick, orange volume on geometry at the same time as Rolland, causing their hands to touch. This simple human interaction automatically kicked both of their baser instincts into gear, forcing their eyes to meet and smiles to be exchanged. "I'm Tina."

Rolland stared into her sparkling blue eyes. Tina was cute, nerdy, and seemed like someone he could hold many conversations with. Her grace, along with her hand, had not moved or shown the slightest indication that she was anything but what she presented herself to be. Tina appeared to be genuine, honest, and refreshing compared to the hoity-toity and secretive other Knights, with their sideways stares to one another.

"Rolland Alan Wright," Rolland said, introducing himself with his left hand instead of his right, which still sat beneath hers on the orange book cover. "Nice to meet you."

"You too," Tina said, her smile and momentary embarrassment tugging at Rolland's flighty teenage heart strings. "Are you new here? I haven't seen you before."

"Uh, yeah, kind of, I suppose." Rolland said half-heartedly, using every filler word he could think of. "My mom and dad used to work here apparently. But they're both gone now so... not exactly sure what it is I'm doing here."

Tina stopped stacking books and pulled her hand away from Rolland's. "Your mom and dad?"

"Yeah, Scott and Taylor Wright. Did you know them?" Rolland asked, noticing the sudden shift in the girl's mood at the mention of his parents' names.

"I never got to meet your mom. Just your dad," Tina said with a finality to her tone that Rolland was not yet comfortable using, even though his mom had been dead for nearly two years.

"Oh..." Rolland said, picking up a couple of the stray books that fell away from her and placing them on her neatly stacked little pile.

"Sorry for your loss," Tina offered, standing up and obviously resisting the urge to put her hand on his shoulder.

Rolland noticed this, but was polite enough to act like he didn't. What he did not have was an appropriate response to the awkward silence that fell between them. Deciding that saying anything was better than saying nothing at all, he turned to face her, only to find her closer than he expected.

And then, they were kissing...

Their lips met with a familiarity unknown by either of them, yet the differences within each paled in comparison to the chemistry brewing under the surface of both. Passion, innocence, and lust all melded together to give both Rolland and Tina a moment, if ever so brief, just for them.

Tina broke away first, opening her eyes to see the dumbstruck look on the young Wright's face. Memories of his father and comparisons to his mother whizzed around in her cranium like boomerangs, but something else remained that was wholly about the boy in front of her, something sweet and kind. Something genuine and noble rang true about this boy in a way that no other had before him. She couldn't quite put her finger on it.

"Oh geez, I'm just not really any good at first impressions," Tina said, a look of terror washing over her face as she pulled away, untangling her fingers from his.

"I wouldn't say that," Rolland said, hoping to lessen the poor girl's tension. She seemed sweet and honest -- almost the complete opposite of Sephanie.

"I just wanted you to like me," Tina moaned, somewhat defeated by her own lack of social skills. Pouting a bit, she turned around from Rolland.

"I do like you, Tanya," Rolland said, only realizing his mistake a moment too late.

"Excuse me?" Tina asked, turning back around and folding her arms across her chest in the all too familiar defiant female position (or D.F.P., as he and Rick had called it). With the raising of her eyebrows, every feature on her face was at full attention, ready to go into battle over a single vowel.

Hoping to cover his mistake, Rolland tried to double back with a quick "I like you."

"No, I mean the other part. Did you just call me Tanya?" Tina asked, her momentary look of indignation gone, replaced with tears in the corners of her eyes.

"Oh, uh…" Rolland stammered, trying in vain to come up with the girl's name he had just seconds before been wrestling tongues with. "Did you hear that I slayed a beast?"

"'Uh' is not my name. I know your name, Rolland Alan Wright, but I guess you couldn't be bothered to learn mine," Tina said, poking him repeatedly in the chest with her index finger. All the while, hot tears ran freely down her cheeks.

On that note, the second cute female in what seemed like so many minutes sped from the parlor and Rolland's life.

"Tina!" Rolland shouted aloud to the empty room.

Both admiring and fearing the girl's tenacity, Rolland found himself switching gears from horny to apologetic in a matter of seconds. This shift, he had been told, was normal when dealing with females.

Storming off in a huff, Tina held back her tears long enough to avoid being seen by spectators as she made her way back to her own sleeping quarters. For her, an uphill climb to replace the team's previous communications director, Taylor Wright, would only become harder as she fell for the late woman's son.

"But I slayed a beast..." Rolland said desperately under his breath.

Having never dated in high school due to his secret homelessness, Rolland had always assumed that, should the right girl cross his path, there would be some kind of sign. Yet in the past twenty minutes he had met the woman of his dreams and been kissed by a beautiful girl in glasses.

This was, of course, nothing compared to the already surreal experience Rolland had been living since waking up to a police flashlight that morning. Only yesterday, heavy subjects like time travel, extra senses, and secret doorways to a magical land were considered fiction at best; now they were simply parts of life he was forced to accept.

Sitting down to reflect on all this, Rolland was granted but a mere moment of privacy before being called upon for dinner.

Chapter 7:
Bureaucracy as a Universal Truth

The re-emergence of Turtledove signaled the gathering of everyone from the grounds and the start of dinner. For the first time since he had arrived, all of the Knights of Time gathered together around the main table in the dining hall for Rolland to see as a group. They were a motley crew.

To Rolland's left sat Victor, who took nearly twice as much space as everyone else at the dinner table. His gaze moved clockwise around the table to Sephanie, Joan, Judah, and Geoffrey, noticing that two chairs were left empty, one directly across from him and the one at one at the head of the table.

Marcus Turtledove waltzed into the room with his usual authoritarian swagger and took his seat at the head of the table. Making himself comfortable, his eyes found Rolland's and he gave the boy a knowing smile.

The last seat in question was soon filled by Tina, who looked more polished, and much to Rolland's relief, was no longer crying. Gone were the glasses, and in their place she wore subtle makeup and an air of rehearsed confidence. She purposefully ignored Rolland throughout dinner, even refusing to acknowledge his presence during Turtledove's toast.

"To the great surprise the universe has shared with us today," Turtledove toasted, holding his goblet of wine high toward the rest of the table, who all returned the gesture as one, their respect for their leader clear.

The meal consisted of beef brisket, rice noodles with tofu and shrimp, couscous, scalloped potatoes, rye bread, and assorted vegetables, all of which were welcome to Rolland's suddenly growling stomach. Realizing that he hadn't eaten in nearly an entire day, Rolland dug into a large portion of brisket as the dinner conversation kicked into gear.

"So Rolland, why is it we've not heard of you until now?" Judah asked, crunching on a piece of celery.

"Pardon?" Rolland asked the room at large, wiping his mouth with a napkin and looking from one set of eyes to another. None of the knights, save for Turtledove seemed to have anything to say to Rolland, but the same awkward question filled each of their eyes.

"It seems," Turtledove began, putting his goblet of wine down on the table before continuing, "that Scott and Taylor had Rolland some time ago and had been keeping him secret."

In most cultures, speaking ill of the dead, especially friends, is considered to be in poor taste. For this reason alone, the Knights of Time were shocked to hear their leader levy such serious and improbable charges against the former 'first couple' of Eden.

"Bollocks!" Judah shouted from across the table, a small piece of potato flying off of his fork and landing near where Geoffrey sat shoveling shrimp into his mouth. "What's your proof?"

"Um, hello?" Rolland said, waving his right hand as he swallowed a mouthful of brisket. "I didn't know anything about this until today. Hell, I haven't even seen my dad since my mom died two years ago."

"It's been two years in your time since Taylor passed?" Joan asked with genuine surprise.

"Yeah, my dad took off not long after," Rolland said. He pierced a scalloped potato with his fork and tried to ignore the pity-filled stares burning into his skull.

Avoiding their gaze, Rolland heard Judah spit out another profanity before muttering to himself and slamming his goblet down angrily.

"So, where have you been living for two years, huh? What's a kid like you do with yourself without parents in what, the 21st century?" Judah asked, getting to the heart of the matter and shining a light on Rolland's greatest, most shameful secret -- the one that cost him all of his friends, classmates, car, and old life on Earth.

"I was homeless, alright?" Rolland said to Judah with gritted teeth, careful not to catch anyone else's eye as he turned back to his plate. With his appetite suddenly vanishing, the red-hot shame and anxiety began to creep in on the teenage Wright.

"Hiding you in plain sight, eh? That's bloody brilliant!" Judah said, nodding his head in sudden approval of Scott and Taylor Wright's deviant and utter disregard for their son's welfare.

There was never a time when Rolland hadn't wished he was someone else's son, a strange thought at that particular moment, given that his lineage had been a cause for celebration only moments before. With every eye in the room on him, Rolland wished for a distraction from their attention; almost all their attention, anyway.

For Sephanie, Rolland would see the earth shift and the room empty. He was sure she was the girl from the bookstore that morning, if only he could get her to admit it. He was drawn to her, like a blooming rose seeks the sun.

It was in every detail of her, from the way her hair fell upon her back and hung there like notes on a page, to way she wriggled her nose every few minutes like clockwork. This was of course followed by the clasping of her hands and repositioning of her legs. Rolland found no small joy in knowing that the girl of his dreams was an obsessive-compulsive creature of habit, just like him.

"So, what's next?" Rolland asked, taking the oversized spoon and scooping another large portion of scalloped potatoes onto his plate. He was careful not to catch the eyes of either Sephanie or Tina, who were both sneaking glances at him as they, too, helped themselves to the succulent dishes on the table.

"I'm glad you asked, Rolland," Turtledove said, selecting a dinner roll from the basket making its way around the table. "Were your parents here, I believe they would be of the opinion that you should attend the Academy and learn how to hone your abilities."

"The what?" asked Rolland, with genuine sense curiosity, happy to find a distraction from his thoughts on the two girls.

"The Academy of Light," Turtledove repeated with the strictest of looks on his face.

"The Academy of what?" Rolland asked again, a mouthful of potato and corn making him cough. Using the napkin from his lap, he covered his mouth and turned his head – accidentally catching Sephanie's eyes. They were so green.

"As a new member of our community you must take a solemn oath to protect Eden, its residents, and the time stream itself," Turtledove said, with an almost indignant pride to his steady voice.

Rolland got the distinct impression that the old man had gone through this spiel many times before. A guess confirmed by an equal yet opposite reaction from Judah, who sat with his arms behind his head, as if trying to catch his breath.

"The Academy of Light will teach you all of this and more. Much more," continued Turtledove. "It is where you will learn how to responsibly use your, uh, talents, in a positive and productive way."

The prospect that Rolland would be making any use of his life was a depressingly foreign one. The last two years had been hard on him, sure, but in the last six months or so, Rolland had resigned himself to the fact that his life ended at 18. While the rest of his friends would be going off to college, he assumed he would be looking for a new place to park his sleeping quarters.

The painful reminder that even his beloved Cadillac Deville was gone was almost more than Rolland could bear. Like all the painful memories he had been bottling up inside for nearly two years, the teenager swallowed it down, deep inside, becoming alert once again and rejoining the conversation.

"Who says I have to go?" Rolland asked, ripping the end of a piece of bread off in his hands. "Who's in charge of all this, anyway?"

Though unexpected, the rebellious spirit inside the youngest surviving member of the Wright family seemed to amuse every one of the Knights of Time and they all, even Tina, smiled at his comment.

"I believe you are referring to The Council of Light," Turtledove said, popping a cherry tomato into his mouth and taking a sip of wine.

"Alright, and what do they do?" Rolland asked, his juvenile impatience on full display.

"They're elected by the people of Eden to decide on legal matters and generally run things," Joan explained, the majority of her food still sitting on her plate untouched. "But once elected, they stop living among the general population and become part of Eden's elite."

"...who only look out for the rich and most powerful," Judah interjected, adding his own two cents to the conversation.

"The vast difference in wealth and quality of life leads to slums, like the one I found you in today," Joan finished, taking a bite of what Rolland recognized as 'Texas Toast'.

The news that he had been found wandering a slum was apparently new information to many people at the table, and no less than five heads turned to look at Rolland with the same quizzical look.

"Political divide, much?" Rolland said with a jovial smile. The grimaces on their faces spoke volumes about the political climate in Eden, and perhaps the state of its inhabitants' morals.

"A bit, yeah," Judah said, his voice dripping with sarcasm. "If it wasn't for the Magistrate and the Protector of Eden, we'd all be as belly up as your mum and dad."

Rolland could feel the vibration in the table as Joan kicked Judah to discourage him from speaking out of turn, a tactic Rolland's mother used to use on his father back in the day. Judah grimaced, and the look of pain on his face confirmed Rolland's suspicions.

"The what?" Rolland asked once again, feeling guilty now for asking so many questions during dinner.

"The Magistrate is the commander of Eden's forces at the Academy of Light," Tina said from across the table, speaking to Rolland for the first time.

"The head cheese," Victor said with one of his large, goofy smiles.

"Oh, cool. And the Protector? Who is that?" Rolland asked, his enthusiasm for the topic mounting with each answer.

This time, the look of silent mockery turned in to a full round of giggles as every knight sitting around the table burst into earnest laughter.

"That would be me, Mr. Wright," Turtledove said, looking over at Rolland from his place at the head of the table.

"Oh, cool," Rolland said, trying to salvage his dignity as he shoveled another large bite of potatoes into his mouth.

"What do you think, kid; think you could make a go of it here?" Geoffrey asked. Having finished his meager helping of brisket, he leaned over and rested his elbows on the table.

"Honestly? So far this entire place sounds like one giant bureaucratic nightmare," Rolland said, placing his fork down on his plate and tossing his napkin on top.

"The kid has a mouth!" Joan chuckled, nodding her head in approval.

"There are those who believe that the bureaucracy established some years ago has become too extreme in their enforcement of the rules, yes," Turtledove said carefully.

Rolland could tell that the old man had not intended to broach this subject with him just yet, but something in the way he smiled told Rolland that his curiosity was refreshing, and maybe even welcome.

"This is… fiction," Rolland said, genuinely at a loss for words. "All of this, Eden, you guys…"

"Hang on," Judah's voice rose over Rolland's rant as he stood up in a show of mock seriousness. "Was that the boy, or has his dad risen from the grave?"

"Judah…" Turtledove said in warning, reminding Rolland of a parent scolding a child about to throw a temper tantrum.

"No, he needs to know this," Judah said sharply to his mentor before turning back to Rolland.

Rolland stood to face the blonde man eye to eye. He was shorter than Rolland by a couple of inches, half a foot at best. His piercing gray eyes fell upon Rolland's and didn't so much as blink as the two men approached one another. Judah reminded Rolland of a wild mountain lion, a calculating predator coldly stalking his prey.

"This is Science, boy-o, not fiction. Science doesn't take sides, it's neutral," Judah said with an eerie calm.

"It is undeniable that nine-tenths of reality is perception," Turtledove said with weary impatience. "It, along with historical fact, is what we base our judgments on."

"So you're saying that you, the Travelers of Light, only work within the parameters of a paradox?" Rolland asked.

"Well, yeah, actually. Bang on," Judah said, somewhat impressed that the boy had inherited his mother's intellect and not his father's oafishness.

Thinking what an incredible jerk Judah was and how beautiful both Sephanie and Tina looked that night, Rolland already had plenty on his mind when Turtledove dropped yet another bombshell on him over dessert.

"Of course, you will have to decide on a career," Turtledove said, helping himself to a generous portion of lime-green gelatin from a white serving dish.

"Huh?" Rolland asked, choking a bit on his own dessert.

"It is standard practice. After you train at the academy, you decide what position within the traveler community you would like to take. Just like on Earth. Mind you, you'll have more leeway given your unique skill set," Turtledove elaborated in an obvious attempt to ease any anxiety Rolland might have had.

Instead of listening to the wisest man in the room, Rolland was once again preoccupied with the females of the species and the many interesting ways they chose to wear their clothing.

After dessert was finished, more light-hearted conversation was swapped amongst them, and the women all excused themselves while the men offered to clean up the dishes. Being a guest, Turtledove insisted that Rolland not bother with helping, and suggested he take a walk around the grounds instead.

Excusing himself, Rolland left the table and walked out into the courtyard.

The night sky was littered with bright stars, undiminished by the moonlight. Rolland walked out onto the balcony and let his arms rest upon the railing.

It was the first time Rolland had found solitude since that morning, and he was more than eager to regroup. But where could he go? He was in a strange land. Eden, they called it. And it wasn't like these people had treated him badly or were trying to convert him in any way.

"It's strange," said a soft voice from behind Rolland, interrupting his thoughts.

Rolland turned to see Sephanie standing in the doorway, her white dress billowing slightly with the breeze. Her eyes were fixated on something behind him. Rolland turned and realized she was looking at the sky.

"The stars look almost exactly the same here as they do on Earth," Sephanie said, walking out onto the balcony to join Rolland.

"When I was a kid, my dad used to take me out to this field in the middle of the country to look at stars," Rolland said, hoping to strike up a conversation with the green eyed beauty that had been such a distraction at dinner.

"I bet he was a great dad," Sephanie replied sincerely.

"HA!" Rolland exclaimed, his crass response catching Sephanie off guard.

"Really?" Sephanie asked with trepidation. "Because that doesn't sound like the Scott Wright I know."

"Knew, you mean," Rolland shot back.

"Right, sorry," Sephanie said, averting her eyes and sitting down on a nearby bench.

Rolland noticed that the wind that had filled the night air had quieted, and was beginning to understand what Victor and Geoffrey had been trying to tell him about Sephanie's uniqueness.

"You're upset, I can tell," Rolland said, sitting down next to her.

"Really, now?" Sephanie asked, looking at him with a glowing curiosity she reserved for only a select few. "What makes you say that?"

"I just have a sixth sense for these kinds of things," Rolland said, using Sephanie's interest as an excuse to scoot within foot and a half away of the treasure he sought. Close enough for an impromptu kiss, but still enough personal space for comfort.

"Yeah, my emotions are kind of tied to things like that, ever since I was a kid," Sephanie said, biting her cheek a bit. It was a nervous habit she had picked up years ago as a way to stop herself from divulging too much information to new people. "Good and bad, highs and lows."

"Highs and lows, huh?" Rolland echoed, a wicked thought crossing his mind.

"Yep," Sephanie said, shifting her feet nervously. He reminded her so much of Scott, but without the baggage or pessimism.

"Are you telling me that you get, like, nature-gasms?" Rolland asked with the kind of confidence teenagers only seem to show as they say the wrong thing.

Sephanie stood up flabbergasted, excused herself with a nod, and went inside for the night. Leaving Rolland alone, awkward and filled with regret.

His pity-party wouldn't last long however, as Rolland's thoughts were soon interrupted by the by the smell of cigarette smoke as Judah lit his post-dinner smoke in the darkest corner of the veranda below.

"What's her boggle?" Judah asked, putting his lighter away and inhaling sharply.

"I asked if she got nature-gasms," Rolland said, drawing a chuckle from the man below.

"That'd do it," Judah said, taking another puff from his cigarette, the end smoldering a bit as he inhaled. Its orange glow hit the night sky with a stunning contrast that fit both the object and the man smoking it. "Enjoy dinner?"

"Meh," Rolland said, closing his eyes as a fresh wave of second-hand smoke wafted through the air around him. "A meal is a meal."

"Yep," Judah agreed curtly, taking another long drag off of his cigarette.

"So, um, what's her story, exactly?" Rolland asked Judah, making sure to avoid eye contact.

"Who, Sephanie? Freaking Mother Nature, that one. Gets off on making me miserable," Judah said with another puff.

"What do you mean?" Rolland asked with a renewed interest in his new colleague's apparent insight into the female psyche.

"Well, she doesn't make any sense, does she? I mean, to do what she can do – controlling the bloody environment and all," Judah swirled his cigarette in a circular motion, the trail of smoke following his hand as he spoke.

"How does that make you miserable?" Rolland asked, dodging a tuft of smoke hanging in midair.

"It's that bloody mouth of hers," Judah began, pausing long enough to take another drag of his cigarette. "Tells my wife everything I do - like some damn sleuthy parrot."

Laughing nervously, Rolland imagined Sephanie taking orders from Joan wearing nothing but feathers.

"Yeah, you're alright kid," Judah said, bringing his cigarette back to his lips and letting it rest there for a moment before inhaling.

"Thanks," Rolland replied, turning his attention back to the night sky he had been enjoying with more attractive company only minutes before.

"Say, that reminds me," Judah said, exhaling a copious amount of smoke and dropping the nearly bald cigarette onto the pavement. "Turtledove told me to test your plasma for variants."

"Huh?" Rolland asked, feeling ignorant as hell and totally unprepared for a conversation with Judah.

Judah smiled, pulling along, deep breath of the Eden night air into his lungs before answering. "I'm going to stick you with a needle, take some of your plasma, test it, and see what it is you can do. Find out how powerful you are."

The bluntness of Judah's intent, while refreshing, still sounded vaguely sinister in relation to Rolland's overly conservative opinion on the matter of privacy. Although he was incredibly curious as to the extent of his newfound abilities, there remained a weary discontent behind Judah's actions in Rolland's mind. Still, it was better than spending the evening obsessing over his lost Cadillac.

"What the hell," Rolland shrugged, sticking his left arm out in front of him and admiring its less than flawless and unmarked skin. "A few more scars couldn't hurt."

Chapter 8:
Dream Phoenix

After living out of a car for twenty months, one begins to recognize certain signs of potential danger. The first of these is when a strange man smoking a cigarette corners you and invites you back to his 'lab' for some 'tests'.

With that being the name of the game, Rolland decided to employ a few tricks of his own that he had learned while bumming his way back from Van Nuys during spring break earlier that year. Digging through his left pocket, he found a cell phone, a quarter, a padlock, two sticks of gum, and a bottle of invisible ink.

"Woah," Rolland said aloud within earshot of Judah.

"I know, this place is gorgeous isn't it?" Judah said in a genuine attempt to make conversation. His usual facade of brash genius was nowhere to be seen as thoughts of forgiveness and starting anew with the youngest Wright ran through his mind, clouding his judgment.

Unscrewing the small bottle of invisible ink with his left pinky and index finger, Rolland began to dribble small amounts of ink behind him as they walked through the grounds of the Halls of Time. While the droplets by themselves were invisible to the naked eye, the real potential for danger lie in the application itself.

Getting caught betraying the trust, or even being weary of a new organization that has welcomed you can be a serious offense when timed right. Rolland knew that he would have no explanation for his actions if he were caught, but he had learned long ago that it was better to be safe than sorry. With that in mind, as they made their way through the maze-like catacomb that was the hall of time, he began to squirt out a drop of the ink every five or six steps.

The four levels of the complex were only matched in their spaciousness and confusion by the number of hallways that seemed to lead to nowhere when Judah wasn't paying attention and went the wrong way. While Rolland couldn't have guessed at the total number of rooms in that place, they must have passed at least one hundred different doors on the first three floors alone before coming to a single red door just off the beaten path.

It wasn't locked, nor did it appear to be unique in any way apart from its color and design. It resembled an old submarine hatch, complete with a little wheel in the center that had to be turned before it opened properly. A strange place for a door like that, Rolland thought, as he followed Judah through it to the fourth floor.

From the way Judah Jacob Raines was walking, one could have assumed that he had just become the father of triplets. Though Rolland had only known him for a few hours, he had never seen this level of enthusiasm from him. Perhaps it was Rolland's positive reaction to finding the ink, but something was definitely different about Judah's demeanor.

In fact, Rolland thought to himself as he tried to keep up with his guide, Judah hadn't cracked a smile or joke the entire time they had been walking, save for some randomly inappropriate yet factual comment here and there.

When they arrived at the end of the corridor, Rolland was greeted by a device he could never have conceived in his wildest dreams. It was metal and pointed into a sort of swirly cone. There was a dim red light at the end, just like a barcode scanner.

Without warning Judah opened his mouth and placed the tip of his tongue on the scanner, alerting a monitor that hung silently overhead to his presence.

"Welcome, Dr. Raines," came a light, feminine voice from a speaker in the wall.

Judah removed his tongue from the device and looked over at his guest sheepishly. He suddenly gave Rolland toothy grin, and the good Dr. Raines opened the large, circular door to his right, saying "Gives me a tingly feeling in me bits."

"After you," Judah said, motioning for Rolland to walk into the dark passageway.

To his surprise, Rolland was not greeted by the dark corridor that he had seen from the other side of the door. On the contrary, the moment he stepped past the security checkpoint there was nothing but bright, florescent lights shining directly into his face from all four of the walls. A cooling fog greeted them as they walked into a brightly lit room completely covered in plastic tarps.

"Clean room," Judah said, waiting for the door behind him to close. Once they were both sealed inside, Judah pressed an unseen button on the wall where a light switch might normally be, causing an odd shaped metal rod to pop out from the ceiling and into Judah's waiting hand. "This little bugger will suck the dirt right off ya. Go ahead. Give her a go."

Taking the cleansing rod in his hand, Rolland felt for the first time like he had truly left Earth. Unsure of exactly what he was supposed to do with it, he rolled the rod across his chest, on his back, and under his armpits before the rod beeped, indicating that Rolland was clean. Handing the cleansing rob back to Judah proved to be quite the task - the Brit appeared thoroughly entertained.

"I can't tell if you're a genius or a dullard," Judah said, shaking his head slightly before continuing onward.

Standing in Judah's laboratory, one thing quickly became obvious to Rolland; this was not the mad scientist's lair that he had envisioned. High above them, the vaulted ceilings curved and ran through several rivets in the sheet metal before stopping at what looked like an automatic ceiling opener. While he had seen automatic garage door openers, and stadium ceilings that opened in a similar way, the intricacy of the opening left him wondering if Judah was more artist than scientist.

"Come along then," Judah said, as he put on a long, white lab coat that read 'J.J.' on the left pocket.

Moving further along the wall, Rolland soon came nose to nose with what resembled a large aquarium housing nothing but a single Petri dish. It sat there, surrounded by nothing more than the padding on the walls and the tiles on the floor. He figured the enclosure couldn't be more than ten to fifteen feet in diameter, and he couldn't even guess as to what the Petri dish might be for.

"Do you like it?" Judah asked as he walked over to peer inside, leaning on the glass.

"Like what, exactly?" Rolland asked sarcastically.

"What, you can't see it?" asked Judah, pointing to the glass with his index finger.

"See what?" Rolland asked, growing somewhat impatient with what he perceived as an evil, Willy Wonka kind of joke.

"Hang on," Judah said, reaching for something on the side of the glass enclosure.

Suddenly a black light that was taped onto the lid of the habitat lit up, revealing a large, mollusk-looking creature with four rows of claws the size of rulers behind the glass. Its large, beady eyes were attached to opposite sides of the thing and blinked in unison as it scratched wildly at the barrier separating it from the two men.

"That's what you call a freak of nature. Extremely loyal, he is," Judah said in a vain attempt to justify his momentary creepiness. "Moving along…"

Their tour continued to the far left side of the lab where a large monitor stood on what looked like a modified Atari.

"Gaming system?" Rolland asked.

"Used to be," Judah said, picking the machine up and unplugging it from the monitor. "Now it's what you'd call a Cause and Effect machine."

"A what?" Rolland asked, eyeing the thing suspiciously. It was black and had wires sticking out of every end. Its outer casing was worn and clearly had the Atari 'A' on top of it. "Dude, that thing totally used to be an Atari system."

"Built it in college on a bet," Judah said, typing a password into the pull-out keyboard. "Oh, to be fourteen again."

"So what does it do?" Rolland asked, deciding to push the limits with his host's patience.

"Ask me why something happened," Judah said, placing his hands on the keyboard as the browser window popped up and the search bar stood empty.

"Like why the chicken crossed the road?" Rolland asked jokingly, not really understanding the point of the exercise.

"Something historical," Judah said slowly and with great mockery. "Like why you were conceived."

"Like the sinking of the Titanic?" Rolland asked, unprepared for a metaphorical question with real world ramifications and desperate to steer the topic of conversation away from his conception.

"Alright…" Judah said, typing in the words 'Sinking Titanic' into the search bar. "Thought you would have gone with something more personal, but whatever."

This hadn't occurred to Rolland until now, but the idea landed in his mind and planted itself there like a tree taking root.

"Here we go," Judah said, clicking on a file titled 'Titanic sinking'.

RMS TITANIC SINKS

The Titanic: An ocean liner that crashed into an iceberg.

Primary Cause: Poor design structure.

Secondary Cause: Ineptitude of crew.

Ways to Prevent: See timeline.

"You get the idea yet?" Judah said to Rolland, clicking on the timeline and revealing a nearly four-hundred-year history, from 1514 to 1914, of decisions, events, and people that had led to the Titanic sinking.

Impressed but not wanting to give Judah any credit, Rolland responded with a polite but terse "Yeah, it's cool."

Leaving the Cause/Effect machine behind and moving further into Doctor Raines' House of Weird, the two of them came upon what looked to be the largest and most secluded part of Judah's lab.

In front of Rolland sat what looked like a hospital bed propped up into a sitting position and attached to a boxy machine covered with buttons and cords.

"And lastly, my most famous invention – this is where you'll be sitting," Judah said to Rolland, motioning toward the makeshift bed.

"This is Dream Phoenix," Judah said in the same manner in which a parent introduces their children to strangers.

"When I designed her I meant for her to be symbiotic, you know, completely cognizant and self-regulating," Judah continued, almost petting the back of the machine next to the bed. "But so far that's just been a dream."

"How does it – I mean, she work?" Rolland asked, careful to catch himself before using the wrong term.

Judah eyed him for a minute before speaking, perhaps scanning for sincerity, perhaps just to be a dick. "Do you know what plasma is?"

"Yeah, that's the stuff in your blood, right?" Rolland asked, pretty confident in his answer.

"Well now! Look who's smarter than the average bear," Judah chuckled. "Everyone's got plasma in their blood; it's what keeps your proteins and antibodies unique to you, protecting you from infection and harm, it's just great."

"Ok... so?" Rolland asked, attempting to follow the blonde scientist's train of thought.

"So since it's unique to you, I thought to myself, well, we live in a freaky world where some of us can fly and others are just awesome. Maybe there's something in our plasma that makes that happen," Judah said, pressing a button on the wall behind him that opened up to reveal a large spinning rack of plastic bags.

The bags rotated in the same manner a dry cleaner would with clothing, except there was little doubt as to what they were. Each one was filled with a dark yellow liquid wrapped in clear plastic with labels on the outside bearing what appeared to be names, ages, and special abilities.

"You collect people's abilities; But why?" Rolland asked, a bit awestruck at the thinly veiled similarities between Dr. Raines and whoever it was that was trying to kill him back at the bookstore.

"Just in case something happens to them," Judah said turning to look at Rolland. "Like with your dad. He was the only time traveler born in the last two thousand years. Now we've got a stock pile of his plasma, but with him dead who are we going to count on to take us safely back in time?"

"The Dream Phoenix can do that?" Rolland asked, becoming more and more impressed with the machine and its inventor.

"It can do whatever the person whose plasma its using could do." Judah said in a manner that sounded rehearsed and exhausted, like he had recited it a thousand times before. "So, yeah, your dad on his best day could time travel nearly 200 years. Without him, we still can, only with less precision."

"Two hundred years?" Rolland asked, suddenly not at all interested in the machine.

"Yep," Judah said, obviously still thinking they were speaking of the machine. "But in order to understand you have to get time travel. You know, really get it."

Not 'getting it' was almost like an art form for Rolland. Although he was good at sports as a kid, he never really 'got' them. The best example of this was his Little League team, where he was an excellent hitter, but insisted on sliding into every base, cleats first. By the end of the team's second game the parents had rallied together and kicked him out of the sport entirely.

"You built a time machine?" asked Rolland.

"Not exactly," Judah stated quickly. "More like a time parachute. Using your Old Man's plasma, or maybe even yours, I could get you where you need to go in time, but in not space. Need a natural time traveler to do that."

"So, this thing is like me, then?" Rolland asked, stepping forward to get into Judah's line of vision. "It can kind of do what I can do, I mean."

"Well, yeah, pretty much," Judah said, offering no objection.

There was a knock on the lab door as Joan walked in carrying a large cardboard box. Judah sprang to his feet and raced over toward her, goading a smile from her full and beautiful lips.

"Allow me to introduce to you the crown jewel of my laboratory, the always beautiful Maid of Orleans," Judah said, walking behind Joan and placing his arms around her waist, his hands wandering slightly until finding their resting spot just below Joan's belly button.

Rolland waited for a long moment to see what Joan's reaction to Judah's advance would be. Certainly she would be angry. Since he had met them both separately this morning, he had seen them in the same room only rarely. Surely this unsolicited pass would upset her.

It was, as it always is, a woman's prerogative to impose her will. With a half-hearted smile and a large exhale of breath, Joan clasped onto Judah's hands resting on her midsection.

Rolland took immediate notice of the diamond ring resting comfortably on her left ring finger.

"So you two are..?" Rolland asked tentatively.

"Shacking up together? Yeah," Judah said with a smile.

"Judah Jacob Raines!" Joan exclaimed, turning around and hitting his chest with her tiny fists.

"Ouch, woman!" Judah cried out, unable to block her blows, hands full of various medical supplies. "I'll thank you not to mess with those."

"And I'll thank you to clean up your workspace more often, Doctor Raines," Joan said, flashing her husband the doe-eyed look that takes most women years to master over their men. "At least pick up some of the more dangerous elements, darling."

"Like what?" Judah asked, using a cotton swab to spread iodine on Rolland's extended arm as he conversed with his wife.

"Gee, I don't know. How about we start with that pile of what looks like dynamite in the corner," Joan replied, pointing to numerous large crates sitting stacked side by side on the far side of the lab.

"I'll get to it, never you worry," Judah offered, sneaking a quick kiss as he moved by her to turn on the machine. "Ready to go, Junior?"

"Just wait a minute now," Joan said, placing the box down on a nearby table and turning to Rolland. "I thought you might want some of your father's things."

Walking over to it, Rolland peered inside the box to find it scattered with various objects. Some he recognized, like his father's flask, college ring, and old brown wallet. Others he had never seen before, like the notebook, black light, and compass.

"Let's do this," Rolland said sharply, moving beyond the box without touching one item inside. Though he knew the time to peruse his father's personal effects would eventually come, he wasn't ready yet.

The injection itself wasn't so bad, Rolland thought as the hum of the Dream Phoenix began the plasmapheresis process beside him. Rolland sat and watched as the little machine went to work extracting his blood, cycling it through a filter, and extracting the plasma from within.

"It's just going to take one rotation. About 200 ml worth ought to do it," Judah said, while monitoring the flow of Rolland's blood as it began to fill the clear plastic tubes. Together they watched the red cells flow from Rolland's arm to the large machine.

"Excellent!" Judah said robustly, a wide smile filling the blonde Englishman's face. "Shouldn't take more than five minutes now."

"Sounds good," Rolland said, the pain of the large needle in his arm subsiding with each passing second.

"What in the bloody hell?" Judah's voice rang out through the lab, prompting Joan to stop poking through Scott's belongings and rush to her husband's side.

"What's up?" Rolland asked from his position on the bed as he felt the saline free-flowing through the plastic tubes and into his body, giving him a slight head rush.

"How did he…" Judah asked in a hushed, but obviously furious voice, followed closely by a shushing sound from Joan.

Judah walked out from behind the Dream Phoenix and held up a small baggie filled with an odd murky white liquid that seemed to glow a bit when the light hit it.

"Mind telling me what this is?" Judah asked Rolland, holding the baggie up to his eye level.

"White gold?" Rolland asked, having absolutely no idea what it was and at a complete loss for what exactly his new British friend was getting at.

Beside himself, Judah marched back behind the Dream Phoenix to where Joan was standing and began shouting obscenities the likes of which would make a sailor blush. He went on and on about how much like Scott Rolland was, and how he didn't have time for nonsense.

Joan, being the good and loving wife that she was, waited for her husband to say his piece before offering possible explanations, none of which seemed plausible to Judah as he logically shot each one down in a fevered whisper.

Rolland heard all of this but could offer nothing in his own defense. Hell, he didn't even know what he had done wrong. Suddenly the inane debate over which girl to pursue was gone, replaced by whatever the hell it was in that little plastic bag.

Judah again popped his head out and leered at Rolland, who was still plugged in to the Dream Phoenix. After a long moment, he turned back toward the little baggie of plasma, whispering angrily at Joan.

"Fine," said Joan in a hushed voice before turning and leaving the lab, flashing a forced smile toward Rolland as she passed.

"Where's she going?" Rolland asked hesitantly, the skin around the needle in his arm becoming itchy and uncomfortable.

Several minutes passed in an equally uncomfortable silence as Judah paced around his laboratory in silent frustration.

"To get Turtledove," Judah said finally, grabbing a chair from a nearby table, flipping it around, and straddling it to face Rolland. "Maybe you'll tell *him* the truth."

"The truth about what?" Rolland asked indignantly.

"Is this a joke to you, boy?" Judah asked harshly.

Behind him, Rolland saw Joan walk back into the laboratory, followed closely by Victor and Turtledove. All three of whom looked considerably more tense than they had just an hour or so earlier at dinner.

"Huh?" Rolland asked, now completely confused. "What did I even do?"

"Are you messing with us? I mean the whole thing with you being a secret child that they've hidden for what, seventeen years, and now this?" Judah ranted. "Do you work for Vilthe?"

"Listen, you trashy piece of pond scum, I didn't ask to be brought here!" Rolland shouted, hoping to get his point across over concerned looks from Joan, Turtledove, and Victor, all of whom now stood between them.

"I think it would be best," Turtledove spoke, raising one hand in the air and silencing all parties involved, "if Rolland went to his room for now. Victor, they are your quarters as well, would you mind showing him the way?"

"Of course" Victor said, walking toward Rolland and patting him on the back. "Come on man."

Refusing to take his eyes off of the blonde Englishman until the last possible moment, Rolland was unhooked from the Dream Phoenix and escorted out of the lab, back to the main part of the Halls of Time. He barely noticed that Victor had grabbed the box containing Scott's belongings as they left the room.

"What's that guy's problem?" Rolland finally asked, as they crossed into the training facility and went around the gymnasium.

"You spooked him," Victor said with a large smile as he held the door open for his new, apparently cool friend. "I've never seen him like that. How'd you do it?"

"Wait, what? How did I do what?" Rolland said, stopping suddenly enough to throw off the much larger Victor's balance.

"Hey, watch it!" Victor said, picking himself up off the ground. "You don't have to tell me if you don't want to."

Confused and beginning to remember the old Louis and Costello baseball routine, Rolland decided to stop, take a deep breath, and begin again.

"Look – I'm sorry I knocked you over, but I really don't know what it is I did to spook him. Would you please tell me?" Rolland asked as calmly as he could manage, looking Victor directly in the eyes.

They seemed to sparkle with curiosity, in brilliant contrast with his dark skin, but even his eyes paled in comparison next to the man's big, bright smile. The gentle giant effect was exaggerated by a long, low-pitched laugh, almost like a bear's roar.

"For serious?" Victor asked, his smile transforming into a look of utter disbelief.

Another long moment passed between them before Victor decided to take the lead and push past the gymnasium to the section of the building where the living quarters were.

Realizing that Victor expected an answer out of him, Rolland nervously stated a simple "Yes. I mean no, I have no idea what's going on."

"Ok, how do I explain..." Victor said, raising his working arm behind his head and bending his elbow. He paused there for a moment before allowing his eyes to squint and his hand to scratch the nape of his neck.

Rolland recognized this as a sign that he was thinking and would soon offer hopefully more useful information, just as he had done in the bookstore.

"That machine that you were uh…" Victor began, obviously at a loss for words.

"Hooked up to?" Rolland offered.

"Yes! Oh man, sorry," Victor said, smiling again and clasping his own hands nervously, sending a small vibration through the floor in which they walked.

"No, Victor, really – you're fine," Rolland said, laughing a bit at his new friend's odd quirks.

"So, that machine," Victor said again, taking a key from his pocket as they turned another corner and stopped in a long hallway filled with doors that somewhat resembled those in an apartment building. "It took some of your plasma."

"Yeah, so?" Rolland asked, coming to a stop behind Victor and trying to decide if his enormous frame could really fit through the tiny, wooden doorway.

"Did you SEE your plasma, man?" Victor asked, pulling the door open and walking into the dark apartment home. "It was white."

"It's not supposed to be white?" Rolland asked as Victor hit the light switch to reveal a quant living area and kitchen.

"More like yellowish-red," Victor said to Rolland, no hint of the previous smile to be found. "The bedroom is down the hallway to the left. I've got the couch. There is something for you on the bed."

"Thanks, man," Rolland offered back to him, still feeling odd about the encounter up in the lab only minutes before.

"It's not from me. But hey - don't stress about all that up there." Victor told Rolland, throwing him a blanket and two pillows he had retrieved from the closet. "They're just surprised by you is all. Your parents were kind of a big deal around here, you know."

There in lay the problem. Rolland DID know. He knew now that his parents were so ashamed of him that they hid his very existence from those they shared every personal moment with. He knew that they were gone, both dead, murdered by someone that no one would tell him about. He knew that he was always an outcast, no matter where he went.

Instead of saying this out loud, Rolland did what almost all seventeen-year-old boys do when confronted with feelings that they don't understand. He internalized them — stuffing them deep within him. Then he took a deep breath, exhaled and answered with a simple and polite "Yeah, looks like you're right."

"Good night," Victor said leaving the room and Rolland alone to himself.

Deciding not to avoid the inevitable, Rolland walked into the spare bedroom and found there, true to Joan's word, his box of possessions from what had fallen out of his Cadillac when the beast flipped it over. Victor had placed the box containing Scott's belongings next to it so they sat side by side. They were similar, yet different. A fitting analogy, Rolland thought, to his father and himself.

While it wasn't much, it was enough to lift the spirits of one teenage boy who was more than a world away from home - he was out of his own time.

Chapter 9:
Walking After Midnight

"GGGnnnnnnnnnAAAAAAArrrrrrrrrrrrrr..." Victor snored loudly as the night dragged on into the early morning hours. The echo he created rocked the bed, which in turn rocked the floors and reverberated through the walls.

Rolland lay in the room next to the large, snoring man and eyed the wall between them with distaste. The rest of the Halls of Time seemed to be as luxurious as Rolland had ever seen outside of Bel-Air. Surely the walls must be up to the same standard, and if not, then why weren't they? As obnoxious as Victor's cacophony was, questions this trivial were nothing to Rolland tonight, not when he knew that Sephanie was somewhere very close by.

Thinking back over his day, Rolland remembered the first few moments after seeing, or at least, imagining Sephanie that morning. With every bone in his body and every fiber of his being, Rolland was convinced that it had been her in front of the bookstore.

"But why would she lie about something like that?" Rolland asked himself silently as the symphony of snores continued to play on through the walls of the apartment. The perplexing thought paled in comparison to the other, more imminent problem of what to do about Tina.

Tina's lips had been soft and welcoming, her embrace was warm and felt natural. Rolland already knew that she liked him, which, to a teenage boy, is half the battle. These, along with multiple other factors were swirling around Rolland's head like small birds in an old Tex Avery cartoon. He wondered if his new-found abilities included forcing appearances into women's dreams, but seriously doubted it. Another loud snore brought his thoughts back full circle.

Victor had proven to be a good and loyal friend to Rolland thus far. That being said, nothing could excuse this snoring. The ebb and flow of the African man's forced breathing fell against the opposite side of the wall like the tide before a hurricane, assaulting Rolland's ears. In the corner of the room was a small night light that lit half of the door and nightstand next to it. On the nightstand were the two boxes that contained the contents of his Cadillac and his father's possessions, including a black light.

Folding back the covers, Rolland retrieved the black light, his father's ring, and his knife from the boxes and walked over to the door, opening it without a sound -- not that making one would have mattered much against the fresh chorus of snores that Victor provided as convenient cover.

Coincidently, Rolland's decision to get out of bed that night would become one of the biggest of his entire life.

Opening the apartment door immediately robbed Rolland of the ability to see anything in the pitch black hallway. Spotting a lighter on the dining room table nearby, Rolland picked it up and stepped out the door, using what sparse light was coming from above the small kitchen's stovetop to guide his way. Quietly, Rolland shut the door to Victor's apartment, blocking off his access to the light, and oddly enough, Victor's snoring.

Silence and darkness surrounded Rolland like a thick blanket, cloaking the world in mystery and leaving little doubt that Turtledove and Judah must not like him after all. Why else would they stick him with the guy whose snores could wake the dead?

Feeling around the hallway, Rolland was able to open the tiny glass door to the lantern hanging on the wall outside of Victor's living quarters and light the eternal wick that lay inside. The fire sprang to life quickly, illuminating more than half of the hallway for Rolland to maneuver around uninterrupted. Or so he thought.

Reaching into his pocket, Rolland felt around for the black light and was in the process of turning it on when he heard a familiar voice behind him.

"Hi there," Sephanie said, standing outside the door across and to the left of where he had just come from.

"Heeeeyy, Sephanie," Rolland offered, pleasantly caught off guard by the girl of his dreams.

"What are you doing sneaking out after hours?" Sephanie asked, knowing full well that her assumptions about Rolland's innate sense of mischief meant he was up to no good. Men in their family were easy to predict, and he was so very reminiscent of Scott.

"Just looking for uh, a bathroom," Rolland said, the lie rolling easily off of his tongue.

Sephanie merely looked at him for a moment, hoping to catch some small sign she could use to force him to reveal the truth. Scott's inability to stand still and moderately excessive blinking had always been small hints that he was fibbing. When neither of these tell-tale signs proved to have been passed down from father to son, Sephanie finally spoke. "Why didn't you just use the one in Victor's place?"

"Well, you see…" Rolland began, apparently prepared for this question "He woke up with an upset stomach like an hour ago and I, well, you know…"

The look of silent comprehension crossed Sephanie's face as she picked up on his lie with ease. Men must emit some scent or pheromone whenever they lie, as women can always tell.

"It's not usually like Victor to wake up in the middle of the night," Sephanie said, walking over to the opposite side of the hallway close to Rolland. "My floor usually vibrates softly all night because of his snores."

"Yeah, tell me about it. It was kind of nice though, him being sick. I actually got some sleep out of it. Hey, how is it so quiet out here, but so loud in there? Are these walls enchanted, or something?" Rolland asked, immediately wishing he had chosen a different word.

Sephanie laughed before reaching for the small, black knob at the bottom of the lantern above them, turning up the brightness of the flame and lighting the other half of the hallway. "No, Rolland, there's no such thing as magic."

"Well, whatever you call it, the quiet is nice," Rolland said biting his own tongue a bit and debating whether or not a post- midnight kiss would be better than exploring on his own.

"The bathroom is down the hall and to the right, by the way," Sephanie said, pointing to a far off door.

"Thanks – wait, what are you doing out here at this hour?" Rolland asked, glad for the opportunity to turn the tables.

"Nothing," Sephanie said sharply, almost like a little girl caught with too many cookies before dinner. The mental image was only intensified when she saw Rolland staring at her hands and thrust one behind her back.

"Oh, yeah?" Rolland asked, praying that a more methodical, confident approach would win her over. "Then, uh, what is it that you have behind your back there?"

At a loss for words, Sephanie bit her bottom lip impatiently and revealed her hand. "It's my retainer."

Unsure as to what to say, Rolland thought back to what the so-called 'preps' and the cool kids would have done, back at school. Opening his mouth, he said, "And you were all embarrassed!"

"You speak to me as if I'm from the 21st century. Simple things to you might have very well been social faux pas when I'm from," Sephanie said, amused, embarrassed, and feeling every bit the child she resembled as she circled the boy attempting to steal her night guard – both of them in their (respective) pajamas.

"Where are you from?" Rolland asked, his face betraying a sense of worry for the first time as he looked Sephanie up and down, perhaps in an attempt to decipher her real age.

This juvenile display of male ineptitude did not go unnoticed, prompting the female of the species to screw with the male's mind just a bit. You know – for sport.

"Not so much where, as when, actually. I'm really old. Older than you can imagine," Sephanie said, much to Rolland's dismay. "I guess you could say that you're just a boy compared to me," she concluded with a wicked grin.

"Ah – ok…" Rolland said, at a complete loss for words and reverting back to his awkward, introverted self. Thinking of Tina, and believing that he could leave to fight another day, Rolland decided it best to lose Sephanie before continuing on with his adventures. "Well, good night then."

Sephanie watched as he backed away, head down, before he turned and went back into Victor's apartment. Confused and uncertain as to who just blew off who, Sephanie retreated back to her own quarters, popped her retainer into her mouth, and curled up in bed thinking about the new, wavy-haired blonde boy suddenly so very present in her life.

For Rolland, the conflict between raging teenage emotions and a once in a lifetime opportunity in a superhero's compound was not a small one. Looking through the peephole into the dimly lit hall, he watched as Sephanie went back into her own quarters, leaving the hallway deserted. Prepared this time, Rolland waited until the end of one of Victor's snores before quickly opening the apartment door, sneaking out into the hallway, and closing it behind him.

Creeping through the Knights' living quarters proved to be simple enough as long as Rolland kept his hand on the wall and traced it through the pitch black. Finding the door in the darkness, Rolland opened it, which led him to the main staircase and front entry of the Halls of Time.

Relieved to have light to illuminate his way once again, Rolland kept one hand on the banister railing that ran the duration of the balcony above the main entry. Looking over it, he could faintly see Eden's night sky from a window off in the distance. It was beautiful in its simplicity, yet grand in its scale.

The sound of clicking heels and popping bubble gum started Rolland from his reverie. Believing it to be coming from downstairs, Rolland jogged as quietly as he could to the edge of the staircase and began his decent downward. Then he saw her.

There, at the bottom of the staircase, stood Tina. But this wasn't the Tina that Rolland had met earlier that day. No, this Tina was something else entirely.

Gone were the formal skirt and blouse he remembered, replaced by much more tantalizing attire. Standing there, leaning against the banister, Tina wore a short, pleated mini skirt and white blouse tied in the middle just above her belly button. Her long hair was parted down the center, and each side was pulled up in a braided pigtail, just the way Rolland liked it.

Not sure as to how to proceed, Rolland stopped and stared for a moment at the beautiful young woman standing in the moonlight.

"Well, hey there, stranger," Tina said in a sing song voice as she gazed up the staircase at him.

"Hey – Tina, right?" Rolland said, carrying the tough, confident act over from the upstairs hallway.

"You know it – stud," Tina said, moving gracefully toward the barrister Rolland clung to. She stopped close enough for him to get a generous view of her cleavage.

"What, uh are you doing down here? This late, I mean," Rolland stuttered, the words spilled out of his mouth.

"Waiting..." Tina said, pulling Rolland closer to her by the collar of his shirt.

"Waiting for whom, exactly?" Rolland said nervously, preparing for another kiss as he leaned in and closed his eyes.

Geoffrey waited until Rolland closed his eyes before morphing back into himself, apparently content in the knowledge he had finally tricked the newest inductee to their little group. Pulling his head back nearly a foot, he looked down at the love-struck young man and almost envied him for a moment. Almost.

"For my Prince Charming!" Geoffrey said in the most masculine voice he could muster.

Opening his eyes, Rolland stared back at the stout, balding little man and realized he had been played for a fool.

"You jackass!" Rolland exclaimed, pushing Geoffrey backward and into the marble vase and podium behind him, causing its contents to spill out onto the floor.

"Whoops!" Geoffrey said, quickly stepping away from the broken vase and the puddle it left under his feet.

"What the hell are you doing anyway?" Rolland asked Geoffrey before common sense had time to register a complaint.

"Going clubbin'," Geoffrey said, straightening the collar of his shirt and catching a quick whiff of his underarms.

"There are clubs in Eden?" Rolland asked with a bemused look.

"Of course there are," Geoffrey said, putting his hands in the air. "We are in paradise, aren't we?"

"So you're going to a club… looking like Tina?" Rolland asked, brushing off the blue petals that had landed on his shirt.

"No, I did that just for your benefit. Saw the way she was looking at you during dinner," Geoffrey said, his eyes scanning Rolland for some hint of an opinion on the matter.

"I didn't notice," Rolland said, careful not to divulge any personal information. Past experiences with gossip had taught him enough to keep his lips sealed unless absolutely necessary.

"Uh huh. Well," Geoffrey said, apparently unphased by Rolland's refusal to discuss the local scenery. "I'll be on my way then. Good evening, Mr. Wright."

"Good night, Geoffrey the Shape Shifter," Rolland replied as he watched the short, rotund man open the front door and walk out into the moonlit night.

Smiling at this rather odd bit of fortune, Rolland decided to press onward with his exploration, clicking the black light in his pocket back on.

Moving faster through the Halls of Time with the increase in light, Rolland was able to maneuver around enough to make his way to the halfway point in his journey as the invisible ink drops led him to the dining room. The long, lavish, dinner table where Rolland's hosts had dined with him mere hours ago lay bare. Gone were the ornate china and goblets.

The black light illuminated the rest of the trail back to Judah's lab with ease. It wasn't a complex route, but Rolland didn't suspect he could find his way back without it. The somewhat steady stream of invisible droplets took him through the building and all the way to the large red door that he and Judah had gone through earlier.

As he walked through the red hatch, Rolland could not help but be impressed by the sheer size of the Halls of Time. 'Halls' seemed to be the correct term for the ever-expanding building, as Rolland again found himself in the twisting and turning corridors that inevitably led to the long staircase ascending to Judah's laboratory.

Once at the top, Rolland spotted the keypad and familiar silver cone that Judah had used to unlock the door earlier. Removing the tape from his pocket, Rolland broke off a two inch piece before taping one side to the other and forming a round 'O' of tape. Next, he sized it to the silver cone and firmly placed it inside.

"Here goes nothing" Rolland said to himself, sticking his tongue out and dipping it into the taped silver cone.

"Welcome, Doctor Raines," the female voice said, triggering the automatic door locks behind Rolland to pop open and allow him entry.

Thankful, but not quite relieved, Rolland pulled his tongue out, then turned around and climbed into the disinfecting room. Waiting until the door shut behind him, Rolland felt around the wall for the hidden button that detected germs. Finding it, he pushed the hidden compartment, releasing the 'cleansing rod' and scanned himself.

Opening up the laboratory door, Rolland climbed inside and breathed a sigh of relief. The first part was over. Now all he had to do was find his father's plasma, figure out how to get the Dream Phoenix working, and send himself back in time to stop his mother's death. Piece of cake.

Creeping through the dark laboratory, Rolland clicked the black light back on and followed it along the far wall to where the Cause/Effect machine sat, still propped up and turned on from the presentation earlier that evening.

Vaguely recalling the sequence Judah used earlier, Rolland decided to go with plan B instead. Clicking on the black light and hovering it above the keyboard, certain keys flashed traces of bright blue finger prints on their surface. The brightest among them were the E R O A S L and N keys.

Running through every possible combination of words using those specific letters, Rolland believed he had very few options. His third guess of 'ORLEANS' turned out to be the winner.

Typing in the words 'Taylor Wright's death' was more difficult than Rolland had anticipated. Although it had been his intention to do this very thing for hours now, actually doing it made him feel... icky. Thankful that none of the Knights could read minds, Rolland took a deep breath, and typed his mother's name into Judah's Cause/Effect timeline.

TAYLOR MICHELLE WRIGHT

Age at Death: 40 years old.

Primary Cause: Murdered by Vilthe.

Survived by: N/A – See Scott Wright murder file.

Ways to Prevent: See timeline.

A line of events popped up on the screen in a timeline. Going backward from Taylor Wright's death it covered almost 200 years of history and roughly seven thousand events. The overload of information needed to be filtered, that much was obvious, but how?

Rolland again searched for Taylor's death, only this time he looked for major events that might have caused it. Only one event popped up, a file marked 'Nabawoo Extinction, 1817, Florida' that Rolland clicked on.

December 11, 1817: Native-occupied Florida (North America).

On this day, General Andrew Jackson, representing the United Stated Armed Forces, led an expedition through Seminole-controlled Florida, wiping out the indigenous population and killing over 4,000 Native Americans. Among the notable killed were Nahoy, Chieftain of the Nabawoo Seminole tribe; his daughter Princess Blaisey of the Nabawoo Seminole tribe; and two British officers who were assisting the natives during their conflict with the Americans.

A picture of numerous dead Native American bodies laying on the ground accompanied the article, although Rolland could not understand why. He searched next for 'Nahoy' but found nothing. It wasn't until he searched for 'Princess Blaisey' that an interesting result popped up. According to Judah's records, Princess

Blaisey of the Nabawoo tribe was Rolland's great-grandmother on his mother's side.

"Interesting," Rolland said to himself aloud, quickly changing gears and typing in 'Princess Blaisey Nabawoo death' into the Cause/Effect machine. These results were quite blunt and to the point.

Princess Blaisey of the Nabawoo Seminole Tribe

Age at Death: 19 years old.

Cause of Death: Murdered by General Andrew Jackson.

Survived By: Three children.

Intrigued by these results, Rolland tried one last tactic, typing in 'Princess Blaisey Nabawoo Death Prevented' before clicking search. His heart raced within his chest at the possibility of what this discovery could potentially mean. Finally, the computer stopped its search, yielding one result.

Princess Blaisey of the Nabawoo

After surviving the attacks on her people, Princess Blaisey went on to lead what remained of the Nabawoo Seminoles against Spanish and American forces.

Date of Death: July 30, 1832.

The dramatic shift in his great-grandmother's fate due to living through one key event gave Rolland an idea. He again brought up the search bar and in addition to what was already there typed in 'Taylor Wright death' and pressed enter.

Another couple of long, excruciatingly agonizing seconds went by before another file appeared on the screen. Rolland clicked it immediately to reveal not a text file like before, but another time-line. This one was different, however, as the closer Rolland looked at it the less he could decipher.

Rolland added one of their deaths back into the equation on the search bar, but when he pressed enter both of their deaths disappeared. It was almost like they were linked somehow, like one death prevented the other. Sensing he might be on to something, Rolland did one final search for Taylor Wright under this scenario where his great-grandmother did not die when she was supposed to.

Another timeline appeared on the screen, this time it showed Taylor's life in great detail. Her birth, marriage, and the birth of Rolland were there plotted out like little stops she made along the way to….nothing.

The shock hit Rolland almost as hard as the beast outside the bookstore had the day before. Under this scenario, the Cause/Effect machine predicted that Taylor Wright would still be alive.

"I've got to get my ass to 1817!" Rolland half shouted under his breath as he stood up from the chair and walked over to the Dream Phoenix.

Coming face to face with Judah's machine left Rolland with an unsettling feeling in his stomach, lurching and sending a pain through his body. This, as much as anything, was probably due to the grim realization that in order to accomplish his goal, Rolland would have to insert the 30 gauge needle directly into his own arm.

The materials were still spread out on the exam table from earlier, apparently forgotten in the commotion. The tourniquet, needles, gauze, iodine, and bandages were all waiting, tempting Rolland to utilize them for his own ends.

Tying the rubber band around his arm proved to be a slight challenge, but one that took seconds, not minutes, to master. After disinfecting the area above the vein on his arm, Rolland slowly but accurately stuck the needle into it before taping the tube attached to it to his arm.

"Tape is so awesome," Rolland said to himself, reaching across to trigger the activation switch on the Dream Phoenix.

The process was immediate and identical to a few hours before. It took a mere five minutes for the plasma to separate and extract from Rolland's arm, giving a little beep sound as it finished.

Relieved that things were going so well, Rolland leaned over to the Dream Phoenix and pressed the 'SYNC' button, allowing it to sync up with the Cause/Effect machine and program the coordinates that Rolland wanted to travel to. The idea that maybe Judah was bullshitting with these instructions did pass through his mind once or twice. These fears were doubled when out of nowhere the machine began shaking violently.

"That probably isn't good," Rolland said, as he watched the Dream Phoenix convulse before shooting out a beam of bright light onto the middle of the tile wall behind it. Before Rolland could react, he was joined by an unexpected visitor.

"What the bloody hell is going on?" Judah screamed as he rushed into his laboratory half asleep and equally as dressed. "How did you get in here?"

"I, uh…" Rolland began, but was quickly distracted by the large tray of medical instruments that went flying past his head and into the bright void of nothingness behind him. "I think there might be a problem."

To Rolland's left, the entire wall where the Dream Phoenix was mere moments ago was gone, replaced by a soft yellow light, just like the one from the library basement that brought him to Eden. This one, however, was not stationary like June Lin's.

On the contrary, the closer that Rolland looked at the light, the more he realized that it was expanding and taking everything it touched with it.

"Hit the emergency alert button to your left!" Judah screamed at Rolland as the shaking intensified and drowned out all other noise in the room.

Sure enough a large red button marked 'EMERGENCY' was there on the control panel under a small sheet of glass. Rolland smashed both the glass and the button with his fist, triggering an alarm that sounded through the entire complex.

With all of the energy he could muster, Rolland closed his eyes as tightly as they would go and began snapping and clasping his hands together in a vain attempt to utilize his time traveling abilities. The blindingly white light that came from the Dream Phoenix had filled not only Judah's laboratory where he and Judah were stationed, but out into the clean room and staircase beyond.

The light moved independently, almost of its own volition. All around the laboratory things began to disappear. First the Cause/Effect machine began to glow a radiant shade of orange before it became one with the light and was gone, vanished into the breach in the time stream.

It was then that Rolland realized what he had done. With one careless mistake, he had unleashed the full power of himself and the Dream Phoenix on the Halls of Time.

While the light moved slowly at first, it picked up pace as it went, threatening to block off the only exit. This was worrisome, as silhouettes of people began to fill the doorway of the laboratory. Still strapped to the chair, Rolland could only vaguely see the outlines of Sephanie, Tina, Joan, and Turtledove.

"What did you do?" Judah yelled out at Rolland, demanding an explanation as he held onto the table top for dear life as the vortex attempted to suck him in.

"I put my plasma into your machine," Rolland began, but was cut off before he could get any further.

"You did what?!" Judah asked, his face falling into a state of disbelief. "Why don't you stop this?"

"I can't!" Rolland screamed while trying to wiggle his plugged in arm. "I'm stuck!"

Cursing, Judah lost his grip on the sleek wood of the table top and fell into the blindingly bright vortex that threatened to take over the room.

"Judah!" Joan screamed, releasing her own grip and flying into the vortex after her husband.

Looking over at Sephanie and Tina, Rolland could see the fear and confusion in their faces. Neither young woman knew any more about what was going on than Rolland did, but unlike Rolland, they were both slowly beginning to walk away from the ever-growing white light.

"Oh, no!" Turtledove said from over Rolland's shoulder. "We must run, now! Everyone go!"

The mass exodus behind him was all but lost on Rolland as he sat there, still strapped to the Dream Phoenix. From this front row seat Rolland was forced to watch everything and everyone he had come to know in the past twelve hours be sucked up into the white abyss that now completely surrounded him.

Still unable to move due to the needle lodged firmly within his arm Rolland was little more than a sitting duck.

Finally and mercifully, Rolland too was surrounded by the light, slipping into the anomaly with one final, solitary thought.

"What have I done..?"

Chapter 10:
Breaking New Ground

December 11, 1817 - Pensacola, Florida

7:45AM EST

It was a muggy, humid morning when U.S. General Andrew Jackson woke to the sound of tribal horns. Immediately identifying their purpose, he quickly gathered both his wits and his pants, grabbing his sword and sidearm as he left his tent.

Known to be tough as hickory, Andrew Jackson was a moderately tall man for his time, standing at six feet, one inch. In this and in his military rank he was compared often to George Washington among elite society in Boston, Washington, and New York, despite his humble beginnings.

Jackson's rigid demeanor was only matched by his sharp attention to detail. His crisply pressed uniform was such that it demanded the attention of all the company's men. Each stood at full attention, showing perfect respect for their commanding officer as Jackson made his way through the columns slowly, careful to catch each and every pair of eyes.

"Today we fight like dogs, and live like kings!" Jackson roared to his men, who cheered loudly in response. Their gusto and appreciation for their General's bravery in the face of danger was not unnoticed by his adversaries on and off the battlefield.

A slave, brought directly from Africa on Jackson's orders, walked Jackson's horse to him around the hustle and bustle of preparing for the day's campaign.

A light rain began to fall on the heads and shoulders of every soul under the barely visible sun, uniting them in nature. They all felt the soft droplets as they landed on both white and brown skin alike.

Lightning struck diagonally across the gray sky, followed shortly by an attention-stealing clap of thunder that rocked the previously dry Florida landscape.

Jackson looked across the foggy clearing and saw the dark brown eyes of Nahoy, leader of the Nabawoo Tribe and speaker of the Florida Seminole Council. The two had met many times, during battle and in the courtroom. While other savages chose a direct confrontation, Nahoy practiced the art of diplomacy, a game of mental jousting that Jackson had been happy to play with the man over the years. Today that would end. This would be their final showdown; both men knew it somewhere within them.

"I told you not to come," Nahoy said without turning around to acknowledge his audience.

"But I wanted to, I had to see you," said a small but assertive female voice behind him. "To at least say goodbye."

Nahoy turned around and looked down slightly to see his daughter, the beautiful and vivacious Princess Blaisey.

"Yazhi, little one. This is not goodbye," Nahoy said, taking his daughter's face between his hands and kissing her forehead tenderly. "Fate is about to bring us a great gift. Feel it in your bones, my cub."

This was much more difficult for Blaisey than for the average Seminole child. Aside from being more skeptical of her people's teachings than most, her studies of world affairs had led her to the conclusion that the man waiting on the other side of the clearing was both ruthless and bloodthirsty. The white man's newspapers had taught her that many years ago.

Yet somehow, just as she had done many times before, Blaisey found herself playing the part of a well behaved, dutiful daughter. Looking up at her father's lined, weathered face, she simply said, "Yes, Papa."

Back across the foggy clearing, many of the American soldiers were gearing up for battle. Jackson saw this, saw the fear and determination in each set of eyes that he passed, knowing that these men were fighters, soldiers trained by him alone. Each and every one of them was at his sole command, just the way he had envisioned it.

"Formation!" Jackson bellowed.

"Though there is smoke on the water, there is also fire in the sky! Let us send these savages to hell where they belong!" Jackson cried, pulling his ceremonial sword out from its sheath and holding it up high for his soldiers to see.

The two forces, American and Seminole, both came charging down the sides of their respective hills. Weapons drawn, each soul on the field knew nothing of the glory and consequences that lie before them. Faster and faster they went, gravity taking hold of their bodies and urging them headlong into the battle.

Blaisey looked on at the scene before her, bayonets, arrows, bullets, and horses filling her senses. In a world where food was something scarce, weapons were as plentiful as they were terrifying.

From the sky above him, General Jackson could see a small, glowing object. Its shape appeared to be round and twisted with no definable parameters, almost as if it was getting bigger the longer he looked at it. It kept swirling faster and faster until it formed what looked like a giant sideways tornado in mid-air. Another bolt of lightning struck, disappearing behind the strange phenomenon.

The clash was imminent.

"General!" came the voice of Jackson's first lieutenant, whose attention had also veered to the sky.

Looking downward, the General did not see the skirmish he was expecting. On the contrary, both the American line and the Seminole warriors had stopped on the spot and all gazed toward the heavens. Some of their mouths were even ajar in surprise and wonder at the bright spot of light that had appeared above them.

In disgust and amazement, the General let out another battle cry, but it fell upon deaf ears. The looks of wonder were turning into terror and fear as the light expanded and began to widen. Jackson had seen this look on many a man's face before, moments before meeting the end of his musket.

"It's a trick! Stand your guard men, stand your..." Jackson shouted, his voice getting lost in the sea of unrest amongst both the American and Seminole forces.

From high above their heads came the sound of thunder accompanied by a bright flash of white hot light from inside the center of the tornado before it expanded into a long, ribbon-like creation at least ten feet long. It pulsated with a fiery glow that blinded the General and forced him to look away.

Witnesses claim that what came next never happened. As it was, on that day in December of 1817, the surrender and subsequent murder of Nahoy of the Nabawoo at the hands of General

Andrew Jackson was delayed indefinitely as three people came hurtling out of the strange hole in the sky.

Judah came down first, landing in the top of a tree about five feet from the portal's exit. All eyes immediately fell onto him as he tumbled and fumbled his way out of the tree's low branches and down to solid ground.

Sephanie and Joan soon followed Judah out of the center of the Dream Phoenix's time parachute, though their landing fell on the American side of the battlefield where they were immediately surrounded by a group of armed and overly friendly men.

They were soon followed by Turtledove, Victor, and Tina, all of whom shot out of the time rip with greater speed than the others. The result of which was a landing behind Seminole lines.

The spectacle above them was now secondary to both the American and Seminole natives as they eyed their new guests with hostile reserve. The Seminoles were especially bloodthirsty, as from their world view, a borderline elderly man accompanied by a white woman and an African had invaded their land from the sky. Before having time to process this, a barrage of items, ranging from small to large came hurtling down on them from above. The stream of books, pillows, training equipment, dishes, cutlery, furniture, and other various household items rained down on them, forcing anyone within its path to duck and cover as quickly as possible.

With such short notice, not all of the soldiers on either side of the battlefield made it, as a well-placed fork took the life of a Seminole on horseback and another met an untimely end underneath a bathtub.

On the American side, an entire line of archers fell prey to an invisible force that lifted them high into the air and snapped off their legs one by one. The invisible creature from Judah's lab was loose, and claiming victims as it went along undetected.

Rolland landed on his feet, although he was not alone. Raising his head slowly, he realized that standing mere inches away were two people. One was a man, tall, and proud with broad shoulders and a square jaw that reminded him immediately of a grizzly bear.

The other was female, a teenage girl, who stood slightly behind the man in a childlike manner. Rolland had to concentrate to get her into focus, but once he had, her identity was unmistakable. It was her, the girl from the picture on the Cause/Effect machine – it was his great-grandmother, Blaisey of the Nabawoo tribe.

But before Rolland could say anything, a loud horse whinny from behind captivated the attention of the large Native American man, causing him to turn and face whatever it was head on.

There, Rolland saw none other than the legendary Andrew Jackson, mounted upon a grey stallion and looking very debonair. Based on looks alone he was every bit the American hero with his sword drawn and spurs glistening. It wasn't until the horse began its gallop that Rolland realized Jackson was charging directly toward them.

Jackson ditched the sword, instead choosing to pull out what appeared to be two crudely made tomahawk axes from either side of his hips. Arming himself with these, Jackson let go of the horse's reins and readied for the attack by launching himself off of the beast and directly at Princess Blaisey.

Thinking quickly (or perhaps not at all), Rolland reacted, grasping the native girl by the waist and pulling her out of harm's way only seconds before she met with the business ends of Jackson's two weapons.

Rolland's calculation was off only by a moment, as Jackson was ready for the counteroffensive that Nahoy launched before Jackson's feet even touched the ground.

The two men fought hand to hand for what seemed like a small eternity as Rolland helped the Seminole girl to her feet and pulled her after him, away from the scene.

Nahoy watched as his daughter disappeared from his line of vision with the white boy who fell from the sky. Surely angels were smiling down upon his family this day.

Watching all of this transpire while attempting to beat back the onslaught of American forces, both Marcus Turtledove and Sephanie Kelly debated whether to follow Rolland or stay and continue fighting.

For Turtledove, the prospect of controlling the already versatile situation was secondary to discussing the incredible fact that somehow Rolland had sent not only himself, but the entire contents of the Halls of Time, including its residents and all of their possessions, back to what Turtledove guessed was the 19th century. While pondering this quandary to himself, he was attacked by not only two American servicemen, but a Nabawoo archer who was out of arrows as well.

For the far less responsible Sephanie, the choice was much easier. After subduing the two brutish guards blocking her path, she ran into the swamplands after Rolland, leaving the rest of the Knights of Time behind.

"Stay together!" Turtledove shouted to his Knights, holding their position with his level- headed will.

"Judah, you must go after them," Turtledove commanded his most loyal pupil.

With a reluctant glare and an exasperated sigh, Judah kissed his wife and ran off into the Florida forests in pursuit of the 'children' who had created this mess.

Nahoy watched in silent curiosity - distracted, yet not fearful of the sky people following his daughter.

A small knife popped out from under Jackson's sleeve and he stabbed the Nabawoo chieftain in the shoulder.

"Hujo!" screamed the Nabawoo second as he made his way through the battle to his leader's side.

With the fight drawing to a stalemate, and the introduction of new players into their game, Jackson decided to fall back and re-evaluate.

"Fall back!" General Jackson yelled over the commotion to his soldiers, riding past the line and noticing a group of them huddled around the passed out Victor. "Take the sky people's slave with us."

Three glassy-eyed American soldiers ran over to the fallen Victor and picked him up by his shoulders before dragging him to a nearby cart and depositing him within it. This purposeful kidnapping was as sinister as it was immoral, yet it was only a taste of the depravity of Andrew Jackson's character.

The Knights of Time were wildly outnumbered, and Turtledove was unable to help his most flame retardant Knight as Victor was abducted by Jackson and his American forces.

"Um, Turtledove..." said Tina with hint of panic in her voice.

"Yes?" Turtledove asked her without bothering to look away from Jackson's retreat.

"I think we've got a much bigger problem than the Americans," Tina said, hoping to convey the importance that the situation carried with it.

The razor-sharp tips fused to wooden arrows belonging to three dozen Nabawoo warriors were bearing down on their small party of three.

"Baloukudon, Nahoy," one of the Seminole warriors said to the group at large. At this prompt, another one of the natives lowered his weapon and rushed to the side of the fallen Nabawoo Chieftain.

"Nahoy, Nahoy means leader!" Tina said, accidently raising her voice in excitement, causing a dozen of the Nabawoo natives standing closest to her to pull back on their bow strings in alarm.

"While I believe you are correct in your assumption Miss Holmes, perhaps now is not the time for casual observations," Turtledove said, careful not to break eye contact with the Nabawoo warrior who had given orders to the others.

This cat and mouse game persisted for many minutes, each man refusing to blink first.

"You think you're tough?" Joan asked, having no problem at all displaying her defiance to their new captors. By refusing to get on her knees, she was refusing to submit, unlike her two companions. "I've fought AND married the British. Go ahead and bring it on, cupcake."

Though he did not understand the exact words spoken by the insolent blonde woman standing before him, the only unarmed Seminole understood her challenging tone. With an odd smile, he motioned with his right hand, summoning four more Nabawoo warriors, all armed with long, , wooden sticks resembling large skewers.

It came as no surprise to Turtledove when the skewers found themselves centimeters from his and Tina's necks.

"Won tushi fhizat," the Nabawoo warrior said to Joan, while holding his hands out and turning them over slowly before shrugging his shoulders.

This elicited laughs from the entire group of Nabawoo, save for their medicine man who was still attending to their 'Nahoy'.

Joan, realizing what kind of interest she held for the Seminole in charge, decided to take advantage of her situation. Unbuttoning the top button of her pajama top, Joan wiggled a bit, hoping to entice the half-naked native man into coming close enough to her to inflict some pain.

The obviously excited and unarmed Nabawoo warrior took a few steps toward Joan before stopping again and calling backwards, never taking his eyes of Joan's chest the entire time. "Von tumigle Nahoy?"

"That's right... come right over here..." Joan said motioning with her finger for the Nabawoo warrior to join her.

"Rut too, vamanos," came the voice of the unseen medic, commanding the attention of the entire group, if only for a moment.

Satisfied with whatever it was the medic said, the Nabawoo continued on, crossing the rest of the distance between him and this exotic and alluring white woman.

Diplomacy knows many languages. Food, drink, sports – all examples of ways that people of different cultures can lay aside their differences and share a bond over something basic, something pure, something elemental.

Instead Joan, in her infinite wisdom, decided to kick him in the crotch.

"Go to hell," Joan said, squaring her jaw and raising her eyebrows.

Ten minutes later, Turtledove, Joan, and Tina had their hands tied behind their backs and were being marched away by a group of Nabawoo warriors carrying the skewers. Following them closely was about a half a dozen other Nabawoo carrying their 'Nahoy' on a long, makeshift gurney.

"He had it coming," Joan said as they were led into the morning sunshine of Western Florida.

Chapter 11: Call Me Lion

Running through the swampland, native girl in hand, Rolland thought of nothing but getting away. Over logs and tree limbs, through muddy puddles, the two of them dashed for their lives through the harsh landscape, not stopping until they reached a large stretch of swampland where the Seminole Princess insisted on catching her breath.

"I think… I think we lost them," Rolland said breathing and sweating heavily. He placed both of his hands behind his head in an attempt to breathe easier, an old tip he had picked up in middle school track practice.

"Peelima du verro?" Princess Blaisey of the Nabawoo asked him, also breathing heavily but not sweating nearly as much. Women have a magical way of doing this, making it appear as if they are less human and more divine than their sweatier male counterparts.

For this, and for not being able to understand her, Rolland felt truly embarrassed to be such an awkward adolescent. He had already held the opinion that females looked good doing anything. Apparently sweating and running for their lives from crazy former presidents fit into that category as well.

"I'm sorry, I don't understand you," Rolland said, dropping his arms to his sides in defeat. "Maybe you could write it down, or…"

Realizing how foolish he sounded, Rolland was suddenly grateful for the Seminole girl's inability to speak English.

The hot, humid Florida air was beginning to make Rolland uncomfortable under his denim jeans and pearl-snap shirt, causing his frustrations to rise with each passing moment. Standing there, staring at the Seminole girl, he could find no sense of resemblance between the two of them. No distinguishing characteristics, aside from her eyes, that gave any indication that the two might share the same Earth, much less the same bloodline.

"Rook tach, vandimat put a lorne," Blaisey said, looking over Rolland's shoulder and past him to the swamp behind them. She began walking towards it cautiously, almost as if she expected trouble to pop out and attack them at any moment.

In Rolland's experience, trouble was not something that announced itself, but instead something that snuck up from behind you outside of a bookstore or laboratory. For that reason, he decided not to follow the Seminole girl, but to turn around and keep an eye out for a potential sneak attack.

No sooner had Rolland turned around than he began to get another wave of the uneasy feeling in the pit of his stomach. The pain was a mixture of bad gas and nervous intuition bubbling together to form a new, painful combination of nervous anxiety and earth shattering stomach cramps.

Falling to his knees with both hands pressed firmly to his stomach, Rolland caught the break of a lifetime. For sitting there, with his head held low and heart full of woe, came into his line of vision two, no three, slow-moving objects roughly fifty feet away and headed toward them.

"Blaisey!" Rolland screamed, prompting the Nabawoo Princess to turn around in surprise and see the snouts of the three alligators quickly approaching their position.

"Oy vey," Blaisey said quietly under her breath, causing Rolland to look at her in surprise.

Not wasting any time, Blaisey sprang into action, running the distance of the clearing before jumping clean over the middle alligator as it opened its mouth to lunge at her. From behind it, Blaisey grabbed the back end of the gator to her left, using her left hand to firmly massage its spinal column up to its head. This left it in a bit of a trance, as she took her free hand and placed it firmly under its head, before closing its jaw by pressing both of her palms down.

"Ghoutozer!" Blaisey exclaimed at the animal, gritting her teeth and guiding it as it began to roll over onto its side. The gator not only complied, it did so without the least bit of resistance.

This display of dominance caused the last alligator, the one in the back, to slowly slither away before Blaisey could fully subdue its fellow reptile. The middle gator, incredibly upset at its sudden isolation, opened its mouth and released a loud growl at the Seminole girl before lunging toward her in fury.

Jumping behind the overturned gator, Blaisey managed to avoid the onslaught of the creature's anger as it bit down hard on the overturned gator's tail. The still-hypnotized alligator lay there, helpless and meek, merely blinking, completely oblivious to the world around it.

Small fingers found their way to the top of the ornery gator's head and stroked the bumpy, leathery skin with the grace that only a female could master, resulting in a second fairly subdued eight-foot alligator.

To Rolland's surprise, Blaisey was not vindictive toward her attacker. On the contrary, she stayed by its side and began whispering into the side of its head in short, simple words of her native language.

Nearly three miles away, on the site of the earlier skirmish between the American and Nabawoo Seminole forces, the three remaining Knights of Time who stayed back to level the odds now stood, not as heroes, but as captives, at the bottom of a very small pit.

"Why can we not communicate with them?" Turtledove asked, his hands bound to the point of circulation loss.

"You gave the universal translators to Sephanie, sir," the intern Tina piped in, annoyance and fear filling her voice. She had never experienced field missions before, but something told her that this impromptu one wasn't going so well.

"How about sign language, has anyone tried that yet?" Joan said, still struggling against her own bonds. The crude leather straps that bound her wrists behind her back dug into her flesh and refused to yield, despite her constant struggling.

"Na toy, va much hoy," the Seminole warrior who stood directly above the pit said to the six armed guards standing behind him. Each of the captives were assisted out of the steep hole and to their feet by the men. Not remaining stationary for long, the three weary knights were placed in a walking formation and driven eastward.

Alongside of them, marched a group of four of the largest Nabawoo warriors, each of them carrying the handle to the makeshift gurney. On top of it lay their leader, Nahoy, still wearing his headdress.

"Their leader is injured," Tina said out loud, hoping to soothe her tension by conversing with her companions.

"Probably not long for this world," Joan said, her chest and head slumped forward as she walked up the steep, rocky hill. "Who do you think they're going to blame for that one, huh?"

"Not us... right Turtledove?" Tina squeaked hopefully, looking over at her mentor for reassurance.

Marcus Turtledove, however, was only barely listening. Before he had been ripped from his comfortable, down feather bed, he had been having the most wonderful dream involving a foreign, far-off beach and a lone, isolated beach chair waiting to be relaxed in. The years had been hard on his tired old bones, and the current situation promised no respite.

The chastised alligator that Blaisey had broken mere moments before lay upside down beside Rolland's feet. With the creature's eyes half closed, and all four legs pointed straight up in the air, the gator Blaisey had called 'Oine' let out a low, constant purr.

This noise elicited from her former enemy brought a smile to the Seminole Princess' face. Rolland could not understand a word the young woman said, but kindness is universal, and he could tell that the two of them had made peace with one another.

Blaisey stopped petting the alligator when she heard a rustling from behind her.

"Did you hear...?" Rolland began to ask her, but was cut off mid-sentence as Blaisey held up her right hand and extended her pointer finger outward to indicate silence. He had seen this same gesture many times from his mother growing up, and in its own odd sort of way, there was a sense of comfort there.

Blaisey snatched her bow from its resting spot beside her and raised it toward the grass, ready to strike at who, or what, might be after them.

From behind the tall grass came Sephanie, carrying a handful of something small, round, and shiny. Seeing her brought a smile to Rolland's face that did not go unnoticed by his new traveling companion.

Awkward looks were exchanged by all three of them before Rolland, acting as the intermediary, began to speak.

"Um..." Rolland said, unsure as to how to translate native speech, much less female.

"Right, there you are," Judah said appearing behind Sephanie and pointing at them both as Blaisey reached for her arrow, bringing it to a firing position before another word was spoken.

"What the bloody hell did she do that for?" Judah asked, appearing to be genuinely offended by Blaisey's protective gesture.

"I think these will help everyone," Sephanie said, slowly distributing two of the tiny devices to Rolland and Blaisey, before tossing another to Judah, and finally putting the last one in her left ear.

The Nabawoo princess and Rolland both watched the other two put the contraptions into their ears before copying their actions; though Blaisey did her best to hold onto her bow at the same time.

"There, can you understand us now?" Sephanie said to Blaisey directly.

"I... I hear you," Princess Blaisey said, again aiming the bow wildly at the two newcomers, gifts of enlightenment notwithstanding. "Who are you?"

"I'm Judah Jacob Raines, ok?" Judah said, taking a step toward the Indian princess before spooking her into triggering the bow and pointing it directly at his jugular. "I'm, I'm the smartest man alive, alright. So I'm sure together, we can all come to some sort of understanding."

"Smartest man, huh?" Blaisey said, momentarily dropping the aim of her weapon off of Judah for a moment. "Well, I'm no man. So I've got no use for you."

Out of the corner of his eye, Rolland could have sworn he saw Sephanie smirk, but upon full glance there was nothing but a steely reserve to her otherwise angelic face.

"Figures," Judah said sarcastically, drawing Blaisey's renewed focus. "I'm sorry – look I…"

"And you – why are you here?" Blaisey interrupted Judah, and turning her focus to Rolland, catching him completely unprepared.

"Uh, well, I'm Rolland Wright and…" Rolland said, but was immediately cut off, as was becoming the custom, by the native princess.

"I did not ask WHO you were," the princess said, taking one hand off of the bow and poking Rolland playfully with the end of it.

"Yeah, how come?" Judah asked, again drawing her ire.

"You, well, you're mine somehow." Blaisey said, a look of mild embarrassment crossing her otherwise steadfast face. "I just know it."

"You're right," Rolland said, taking a step toward Blaisey "I'm your great-grandson, your descendant. I'm from the future, Princess."

"Don't call me princess." Blaisey said, pointing the bow at Rolland one more time before finally lowering it for good. "It's Blaisey. Call me Blaisey, all of you."

"Alright, Blaisey," Sephanie said, speaking for the first time since they could understand each other's languages. "Where are we exactly?"

"In the Gyro Nikko swamp, near the creek lands. About five miles or so from my village," Blaisey said, looking over at Rolland once again. "My great-grandson, huh?"

"So, you believe me, then?" Rolland asked while raising his eyebrows in hopes that their entrance had made enough of an impression to warrant believability.

"Bad idea, Cinderella," Judah said, ruining the moment. "You just can't go around changing the past."

"I'm not changing anything," Rolland shot back, defiance toward anything even resembling an authority figure deeply rooted within him.

"So you're saying she wasn't supposed to die before you two ran off and left my wife and the rest of our team back there for her people to do, well, who knows what with," Judah retorted, his indignation overpowering his penchant for reasonable argument.

"My people?" Blaisey asked him indignantly. "What, do you think they're going to eat your friends or something?"

"Well, some early native American tribes did practice cannibalism," Judah said, staring straight ahead and pulling this nugget of wisdom from his never ending repertoire of knowledge.

"And most British procreated with their cousins. Keeping their royal blood pure, yes?" Blaisey countered, catching the three travelers off guard with her knowledge, quick wit, and sharp tongue.

"Suggestions are welcome, J.J.," Sephanie said, hoping to move the conversation in a more measured and productive direction.

"Look – the way I see it this is a classic Wizard of Oz scenario," Judah said, cracking his knuckles one at a time in a calculated attempt to deal with his stress and assert his dominance.

"Wiz ord of oz?" Blaisey asked, looking at Rolland for clarification.

"So the four of us march our happy little selves through the swamps and forest and back to wherever it is you come from. We'll straighten this mess out there, everyone good with that?" Judah asked, looking from one female to the other, but making no notice of Rolland.

"You're pissed at me, aren't you?" Rolland asked, deciding not to beat around the bush. "For breaking into your lab."

For a moment, Judah resembled a wild mountain lion that Rolland had once seen roaming a hiking trail when he was a boy. With his cold, iceberg blue eyes and the random whiskers on his face, Judah resembled a feral feline that was about to annihilate his prey for sneaking into its den.

"So, that makes you Dorothy," Judah said to Rolland mockingly, as he took out a pack of cigarettes from his front bathrobe pocket.

"You name is Dorothy, not Rolland?" Blaisey asked Rolland, confused by Judah's references to popular culture.

Rolland, for his part, kept his cool during Judah's mockery. He had after all, broken into the man's laboratory and messed with his invention, sending them all nearly two hundred years into the past. The least he could do was put up with a bit of good natured ribbing.

"ROLLAND!" said both Sephanie and Rolland to Judah's utter delight.

"What about you?" Sephanie said to the blonde genius who was still sporting his pajamas in the middle of the forest.

"You can call me Lion," Judah said in a voice that reeked of cockiness and wit as an unlit cigarette bounced between his curved, smiling lips.

Approximately two miles away, in the makeshift American encampment, Victor was beginning to wake up from bludgeoning he had taken at the hands of America's future seventh President.

Though he had only been there for an hour, Victor had already been subject to Jackson's cognitive questioning, leaving his head feeling more like a large melon with the insides missing. All around him the other slaves were getting their daily ration of porridge as they lined up to accept it from one of the less popular American cooks.

Being from the 20th century himself, Victor never knew the hardships of slavery or the indignation it created. The line of slaves before him had very little in common besides their shared bondage. Their skin colors were very different, as he spotted black, white, yellow, and every shade in between making an appearance in line, waiting for a much-deserved hand out.

Victor, being the newest, was last.

"Best get your food and move on, laddie," said the middle-aged slave ladling out cold porridge. He poured two bowls, one for each of them, before stepping away from the pot, and motioning toward a nearby clearing for them to sit. "My name is Mansa. Stick with me and you won't get noticed."

"Look, there's something I need to tell you," Victor said to Mansa in the most serious tone that he could muster.

"You want my porridge, yes? But you cannot have it," Mansa said, greedily slurping mealy gray goop into his mouth and down his throat.

"No," said Victor with a sense of urgency he had never felt before. "That's not it."

The tone of voice Victor used made Mansa uneasy, as he had not heard the stranger use such a large speaking voice since his arrival.

"You'll want to be careful," Mansa said, using his finger to scoop up any remaining fragments of food left behind in his copper bowl. "You don't want to attract attention here."

"But I do," Victor said in a much lower tone of voice.

"Then you will be killed," Mansa said, fingering the last bit of porridge from his bowl and inserting it into his mouth. "Of this I am sure."

"By the guards?" Victor asked, eyeing his new acquaintance suspiciously.

"No – it is Hickory," Mansa said, a far-off look collecting behind his eyes. "The man in charge, he will beat you to death to amuse."

"But I..." Victor began, but was cut off.

"Please, no more. Of this, I cannot speak more," Mansa said, turning away from Victor and re-depositing himself upon the splintered bench and table where they sat.

Staring straight ahead, Mansa replayed the images of Aljo, the last friend he had made as a captive runaway. They had met each other up in Georgia before being taken by Jackson's men and forced back into slavery. Nearly a month had passed since Aljo was taken early one morning and brutally tortured to the point of death by Jackson. This, of course, was done for mere amusement.

Mansa's concentration was broken by the arrival of a full copper bowl of porridge landing with a thud on the table before him.

191

"You can have it," Victor said, laying the trap.

Victor sat down and readied himself for the obviously crazy statement he was about to make. It broke every protocol he knew of, but if this didn't qualify as an emergency, nothing did.

Looking at the somewhat older Mansa in the eye, Victor opened his mouth and said simply "My name is Victor Aquasi III, and I'm from the future."

Chapter 12:
Untapped Potential

With her hands tied behind her back and legs folded beneath her, Tina Holmes felt the very definition of the word "helpless." It was, she guessed silently to herself, a condition she would be getting used to. Though she had never been in the field before, something told her that things weren't usually this… grim.

Directly to Tina's right, Joan shared a similar fate, as she, too, was tied up and defenseless. The difference, however, was the amount of attention that Joan attracted from the Nabawoo warriors as they watched in silent amusement.

"Let us go, you pug-ugly son of a bitch!" Joan shouted at the top of her lungs. She struggled at her bonds, stirring up dust from the dry ground beneath her bound feet.

None of the Seminoles, warrior or civilian, would go near her.

"When I get out of here I'm going to teach you a thing or two about respecting women, you insufficient excuse for a man!" Joan said, hurling a fresh round of foreign insults at the Nabawoo warriors, particularly the one she had kicked in the crotch.

"I believe they are going to kill us now," Turtledove guessed, looking over at Tina. "Wouldn't you say?"

Wishing that she didn't agree, Tina concentrated as hard as she could, listening to the voices coming from all around her. They were fast and blended together, yet she could hear them over lapping and creating a linguistic symphony to her ears.

"Cursing will do you no good, Joanie," Turtledove said, using a familiar pet name for his second in command instead of her formal title.

Some people might not have noticed this dramatic shift -- hell, even Joan herself didn't bat an eye. But for Tina, who had studied the proper Knight of Time protocol so much it had almost made her head explode, this was a major turning point.

To Tina it meant he was giving up. That Marcus Turtledove, leader of the Knights of Time, was giving up hope that the three of them would get out alive. The Protector of Eden and the man she had grown up admiring was abandoning his post because all he had was his second in command and her. She got the distinct impression he thought she wasn't good enough to be a part of his team, much less in a situation as dire as this.

"I miss Taylor..." Joan said, offering her first honest sentiment other than rage since they had become captives.

"As do I," Turtledove said softly, perhaps admitting it to himself for the first time. "She was quite the linguist."

The words angered Tina, cutting into her psyche with a wicked shine. Turtledove's words were enough to finally push her over the edge.

"Enough!" Tina screamed, her fists clenched tightly by her sides as she stood, the slack on the ropes enough for her five-foot, three-inch frame to do so. "I have had enough of you people always second guessing me and comparing me to her!"

Every head, Traveler of Light and Nabawoo alike turned to Tina, a theatrical curiosity blossoming around her and drawing them in. Their looks of bemused surprise were evident only to their one blue eyed audience member. But the girl with the dirty blonde hair didn't care anymore. With pulsating adrenaline rushing through her veins, her decision was made on instinct, not reasoning.

"Tina," said Turtledove with a calm that even surpassed his normal demeanor, "I think it's best if you just sit back…"

"No," Tina said with a small stomp of her foot, not unlike that of a child. "We are going to do things my way, or else nothing will get done!"

For the first time in her life, Tina Leigh Holmes commanded the attention of every person near her. She glanced around quickly, from right to left. Every soul was focused on her… and she planned on making the most of it.

"Nahoui von too muckva deen," Tina said, looking directly into the eyes of the Seminole who had been giving orders to the others. She motioned toward herself, Joan, and Turtledove – paying special attention to emphasizing his role within their group as appointed leader.

This small statement appeared to be very enlightening and completely understandable, as the Nabawoo in attendance let out a collective gasp. The young natives ran behind their mothers while the old showed no surprise at all, seasoned as they were to the erratic ways of the world.

Nearly all of the warriors who had been ready to fire at all three of the Knights at a moment's notice now put down their bows, leaving all but the four warriors standing closest to their new leader undefended.

Refusing to turn away from the young, white girl's gaze, the Nabawoo warrior giving orders finally opened his mouth and said "Von too mesh yopp vadeen?"

All eyes again turned back to Tina, who broke out into a big smile and nodded her head. "Yeah. Yes, naktich."

The Nabawoo warrior nodded his own head in return with the words "Gra Nada", prompting the four warriors still holding their bows to finally lower their weapons. He then walked the short distance to the three strangers, signaling to an unseen group stationed behind them who rushed forward and cut their bonds.

Arriving just in time to assist Tina to her feet, the Nabawoo commander cupped her hand in his and said the word "Charlton", touching his chest with his free hand.

This introduction elicited another broad smile from Tina. Never in her life had a boy been so formal in introducing himself to her. It felt wonderful and confusing all at the same time, like a first drink, or a kiss.

The moment did not last, however. No sooner had Tina learned his name than Charlton ran off with no explanation. From far away she could hear murmurings from the crowd of Nabawoo who witnessed the entire exchange. One word kept popping up amongst their sea of gossip: 'Nahoy'.

"Just one moment," Turtledove said to the Nabawoo guard before turning to Tina "May I have a moment of your time?"

"Of course," Tina said, wary of what her team leader wanted to discuss with her.

"Truly excellent work my dear," Turtledove said, putting his right hand on Tina's shoulder. His pale green eyes were old and tired, but held pride behind their jubilant surprise. "I wonder if you could –"

"Get to work on making more translators?" Tina asked, holding up her left hand to reveal a couple of cogs and metal pieces she had found in the dirt when they had arrived. "Already on it, boss."

"Keep up the good work then," Turtledove said, turning back to the guard and motioning forward in a 'lead the way' type gesture.

The rest of Tina's afternoon went by in a flurry of searching, salvaging, and fitting parts together to create makeshift translators for her and her fellow knights. The tedious process went smoothly enough as her hands and mind synced into an assembly-line-like trance, the result of which was over two dozen translators, each the size of an American nickel. Her concentration was only broken by the steady stream of Nabawoo that kept invading her working space, their attention fixed elsewhere.

Turtledove walked past Tina, following another man as they made their way into the large, open space by the fire. It seemed as if they were preparing to address the mass of people gathering around them.

Tina looked at this 'meeting of the minds' taking place before her in front of both the Nabawoo warriors and village people alike, and envied the two men their leadership qualities. Not only the transparency they allowed in discussing their business out in the open, but the remarkable tact Turtledove was displaying, despite being dragged into the camp by Charlton at arrow point only an hour before.

"Hey, kid, how did you do that back there?" Joan asked, unable to suppress the smile on her face as she pulled what appeared to be two thirds of a computer monitor out of a large mud puddle.

"Same way you know just when and where to be," Tina said, relishing every moment of adulation that her superior officer afforded her as she finished fitting the scattered cogs and gears together. Thoughts of recommendation letters from both of her commanding officers raced through her head and brought a smile to her face.

Joan chuckled and walked back to where Turtledove, Charlton, and the newly awakened Nahoy were conversing.

Around dusk the American forces rounded up all the slaves and confined them to a separate site outside of the main camping area. Though they were given no more food rations, a private did light a small fire for them before abandoning the thirteen souls to the dark of night.

Until that evening, Victor Aquasi III had spent his entire life within the confines of the law. Never much for breaking the rules, he preferred the role of class clown and spent his days getting people to laugh. But now, after revealing to this group of escaped slaves that he was a traveler of light and therefore came from the future, their laughter felt like hot humiliation on his cheeks.

"You had me worried there," Mansa said, slapping Victor on his bare shoulder before settling down with the small group that had gathered together beside the fire. While all of them were tethered within a fifteen foot radius, none seemed to be obviously upset about their circumstances. It seemed more like it was an unpleasant, yet unavoidable fact of life, not dissimilar to mosquitoes or advertisements of animals dressed as people.

"Stories. Nothin' but stories," said another captive, who oddly was still wearing shackles around his wrists.

"They're not stories," Victor said, his deep baritone voice resonating through the small clearing. "It's the truth. I am from the future and we all need to get out of here. Who is going to help me?"

Silence filled the air between them as memories of past attempts at insurrection drifted to the surface of their minds.

"What exactly is it you want our help with?" asked the Hispanic man sitting across from him.

"I need help breaking out of here," Victor said, causing a series of eye rolls and resumed mumbling. "It's not a problem for me to get out alone, but if you all want to come we'll have to work together."

Laughs broke out from no less than a half a dozen of the men.

"What's keeping ya here, then?" asked one of the older slaves, coughing a bit as he spoke.

"Yeah – best be on your way, pup!" said another, hiccupping halfway through his sentence.

Victor had expected this and had hoped he wouldn't have to resort to what he was about to do. Unfortunately, he saw no other choice. Standing up, Victor walked through the line of slaves, forcing them to part as he walked by.

Then, without stopping, he balled his fingers into a fist, straightening his arm, and striking it against the ground. The friction caused by this created sparks that quickly ignited Victor's forearm like a slow-burning matchstick.

Mansa and the other slaves watched in astonishment as the newest captive literally turned into a large fireball before their eyes.

As Victor approached the fire, the steel shackles that bound him grew weaker, practically begging him to snap them off. He resisted however, wanting to make a necessarily dramatic impact on his fellows. He turned to face them, his entire upper body engulfed in red-hot flames, impressing even the most skeptical of the slaves.

Clasping his hands in front of himself and bowing his head, Victor prepared for his big finale. He counted to three before standing straight up and throwing his arms in the air in triumph, both of his shackles snapping off in the process.

Within seconds, the flames began to die down, disappearing from Victor's legs almost immediately. In the span of half a minute they were gone, replaced by his familiar dark brown skin.

Victor didn't bother looking down at the men still watching. He didn't need to. The matter was out of his hands now, just like the shackles that had been placed upon him. Now he was back to being Victor, back to being Flint. Back to his normal self.

The Nabawoo feast held in the Knight's honor was as bountiful as it was luxurious. The guest of honor, the young woman known as Tina Holmes, sat at the opposite end of the table from Nahoy. For Turtle-dove, a seat next to Nahoy made for some great dinner conversation thanks to his new, remarkably well constructed universal translator.

Joan meanwhile, was making conversation with the Seminole warrior known as Charlton. As leader of their defensive forces, Charlton was adept with the bow, a feat in which he took extreme delight in bragging about to his new acquaintances.

Joan humored Charlton, listening to his tales of this hunt for boar and that hunt for deer -- that is until his conversation turned toward the topic of mating.

"Sorry, I'm married," Joan said, holding up her left hand. She had hoped that in addition to being 'forever', diamonds were universal in meaning as well.

"You have a mate?" Charlton asked skeptically.

"Yes, out there," Joan said, motioning toward the dark forest behind their camp. She thought of how foolish she must look at that moment. If Judah were there, he would make a comment about how her 'mate' from the 'woods' should be along any minute now to drag her back to his lair. True love, it seems, knows nothing but tolerance.

"Then why did you kick me?" Charlton asked, confused and apparently thinking that this sort of action was common in mating wherever Joan came from.

"Yeah, I'm awful sorry about that," Joan said, hoping that the subject could have been avoided.

"I have a mate, too," Charlton said, standing next to Joan and staring up at the night sky.

Remembering that perception was everything, Joan chose not to grill Charlton for his questionable ethics and instead decided to go a gentler route. "I'm sure she's alright."

Among all the joy and celebration at the feast that night, not one soul suspected that a sinister eavesdropper crept within their midst. The tar black shadow that had been listening to them for the better part of the evening made an unseen move, creeping along the tree line at a silent pace.

With each passing second, the shadow grew larger. Like a water stain on the tapestry of nature, it spread to every corner that it conquered. With a lethal touch that wilted all that it consumed, the shadow moved around the Nabawoo encampment with ease before traveling the mile and a half back to the Spanish made gravel road and to take solid form.

Though it was still nearly three or four hours until sundown, the shadow mimicked the darkest, most primal features that the cover of night had to offer. It formed shoes, black, in a men's size eight, followed by feet to fill them, legs, slacks, a torso, and finally a head.

Walking down the East Florida pathway, the skinny, sweater-vest-clad Edward Vilthe smiled to himself as he thought of how silly Turtledove and Nahoy looked talking to one another, like two old men sitting outside of a general store.

"Just waiting to die," Vilthe said aloud as he placed both hands in his side pockets and began whistling an incomprehensible tune to himself as he walked along nonchalantly, as if he were any normal 19th century settler out for a stroll.

For the briefest of moments, Rolland found himself completely alone. The lack of people around was a refreshing change from the constant company he had been keeping since the bookstore, though it did feel a bit odd to be so alone with nature. Maybe it was hypocritical, but the entire time that Rolland had spent homeless he had only slept outside once.

The El Dorado seemed like such a luxury to the dirty-blonde haired teenager who now found himself so exhausted that the dirt suited him just fine.

"Sleeping already?" said Turtledove's voice in a strange echo inside Rolland's head.

"What the hell?!" Rolland exclaimed, jumping up off of his back and getting to his feet. But no one was there. Not Turtledove, not anyone.

"What the hell is going on?" Rolland asked aloud.

For Turtledove, it was a mixed bag. On one hand he, like Rolland, was not born in Eden and therefore did not have the luxury of growing up exposed to the otherwise fictitious behavior of Eden's inhabitants. But on the other hand, well, it was always fun to pick on freshmen.

"It seems you've created quite the stir, Mr. Wright," said the voice of Marcus Turtledove from behind Rolland.

Much to Rolland's dismay, it was not the actual Marcus Turtledove that stood before him when he turned around; it was not the gray man he expected to be poised to deliver a lecture on the finer points of basic human consideration. Instead, a shiny, translucent, yet colorfully holographic version of Turtledove hovered feet above the lit fire, looking down on him with the same smile he had outside of the bookstore the day before.

"What...?" Rolland asked, taking a few steps back and tripping on a rock the size of a football. "Just... what?"

"I suspect that you have not yet had much, if any, exposure to astral projection," Turtledove's disembodied voice said, his feet merging together.

"Nope, can't say that I have," Rolland offered, hoping to forgo the usual acceptance of being dumb because he wasn't from Eden spiel.

"You are an interesting breed, Mr. Wright," Turtledove said, joining Rolland at ground level, though the apparition's feet still did not touch the ground.

"You mean like a purebred or something?" Rolland asked jokingly, hoping to speed the lecture along.

"No, not exactly," Turtledove said with a low, genuine chuckle that conveyed a much-needed sense of whimsy.

"Shucks," Rolland said passively.

"Your father used to find great joy in saving the lives of others," Turtledove's apparition said, circling back for another lap around Rolland. "To him, it was a like a drug, a high that was on par with riding a motorcycle dangerously or driving your automobile too fast."

Thinking back on the few sporadic memories he had of his father, Rolland was inclined to agree with the sentiment, though he still failed to see the point.

"Yeah, so?" Rolland asked somewhat rudely.

"So, I've completed enough empathic scans on you to know that you and he are not of the same cloth," Turtledove said, holding up one of his foggy, ghost like arms into a stopping motion. "That isn't to say that you yourself do not enjoy saving lives. It is just that while he sought the danger that came from helping others, you possess more of a sense of responsibility."

"You're saying all this is because of Blaisey?" Rolland asked, slightly annoyed at this unwarranted psychiatric evaluation.

"Because of the girl and the bookstore," Turtledove said before his ghostly face turned slightly sour. "Danger is coming."

A rustling from the bushes behind Rolland confirmed the apparition's suspicions. Another moment passed before a laugh and the sound of running feet made their presence known.

"Did you hear...?" Rolland asked the appreciation of Turtledove, but it was gone, replaced only by the crackling fire and the sounds of the Florida night.

Deciding to investigate, Rolland walked toward the noise only to find nothing out of the ordinary. Rows of bramble bushes stood beyond him in the darkness. Having only the light from the nearby fire, it was difficult for him to see much except for a random piece of what appeared to be blood-red rope.

Rolland picked it up and noticed that it split down the middle, falling apart in his hand.

"What?" Rolland asked aloud to himself as he fingered the strands of what appeared to be red hair. A strange thought occurred to him, and he decided to tug on the ends of the strands, meeting with extreme resistance and a high-pitched squeal reminiscent of a pig. In Rolland's mind it could only mean one thing: the hair was still attached to its owner.

"Come out!" Rolland screamed, reaching for his father's knife at his side as he pulled on the hair again, wrapping it around his knuckle and elbow like a cowboy would a rope. He did this several times, wrapping what had to be several feet of hair around his arm before its owner made himself known.

Slowly, the bushy strands of red were followed closely by a long, bent nose and a crooked smile. It appeared to be a small, ginger haired man dressed in what resembled an old gray couriers' outfit from the revolutionary days, moving forehead first toward Rolland as he mindlessly continued reeling the stranger in like a fish. When he was free of the bushes, Rolland cut the hair clean through with his knife, freeing the little man.

"Hello, Mr. Wright," the ginger-haired man said with a coy smile and wily eyes.

Chapter 13:
Myth vs. Legend

There are some people in life who you know you aren't going to like just by looking at them. In a world that demands tolerance of religion, race, and gender – the right to refuse pleasantries on the grounds that someone looks 'annoying' is one of the last politically correct rights left. This option suddenly seemed very appealing to Rolland as he gazed upon the stranger who greeted him in the woods, as if from nowhere.

"Greetings, my mortal friend," said the red-headed man, stepping out from behind the brush and joining Rolland in the clearing.

"Uh, hello," Rolland said awkwardly. While he wasn't sure what to make of the man based on first impressions, one thing was for sure - the man was as out of place here as he was, even if it was in a very different way.

"You aren't from around here, are ya?" Rolland asked, half-sarcastically in his best 'Deliverance' accent.

"Smart one, this," the ginger-haired man said, creeping further out of the shadows and closer to the fire.

Over his shoulder, Rolland could hear Sephanie and Blaisey looking for him.

"You aren't going to run off now, are you?" Rolland asked the little man in earnest. No such assurance was given.

"Oy, Scott's kid, where'd you get to?" Judah shouted as he came around the bend. "...the hell?"

Rolland could see the little man more clearly as he moved closer to introduce himself. Dressed in a crisp, military uniform he stood all of about five-feet, two-inches tall. He was skinny to the point of malnourishment, and his bright red hair was suck out wildly in all directions, including straight up.

"Over here," Rolland finally shouted back to his companions, "And I'm not alone."

Hearing this, Judah put his left arm out, stopping both Blaisey and Sephanie in their tracks as he walked behind the tall grass that separated them from Rolland. "Wait here."

On the other side of the grass, Rolland and the ginger-haired man continued to stare each other down.

"So, how do you know my name?" Rolland asked the ginger-haired man.

"He's from Eden," Judah said, walking into the fire light and seeing the little man for the first time. "I can smell it."

"Hang on now," Rolland said to Judah. "What makes you automatically assume that he's from Eden?"

"Well, for one thing he's floating, you dolt," Judah called snarkily back to Rolland, slightly chagrined at the teenager's obliviousness to the obvious.

"Friend of yours?" Blaisey whispered to Sephanie, immediately noticing that the man's two legs were not touching the ground.

"Nope," Sephanie replied, tentatively listening to the three male voices on the other side of the tall grass.

"So you're our contact, then?" Judah asked skeptically, eyeing the short, floating man with apprehension.

"I surely am, my British comrade," the ginger haired man said lifting himself another six inches into the air as a smile fell upon his face, somewhat resembling a child's toy that requires you pull a string to illicit a reaction. "And if it is the Nabawoo that you seek, I know of a short cut that will get you there by morning."

Seeing this as no stranger than anything else he had observed in the last twenty four hours, Rolland decided to speak first; short and to the point. "Look, I'm not saying that we should trust him, just that we don't have any other choice," he said, looking at Judah.

Judah Jacob Raines looked at Rolland with mild indignation, but before he spoke he turned his head toward the tall grass where the females of their party were still silently watching. Though his eyes were not focused on anything in particular, they darted back and forth at lightning-quick pace, causing Judah's face muscles to twitch and contract every couple of seconds.

Rolland recognized this as a sign that Judah, the self-proclaimed smartest man on Earth, was considering all of the variables associated with following this man and would soon come to a conclusion as to why it wasn't a good idea. Wandering aimlessly would be Judah's suggestion, Rolland was almost certain of it.

"We can follow this git, for now, at least," Judah said with a piercing glare to Rolland and their new companion, causing the ginger-haired man to lower himself to all but two inches off of the dirt out of sadness. "Girls!"

Both Sephanie and Blaisey made their way through the tall grass and joined the three men, and the stranger bobbed a few inches higher. Not sure if they should be flattered or offended by this, the two females merely ignored it.

After putting the fire out, the five were on their way.

"So, you make your way into Eden often, then?" Judah asked the little man while taking large, wide swings at the surrounding trees with his machete. Plant and forest vegetation flung around them as they passed by, their feet littered with the remains of their blaze through the wilderness.

"Not as often as I'd like, Dr. Raines," the ginger-haired man said with a sideways spin in midair, landing in a crouch and descending down to Earth. "Allow me to introduce myself. My name, dear ladies and gentlemen, is Puck." He executed an elaborate bow.

With dusk settling over the land, Marcus Turtledove found himself growing increasingly uneasy about the fact that his people were split up, scattered to the four winds across the swamplands. To relieve this anxiety, he ordered Joan out on a scouting mission to report back with troop movements around Jackson's camp, where he at least knew Victor to be.

Hearing this, Charlton of the Nabawoo offered to accompany Joan, this time as her protective detail. The two groups rode out together. Though neither Joan or Charlton trusted each other, a strange sort of mutual respect was forming just beneath the surface. The two did have quite a bit in common, after all. Both served as second in command to their respective leaders, and were of a similar mind when it came to battle tactics and conditioning. Both had been separated from the people they loved.

On the left rode the Knights of Time (Joan and Tina) while to their right galloped the horses of eight more experienced and battle tested Nabawoo warriors, Charlton in the lead. All of them were armed with rifles and bows, all except Charlton, who refused to equip himself with anything but a single blade; a knife that he claimed was given to him by Nahoy himself.

"On my wedding day," Charlton explained, flashing the knife to Tina as they rode their jet black horses up the hillside to get a better view on Jackson's camp.

Their vantage point gave them a clear view of the comings and goings of Jackson's camp, though nothing seemed to be happening as the sun set for the day. The horses that were usually kept out front were gone, roughly two dozen of them or so would usually return before dark according to Charlton. Apparently tonight was the exception.

"So they'll all be on foot when we attack. Great! Let's go," Joan said, her impatience irritating Charlton to no end.

"No, we will stay here until dark, then go back to Nahoy," Charlton said, grabbing Joan's wrist in an unfortunate attempt to impose his will. He was about to learn exactly how unfortunate.

Using Charlton's own momentum against him, Joan pressed her weight against his wrist. He smiled, amused at the blonde woman's impudence. This merely sealed his fate as Joan switched gears, jerkily twisting Charlton's arm in the opposite direction, forcing him to shift with it and act as a shield between Joan and his seven guards, all of whom were armed and ready to shoot either Joan or Tina.

"Woooahh, ok, this situation just got intense," said Tina, putting her arms up in the air and offering no resistance to the bows pointed at her face and stomach. "Joan, maybe you should stop."

"Quiet, kid," Joan said, still struggling against Charlton, and the constant motion made it too difficult for the archers to get a bead on their target. A moment later Joan gained the upper hand, getting her foot over Charlton's chest and kicking him hard to the ground, knocking the wind out of him. Standing over Charlton as he gasped for breath, Joan considered her options for a moment before extending her hand out to him and saying, "We are not your enemies."

Charlton seemed to consider Joan for a moment, looking up at her through shallow breaths and random coughs. She fascinated him, this woman who appeared from the sky and bested him, a Seminole man, in combat. He waved the archers off, alleviating the tension for the moment. Then he accepted Joan's hand in friendship and she helped him to his feet, the entire display holding the complete attention of the Nabawoo archers.

"You may be a great warrior," Charlton said, brushing off the soot covering his backside, "But that 'kid' is smarter than you are — you would be wise to listen to her."

Rules are rules for a reason. If it were not for basic rules and conduct we would fail to be a society, and would have continued on as a bunch of hunter-gatherers looking out for numero uno. For this reason, Victor had always obeyed the rules, and because he had always obeyed the rules, he had never even considered the idea of revealing his powers to anyone, something he had now done and wish that he hadn't.

Since Victor had set himself ablaze nearly an hour ago, no one had come to talk to him. His actions, it seemed, had had the opposite effect of what he had intended. Sitting against a tree with his head held in his hands, Victor closed his eyes and thought of a plausible way to save the lives of all the misguided, enslaved people suffering under Jackson's oppressive thumb.

Among all this fear and loathing for Jackson came a voice in support for Victor's unbelievable claim. Strangely, it came from the group's only white man.

"Excuse me," said a meek and beleaguered man from several feet away.

Victor looked over to see a middle-aged white man staring back at him, his hands free of the chains that still bound the others in place. He moved slowly but surely in Victor's direction, his bottom half obscured by the grass.

"How did you get free?" Victor asked, not moving a muscle in case the man had also been gifted with an extra ordinary ability.

"Oh, I picked the locks," the man said to Victor with a cheery disposition. "I'm a colonel in the British forces you see. Or I was…"

The look in the man's eyes screamed of honesty and reminded Victor of the lost look a parent gets when they lose a child. This man had lost something as well, his freedom.

"I believe you," the man said, stepping forward toward Victor.

"You do?" Victor said, his deep voice betraying his surprise; he felt almost giddy at the prospect of finding a possible ally in escape.

"Yes, and I too would like to escape," the man replied, scooting closer to Victor slowly.

It wasn't until the man came closer that Victor realized why he had been moving so slowly. His legs had been slashed and chopped, like giant jungle cats had clawed at him for an afternoon or two.

"What in the blue Hawaii happened to you, man?" Victor asked him, forgetting courtesy in the wake of the grotesque open wounds on the man's legs.

"Jackson tortured me for information on the King's ships when I got here a week ago. When I wouldn't give him any, he took it out on me' partner and…" his story was interrupted by the overzealous Knight of Time.

"What was her name?" Victor asked, hoping to get to know the man better before deciding whether or not to trust him.

"His name was Arbuthnot," the man responded with half a smile and a small tear in his right eye.

Surprised, but not offended by this revelation, Victor offered one of his toothy grins, hoping to put the soldier at ease.

"What's your name?" Victor asked the man awkwardly, hoping to change the subject.

"Colonel Robert Ambrister, at your service," the man said, extending a hand to Victor, who accepted.

"Well, Robert," Victor said, bringing his hands back down and holding them over the fire, drawing a spark. "We would still need the others in order to successfully escape, so unless you have any ideas…"

"Actually mate," Ambrister said, looking closely at Victor's scaly, almost charcoal like forearms, "I think I do."

"This yahoo doesn't know where we're going!" Sephanie exclaimed loudly to the rest of the group, though she didn't bother to stop.

"Ya who?" Blaisey asked, rounding out their party from the back. She looked at Rolland who merely shook his head and waved the comment off.

The five of them had been walking up the rocky hillside for nearly two and a half hours in the hopes that the short cut Puck had told them about would deliver them to the Nabawoo camp by dark. So far though, all they had to show for it were blisters and bitching.

"I just don't trust him," Blaisey half-whispered to Rolland as they passed another dry creek bed.

"Why?" Rolland asked her, dodging another low-hanging tree limb.

"Just something about him makes me uneasy," Blaisey continued, trying to keep her balance as they walked over terrain more rock than dirt.

"Oh, I know what you mean," Judah interjected to an astonished Blaisey, "That red hair creeps me out as well."

"Uh, what?" Rolland asked, surprised by the grumpy Brit's sudden interest in their conversation.

"He's a ginger," Judah stated in a matter-of-factly, motioning toward Puck with his head. "I'll bet you anything he's a plant."

"A what?" Blaisey asked, but their moment of privacy was again interrupted by Puck and Sephanie's bickering over proper tracking technique and the path to the top of the hill.

"My fair lady..." Puck said, but was interrupted by a back-handed slap from Sephanie.

"Don't you 'fair lady' me!" Sephanie said, feeling no pity for the hovering stranger who was obviously leading them on a wild goose chase. "We're stopping for now."

With four pairs of eyes locked onto her, Sephanie placed her hands on her hips and stared right back at them, looking for any sign of resistance. When none came, Sephanie spoke again, "For the night. We're stopping here for the night."

"We're only half way up the rock." Judah said, but after another dirty look from his wife's best friend, he thought better of arguing and quieted down. "Well, then, I'll go find some wood."

"That's a great idea," said Sephanie as she watched Judah walk off into the trees and out of sight. "We're actually going to need a lot of wood. Rolland –"

Jumping at the sound of his name, Rolland stopped staring at Sephanie's backside long enough to respond. "Yes?"

"Would you mind going to find some wood, too?" Sephanie asked him, biting her lower lip.

"Yeah, yeah, alright," Rolland said, following Judah's path into the forest.

"And take him with," Sephanie said before Rolland could get away, prompting Puck to spin in cartwheels after the less than enthusiastic teenager.

Once they were alone, Blaisey approached Sephanie and, placing a hand on hers, caught her eye. "Seriously, Sister, how long do you think that will last?"

"Honestly," Sephanie said, looking back down the trail and listening to the sounds of Puck's laughter, "I don't know."

Meanwhile, back at the Nabawoo camp, the evening's festivities were transitioning from traditional activities to more mature ones. Among these was the private meeting that Nabawoo Chieftain Nahoy shared with the leader of the Knights of Time, Marcus Turtledove.

The inside of Nahoy's tent was spacious; he was accustomed to housing no less than ten people at a time. The walls and ceiling were made out of a thick hide that had been stretched and smoothed out, making it look clean and sturdy.

"Your generosity is only matched by your hospitality," Turtledove said with distinct sincerity as the two men sat and shared wine.

Perhaps it was Turtledove's innate empathic qualities, or maybe it was his own experience as a father, but something inside of Turtledove recognized the worry that weighed on his host.

"Your daughter is in good hands," Turtledove said, taking Nahoy off guard.

"How do you know what haunts my thoughts?" Nahoy asked, his curiosity extending beyond the social norms of his people.

"It is within me to understand the feelings of others, just as it is within you to predict events about to transpire," said Turtledove, putting his cup of wine down on the table between them; it was then that the long, curved pipe that sat opposite the tea cup caught his eye. "Do you smoke?"

The question, though not off-putting, seemed like a diversion in Nahoy's mind. Still, courtesy and custom dictated he oblige his guest with any reasonable demands. "Yes, would you like to partake with me?"

As the bowl of friendship was lit between the Travelers of Light and the Nabawoo Seminoles, a fraternal bond was solidified between the two organizations forever. Yet, as it always is with those closest to you, great trust brings a sense of over-familiarity.

"Where are you from, exactly?" Nahoy finally asked his slightly younger new friend.

"A land called Eden," Turtledove said, taking another long drag off of the tobacco pipe.

"Are you from the future?" Nahoy fired back, maybe a little too impatiently.

Chuckling slightly, Turtledove accepted the pipe from Nahoy and said "Not exactly. Eden exists outside of time and space as you know it."

Nahoy seemed to ponder this for a moment, gazing longingly into the fire before asking again, "And you, where do you come from?"

Taking another puff off of the bamboo pipe, Turtledove considered his answer carefully before responding. "I am quite old, actually. From the time of your ancestors, no doubt."

"But you left your own time, your home, for Eden – yes?" Nahoy asked, taking the still smoldering pipe back from Turtledove and arranging himself comfortably in his chair.

"Yes, but not of my own volition, err, free will," Turtledove said, not knowing just how powerfully Tina had rigged the universal translators. "I, much like you, am special. That is to say, my genetic structure differs from that of a normal person by four chromosomes."

"Chromo zone?"Nahoy asked, choking a bit on the smoke in his lungs.

"Yes my friend, what makes human beings like you and I different from the birds or four-legged beasts," Turtledove said, handing Nahoy his untouched cup of water from earlier in the evening. While far from the sanitary standards of Eden, or modern society, it soothed the Nabawoo chieftain's sinuses just the same.

"You were recruited then, yes?" Nahoy asked, clearing his throat and recovering his authoritative stature.

"Correct, yes," Turtledove said, pressing his thumb into the bowl of the pipe and feeling only ash.

"In whose war?" Nahoy asked, defiance reigniting the fire behind his wise eyes.

Turtledove picked up his cup of wine, swirled it around a bit, and brought it to his lips before answering simply "In humanity's war."

Never in the history of time and space had male bonding gone so horrifically wrong. Rolland could not believe his ears as he walked down the dimly lit path between Judah and Puck, listening as they argued the philosophical implications of someone named Descartes.

The three men turned the otherwise dark corner blindly save for the precious little light they conjured against the dead of night with Judah's lighter.

"Stop! Who goes there?!" came a voice from beyond their line of sight. The half visible outline of tall man with fading brown hair and a dominant swagger to his walk gave them all the clear impression that it was someone of authority and importance; none other than Andrew Jackson.

"Nice job leading them to us," Judah said, raising a hand to stop Rolland in the middle of his stride.

"I'm sorry I..." Rolland stated with genuine regret before he was interrupted by the sound of gunshots.

"I was talking to the ginger, you dolt! But come to think of it, I...ow!" Judah was silenced by a size twelve boot connecting with the back of his knee as Jackson silenced the Englishman the only way he knew how.

"British filth!" Jackson snarled, standing rigidly, sword drawn and pointed at Judah's neck.

"Hold it right there, jackass," Rolland said, raising Blaisey's bow to Jackson's midsection. "I don't like him either, but I need him alive. So, why don't you take your hand off of that sword?"

"Dorothy..." Judah said, antagonizing the boy further.

"Wha-" Rolland began, but stopped short as he saw a dozen or so figures behind Jackson. It wasn't their presence that spooked Rolland, but their eyes. The dull, white emptiness where their corneas should have been chilled him to the very core of his soul, making him put down the bow and surrender.

The rugged General Jackson smiled at this and strode confidently over to the boy, picking up the bow. Holding the weapon in his hands, Jackson realized just how close he was to Rolland and how easy it would be to take the life of this obscenely insolent young man.

"I won't bother asking who you are, or what you're doing," Jackson said, examining the bow further for hints on the mixed company of what looked like a Brit, an Irishman, and a teenage American defector.

"The name is Rolland Wright," Rolland said confidently, his breathe steady against the night air as the words fell from his lips with little forethought as to their repercussions. "And as for what I was doing, well, you'd have to ask your mother. Gentlemen don't kiss and tell."

"You little shit!" Jackson said, walking briskly to Rolland before getting uncomfortably close to the teenager so that the two were almost nose to nose. "Do you have any idea WHO I am?!"

"I don't know what you are, actually," Rolland said to Jackson without as much as a blink.

Jackson, eyes widened in offended shock, quivered his upper lip a bit before backing away, finding his horse in the darkness, and climbing onto it before drawing sharply upon the stallion's reins. Stirring in place, Jackson rounded the creature about in an attempt to pacify both of their restless spirits; it was a fitting allegory for a man who would go down in history as one who would impose his will on the less fortunate.

"You there, soldier," Jackson said, pointing to Puck with his free hand. "What is your name and rank?"

The ginger-haired Puck glanced nervously at Rolland and Judah, as if they could offer him some sort of protection from Jackson's questioning. His face went white, and then a light shade of strawberry pink around his cheeks before he answered. "Private Puck, Master Jackson."

"Puck?" Jackson asked the freckled faced man kneeling before him. "As in Puck from Shakespeare's Midsummer? That is but a myth."

"And you are but a legend," Puck said to General Jackson, smiling giddily as he caught the man in a word trap, his perverse sense of humor on full display.

Chapter 14:
Jackson's Art of War

In December of 1817 Andrew Jackson was a cocky, brash man with a quick temper and an infectious charm. Having grown up poor as the son of a soldier's widow, he had learned to overcome life's obstacles at West Point, before going on to accomplish amazing and death-defying feats at the cost of others.

Proclaiming himself a patriot in the same spirit as General George Washington, Jackson quickly excelled within the ranks, despite his family's lack of belief in formal education. He accomplished this the old fashioned way; by being polite, following most of the rules, and never getting caught in any wrongdoings.

"Alright Private Puck, if that is your real name. What be your orders?" Jackson asked, rounding about and getting off of his horse. He did this without fear of ambush as about half a dozen rifles were peeking out from behind his shoulder.

"My name is Rolland, sir, and I…" Rolland managed to say before Jackson punched him squarely in the jaw.

"Speak only when spoken to," Jackson said, lifting Rolland's face with his gloved hand before tossing him aside with a sadistic smile. "I want to hear from the soldier, not the boy."

"Well, sir, I am what you would call a soldier of fortune. That is to say that I, well…" Puck stammered, shifting uncomfortably.

"What he's trying to say is that he's not really a soldier at all," Rolland interjected again. Jackson turned around and fired a warning shot in Rolland's direction, grazing the teenager's shoulder.

"Next time I take your heart. Is that understood?" Jackson said to Rolland, his gun pointing at his captive's chest. He knew that sometimes psychological warfare is more effective than physical confrontations. "What is your business here?"

"I like this place, and willingly could waste my time in it," Puck said, smiling a bit wider and suppressing a giggle.

"Pretend inferiority and encourage his ignorance, I see," Jackson said, returning the verbal volley of quotes from the conflicting ideologies of William Shakespeare, and Sun Tzu. The General circled back around to Puck slowly, careful to exaggerate every step.

"This is exhausting," said Sephanie, walking out from behind the brush with Blaisey trailing after her with obvious unease. She looked over at Puck and wondered if the small ginger man might begin purring to curry favor with his new master.

"All war is based on deception," Jackson said, again quoting Sun Tzu in an attempt to intellectually one-up his challenging new rival.

"Dost thou protest?" Puck said coyly to the weary Jackson, rising off of his feet in one fluid motion and continuing his odd mid-air skip around the campfire.

With a forceful and commanding hand, Jackson delivered an unexpected punch directly to Puck's left orbital bone, leaving his intention clear – he was not to be fooled with.

Lying on the ground, the demure man known to the group as Puck now resembled something similar to road kill.

Tilting his head slightly, Jackson placed his boot on Puck's neck and began to press down firmly.

"Know this, mongrel," Jackson said, moving even more of his own weight onto Puck's neck, "Your life means nothing to me. So either give me answers, or die here and now."

"I'm a traveler of light," the frail Puck confessed to the bully Jackson. With his bloody nose and missing teeth, one could almost feel sorry for the pitiful man. That is, if they truly understood what kind of man Puck was.

"A what?" Jackson asked, adding additional pressure to Puck's neck.

"Don't say anything!" shouted Judah, drawing the aim of Jackson's guards.

"Silence!" Jackson hissed "Where are you from, truthfully?"

"Eden. I'm from Eden, sir," Puck said weakly, curling into a ball by Jackson's feet.

"I've heard this name before, from one of the slaves that came from the sky," Jackson said, finally directing his comments toward Rolland. "Tell me, who is Vilthe?"

For his part, Rolland assumed that this sudden attention was not because he appeared the most capable of the group, but due to Jackson's strongly held prejudices against women, the British, and Native Americans.

"Our, uh, sky captain. Yeah, the guy in charge. You know, the one who sent us here with plans to help the natives defeat you with our, uh, Tom Cruise Missiles," Rolland said, hoping to discredit Puck by sounding crazy himself. "He's telling the truth."

"What the bloody hell is wrong with you two?" Judah demanded, irate at the mention of Eden, the Travelers of Light, and Vilthe. He fought against the bonds that tethered him, but it was no use. There was little choice for him now but to watch, and log every instance of abuse of the time stream.

Rounded up, tied up, and marched through the woods in the middle of the night, the five companions felt their situation could not get much worse. Their clothes were soggy from a full day's worth of sweat and exhaustion. Their spirits were broken, and their stomachs empty.

Jackson had taken a special interest in the two females of their group, especially Sephanie. Rolland watched as the General rode alongside her, only stopping once to take the young woman's face in his hands, ripping the earpiece from the right side of her head.

"I'll be taking this," Jackson said, fixing the universal translator into his own ear before turning to Blaisey and asking her "Do you understand me?"

"Yes," Blaisey acknowledged reluctantly.

For Jackson, the language barrier had been the only challenge he had not overcome since arriving in Florida. Being from Tennessee, he had previously only dealt with assimilated natives, not any with their own culture or language. This peek behind the curtain would give him more leverage for the coming clashes with the girl's father. "Good, now move your ass girl, before I make you cannon fodder!"

As they entered American territory, Rolland noticed one of the guards running ahead of the group. Finding this curious, he watched the man run off to a spot roughly one hundred yards in front of them and cup his hand to his mouth to amplify his voice. Next came what Rolland would swear sounded like a duck call.

"Did you hear that?" Rolland asked Blaisey behind him.

"Armed guards," Blaisey said, moving slowly and dragging her feet.

As they approached the spot the sentry had run to, Rolland saw the two armed guards waiting silently for them in the brush. Their rifles were still raised level with their solid white eyes, ready to strike as the convoy inched by slowly.

The five of them were treated like slaves, no better, no worse. Each was tied forcefully to a long, steel chain that ran the entire length of their human convoy. It was demeaning beyond words to be treated as nothing more than cattle being led to slaughter. Yet, in each of their minds freedom was still tangible, a reachable goal of finding something each of them had taken for granted a mere hour before.

"Target the children first," Jackson said to his three captains, all of whom looked up at him with vacant, expressionless white eyes.

More soldiers approached. Rolland guessed that they were all under Jackson's hypnosis somehow. Since coming to Eden and re-alizing that superhuman abilities he had previously thought of as fictitious were real, Jackson's use of hypnosis on large crowds of people was by far the weirdest. It reminded Rolland of a queen ant and the way she would order the entire colony to do her bidding. The thought of Jackson as a queen made him chuckle, but the moment of joy was fleeting.

"No sense in letting the weeds grow any taller, eh, boys?" Jackson bellowed, pulling on his horse's reins, eliciting a pain-filled whinny from the poor animal.

Blaisey watched this with a silent fury building within her. Since she already knew this to be the man who killed her mother before kidnapping her two brothers and little sister, it was no surprise to hear her own suspicions about Jackson's agenda straight out of the villain's own mouth. A hand found hers in the darkness, and Rolland squeezed it firmly, reassuringly.

Jackson looked at each captive, analyzing them one by one, ending with Puck. "Take the ginger away. Beat him for more information."

At this, the skinny Puck began thrashing and pleading for mercy, but the hypnotized American guards dragged him away from the main camp to parts unknown.

Blaisey tapped Rolland's thigh with her shackles, getting his attention and pointing over to the slave's pen. "There, do you see those people huddled underneath that rock overhang?"

"Yeah," Rolland replied, his eyes finding the spot she described.

"If my brother and sisters are here, that's where they'll be," Blaisey said, before her thoughts were interrupted by Jackson's low, yet shrill voice.

"Take the native girl to my tent," Jackson ordered, smiling down at Blaisey and cupping her chin.

"No!" Rolland shouted, earning a punch to his stomach for his insubordination.

"It's alright," Blaisey assured them before two guards approached and unlocked Blaisey's shackles, leading her to Jackson's tent.

Knowing that his entire purpose for being there was to protect Blaisey, the guilt riding on Rolland's shoulders consumed every spare thought, even those reserved for ogling Sephanie when she looked away. No sooner had he began thinking of a plan than half a dozen additional clear-eyed guards approached the three

Travelers of Light and herded them toward the slave pen, where their arrival drew little attention from the men already there. All save one.

"Hey, ugly!" said a voice that Rolland knew had to be his missing friend. Though he could not see Victor from where he was chained, Rolland took great comfort in knowing that he had another ally nearby.

Never happier to hear an insult, Rolland cupped his hand and whispered loudly back to his friend "Hey, goofy-lookin'."

"What's the haps, yo?" Victor asked, delighted to speak in a language that would both confuse and validate his preposterous stories to the other captives.

"Not good, hombre," Rolland replied, lifting his arms enough to jingle the shackles that held him. "Hey, have you seen any kids here?"

"Why? Trying to create a Jackson youth?" Victor said jokingly. "No, there are no women or kids here, or at least there weren't any until you guys showed up. Hey Sephanie!"

"Hey Victor," Sephanie offered back to her jovial friend, though she like Rolland could not physically see him.

"Is that your girl they took to Jackson's tent?" Victor asked, looking over to the darkest, most isolated part of woods.

"In a matter of speaking, yes," Rolland admitted, hoping for some sort of inside knowledge of their surroundings. Unfortunately, aside from confirming Rolland's suspensions about Jackson's extraordinary abilities of mass hypnosis and persuasion, there was none to be had. "What does he do to people in there?"

A cold breeze ran through the camp and Sephanie, Rolland, and Judah crammed closer together for warmth.

"Let me just put it this way" Victor said, his voice tight with apprehension. "That's the first place he took me and I cracked in under a minute. He knows about Eden. He knows about us."

For Princess Blaisey of the Nabawoo, a private audience with Andrew Jackson was tantamount to a death warrant. Jackson, who felt quite at home in his private tent, was thrilled to add the eldest of Nahoy's children to his collection.

A pensive look washed over Blaisey's face. She shifted uncomfortably in the creaky wooden chair as Jackson pushed his own back and stood up across from her. Their eyes met again before she asked "Where are my brothers and sisters?"

"Oh, you'll see them again soon," Jackson said, unbuttoning his officer's jacket. "I have a proposition for you, my dear Princess. Marry me."

"Excuse me?" Blaisey asked, completely taken aback by his sudden and unexpected proposal.

"I mean to take over this region eventually, we both know that to be true," Jackson said, making no qualms about his own aspirations. "And this is the traditional way of doing things. Marriage, I mean. My family, your family, both conquering together."

"After all you've done to the Creek? To my people? Taking my brother and sisters?" Blaisey said, trailing off and shaking her head. Tears were pressing themselves against her eyes, but she would not give Jackson the satisfaction of seeing her cry.

"So, what do you say Princess?" Jackson asked Blaisey, looking deep into her eyes. She saw a slight twinkle in his, not unlike that of a very good salesman, just under the surface.

"Hell no, I won't marry you," Blaisey said flatly, no further explanation necessary. "But make no mistake; I will give you what you want if it means the freedom of my brother and sisters."

"Is that so, Princess?" Jackson asked, smiling again and shaking his head slightly. He moved around the table between them and over to her.

"It is so," Blaisey said, swallowing hard and closing her eyes. The safety of her siblings meant everything to her, everything to her father. They were the future of her people, and she could not return home without them.

"You do look good enough to eat, my dear," Jackson said, moving ever closer, his left hand unbuttoning his trousers.

Jackson's right hand found its way to Blaisey's vest, slipping it off of her shoulders and dropping it to the ground below, leaving only her chest wrappings to separate her from Jackson's wandering hands.

"I think you want to take that off, my dear," Jackson said, his eyeballs boring into Blaisey's brain, pushing away any resistance or ambition that stood in the way of his goal.

But unlike the masses that usually fell prey to Jackson's wicked schemes, the Nabawoo Princess held a supernatural secret of her own.

"No," Blaisey said, shaking her head. "This I cannot do. My heart belongs to another."

Jackson advanced on her, placing his hands on hers and pulling them back so that she was immobilized. "I don't think you heard me, Princess. You want to take it off."

Blaisey's eyed flashed white, just as Puck's had in the woods earlier in the evening. Her arms went slack and fell to her waist listlessly, her free will slipping away.

"Why, hello there, my dear," Jackson said. "What's a pretty little thing like you doing out here with those people who fell from the sky?"

Deep in Jackson's trance, Blaisey's mind took a backseat to the constant barrage of pressure and melancholy that clouded her thoughts. She felt that if she were to try and fight it, her nose might bleed out of frustration alone. It was futile. She gave in.

"Helping them, they are from the future," Blaisey said in a slow, revealing tone.

"Oh, I've heard that. The real question is, are they telling lies…" Jackson asked, circling Blaisey as a shark would its prey.

"It's all true. You get the whole country. All of it – after you kill my people," Blaisey said, the tears flowing freely from her white, unblinking eyes.

"Oh I am going to kill you, and your brother, and sisters," Jackson said, smiling sadistically as he traced his hands over Blaisey's chest wrappings "Slowly."

Deciding to rob the girl of her remaining dignity, Jackson turned back to his dining table to find his knife, thinking to himself, 'If the little bitch won't strip, I'll destroy her clothes myself.'

With one hand riding up Blaisey's buffalo tan skirt and the other wrapped around her back, Jackson never saw the rock Blaisey used to knock him upside the head.

With her free will returned and the white disappearing from her eyes, Blaisey picked up Jackson's gun, knife, and a foreign item that she would later learn was called an elastic band before bolting out of the tent and back towards where Rolland and the others were held captive.

Out of the darkness came a strange sound, not unlike birds calling to one another in the early morning hours. From the corner of her eye Blaisey could see shadows moving in the darkness. Layers of blackness became more pronounced and moved about all around her.

A small fire near the horse stables was her first stop, but Blaisey found it empty save for one soul, a small, pathetic ball of a man, blocking both his eyes and ears with his elbows. It was Puck.

"Do you want your freedom?" Blaisey asked the ginger man who lay curled in the fetal position behind a few crates of hay.

"Tempt not a desperate man," Puck said, moving his still bound hands from his mouth and eyes.

After cutting the rope binding Puck, Blaisey dropped her knife and bent down to retrieve it. "Now help me free the others."

When she stood up, Puck was gone, disappeared back into the forest from which he came.

"Great," Blaisey said to herself, pocketing the blade and moving closer to the center of camp to find her new friends.

The officers' fire illuminated the path for Blaisey once she got close enough. Moving along a stone wall that she once used as 'base' when she played hide and find as a little girl, Blaisey was able to get a clear view of Rolland, Sephanie, and Judah. After she had settled into an advantageous position, she saw the figure in the distance.

It looked like a man, dressed from head to toe in a black bodysuit, moving along the boundaries of the night, and keeping to the shadows to avoid detection. Then he moved again, but far away, too great a distance to have covered so quickly. A black face-mask, followed by another, and another, emerged from the cover of night, making their way toward the main camp.

Blaisey watched as they poured into the camp like a tidal wave, altering everything they touched. They were tall and muscular, but their black bodysuits left no detail, absolutely nothing to distinguish them as humans except for their shapes. They were armed with hand weapons, no firearms; yet strength in their numbers was clear as scores of them flooded the camp.

Immediately clashing with the American soldiers, the men in black burned, killed, and pillaged everything in their path, which seemed to be leading them directly to the slaves, and the Travelers of Light.

Rolland watched as, one by one, everyone fell to the wave of men in black. His eyes attempted to focus on one, study it, decipher if it was a human being under the hood, but against the backdrop of the night sky it was near impossible. He tried again, and again, watching each individual fade into the shadows, and reappear as part of a small group, making it impossible to distinguish them apart from one another. What was possible to distinguish, however, was the native girl who stood out amongst them as she jogged back toward the slave pens.

"Blaisey!" Rolland screamed over the noise and confusion. The sound of his voice traveled through the air, catching her ear and attention.

Running over to Rolland, Blaisey pulled out the key ring she had taken from Jackson's tent.

"Hope this works," Blaisey said, unlocking Rolland's shackles first. To her great relief they popped right off his wrists, freeing him instantly. She went on to do the same for Sephanie, and finally Judah.

"Right, I'll get Victor," Judah began before something caught his eye.

"Let's get the hell out of here before anything else happens," Sephanie said as the sound of gunshots filled the air.

There, behind them, with blood dripping down the right side of his face from a gash where Blaisey had clocked him upside the head minutes before stood General Jackson, disheveled yet defiant.

Two gunshots, only two, rang out, as that is the number of bullets the concussed and wobbly Andrew Jackson had left. They went off, one hitting the ground, the other a nearby tree.

"Damn it all!" Jackson shouted, his trigger finger still clicking away on his revolver as he fell to his knees, blood dripping from his open head wound. That noise was all that could be heard now as the haunting silence of the recently departed filled the air.

A rifle between them caught both Rolland and Jackson's eyes, baiting each to draw upon its power in the moment.

Anyone even remotely prepared would have taken seconds to take advantage of such a lucky occurrence. Perhaps it was because it was Sephanie who was talking when Jackson started shooting, but that day Rolland Wright responded first, and quickly.

In that second, Rolland knew that he must make a choice. He could end the life of this miserable old man before he had the opportunity to kill thousands more with his brutality, or let history take its due course and elevate him to the status of a modern legend.

"Rolland, let's go!" Sephanie's voice rang out, falling upon deaf ears.

Turning the rifle sideways, Rolland raised the back end of the gun up, and then brought it down hard, whacking General Jackson upside the head with as much force as he could gather.

Jackson fell to the ground unconscious as his camp burned all around him. The captains and remaining officers were all dead. The free-thinking men that had chosen to flee were either gone, or lay dead along with their commanding officers. All in all, the thirty men under the command of General Andrew Jackson met with a grizzly end that evening.

Just another senseless act of violence in humanity's war of ideas...

Chapter 15:
Bright Spots

With Victor nowhere to be found in the immediate aftermath of their escape from the American's camp, the four companions ran through the flat, unyielding swampland and away from what was left of Jackson's forces. Dodging the sinkholes lining their path, Rolland, Blaisey, Sephanie, and Judah ran as fast as their legs would carry them.

Leading the pack, Blaisey darted through the night like it was second nature. Rolland watched from third place as she expertly maneuvered through the harsh, mossy terrain. Her footing, Rolland thought, was as sure of itself as her mouth was.

"Left step, watch for the sink sand to your right! Three meters!" Blaisey shouted over her shoulder as she hopped along with the grace of a cheetah through the swamp.

Rolland didn't dare look up at her for fear of losing his footing and ending up in the 'sink sand'. It had been nearly twenty-four hours since he had met the Seminole girl, and while there were obviously some translation issues, Rolland had taken quite a shine to her.

Running cross country was never one of Rolland's strong suits, but neither was purposefully looking foolish in front of the girl of his dreams.

Successfully dodging the 'sink sand', Rolland smiled and looked up to thank his guide, but instead saw the backside of the brunette beauty directly in front of him. Allowing his eyes to linger there for a moment, Rolland thought of what it would be like to embrace her, to smell her hair and feel the softness of her cheeks on his.

It came as no surprise to him when, after only a few moments of this, Rolland tripped, barrel-rolling into a soft patch of mud which waited for him with a wet, grainy landing spot in the Earth. While humiliating enough to trip in the first place, the addition of mud could only serve to further his one man mission for self-sabotage. An odd thought given the reverse standard and high level of esteem most men hold for female interaction with mud.

"Keep up, pup!" Judah huffed out from worn out lungs as he passed by the sopping wet Rolland, who quickly stood up before slipping again, righting himself, and taking off after his three traveling companions.

Sephanie had kept close to Blaisey since they had made their escape. After seeing how eager the strange figures in black bodysuits were to release Blaisey, Sephanie could not help but wonder if the Seminole girl might be luring them into a trap, a thought she assumed was shared by Rolland as he kept catching Sephanie's eye in the dark.

After a couple of miles, Blaisey stopped them when they came upon a wall of limestone peeking out from a wooded hillside. It stood about thirty feet high, and had a large hole on the side facing them. Rolland thought of sitting on it, but quickly discovered how uninviting its jagged edges were to human skin.

"Stop here for a bit, loves?" Judah asked, placing his hands behind his head in an attempt to catch his breath.

Rolland saw this and mimicked the motion, but Judah noticed him and fired off a look of intense loathing, forcing him to stop. It didn't much matter, as within moments Rolland's attention was directed towards something else, something incredibly normal, yet familiar only to him.

At the bottom of the limestone formation, he spied an opening to a hidden cave. The opening was wide at first; Rolland guessed it to be six feet across, but it quickly narrowed and curved after about eight feet, leaving nothing beyond visible to the naked eye.

But Rolland did see one thing. There, in the deepest part of the cavern, shone the same bright white orb of light that he had seen in the bookstore. It hovered there not physically touching anything, almost as if it was waiting there for him to see it and follow. Just like last time.

"Huh," Rolland said aloud, and his three travelling companions dropped what they were doing to look at him curiously. "I think I know what we're doing next."

Back at the abandoned American camp, General Andrew Jackson began to stir. No longer satisfied with his blanket of stars, Jackson woke groggily and inspected his surroundings. He felt a great deal like he had overdone his drink the night before, but of this he had no memory. Slowly, he began to put together bits and pieces of the raid, and the escape of his 'sky captives.'

Thoughts formed in Jackson's mind - Of that insolent teenager and that beautiful young thing that was with him, of the pain and humiliation he had suffered at the hands of the young buck, the

Englishman, and the native girl. All around him, his once impenetrable camp lay in utter destruction. A fire crackled nearby, drawing his attention.

There lay his former second in command, still clutching his long hunting knife and musket. Even in death, he was unable to let go of the tools he had taken such solace in while defending his own life. Slowly, Jackson crawled the short distance and pried the items from the dead man's fingers, something he had done too many times before.

The fact was, there was very little remorse within the soul of the man the world knew as Andrew Jackson. With a rocky upbringing and a career that largely consisted of military exploits, he was not given to exhibiting sympathy or showing emotion. Never one for self-pity, Jackson clamored uneasily to his feet.

"Where'd you get to, boy?" Jackson asked himself. Using the musket as a crutch, Jackson lifted himself to his feet to get a better view of his surroundings. The ground was littered with cloth, bodies, and weapons of all sorts. It was a sight Jackson had seen many times, though never from this perspective.

Then he saw them. Four sets of footprints heading due east.

The howling could be heard for miles around, if ears were present to listen.

Puck's face contorted in pain as his outstretched arm was mutilated by the sweater vest clad villain, a perverse smile plastered to his clean-shaven face.

"One cannot help but wonder; If a man is tortured in the woods, does anyone hear it?" Vilthe asked the almost infantile looking Puck as he cowered in terror.

Hours passed, and Vilthe's sadistic torture went on - ever in search of some measureable amount of flesh to extract to equal his volatile temperament.

"You were warned," hissed a voice from the shadows, and Puck turned toward the spot where the voice originated.

"Please, please master! I didn't mean to disrespect you. I... I promise I'll..." Faster than light, Vilthe appeared behind his anguished target, cutting him off mid-sentence and pushing the small man's left thumb back until bones shattered and tendons snapped.

"It is done," Vilthe said, letting go of the still screaming Puck. The rollie-pollie of a man fell at Vilthe's feet, and the Harvester of Souls towered over the small red-head. The hazel of his eyes faded away slowly as the deep copper hue of his true form peaked out from behind its façade.

"Good," hissed the voice from the shadows. With dawn approaching it wouldn't be long before the faceless void would need to seek shelter from the sun's might. "Now bring me the boy."

"Figment of your imagination," Judah said, taking a pack of cigarettes from his left pants pocket.

This action attracted the attention of both females of the party. Their stares were for different reasons, yet Rolland saw the same problem with both of them. While neither Sephanie or Blaisey had completely made up their opinion of Rolland, he could tell this particular topic was not helping his image. It seemed that no one believed him about the light within the cave.

"Maybe you're right," Rolland said, the absurdity of his claim resonating within his mind. He decided that perhaps a walk around the rock formation would help him re-focus, its football stadium circumference offering him a chance to clear his mind of what Judah called 'figments of his imagination'.

As Rolland walked away, Judah searched his pockets for his lighter. This proved to be a more challenging task than he anticipated. With no results in his left coat pocket, he switched to his right one, his eyes briefly catching the daggers that Sephanie was staring at him.

"You better not," Sephanie said to Judah, her hands going straight to her hips.

Ignoring her, and wondering why all women of a defiant disposition choose the exact same pose, Judah continued his rummage through his coat. Each search, however, resulted in no lighter. Cigarette still resting between his lips, Judah answered without looking at her. "Why the bloody hell not?"

Prepared for his rebuttal, Sephanie quickly fired back a curt, "You know your wife doesn't approve."

Blaisey watched all of this unfold while keeping one eye on the disappearing Rolland. She could not decide which spectacle merited her undivided attention. She guessed it would be another five minutes or so before Rolland found his way around the large rock formation and back again, so she decided to make a genuine attempt to get to know her other, less impressive travelling companions. Surely these white people would stop arguing soon. Surely.

"What do you think, then?" came Judah's voice, as Blaisey zoned back into their conversation.

Blaisey looked at him and saw him staring back at her. To her astonishment, Blaisey realized that Judah was asking for her opinion. Aside from his rather informal introduction, this was the first time that Judah had addressed her directly. Her surprise must have been evident to him, as Judah's lips crept into a thin, lopsided smile around the cigarette.

"I knew a man once," Blaisey said, in a calm, soothing voice. She had been told by her father, Nahoy – leader of the Naba-woo, that white people prefer when natives speak in a calm, slow, relaxing tone. He believed that it goaded the white man into a false sense of superiority that their people could use as an advantage.

Blaisey, who was never any good with people (just animals), had seen this as slightly sneaky and underhanded, but those were thoughts from before the days of Jackson's terror, before the days of being kidnapped by American soldiers in the middle of the night, and people falling out of the sky at daybreak. Now she saw the need for an 'ace' up her metaphorical sleeve.

"This man, he rolled and smoked his tobacco, like you," Blaisey continued. She looked deep into Judah's blue eyes and sensed no intent of malice, or evil. Quite the opposite, within the soul of this man were the most redeeming characteristics of all: love and loyalty. She guessed it was a woman's influence that led the blonde man with the funny speech to a life like this. As such, Blaisey decided to let him off the hook gently.

"Oh, yeah?" Judah asked, the cigarette in his mouth bobbing between his lips as he spoke. "What brand? I'm a Luckys man myself." He sniffed and lifted his head proudly, his chin held high. When in doubt, it was always easier for Judah to rely on his quick wit rather than admit he was wrong – no matter the subject.

"This I do not know," Blaisey said, smiling out of politeness. "And we cannot ask him, for he is dead."

At this, Judah stopped his search for the lighter and looked at Blaisey head on, giving her his full attention for the first time. "From smoking tobacco, right?"

"No," Blaisey said with vigor. "He was an ass like you, and somebody shot him."

Sephanie could not stop laughing for three full minutes. Neither she nor Blaisey noticed Rolland's return, their moment of shared interest in subjugating the nearest male among their group giving them a welcome chance to bond.

No sooner had Sephanie realized that she had incorrectly thought of Blaisey as the 'foreign' one than she noticed the smile on Judah's face as well.

"Judah, I'm glad to see that you still have a sense of humor!" Sephanie said, taking a seat on the rock and motioning for Blaisey to join her. The offer did not go unnoticed by the Seminole Princess, who quickly joined Sephanie near the cave opening.

"Oh, no worries, love. I'm not smiling because of her," Judah said, removing a lighter from his back pocket and lighting the cigarette. He inhaled its contents with a jubilation that was as short lived as it was sudden.

Sephanie watched this foolishness and decided to take action. Using his moment of pleasure against him, Sephanie pried the cigarette from between his lips, threw it on the ground, and stomped on it before returning her hands to her hips.

Before Judah could respond to this insult, the group's attention was called back to their fourth member.

"It's still there!" Rolland screamed from behind them. The three turned to see Rolland running in their direction. With both of his hands on his head and his eyes fixated past them into the cave, he looked every bit the madman Judah made him out to be.

"What is?" yelled Sephanie.

"The light! In the cave!" Rolland shouted back.

"Oh... that again," Judah said, under his breath.

Finally reaching them, Rolland stopped and bent over to catch his breath.

"Rolland, I really think it's best if you just let this one go," Sephanie said, placing one hand on his shoulder.

Blaisey wasn't sure, but she could have sworn that in that moment Rolland's breathing become faster, not slower as he would have intended.

"I have to go in," Rolland said, standing upright and walking past them. Fear be damned, he was going to go into that cave. He was going to find answers.

At West Point, Jackson had made a name for himself as one of the quickest runners, highest jumpers, and best belly crawlers in the fine academy's history. Although he had plenty of opportunity to display the first two, for the first time in his otherwise distinguished career Jackson would be getting an opportunity to utilize his most overlooked skill.

In order to catch up with Rolland and the others, Jackson ran, only glancing down occasionally to verify that he was still following their tracks. With eight separate prints to guide his path, it was easy to make quick time, going the three and a half miles in just over half an hour: an incredible feat for a man in his middle age, regardless of the century. Guided by intuition as much as his tracking abilities, Jackson made his way to the wooded area where a clearing housed an old cave opening. Sensing danger close by, Jackson dropped to his hands and knees in a push up position before expertly belly crawling around a series of small boulders before the tree line.

Upon entering the clearing by the cave, the beaten, yet determined Jackson immediately heard the voice of someone familiar.

English accent, distinct lack of authority toward superiors in his tone, must be the blonde man who traveled with the boy.

Scurrying on hands and knees to the side of the limestone rock formation that surrounded the cave, Jackson flattened himself as low to the ground as possible. He watched as each of them squeezed into the cave at the end of the limestone, disappearing from his view. He counted to thirty before following them inside.

Reaching around in the darkness, the first thing Jackson felt was a small, smooth package. Picking it up, he turned around and held it toward the opening of the cave, shining light onto the wrapped bundle. The message 'DANGER: EXPLOSIVES' was written in large, red letters several times. Believing the cave to be a possible weapons stash, Jackson silently crawled further into the entrance, listening for the sky people's position.

The opening was no bigger than a bicycle wheel, but with the right positioning it could easily accommodate a fully grown man. The dark, narrow cave seemed to go on forever. Rolland's only known fear was claustrophobia. Torn between a need to discover the white light's meaning and a crippling fear of the uncharted chasm that lay before him, things could not be any worse.

Looking behind him, Rolland could see very little, if any, daylight. He had gone deeper down the rabbit hole than he had thought possible. The pang of fear in the pit of his stomach grew with his unease and restlessness. He clicked on the light attached to the strap on his head, and for the first time saw the mountain that lay before him, waiting to be conquered.

The cave narrowed about twenty yards ahead of him into a small, rocky passage that opened widely at the end. Daunting though it was, Rolland couldn't take his eyes off the odd, white light that waited on the other side.

"What the hell," Rolland said to himself, taking a deep breath and releasing it slowly. This exercise had been taught to him by his mother at a young age, but since her death...Well, Rolland rarely used it.

From behind him, Rolland could hear the familiar sounds of his friends struggling through the cave.

"Rolland?" came a soft voice from the darkness. Blaisey, it seemed, was just as much of an adventurer as she was a princess.

"Yeah, I'm here," Rolland answered, a bit embarrassed about his lack of progress through the cave.

"Are you alright?" Blaisey asked, still inching along in the dark toward him. She, too, was moving with her arms extended in front of her, leaving her stomach to do most of the work.

"Yeah, I'm just..." Rolland thought for a moment of an appropriate way to finish the thought without sounding like a complete coward. Then, from behind, someone ran into him. "Ouch!"

Moving through the dark like a silkworm, Blaisey had covered the same ground in moments that had taken Rolland nearly a quarter of an hour. Silently, he thanked the darkness that surrounded them; it hid his embarrassment quite well.

"Oh, come on," came Judah's voice from behind Blaisey. He, too, had found his way through the cave and lay trapped behind the two-person traffic jam.

"Lay off him," said Sephanie from the back of the pack. Her voice was soothing to Rolland's red, anxiety-filled ears.

Taking another deep breath, Rolland began moving forward with his abdominal muscles, inch by inch. He could feel the warmth of

Blaisey's hand on his ankle as he went. With his eyes closed and teeth grinding, Rolland inched along the narrow opening until he could feel the cool, stale air of the inner chamber that lay before them.

In the world of hidden treasures, these would take the blue ribbon as most unexpected. Two large limestone fountains lay before Rolland. The one closest to him was plain, and contained a pool of water with a small spring in the center. The other was taller and more ornate, with what looked to be hand-carved depictions of an ancient people running all along its rim.

Toward the top of the rim was the first drawing of small stick figures, each with different features. Right beside it was another, this one with more color – green to be precise. It seems that whoever carved into the fountain's side was familiar with the existence of Elemenos, as the carving portrayed the two meeting and sharing a tranquil meal.

Rolland took a step back and gazed at the fountain in awe. Assuming the carvings told a story, he scanned lower and came across what he had suspected might be there. He recognized it from the basement of the library and the river of time that flows through Eden; the soft, glowing hue of the time stream.

Carved into the limestone fountain was an engraving of the fountain itself, surrounded by both humans and Elemenos waiting happily for it to grant them entrance into Eden.

"I bet they build a library here someday," Rolland said to himself before he heard a loud thud signaling Blaisey's arrival into the chamber. Her eyes found Rolland and the two fountains almost immediately.

"What are they?" Blaisey asked, drawn to the more elaborate fountain. She ran her hands across the symbols and characters carved into its limestone surface.

"Wait, you don't know?" Rolland asked "But I thought that you...?"

"No," Blaisey said, breaking her gaze away from the ornate fountain for the first time since entering the chamber. "I've never been crazy enough to actually climb down here."

Walking around to the far side of the chamber, Rolland decided to get a closer look at the second fountain. It wasn't completely limestone like its counterpart, but part ceramic with marble trim, and cold to the touch. Its round, uneven shape seemed primitive and rushed, like its creator had left in the middle of its construction. In the middle of the fountain sat a single steady spring of the purest, bluest water Rolland had ever seen. It captured his attention, reminding him of simpler days.

Another loud crash from the entrance broke Rolland's concentration. Turning his head, Rolland got a clear view of Judah's blond mane toppling in over his dusty robe.

"Bloody hell!" said Judah, righting himself. "Like a birth canal in there."

"Shhh," Blaisey whispered, but it didn't matter.

Like the two who entered the chamber before him, Judah fell silent as he realized what lay inside. Unlike them, however, Judah knew exactly what the two fountains were.

Dismissing Judah as an arrogant putz, Rolland leaned in closer to the plainer of the two fountains. Sitting on the edge, Rolland studied the sides of the ceramic structure. There didn't seem to be anything special or extraordinary about it, aside from its placement. Deciding to put these perplexing thoughts out of his mind for a moment, Rolland thought of more basic needs, like the lump in his throat and cuts to his hands, inflicted while he was squeezing through the 'birth canal'.

Standing above the clear, blue water Rolland looked down into it. No reflection stared back at him this time, only the ceramic bottom, solid but for a little hole in the center where the spring came through. Rolland cupped his hand and reached for some water.

"Wright – get away from there." Judah said in a slow, yet oddly urgent tone.

"Why?" asked Rolland, so close to the water's surface that he could almost taste it. His thirst and anxiety had almost gotten the best of him in the enclosed space Judah had dubbed 'the birth canal'. All he craved was some refreshment.

A final thud came from behind them as Sephanie entered the chamber. Ever graceful, she promptly stood and readjusted her clothes before briefly scanning the room. To Rolland's astonishment, her eyes did not linger on the fountains like theirs did. Instead, they fell squarely upon him.

"Rolland, please get away from there," Sephanie said in a voice usually reserved for dealing with children and the infirm.

"What the hell?" Rolland questioned, feeling ganged up on and defiant.

"You don't know what you're doing, boy," Judah said, taking another step toward Rolland. His squeaky shoes echoed, grating on the nerves of everyone in the small cavern.

With flashbacks of white plasma and feeling like an outcast, Rolland took major exception to this treatment, deciding instead to take his chances with his thirst quenched. He cupped his hand and dunked it in the cool, refreshingly blue water before looking at Judah and saying "Mind your own business."

No sooner had Rolland submerged his hand than the sounds of cursing and squeaking filled the entire chamber, as both Judah and Sephanie flung themselves at Rolland before he could bring the water to his lips. Unfortunately for Judah, he got there first.

Tumbling away from the fountains, Judah tackled Rolland, spilling the water all over Rolland's stomach and Judah's chest. Judah swore again, throwing a punch that landed squarely below Rolland's eye.

"Orbital bone," said the blonde Englishman, bringing his hands up to a fighting stance.

"You attacked me, jackass!" Rolland exclaimed, his voice echoing through the chamber and accosting their ears again and again.

"Rolland," Sephanie said, moving closer to him and grabbing his hand. "Look."

This, like every brief moment of happiness in Rolland's seventeen years, was taken with a grain of salt. At that moment, Rolland felt every bit the fool they were making him out to be. Examining his hand, Rolland saw nothing wrong with it. Nothing at all in fact; his cuts and scratches from the cave were gone.

"Wasn't your hand...?" Blaisey began to ask Rolland, speaking up for the first time since Judah and Sephanie's arrival into the chamber.

"Come on now," Rolland began, addressing all three of them. "You can't really be suggesting that that water actually HEALED me?" Listening to himself, he couldn't help but think that his own voice betrayed his insecurity.

The other three said nothing, but their eyes spoke volumes. Exchanging glances with each other, the four travelers came to a silent agreement.

Removing a flask from his coat pocket, Judah approached the plainer fountain and carefully dunked its opening into the blue water until it was submerged enough to welcome its contents. He then pocketed the flask once more before turning his attention to Sephanie with the same expression that a cat would a goldfish.

"May I have this dance?" Judah asked, extending a hand to Sephanie, who looked at it, and him with mild amusement before sighing softly, rolling up the leg of her pants, and removing a flask identical to Judah's from a previously unseen Velcro strap wrapped around her ankle. She handed it Judah before turning to Rolland, and quickly looking away.

"Think I'm beginning to understand the Knightly culture," Rolland said sarcastically.

With a smile, Judah dunked the second flask into the water, allowing it to fill every part of the metal enclosure before twisting the lid back on and handing it again to Sephanie.

'Such an odd thing,' Judah thought to himself. The idea of water with natural healing powers. 'Almost like it was a fou-'

Judah's thinking was interrupted as he accidently submerged his right pointer and middle finger beneath the water. He jerked them out quickly, jumping back a bit and startling a zoned out Blaisey.

"We're in Florida, right?" Judah proposed to the group at large.

"Yeah. So?" Sephanie offered constructively.

"So, has anyone given any thought as to whether or not this is the… well, you know," Judah said. The two females looked at him as if he was alluding to something awkward, but waited for him to muster the courage to say it.

"He wants to know if this is the fountain of youth," Rolland said petulantly, without looking at the other three. He had not been invited to join in the conversation. Teenage brooding is a full time job.

"Turtledove will know." Sephanie added confidently.

"Yes. Yes, as will my father." Blaisey said in agreement.

"Alright then, so we go get the grownups to come take a look at it, eh? All in favor say oi," Judah stated, raising his hand above his head in a cheap play to see if Blaisey would do the same. She didn't.

Though neither of the females said anything, the consensus among them was to go with that strategy.

One by one they began to filter out of the main chamber . Rolland went first, for just as when they went into the cave, he needed the encouragement of at least two people behind him. Blaisey followed, then Judah and finally Sephanie.

Crawling out from behind his hiding place in the first chamber, Jackson watched the last pair of shoes disappear through the birth canal, counted to three, and made his move into the cavern containing the two fountains.

What Jackson saw surpassed his wildest expectations. Before him lay the answer, nay, the very key to ultimate victory against the natives and the British…

"Hell, anyone I want," Jackson said aloud to himself.

Rummaging through his bag, Jackson pulled out a standard issue US Army flask and dunked it into the plainer fountain's pool of water, filling it to the brim with the clear liquid. He then secured the top and placed it inside of his bag before removing another flask.

Just as Jackson went to scoop the second flask into the fountain, he was hit upside the head with a large, metal object.

"You really shouldn't talk to yourself," said Sephanie as she took the opportunity to give Jackson a good kick to the ribs. "It gives away your position."

A loud moan rolled off the lips of the future president as he rolled onto his back and slithered away from Sephanie.

"You, woman!" Jackson managed to say through gasps of air.

"Me," Sephanie said, crossing her arms in front of her and looking down on him with complete authority. "Whatcha got there in your satchel?"

Her tone dripping with mockery, Sephanie moved in on her captive and soon had his bag open for display.

"Just as I thought," Sephanie said, pulling the flask out of the side bag.

"It will help me stop them," Jackson sputtered, a tiny drop of blood escaping from his busted lip.

"You'll stop no one," Sephanie said, grabbing Jackson's collar and lifting him to his feet. "Now let's go."

As she pushed the hero of New Orleans out of the narrow passageway ahead of her, Sephanie could not help but silently curse herself for not realizing that he had followed them there in the first place. In hindsight it made sense, given Jackson's reputation and arrogant attitude. Though she hated to admit it, the thought that Rolland had killed Jackson and changed things somehow, had excited her to the possibilities of his power.

Dismissing the notion as quickly as it had come, Sephanie was brought back to reality by a recognizable voice.

"Sod off, you bloody hogs!" came Judah's voice from beneath the rock formation outside the cave.

"You'll do as you're told or you'll get dragged outta here!" said a man that Sephanie recognized as belonging to Hess, Vilthe's right hand man. If he was here, Sephanie knew another person stood with him, a red-headed woman with the same crooked nose and iguana-like features as Hess. Sephanie knew the woman was Alora, Hess' sister, and one of the most vindictive bitches she had ever had the misfortune of tangling with.

"Stay right here and don't you dare move!" Sephanie whispered to Jackson before inching back through the first passageway.

Though she couldn't see them because of the twist in the cave ahead that Judah had nicknamed the 'birth canal', Sephanie heard Blaisey scream as two shots were fired and Alora gave orders to prepare them for transport.

"This is wrong," Sephanie said out loud to herself before turning around and heading back into the chamber.

No sooner had Sephanie gone to check on the status of her friends than had Jackson gone back to the fountain. He was scooping both hands into it, splashing his face, washing his chest, and drinking from it gleefully. The cuts he had sustained during the raid healed instantly, but the pain in his ribs from Sephanie's kicks lingered on despite the water's cooling relief. This time he saw her coming.

"I've been thinking, a delicate thing like you running around in the forest, just isn't proper. Let's run away, you and I," Jackson said, wrapping one arm around Sephanie in an attempt to draw her closer. His father had taught him at a young age that cleanliness was next to holiness and that women liked that before coitus.

This gesture was met with a most 'delicate' elbow directly to his stomach, sending him into a coughing fit.

"We've got to get them back," Sephanie said to Jackson, noticing how sopping wet he was. "Maybe you should dry off first."

Chapter 16:
Inherit the Wind

The three of them, resembling Dorothy, The Lion, and The Scarecrow, were marched at gunpoint through the dried up riverbed that separated Vilthe's camp from everywhere else they'd explored since they had arrived. Having never before been at gunpoint long enough to analyze the situation, Rolland wondered what sort of tricks he might be able to get away with. Blaisey seemed to be considering the same thing as she caught Rolland's eye and shook her head discouragingly.

It became abundantly clear to all three of them as they entered the site that Vilthe also possessed the ability to time travel. Inside the gates stood three Elemeno guards, all armed with AK-47 assault rifles and wearing Kevlar armor, a strange sight for the year 1817, or any other year, for that matter.

Individuals that possessed extra ordinary abilities like the three travelers were also scattered across the camp, but every one of them looked malnourished, cold, or generally miserable. They sat around tables covered with busted up old technology, such as televisions without a signal or viable plug, and radios picking up nothing but static.

Without warning, everyone, human and Elemeno alike, fell flat to the ground in anticipation of their masters arrival. With only Rolland, Judah, and Blaisey standing at eye level, the man known to them all as Vilthe entered, strutting confidently to his captives.

Vilthe eyed Rolland, remembering the boy from the picture in the time traveler's hand. He next saw the Seminole girl, Nahoy's eldest, before his eyes fell on the oldest, and most familiar member of their party. "So we meet again, Mr. Raines."

Judah was presented to Vilthe, his blonde hair matted, hanging lazily over his pale British face.

"That's Doctor Raines, actually," Judah said defiantly. "And I'll thank you to not go sullying up my name with your 'misters'."

"Give him to Alora to play with for a little while," Vilthe said to a group of Elemenos standing nearby, waiting to do his bidding. "Her as well," he added, waving a careless hand at the Seminole princess.

"She stays with me." Rolland said, throwing one arm over Blaisey as the AK-47 wielding Elemenos advanced on the small group.

"Very well," Vilthe responded unexpectedly. "Though for your next pet, might I suggest a bird of some sort? They're extremely loyal for creatures that used to rule the planet."

The three were left alone, and although Blaisey was by his side, Rolland still felt overwhelmed by the intimidating yet demur man. "Allow me to introduce myself, I am Edward Vilthe."

Rolland offered him no response, merely watching the man, analyzing him as one would a foreign life form.

"What are you thinking?" Vilthe asked Rolland directly.

"Honestly?" Rolland asked, speaking again.

"Yes" Vilthe responded.

"Huh. So you're the one who killed my parents?" Rolland asked looking deep into the man's eyes, their black depths almost sucking him into their void of despair.

"My boy, I did no such thing," Vilthe said, not moving a muscle. The lines on his face betrayed a sense of morbid wisdom and experience.

"I was told," Rolland interjected. "That you murdered my mom and then later..."

"Your father?" Vilthe asked sharply.

"Yeah" Rolland said, swallowing the lump in his throat. "But I don't care about him, he abandoned me. Her though."

Rolland stood up from the chair and walked toward the man, staring him down. Having grown up on the likes of Adam Copeland and Phillip Brooks, Rolland had almost perfected the art of intimidation. Although he had no real plan past this immediate display of dominance, Rolland had hoped to make his intentions clear. However, aside from establishing the fact that he was taller than his parents' murderer, he accomplished very little.

Rolland's action was not met with a swift blow from the evil mass murderer that Turtledove had spoken of. On the contrary, Vilthe stood before Rolland, perfectly if not annoyingly still. With his grey flannel sweater vest buttoned tightly and his maroon tie tucked underneath, Vilthe appeared in complete control of the situation. The two could lock eyes all day; Vilthe would not let his body betray him.

"Yeah, I get it," Rolland said, sitting back down in the chair.

"No, you don't," said Vilthe with an eerie calm as he broke the rigidity he had imposed on his body. "You have it wrong, son."

Despite the fact that Rolland despised being called pet names like 'son', he had little choice but to listen to the man speak. "How do you figure?"

"You come from Eden, yes?" Vilthe asked, bending his legs into a sitting position. Suddenly a folding chair from within the encampment came flying out, propelled as if by nothing, un-folded, and placed itself in the spot where Vilthe was about to sit.

Having learned to expect the unexpected, and attempting to bluff his way through the situation, Rolland decided to play along. "No, actually, I'm from the future."

True to form, Vilthe did not flinch at this answer. "Really now? What year?" he asked, a hint of genuine curiosity in his voice.

"Oh, roughly ten minutes from now," Rolland said, smiling as politely as he could.

This response seemed to rock the previously stable man, who up until that moment had looked at the boy in the same manner a cat would a mouse. This mouse, however, seemed to be offering greater things. "Go on."

"How did you find us?" Rolland asked, genuinely curious in the event that he might actually survive this meeting and escape.

"You insufferable boy, do you still not understand?" Vilthe asked, standing up before circling Rolland again with his slow, methodical pacing. "I can sense every negative and impoverished thought you have."

"You can read minds?" Rolland asked to a round of cack-les from the man who so resembled a good natured next door neighbor.

"I said sense your thoughts boy, not read," Vilthe quipped, coming to a stop from his pacing. "Not unlike the one you call Turtledove."

"So, you're empathic then?" Rolland asked, a dark cloud forming overhead. "You can feel what others feel?"

"In a matter of speaking," Vilthe said, flashing a yellow-toothed smile. "I have existed since your kind was in its infancy, Mr. Wright. I've watched the lowliest human rise up with the use of tools and vanquish their enemies completely via a Scorched Earth policy, killing everything and everyone in their path. I am the bringer of destruction, evil incarnate."

"Sounds scary," Rolland said, his teenage tongue having not yet caught up with the rest of his body.

"Scary, Mr. Wright, is continuing to live without an equal," said Vilthe, finally ceasing his circular pacing and taking a seat directly across from Rolland.

The way he sat was unlike anything Rolland had ever seen; it could be described as similar to watching a dog lie down. It was surreal.

"Hang on, are you asking me to join you?" Rolland asked, hardly believing his ears. He remembered the dire warnings that both Turtledove and Judah had given about Vilthe. The idea that the 'sweater vest wearing old goat was only interested in the worst of the worst' troubled Rolland as he sat and listened to a recruiting proposal.

"Precisely," Vilthe said, a slight lisp sneaking through his sophisticated veneer. "Become my partner - train with me, and together we can travel through recorded history and change the injustices that have fallen on mankind."

"What's in it for me?" Rolland questioned, feeling a rare moment of offense.

"Right to the point, I like that," Vilthe said, bringing his left hand to his chin and scratching it lightly. "How does complete honesty sound?"

"Pardon?" Rolland asked, thinking he must have heard incorrectly. Surely in a world where everyone keeps their secrets better hidden than most wireless internet passwords, transparency from the crowned prince of evil would be unthinkable. Right?

"Ask me anything, and I swear to answer it truthfully and correctly," Vilthe said, looking Rolland directly in the eyes. The golden ring around each of his corneas glowed and pulsated with menacing intention.

So many questions buzzed and fought their way to the surface of Rolland's conscience it was almost like an instantaneous head rush.

"Did you send that monster after me in the bookstore?" Rolland asked bluntly, testing the waters.

"Yes," Vilthe responded, the yellow fleeting through his eyes in small bursts.

"Kind of screwed up, don't you think?" Rolland asked. "For someone who wants to be partners."

"Perception is nine-tenths of reality, Alan." Vilthe said, calling Rolland by his middle name.

"My name is Rolland. Alan is my middle name," Rolland said, both confused and annoyed at this error.

"It was... but like so many travelers, I'm sure they made you stage your own death, yes?" Vilthe asked playing upon all of Rolland's deep seeded doubts about the travelers of light, Eden, and its real purpose. "Fake body and all?"

"Yeah, yeah, they did," Rolland answered meekly, having no choice but to play right into the hands of this obvious spin artist.

"I bet you were tricked into walking willingly into a bright light as well," Vilthe asked, shaking his head and cracking his knuckles.

"Yeah, actually," Rolland said, furrowing his brow and thinking back to the library basement. At the time nothing seemed amiss, but the more he thought of the old wives tales of 'going into the light' the more the entire scenario began to make sense.

"They killed Rolland Alan Wright. But together, you and I can create Alan Wright – the greatest natural-born time traveler that's ever lived!"Vilthe said, his manic excitement getting the best of him for the briefest of moments.

"Did you get that perception quote from Turtledove, too?" Rolland asked, suddenly feeling free to ask anything he desired for the first time since he'd learned that fact and fiction bled into each other every day.

Vilthe barked the largest, deepest, loudest cackle Rolland had ever heard, saying "Got it from him? Boy, he got that line from me. I made that up."

"Oh…" Rolland said, a tad bit embarrassed and surprised by Turtledove's lie by omission. "But why me? Couldn't you just as easily kill me like you did my mother and father, taking my abilities, or whatever they are, for yourself?"

"I could, I suppose," said Vilthe, extending his arm and putting it on Rolland's shoulder. "But like I said, an eternity without an equal is hardly an eternity worth living at all. I have no need for friends, merely brothers in arms. And as to the death of your parents –"

Rolland looked up at Vilthe and attempted to divert his eyes to the spot right above Vilthe's nose.

"I merely killed your father. Your mother, well, I have my suspicions as to how she died, but…" Vilthe said, his voice trailed, having the desired effect.

"Wait, what?" Rolland asked, making eye contact with Vilthe again. "You didn't kill my mother?"

"No, no, of course not," said Vilthe, his eyes contorting with a look of mock disgust and horror. "I would never do such a thing."

"But Turtledove said that..." Rolland began, but already knew that this line of logic would be lost of the man's apparent mortal enemy.

"It is easy for someone like Marcus Turtledove to be afraid of my condition," Vilthe said, breaking his naturally intense gaze and casting his eyes downward in an obvious attempt to illicit sympathy.

Rolland, who had volunteered numerous times at the senior assisted living centers, had seen this act before.

"My condition dictates that I consume souls of others in order to survive, yes," Vilthe said, his matter-of-fact tone unapologetic. "But I only take from those I yearn to kill the most; mainly those individuals who have wronged me, and only humans with great power. Your mother fell into none of those categories so no, Mr. Wright, I did not murder your mother. Only your despicable, child-abandoning, drunken oaf of a father; if you ask me, I did you a favor."

Unsure whether or not Vilthe was telling the truth or just sensing his own doubt and running with it, Rolland decided to press him for as much information as he possibly could, asking "But why me?"

"We're both... survivors, you and I. We are the head, not the tail," Vilthe said. "Besides, none of this matters anyway."

"Why do you say that?" Rolland asked, sitting down next to the man who admittedly murdered his father.

"Think about it boy. This, all of this, does any of it seem real to you?" Vilthe asked, looking around slightly before focusing once more on Rolland.

"Well…" Rolland said, knowing full well that since he'd stepped out of his car in the bookstore parking lot, the line between fact and fiction had been blurred so many times it might as well be forgotten.

"Face it, boy," Vilthe said, placing one of his icy cold hands on Rolland's shoulder. "You're dead."

Of all the things he was expecting to hear, the prospect that he might be dead was one of the last. "What, dead? What are you talking about?"

"Think about it," Vilthe said, squatting down so that he and Rolland were again eye level. The subtle cue in mannerism might go unnoticed by anyone else, but not Rolland Wright. "If you died in that bookstore fire than all of this would make sense, would it not?"

"Because it would all be in my imagination?" Rolland ventured a guess, hoping to find a needle of logic in a haystack of supernatural.

"Correct," Vilthe said, pressing down on Rolland's shoulder even harder.

It hurt like hell, but Rolland's face refused to show it. His mind had channeled pain out long ago, and was now entangled in a battle over his own life and death.

"Why didn't Turtledove tell me that then?" Rolland asked, not mincing words.

"Turtledove is a figment of your imagination," Vilthe said, removing his hand and circling around to a long picnic table covered in a multitude of gadgets. "He's trying to keep you here, trapped like the rest of us, in purgatory."

"Purgatory?" Rolland asked, the very thought sounding ridiculous as… well… anything else he had witnessed in the past forty-eight hours.

"The man you know as Turtledove hates me for speaking the truth," Vilthe said, taking a seat upon a large ornate chair somewhat resembling a throne. "I free souls by consuming them, allowing them to pass on."

"To where?" Rolland asked, not thinking about the repercussions of his quick tongue.

"The hell if I know," Vilthe said, smiling his large yellow smile.

It was an odd thing, but Rolland could swear he saw four extra canine teeth on both sides of Vilthe's under bite.

"Join me, Alan, and together we shall save every soul in purgatory, and help them all move on," Vilthe continued, excitement growing in his voice.

This expedited proposal from the man who everyone had claimed an hour ago had killed his parents was making Rolland's head spin. He needed time to think, and process all this information before making any decisions. But would Vilthe accept that, or would he kill Rolland on the spot just for questioning his authority, just like his parents?

"Let me sleep on it…. Partner?" Rolland said, standing up and making himself taller than Vilthe.

"Very well," Vilthe said, his blood lust now fully exposed. "But know this; within you lies the power to do great things, world-changing things. You could quite literally inherit the wind!"

"I think," said Rolland, cracking his knuckles and yawning forcefully "That I'll go to bed now."

As the sun set on the knight's second day in western Florida, Tina found she was a fish completely out of water. All around her were the sounds of people being productive, helping out the Naba-woo community in some way. Turtledove was lending his leadership skills and strategizing with Nahoy and Charlton, and Joan was... where was Joan?

Utilizing one of her less-discussed abilities, Tina cupped her hand to her ear and listened throughout the valley for Joan's unique sound.

"Whatcha doing?" Joan asked Tina from behind, sneaking up on her for sport.

"Just listening for people," Tina said, hearing the notes of Turtledove's theme as he packed up and left the camp on a mission of great importance with his two native companions. She knew this because the notes were accented and punctuated as he walked, giving purpose to his actions instead of the mundane easiness he usually possessed.

"What does he sound like?" Joan asked, not really paying much attention to the youngest, and in her mind, dumbest of the Knights of Time. Admittedly, Joan had very little in common with Tina, especially compared to Sephanie. The fact that Tina had seemingly replaced Taylor in their trio of friends didn't help matters either.

"It sounds like that concerto by Armand. You know, the one they use in the Olympics? The do-do-doo-doo-do-do," Tina sang poorly, but with great enthusiasm. It was not appreciated.

"Uh-huh," Joan said, taking a seat to the girl's left and opening her brown leather log book. The edges were embalmed with a light golden hue that seemed to glow against the darkness of the night.

Tina had seen logs like that before. It was the standard issue TOLL (Traveler of Light Log) book, but to Tina it represented more than that, much more. For her it embodied respect, admiration, courage, independence, and perhaps the embodiment of her goals in life. While most children of Eden dream of being sports figures, entertainment starlets, or elite fighters defending the realm, she had always been enamored with the Knightly way of life, espousing virtues long forgotten in modern society. Virtues like courage, conviction, and honor: three adjectives among many written on each TOLL log's cover. Though she wanted to compliment Joan, telling her how much she admired her colleague, and wanted to be a great deal like her, the level of intimidation was too high, and all that came out was an overenthusiastic "I like your log book."

"Uh-huh," Joan said again, with even less interest.

Perhaps it was the shadows that prevented Tina from seeing the look of annoyance on Joan's face, or maybe the noise. Either way, Joan was quickly beginning to suspect that the only way to get the girl to stop talking was to distract the young intern and drown her out during the next rant about, well, anything.

"Judah is alive, you know," Tina said warmly, hoping to open a dialogue.

"I'm sure he is," Joan said, ceasing to write in her log and actually engaging Tina in normal conversation. "But why would you say that?"

"I heard him," Tina said meekly.

Joan had been briefed by both Turtledove and Scott Wright the day before Tina had started working at the Halls of Time, but she couldn't for the life of her remember what extraordinary skills the girl possessed.

"Excuse me, but did you say that you heard him?" Joan asked, hoping that it was she who heard Tina wrong instead.

"Yeah, I heard him," Tina said, sipping casually on her beverage.

"Well, what the hell does that mean?" Joan said, abandoning any tact or grace she might have had going into the conversation.

"It's this thing I do," Tina said, her cheeks burning with embarrassment. "I hear music specific to each person."

"Like theme music?" Joan prodded, hoping to harass the girl into honesty.

"Yeah, sort of…" Tina said bashfully.

"That's cool… I guess," Joan offered, before picking up her log book. "So what noise do I make?"

"Not a noise… an instrumental. Sort of like entrance music, only it's exuded outward, from within one's soul, I guess."

"Ok, what music is my soul playing?" Joan asked, her patience waning.

"Well it's interesting actually," Tina said, obviously avoiding the question. "You see, I look out there on the forest and I can tell where Rolland and Judah are."

"Where are they?" Joan asked, casting skepticism aside for a moment in the hope of news of her husband's whereabouts.

"Over there somewhere," Tina said, pointing north. "I can hear a sax solo, which is your hubby. And sometimes when he's angry or really passionate about something Rolland sounds like trumpets."

"Trumpets? Saxophones?" Joan asked, placing one hand on her hip and one on Tina's forehead. "Sweetie, did you smoke anything those natives gave you?"

"What?" Tina asked, pulling back from her commander's touch. "No! Ugh, never mind."

Tina got up to leave, but Joan wouldn't let her.

"Not so fast, cupcake," Joan said, blocking Tina's path. "You didn't tell me what I sound like."

"Why do you care?" Tina asked, lifting Joan's arm and going underneath her to get by.

"I just do!" Joan said, feeling very much like a bully.

"Bells," Tina said, with no further elaboration.

"Bells?" Joan asked her.

"Yep, bells. Don't know why, but there you go." Tina said, finally walking away.

With six Nabawoo warriors riding close behind them, bows at the ready, neither Nahoy nor his guest Turtledove feared an attack while they travelled into the designated Creek lands.

"Sad tale," Nahoy said to Turtledove, pulling on his horse's reins until it slowed to a brisk pace.

"So I've heard," Turtledove said, doing the same with his own steed. "How long ago were they forced here?"

"A year ago, they came," Nahoy said to the small group as they slowed their horses to a walking pace before coming to a complete stop between two large bushes. "In seclusion ever since."

Not more than five seconds passed before the long, slender barrel of a rifle found its way to Turtledove's temple without him noticing. This alone warranted respect in his line of work, even more in the year 1817.

Fifteen natives, all carrying rifles -- not bows --emerged from their hiding places in the brush, flanked by an old, white haired man, unarmed but for the smile he wore.

"Welcome, my brother," the Creek Chieftain known as Black-foot said, extending his arm to Nahoy. "I apologize for the precautions, but when they told me a white man traveled with you I thought it necessary."

The blatant racism was strange to Turtledove, as he realized for the first time that every weapon was pointed at him and no one else.

"I'm sorry, but he can go no further without paying for it with his life." Blackfoot said, his face stern with resolve.

"Be reasonable Blackfoot," Nahoy urged his fellow leader "He is merely trying to help us keep what is ours. Perhaps you have heard of his people, the ones who fell from the sky."

"Perhaps your eyes fail you, Nahoy," said a voice behind Black-foot as Levi, the Creek leader's son and second in command came into view. "Sky people or not, he is still white."

"Very well, then," Nahoy stated, his voice flat and emotionless. "We shall take our leave without your support."

"Know this," Turtledove said, drawing renewed attention from the fifteen rifles aimed at him. "The Americans will come again, and without or without your help, we will fight them."

"Then you will die," Blackfoot said, hatred clouding his judgment.

"Perhaps," Turtledove said, looking around at the Creek natives who held their guns tightly in their hands, their fingers centimeters from the triggers. "But you will be next."

"That cad called me a pet!" Blaisey shouted at Rolland through the tent where she was changing. Although they had developed quite the friendship since his arrival, Blaisey insisted on some privacy while she changed - a request Rolland was happy to oblige, except he had assumed it would give him a few moments of peace and quiet. "Who the hell does he think he is?!"

"From what I've been told, he's evil incarnate," Rolland said through the mesh netting separating their faces. "But I don't know. He seems oddly honest about all of this."

"We have to get out of here," Blaisey said to him, stepping out of the tent dressed in a more traditional, less conspicuous dress.

"Then let's go," Rolland offered, acting as if it was as simple of a matter as walking out halfway through a bad movie.

"How do you propose we do that?" Blaisey asked, sneaking a peek at the fortified walls surrounding them.

"Wait until things settle down, grab Judah and the kids, and go," Rolland said, thinking that once again clicking his fingers might give them the advantage they needed to escape.

"We can do that?" Blaisey asked him, taking a step closer.

"We can do whatever we want, I imagine," Rolland said, confidence in his new found abilities making him overly optimistic. "Or so Vilthe was telling me, right?"

No matter how uneasy she was, Blaisey was adamant about rescuing her siblings, an urge that overrode her desire for personal safety by half and forced her to agree with Rolland, no matter what his plan of escape was.

Precisely one hour later, they set their plan into motion. Tiptoeing around an artillery shed heavily guarded by drowsy Elemenos, both Rolland and Blaisey found Judah bound with bungee cords and covered in small electrical burns that ran down his arms and legs.

There were no other captives; the other slave pens were completely empty.

Though he was alive, Judah looked as if he had been badly mistreated and refused to wake. The two of them were forced to carry him much in the same way Rolland and Turtledove had carried Victor only a few days before. The 'slow and go' process of sneaking out of Vilthe's camp was only made more difficult by their lack of weapons, and the constant vigilance of the Elemeno guards.

Fortunately for them, the Elemeno didn't seem to be too wise when it came to matters of warfare, and the three of them were able to sneak out of the camp without using Rolland's new trick, a fact which left him feeling very grateful.

Their unbelievable luck continued, and Sephanie was waiting for them just outside Vilthe's camp. Although Jackson was with her, he offered no resistance to once again being face to face with Rolland and Blaisey. Not immediately, anyway.

"What's up?" Sephanie asked, holding a rifle in firing position and covering Rolland's rear as they approached her.

"Nothing, just walked out," Rolland said cheerfully, as if he was personally responsible for this great feat.

"Just like that?" Sephanie asked, lowering her rifle but continuing to look around them for potential threats.

"Well, we did have a bit of trouble getting Judah out," Rolland said, grabbing the top of the blond genius' head and propping him up like a rag doll.

"That Alora liked him a lot," Blaisey said, pulling the groggy Brit to his feet. "Come on, Lion."

"Yeah, wake up and earn your stripes," Rolland said sarcastically.

"That's tigers, you dolt," Judah mumbled. He was barely aware of his surroundings but he still managed to get a zinger in on Rolland, not only giving the impression that Judah would be fine, but also reminding the group that they needed to get as far away from Vilthe's camp as possible.

"Still one problem," Sephanie said, looking over at Jackson.

"Where are my siblings?" Blaisey demanded, eyeing Jackson.

"My compound due east of here, near the beach," Jackson offered, hoping to barter a deal. "There I have supplies, food, protection. But you need me to get inside."

"Works for me, how about you?" Rolland said to Sephanie, who turned and raised her weapon toward Jackson.

"No, not again. I'm useful. Don't leave me here, I…" Jackson pleaded, but it was too late. Blaisey delivered another blow to the side of Jackson's head, knocking him out cold.

"This time I definitely knocked him out," Blaisey said. She again threw Judah's right arm over her neck and together with Rolland, dragged him along down the hill and over the dried riverbed that led back to the area closest to the beach.

"Let's hope so," Rolland said.

"Not a good day to be that guy," Sephanie chuckled, stepping over Jackson as they made their way away from Vilthe's camp.

Chapter 17:
Home

The lush foliage that graced the vast Florida landscape in 1817 cared nothing for age, gender, or experience, yet for the teenage Tina Holmes, it felt like a constant enemy pushing against her in the darkness of night.

After her awkward encounter with Joan, Tina sought nothing more than a quiet place for solitude, a place to sort through the day's developments. Slinking around an unusually large tree, she spotted a clearing fifty yards ahead that looked solid, dry, and free of vegetation. The closer she got to it, the more aware she became of what else she was she was zeroing in on.

Light was coming from just beyond the tree line, bouncing off of the large leaves and washing over Tina's middle section. She approached, a bit apprehensive at first, but soon found a reason not to be - a six-foot, one-inch reason with wavy blonde hair and a tattered pearl snap shirt. It was Rolland, sitting across from Judah, Sephanie, and the Seminole girl they had run off with.

Tina watched the group in silence, unsure how they would react to her unexpected presence. The moments dragged on, filled with small talk but little else. Moments turned to minutes, and minutes blended together until Tina no longer knew how long she'd been watching them.

For nearly an hour Sephanie went over every bit of strategy and battle preparation she could think of in the event that they were attacked again, but eventually the attention of the others began to shift steadily away from Sephanie's precautions and toward more mundane things like hunger and exhaustion. Sensing that her audience was lost, Sephanie eventually gave up and sat down on a rock next to Judah.

Silence filled their camp for the first time as the sounds of the night spoke to them. The soft hoots of an owl, the gentle shuffling of twigs and grass, and the sporadic splashing of nearby water filled the conversation over the crackling fire, turning it in to a symphony of sound.

"What's up with you, green eyes?" Judah asked Sephanie, poking her a bit with a walking stick he had been drawing in the dirt with moments before.

"Just thinking of home, I suppose," Sephanie said, hoping to start a conversation with her otherwise silent companions. Since she didn't want to be the first one to bring up the subject of the cave, she thought maybe a more general topic would get the ball rolling.

"I remember once," Judah chimed in, his thick British accent piercing the air with its unique and splendid drawl. "When I was a pup, 'bout seventeen, I'd just gotten my driver's license."

"Your what?" Blaisey asked, about one hundred years too early to understand the reference.

"A written notation that says I can operate an automobile," Judah said, using his hands to mimic the turn of a steering wheel.

"Huh?" Blaisey asked him more confused than ever.

"A really fast horse!" Judah hollered louder than he intended to, causing a chorus of stifled laughter from both Sephanie and Rolland that eventually turned into open laughter from the entire group, including Blaisey, as they all found joy in Judah's frustration. Even Tina, hidden in the bushes, couldn't keep a straight face.

"Anyway," Judah said, composing himself "I was driving with me mate when I see, out of the corner of me eye, this fit little bird driving in the lane next to us."

Rolland watched Judah's hands as he further illustrated the positioning of the cars using wide, vivid gestures and attempted to count how many times the man said the word 'me' in one sentence. It was a mild pet peeve of his, but one that Rolland had come to associate with being egomaniacal and selfish, similar to the way valley girls at his school used to say the word 'like' as filler for their otherwise pointless stories about shopping, boys, and popular fashion accessories.

"So I ever so slightly bumped the front of me car into the back of her bumper, you know, just to get her to pull over." Judah said matter-of-factly, as if it was a common practice. "We got to talking, went on a few dates, and bam – my first wife."

Laughing, Rolland looked around, noticing guiltily that neither Sephanie nor Blaisey so much as cracked a smile at Judah's story. Turning his attention to them, it became obvious that something was bothering the two girls, even though neither of them would admit to it. "What is on your mind?"

"Just worried about my brother and sisters, I guess," Blaisey replied, her hands hiding beneath the long, hand-woven cloak she had brought on their journey.

"It's not so much their safety I'm worried about," Blaisey continued, her spirit springing to life as the fire danced in the light of her eyes. "They're probably really scared, not knowing when, or even if they'll see home again."

"Blaisey..." Rolland said, offering her his hand in sympathy.

"I was kidnapped as a kid, too," Sephanie said to the great surprise of everyone listening.

"You were?" Blaisey asked her, shooing away Rolland's hand in exchange for the more comforting prospect of Sephanie's story.

"Yeah..." Sephanie said quietly.

In the bushes behind Sephanie, Tina still sat crouched and listened to every word that passed between them. She knew where their conversation was heading and thought of intervening, but someone beat her to it.

"I wouldn't..." Judah warned, but he was quickly overruled.

"It's fine, J.J.," Sephanie said, pulling her hair back into a ponytail and tying it with a leather band. "I was twelve years old when it happened. I went out to collect milk from the barn and was abducted. Simple as that."

The shock that Sephanie's last comment inspired in the group, even Tina hiding unseen in the bushes, was considerable. Her apathy toward a life-altering event left them all reeling, desperate for some sort of elaboration, but social custom dictates that one show respect for the victim's ordeal and not bombard them with questions. All but one member of their party extended this courtesy. All but Blaisey, who did not share their culture, and therefore did not know any better than to ask.

"Who took you?" Blaisey asked, earning a dirty look from Judah who sat opposite her.

Rolland could not understand why Judah kept shaking his head at Blaisey, as if to indicate to her to stop. Guessing that she was not familiar with this cultural norm, Rolland found it extremely amusing that he had figured this out before the so called 'smartest man alive'.

The joy did not last long, however…

"It was a tall man with short, light brown hair," Sephanie said, taking a deep breath before finishing. "And he smelled like bourbon."

Before she finished the sentence, Rolland knew that Sephanie was talking about his father.

"My dad abducted you?" Rolland asked in complete disbelief. Hearing accusations that his father might be responsible for his mother's death was one thing, but to hear that he was a child abductor, too…

"Technically, yes," Sephanie said, suddenly wishing the topic had never come up..

Silence filled the campsite, and the four of them sat there for a few minutes, all of them staring at something different and lost in their own thoughts.

"Told you not to say anything," Judah grumbled, poking Sephanie with the stick he had been fiddling with since they sat down.

"No, it's alright," Rolland said, looking from one of them to the other. "It's not like I'm my dad, or anything. He did what he did, and now he's dead."

Blaisey looked at Rolland with quiet, apprehensive shock at her great grandson's harsh and disrespectful words for his own father. "I'm your mother's grandmother, right?"

"Yeah," Rolland said, a bit surprised by the question.

"You're lucky," Blaisey said, standing up and arranging her cloak around her. "I wish to sleep now. I bid you all good night."

Princess Blaisey of the Nabawoo tribe walked eight feet to a small pile of leaves and lay down without another word.

Anticipating their movement, Tina slinked quietly back into the brush around her and made her way back to the Seminole camp. The hike back was nearly a mile and a half, but only one thought crossed her mind the entire way: that she wished she could comfort Rolland after that bitch Sephanie accused his dad of being a kidnapper.

When she arrived back at the Nabawoo camp, Tina expected it to be a quiet, peaceful place, allowing her to slip in under the radar. Most of the camp was quiet, but not in the way she had expected.

The main area, where they had held the banquet in the Knights' honor, was completely devoid of people. They had all either gone to bed, or had gone to the large gathering that seemed to be taking place in a well-lit clearing nearby.

Walking to it, Tina had to fight her way through a herd of Nabawoo just to get a look at the spectacle. So many Nabawoo, including many women and children, wanted a glance at whatever it was that was happening in the center. With the hour being so late, Tina knew it couldn't be one of the elders making a declaration. She pushed and excused her way past a few of the people before getting a good look at the action. It was enough to make her wish she had stayed back at the campfire with Rolland.

In the center of all the attention stood Joan, wearing what appeared to be a pair of cut-off shorts and a chest wrapping. Both of her wrists were taped up with makeshift buffalo gloves, oversized and filled with straw. Her feet were spread out in a fighting stance, obviously ready for any challenge that might come her way.

As it stood, there were plenty of challengers, but no actual challenges. Tina was startled, but only for a moment as she watched Joan expertly handle each one as if they were little more than stuffed animals. One of the Nabawoo fighters had had the misfortune of bringing a shield into the fight with him, a weapon Joan was quite fond of finding creative uses for.

"Who's next, huh? Who here is man enough to face the Maid of Orleans?" Joan shouted at the crowd surrounding her, all of whom were calling for her head.

The grunts and hollers from the scores of Nabawoo warriors who had lined up to take their shot at dethroning the almighty blonde warrior were deafening to Tina's ears, making her uncomfortable and claustrophobic.

"Come on, you won't beat Jackson like that! What are you, British?!" Joan screamed, barely dodging another barrage from a Seminole man almost twice her height.

Turning around, Joan took full advantage of her agility and extensive knowledge of the human circulatory system. Dropping to a push-up on her hands and knees, Joan looked up at the overgrown Nabawoo warrior towering over her like a skyscraper.

"Hey, ugly!" Joan taunted, drawing the man's attention long enough for her to throw a handful of dirt into the man's eyes, forcing him to drop his weapon.

Joan rolled over to retrieve it and sprang upright, kicking her feet and using their momentum for balance. The impressive feat threw her opponent off guard, allowing her to trap his head between her arms and deliver a final, incapacitating head butt square to the man's face.

Although many of the men were lining up to take their shot, not one of the two dozen or so that had tried had even managed to knock Joan off of her feet. Yet still they came in droves, one, two, three at a time, lunging and attacking her with an assortment of makeshift weapons and talismans, intent on stopping the 'Maid of Orleans'.

One of the Nabawoo, a lanky, tattooed man with an oddly constructed hat, was walking amongst the onlookers and offering his hand, which clutched long strands of beads and coins.

Tina guessed that he was a bookie of sorts, profiting off the ineptitude of those around him.

Fearing that some of Joan's heat from the crowd might rub off on her simply for being there, Tina decided to retreat back to her tent before it was too late.

"Hello, white woman," the Seminole bookie said to Tina, grabbing her forearm and stopping her from leaving. "You want to place bet on your friend?"

"Hi... do you like, um..." Tina said to the suddenly bewildered bookie, walking in step with him until they were well away from the mob of Nabawoo spectators. "Okay thanks, bye."

Breaking off from him, Tina walked across the vacant stretch of land that separated her from her tent as quickly as her dignity would allow her. The tent was easy to recognize; it was the only one that wasn't purple.

Hopping over the sleeping Turtledove's ankles, Tina stepped into her tent, removed her jacket, and began to settle under the cover of skins that had been provided for her.

"Sephanie is such a bitch," Tina said out loud before closing her eyes and attempting to think of more pleasant thoughts.

The sound of trumpets, like a warm embrace or the feeling of a first kiss, fell from the air as Tina's mind went further away from the boy she was sure was the love of her life.

Just miles away, under the same sky Tina was falling asleep under, the boy she pined for found himself just as listless.

Rolland lay on the ground, pretending to be asleep for what seemed like an eternity. The last forty-eight hours had seen him face to face with a giant beast, captive by Andrew Jackson, nearly bathing in the fountain of youth, and recruited by evil himself. To top it all off, he'd just learned that he came from the loins of a man capable of two of the worst sins known to man. Kidnapping and murder.

Sephanie waited out her three companions before crawling the short distance to her tweed knapsack and retrieving her Traveler of Light Log. Removing a pen from a side pocket, she opened the journal. After flipping through the first couple of pages, she read:

TOLL of Sephanie Kelly:

Age 11

I remember the night you died, Daddy. Well - I suppose it was just the night that we found out about your death, Momma and me. I was in the wheat field, looking for Gracie. She's my cat. You never got to meet her. She came to us after you went off to fight.

Gracie kept me warm at night when I thought about you. She would curl up next to me and purr. Maybe it was because of the warmth, or maybe she knew I missed you.

The clouds were moving so fast across the sky, like they were on a collision course with each other. Blue was fading to gray along with my spirits. I felt a knot in the pit of my stomach. I couldn't find Gracie anywhere.

Momma was crying. I had never seen her cry until then. Her tears were like small puddles that fell to the Earth and formed into one long river.

The rain kept coming, and coming. That is, until the day that he came to visit. He was a kind man… more like an older boy really. I guessed he must be in his early twenties.

He talked to me, held my hand, and listened as I talked about my feelings. I remembered him looking out our cottage window a lot. The rain stopped when he arrived for his second, third, and fourth visits, but it would always start up again after he left…

It wasn't until his sixth visit that the man stopped listening and finally began talking to me. He told me that I was special and could do things. That I held a certain influence over nature around me.

I liked that idea. I liked being in control ever since you were taken from me. That day, for the first time since you died, the sun came out above our cottage.

Age 13

I've been here for nearly four months now and haven't been able to go outside once due to the weather.

I miss Momma, but I know I'll see her in the spring. She's always the happiest in the springtime. You think she would be used to it by now, the snow melting at the end of every winter – especially at her age.

Age 18:

Met a cute boy today, but there's already a lot of complicated baggage attached to him. Nothing that's his fault really, just sort of born into trouble – which sounds a lot like me. Wonder what else we have in common.

Sephanie closed her log book and cradled it in her arm as she laid her head down to sleep. With thoughts of the past and future running through her head, and the troubles of the day weighing down her body, it was nice to just be still for a couple of hours.

Rolland watched her do this and wished with all of his might that he could do something to apologize, or even begin to explain his father's actions. But as it stood, Vilthe's argument was beginning to make more and more sense with each passing event.

'This must be hell', Rolland thought to himself, forcing his eyes to close and his brain to rest.

Chapter 18:
Taking the Beach

As the Travelers of Light and their Seminole guide woke up on the second morning in Spanish controlled Florida, they were greeted by the soft rays of the morning sun beaming down on them from high above. Their chance to bathe in the sunshine was short lived however, as the lightest sleeper in the group stirred with the sound of the early morning birds.

The first to wake, Sephanie opened her eyes groggily and let the scope of their situation wash over her like a flood of Gulf of Mexico seawater. She sat up and brushed the hair out of her eyes with her fingers. It wasn't until her line of vision was clear that she saw the dark patches hovering in the distance beyond their camp.

There it was, nearly a mile away, forming somewhere just past the tree line. A pillar of black smoke rose slowly toward the sky, forming ominous shapes as it disappeared into the wind. Sephanie watched it for a moment, lost in a haze of confusion and weariness.

"Up, up! Get up!" Sephanie shouted suddenly, her voice squeaking a little. The impromptu display of childishness sent an embarrassing tingle through her body, causing her face to redden and her heart to beat faster.

"Nehan, white girl, shut up," Blaisey said, playing on Sephanie's embarrassment to buy herself a few extra minutes of sleep.

Overcome with a familiar childhood anxiety, Sephanie could not help but fall into old habits for a moment. Biting her lower lip with her top row of teeth, she thought hard on the situation before she saw Rolland, a curl of his wavy, dirty blonde hair falling into his face as he rolled onto his side to avoid the chatter. Watching him was comforting somehow, a welcome change within the moment.

"Filthy habit there, love," Judah said groggily, barely bothering to open his eyes at all.

Sephanie looked at Rolland and Blaisey nervously to see if they had witnessed her moment of insecurity, but they both seemed to be lost in their own unconscious worlds.

Composing herself, Sephanie began shaking the tarp underneath the three of them. Her command of nature's forces aside, she did not possess the strength to move all three of them, and only succeeded in annoying Judah, who lay closest to her.

"Down to one pack," Judah said, waving her off with his hand without opening his eyes.

"Wake up, dummy!" Sephanie hollered, swapping her shaking for some good old fashioned pinching. "I think that's the contact signal!"

Judah's eyes opened instantaneously. He straightened himself and sat up, turning to see the black intruder rise into the sky above them, though from his vantage point he could see the fire in question clearly.

"The smoke is coming from a signal fire over there," Sephanie said, pointing to the beach.

"You're right. Better wake up Sleeping Beauty over there," Judah said to Sephanie nodding in Rolland and Blaisey's direction. "And the native girl too, while you're at it."

Judah's good-natured jab made Sephanie smile as she loaded a few of her belongings before stopping to rethink her strategy. She went back to shake the other two awake.

After loading their things back into their sacks and bags, they scanned the area before filing out.

"Leave nothing behind but memories..." Rolland said with a yawn and a stretch of his arms.

"What the hell is that supposed to mean?" Judah asked, the lack of caffeine or nicotine causing him to lash out at the slightest provocation.

"Hush, both of you," Sephanie said, shooing them out of the camp and trudging down the hillside behind them. "We'll head to the beach. I'm sure Turtledove is already up and sees it too."

The four of them made their way through the rocky terrain bordering the beach for a quarter of a mile, slowly and cautiously. Behind Sephanie, the other three fell in step with their self-appointed leader as she plotted the smoothest path to the soft and inviting sand that lay just beyond their reach.

When they arrived, every one of them was happy, but utterly confused. The relief that the warm Florida sand provided their sore feet paled in comparison to the large, abandoned fire that lay dying one hundred yards or so in front of them. It had obviously been built to make smoke signals, large and well-constructed.

"Who do you think made it?" Sephanie asked no one in particular as they trudged over to it and circled around to inspect the still red-hot coals within. She put her pack down, opened a flap within, and pulled out a compass before holding it up to get a reading.

"Could be our contact," Judah said, bending down to take a closer look at the pit. He picked up a stray stick and began poking a few of the burnt out coals, turning them over and reigniting them once again. "This is definitely a smoke signal fire."

"We already knew that," Blaisey said impatiently, the exposure of being out in the open making her weary.

"I'm going to go farther down the beach to get a better view." Sephanie said, picking her pack up and throwing it over her shoulder.

"I'll go with you," Blaisey said, doing the same. Together the two of them set off down the beach, leaving their two male companions behind.

Both Rolland and Judah suddenly felt very self-conscious. Tension filled the air between them, as both men realized that they had not been alone with one another since arriving in Florida. Each of them took very different approaches to releasing the stress; Rolland cracked his knuckles while Judah lit his disposable lighter over and over again. After each finger, Rolland moved on to his arms, neck, and back before burying his feet in the sand and thinking about how much he hated the sound of Judah's lighter compared to the ocean as it crashed into the sand. This went on for several minutes, neither of them saying a word.

It wasn't until Rolland picked up a long, skinny stick and began poking at the fire that Judah finally broke the silence between them.

"So there's a good chance we'll be getting company soon," Judah said, clicking his lighter again, much to Rolland's disdain.

"Yeah, so?" Rolland asked, as he tried to block out the annoying click, click, click of Judah's fingers lighting and relighting the disposable lighter.

"So, I've decided to forgive you," Judah said with a resolute tone, clicking the lighter once more before placing it in his left pocket.

"You what?" asked Rolland, raising his eyebrow and turning to face Judah full on.

"Forgive you. You know, for breaking into my lab and sending us to bloody Mexico," Judah said, twirling his arms about as if to highlight their tropical surroundings.

"Okay, jackass," Rolland said, standing up and tossing aside the stick he had been using to poke the fire. "First of all, I don't want your stupid forgiveness. There's nothing to forgive. It's not like I asked your wife to bring me home with her."

"What did you say about my wife?" Judah asked, his voice low and hollow.

"Ask her yourself," Rolland said, taking another step towards Judah. "She saw me on the street and couldn't resist me."

Bracing for the punch, Rolland steadied his feet and was able to dodge the strike that J.J. had been practicing since the age of twelve. When that didn't work, British legs found American ones – resulting in a flurry of punches and kicks between the two men.

This refusal to get along, coupled with the absence of anyone sane enough to stop them, resulted in a storm of distraction that allowed the creators of the smoke signal easy access to their prey. Neither Rolland nor Judah noticed as the ship, or the ship's passengers, a group of Barbary thieves, drunkards, and pirates, as they snuck up from along the water's edge, crawling on their bellies.

They were nearly thirty men, dressed in rags and as silent as they were filthy. Their trails were washed away by the tide as they army crawled closer to the travelers.

"She couldn't, even, remember, her name!" Rolland hollered as he kneed Judah hard in the side of the scientist's left leg, rendering it numb.

Meanwhile, nearly a half a mile down the beach, Sephanie reached into her knapsack and pulled out a small telescope. Looking through it, she could see certain characteristics of the ship as it came into view. The first was the Portuguese flag that flew high above the ships masts.

"Sephanie..." Blaisey said, with caution to her voice as she tapped her companions shoulder.

"Hmmm?" Sephanie asked, brushing her aside and continuing to study the vessel.

"What did you call those green spotted things that attacked us when you first got here?" Blaisey asked, switching from tapping to shaking.

In her defense, Sephanie believed that this was merely another cultural difference between the two, one she had experienced before with the Aborigines and the Spanish, where the rules of etiquette demanded eye contact when speaking. Because of this she responded with a curt "Elemenos. Why?"

"There is a large herd of Elemenos moving this way," Blaisey said, shaking Sephanie harder and finally succeeding in catching Sephanie's attention.

Spinning around Sephanie saw them. Sure enough a large pride was on the move on the far side of the beach. As they were naturally afraid of water, Sephanie did not understand their intentions, but knew immediately what she should do.

"Run, run now!" Sephanie shouted at Blaisey, pushing the Seminole princess to move.

Bullets ricocheting off of the rocks beside them, both Sephanie and Blaisey ran back down the beach toward where Rolland

and Judah were still fighting. Screaming and hollering, neither one of the females managed to capture their companions' attention before the gunfire coming from their Elemeno pursuers did.

Joining them just in time to see the pirates, Blaisey shouted to Rolland, "Behind you!"

Turning quickly, Rolland narrowly avoided an attack from a one-eyed man wielding a crudely made sword before doubling back and joining the other three, who had formed a tight circle between the angry looking Elemenos and pirates.

"Attack formation six beta!" Sephanie screamed out at the others before bending down and retrieving the fallen pirate's crudely made broadsword.

While he appreciated the enthusiasm, Rolland had no idea what Sephanie was talking about. He was just glad that after she had called them into formation, she had not made him move from where he stood behind her.

To Sephanie's right was Blaisey, then Judah. Each of them was clearly armed and gazing into the eyes of a man, or beast, that wished to do them harm.

For Judah, who was being heckled by a group of three slovenly gentlemen, none of which had any of their natural teeth left, it was becoming quite tiresome. Luckily, his photographic memory and selective hearing worked in his favor this time. "Beta six, okay. Got 'em, Coach."

"On my mark," Sephanie said, turning her weapon over in her hands. Before she could make her move, a loud, crunching noise from the forest behind them alerted the three sides to another entrant to the battle.

From out behind the brush came a magnificent gray stallion, dressed in full military garb. The horse's rider, General Andrew Jackson, had already drawn his sword and now eyed the group with an intense desire.

Rolland could see that Jackson carried a sidearm, a bow and a quiver full of arrows with him. With the pirates cutting them off on the right, and the Elemenos marching slowly toward their band from the left, Jackson's forces entered the fray hastily, not realizing that they themselves were surrounded by hostiles.

Despite all of this, Jackson rode on toward the beach, toward Rolland. With his sword raised high and the sun rising behind his back, Jackson stood up in the stirrups as he galloped toward them, eyes filled with wild abandonment.

"Blaisey, you've got Jackson," Sephanie directed under her breath so that only her allies could hear her. "Judah you've got the hardest job, so be ready!"

"Fan-fucking-tastic," said Judah, tightening his grip on the hilt of his dagger.

As the circle grew tighter around them, each beleaguered companion readied themselves for the inevitable confrontation.

"Now!" Sephanie shouted, and they each sprang into action.

Six Beta, otherwise known as a 'Hail Mary' plan, is a last ditch attempt to redeem a win for your team at the last second of play by doing something both effective and shocking. In the case of our travelers, this first meant establishing who was covering who.

Judah, knowing full well that the pirates would be following his every move, did not run straight toward them. He instead took four large paces backward before running behind the other three to launch an offensive on the line of Elemenos approaching Rolland. The pirates instinctively ran in the same direction, coming sword to sword with American cavalrymen and their bayonet blades.

Like Judah, Sephanie launched an offensive of her own, though not at the Americans who stood before her. Instead she launched herself into the conflict between the pirates and Americans on the other side of Rolland, stabbing one of each and causing more havoc between the two sides.

Sensing their cues, Rolland and Blaisey launched themselves into the fray as well, directly in the line of fire between the two remaining pockets of Elemenos and pirates not fighting the American soldiers.

For Blaisey, fighting men was not a new experience. Aside from having an older brother, she had met her husband at a young age and grown up wrestling with him. These men, though white, were no different in their techniques. They might have been easier in fact, given that not a single one of them appeared to be completely sober. Using her superior intellect and the fighting skills her father had taught her as a child, she successfully fought off half a dozen of the pirates with relative ease before Jackson was close enough to attack.

Jumping off of his horse as it approached the water, Jackson lunged directly at Rolland. Blaisey intervened, aiming the dagger in her left hand and letting it fly on a direct path toward the General's neck.

Seeing the sun's reflection off of the dagger's steel, Jackson turned in time to deflect it with his own sword, both weapons falling to the ground nearby. Landing hard on his side, Jackson rolled out of the line of fire and removed his two pistols, pointing them directly at Rolland.

"I've got you now you little shi..." Jackson said, as his eyes rolled back into his head and he fell unconscious into the sand.

Directly behind the falling Jackson stood a very large, very dirty-looking bearded man wearing what appeared to be a bed sheet doubling as both his headdress and his shirt. He carried with him a large wooden club quite like what a stereotypical caveman would drag around for protection.

"Run!" Blaisey screamed to Rolland over the noise of the battle as the large, oddly-dressed pirate approached him, swinging his club wildly along as he went. Sand, debris, and people flew effortlessly through the air as the wooden club missed its mark each time Rolland dodged a fresh attack.

Realizing what a bad runner he was on sand, Rolland zigzagged around Judah and Sephanie, heading inland and hoping to draw the large pirate with him. Though his plan worked, it had the unintended effect of leaving Sephanie in the club's path as he ran past her. Not having any time to stop, Rolland kept onward, leading the large pirate past every Elemeno or American he could get close to.

Rushing to Sephanie's side, Judah quickly helped her up and out of the way of American gunfire. The air was filled with dust raised by the large pirates club, and they were both temporarily blinded, leaving both Knights easy prey for any would-be assassin.

"Bloody hell!" Judah let out, rubbing his eyes with both hands. "Think I dropped me cigarettes."

Perhaps if he had been able to see, he would have noticed the large pirate carrying the club double back and head right for them. As it stood, that was not the case.

Assured of Sephanie's safety, Judah hit his knees and began crawling around for his lost pack of Lucky Strikes, hoping to take the edge off of the situation. Though he was nearly blind, he was determined, like all addicts.

"Me cigarettes!" Judah said, bending down a little more just in time to run into the large wooden club swinging centimeters from his ear. Instantaneously knocked unconscious, Judah fell forward into the sand, dropping his cigarettes and losing them once more.

This time, the hairy man carrying the club decided to focus on Judah's legs, raising the large club over his head and bringing it crashing down onto the sand where Judah's legs had been a moment before.

"No reasoning with you, eh?" Judah said, rolling over in the sand and attempting to get up. This proved very challenging, as the handle of the hairy man's club met the middle of Judah's forehead, leaving the self-proclaimed smartest man in the world unconscious in the sand.

The dust still settling, the large, hairy pirate pulled the bandana atop his head down to cover his mouth and nose before he went to work. He retrieved a long piece of rope from one of his front pockets, and wrapped it around both of Judah's legs numerous times before tying the ends together. This created a sort of handle he could use to drag the man's body along the beach and back into the water.

Perhaps if Judah had still been awake, he would have heard Blaisey's pleas as two other Barbary pirates held her down and a third removed a long strand of rope not dissimilar to the one his colleague had used on Judah's feet.

The old saying goes that misery loves company – a statement acting itself out before Sephanie's very eyes. Looking around her, she could not immediately find Judah or Rolland, but could see Blaisey furiously fighting off the pirates and American troops that were brawling around them. She saw the Seminole girl fight off one, two, three of the pirates before falling down beneath a group of them. She didn't get back up.

Flashes of green dotted the scene as Elemenos fought random individuals throughout the fray, taking out equal numbers of Americans and pirates alike with their razor sharp teeth and cat-like claws. Though their numbers more than doubled that of the pirates or American forces on the Pensacola sand that morning, their inferior intellect and severe mishandling of their weaponry put them at a distinct disadvantage. It was no surprise that their numbers dwindled faster than any other group..

Finding herself at the mercy of the pirates, Blaisey struggled with all of her might against the ropes they were binding her arms with. Next to her, an unconscious Judah was being dragged unceremoniously by his feet across the sand, his arms hanging free behind him, leaving trails in the sand. A moan escaped his lips as he was dragged over a sharp rock. Blaisey saw an opportunity.

Hoping to escape the same fate as Judah, Blaisey rolled over twice until she clasped the rock, roughly the size of a baseball, in her left hand. She then began angling and cutting the ropes with the hastily acquired rock, once again proving to herself the usefulness of nature. Feeling the ropes between her wrists give, she tugged at her bonds, freeing herself before turning her attention to Judah.

Unfortunately for Blaisey, fate had different plans this day. Rounding about, the large pirate carrying his club chose to drop it as he passed by the spot where Blaisey had just cut herself free. Though she managed to avoid being squashed by the massive wooden stick, it pinned her against a stack of fallen Elemenos, obviously shot in quick succession, causing a pile to form. Trapped, Blaisey felt there was little she could do but wait for things to die down and hope that she would be rescued by one of her people.

Her people.

Blaisey was beginning to think of Rolland and his friends as her people. They weren't Nabawoo, or natives of any kind, nor was she particularly fond of any of them besides Rolland, but she couldn't deny that she'd had the thought. Her momentary reverie was disrupted by a stark and ominous sign of disaster.

The ground was vibrating.

The violence broke temporarily as those alive and still fighting on the beach all looked around furiously for answers. Though every face seemed to be wearing the same mask of confused panic, some of the remaining American soldiers shouted to scouts they had left further uphill. Nothing could be seen.

"Ballua!" came the groggy, high-pitched voice of one of the Elemenos as it pointed its furry green paw into the air, one claw extended.

"What is that?" Sephanie asked Rolland, holding the sword in her hands high above her, ready to resume fighting at any moment.

"I have no idea," Rolland said above the commotion all around them.

"Ballua!" a second Elemeno screamed, as his fellow creatures tried unsuccessfully to flee back down the beach they had appeared from. The Americans, with their white eyes and orders given, had other plans. Even the injured Elemenos slowly moved, as the ground vibrated beneath them.

Tree tops shook violently in the distance. Though Blaisey could see this, Rolland and Sephanie couldn't due to the slope of the beach, and rock formation overhead. The sound of snapping tree trunks followed shortly thereafter, alerting everyone to the beast's presence.

A strange tingling feeling crept over Rolland as all the hairs on both of his arms stood upright, followed shortly by those on the back of his neck. Looking over at Sephanie, he could tell that she shared his confusion.

Another vibration in the ground lead to a mass exodus of birds evacuating the forest as Sephanie eyed the tree line suspiciously. Not a single sound could be heard from the winged creatures above them, the noise from trees breaking and men screaming in terror overwhelming everyone still on the beach. The shaking was becoming steadier now, more prominent, as if the cause of the commotion was gaining momentum, or getting closer.

Both assumptions turned out to be true. The beast that the Elemenos had called Ballua emerged from the forest with thunderous fanfare, pawing at the sand and scooping up heaps of dying Elemenos in its wake. Thrashing its head around, it surveyed the entirety of the beach, ignoring the dozens of men and Elemenos attacking its feet with their knives, swords, and bayonets. Not a single weapon left so much as a scratch on the creature's thick, armored hide.

Rolland immediately recognized the beast as the same one that Vilthe had sent to attack him outside of the bookstore. Seeing it again, Rolland's eyes immediately shot to its front right paw, the one he had stabbed days earlier. There, in the middle of its simultaneously fury and scaly paw was the knife wound that he had given the creature days before.

"Excusez moi," said a slow, booming voice from above the destruction. The large pirate who had been carrying the club stood tall as he spoke to Ballua, moving closer to the creature with each syllable. Completely unarmed, the pirate reached behind his head and undid the sheet that formed his headdress and shirt, allowing it to fall freely around his waist. It revealed a completely bald head and a large, hairless chest covered in scars of every shape and size.

Ballua wasted no time in eliminating the short distance separating it and the more than seven-foot-tall, bald pirate. It towered over him and roared, loud and unforgiving, but the large man seemed unphased. On the contrary, the large, bald pirate looked almost serene as he cracked his knuckles and readied himself for the onslaught only moments away. With one almost thoughtless gesture, the beast lifted its massive, scaly paw high into the air. The swing brought with it a gust equal to a gale force wind.

To Rolland's utter and complete shock, the large pirate was not knocked away like the Elemenos that now littered the golden shore. Instead, he caught the Ballua's massive scaly paw in midair with incredible strength and poise. The Greek story of Atlas sprang to the forefront of Rolland's mind as he watched the two strong-willed mammoths go head to head for the right to claim the beach for their masters.

With gritted teeth, both the tall, bald pirate and the beast struggled to assert their will. Ballua began to lose its footing, lifting its injured front leg off the ground in an attempt to gain leverage, relying on its two back legs for support. The bald pirate too re-shifted his concentration of muscle use, though he was shaking badly under the weight of his own strength.

With a final push, the man overpowered Ballua, lifting the creature's limb up over his head and tossing it aside. Without warning, Ballua whipped its tail around, knocking the bald pirate off his feet, and flat onto his back. Believing its prey to be down and out, Ballua immediately capitalized on the situation, extending its massive claws outward before raising them menacingly.

The pirate shot up to his feet and without a second thought, punched Ballua as hard and as square in what he believed to be the creature's chest as possible. The ferocity of the knockout punch sent the beast flying backward through the air towards the open water. Ballua's tail whipped madly, wrapping itself around the bald pirate's midsection, claiming him as it clung on to its would be victim.

Once airborne, the pair flew a few hundred yards past the visible horizon before a single, solitary splash let both Rolland and Sephanie know that the beast, along with the ridiculously strong, bald pirate, were gone. All that could be heard were the natural sounds of the ocean, which had been absent since their arrival nearly half an hour ago.

The few American soldiers that remained fighting did so mainly with pirates, all of the Elemenos having either fled or died in Ballua's attack.

Rolland turned toward Sephanie with a look of surreal disbelief that mirrored her own. Neither had time to voice their concerns; they were interrupted by a loud scream behind them.

"Yaaaaaah!" the bleeding Jackson roared, drawing his bow into firing position and loading an arrow from the quiver on his back.

The years of practice had made the General a quick draw, giving neither Rolland nor Sephanie any time to launch a counteroffensive.

"Rolland…" Sephanie said, as her hand sprang out to find his.

Their touch, though unexpected, seemed to give Rolland a second wind, filling him with a confidence he had never felt before. It was odd, though fulfilling in a way he could not quite define. He looked over at Sephanie, hoping that she would find comfort in his gaze, but her face displayed none of the cheer that their entwined hands had given Rolland. All he saw in her eyes was terror, fear, and worry.

The weakness Jackson perceived in joined affection peaked his curiosity enough to make eye contact with Rolland as he sighted the arrow to Sephanie's chest, his lips quivering into a dishonest smile.

Rolland immediately decided that he would deal with the consequences of his actions after Sephanie's safety was assured; though had he given some thought to what might happen should he intervene, he might have saved himself a world of hurt and trouble.

"Hey, Andrew!" Rolland screamed over the few individuals still fighting around them. "You suck!"

The smile on Jackson's face disappeared as the General turned his face to Rolland. His hands didn't move a millimeter, just his finger as he loosed the arrow.

As the arrow flew through the air toward Sephanie, Rolland felt genuine gratitude that he possessed this particular ability instead of Victor's super strength or Turtledove's ghost talking. Releasing Sephanie's hand, Rolland 'snap clapped' his fingers and hands, closing his eyes, and concentrating on slowing time down to a slow motion version of itself.

To Rolland's pleasant surprise, it did. Wasting no time, he walked briskly toward the arrow and tried moving it with his left hand. It wouldn't budge.

"What?" Rolland said out loud to himself as he again attempted to force the arrow off its trajectory. Confused, frustrated, and estimating that the arrow only had another foot or so to go before the girl of his dreams became a shish kabob, Rolland weighed his options quickly.

Sephanie would not move beyond her slow momentum, and neither would Jackson, or the sand surrounding them. It was almost as if someone had suddenly imposed new rules about altering things when time was slowed down, like some cosmic force wanted Sephanie to be killed, a thought too frightful for Rolland to contemplate in that moment. All he could do, is seemed, was watch them watching him, or at least what they must have known was a blur of him moving amongst them.

"Why won't anything move?!" Rolland shouted out loud, hoping for another unaffected superhuman like Turtledove to waltz in and assist him. Unfortunately, he knew deep down that he wasn't going to be so lucky this time. Now, the burden of responsibility fell on Rolland's shoulders alone. Sink or swim, it was all him.

With each minute, the arrow inched closer and closer to Sephanie's heart, threatening to shove it's vindictive, pixie-stick-sized body straight through her. Perhaps it was Sephanie's summoning of the wind, or Jackson's adamant refusal to be defeated, but something in the situation had to give, and quickly.

Rolland, keenly aware that time was running out, set his mind on an incredibly noble but foolish plan to ensure Sephanie's safety. He looked around for the bag that Sephanie had been carrying with them, finding it lodged between a pair of Elemenos who were both badly beaten, but still fighting each other tooth and nail for the bag's contents. He pried it from between them and brought it to where Sephanie stood, placing it next to her feet in hopes that she would get the message that he was trying to send about the healing water within.

Looking into her sparkling green eyes, Rolland saw his own reflection against the sunlight, the same gentle rays that had woken Sephanie up that morning. Her eyes were elegant in their imperfections, and seemed to both create and decide the future of the young man who gazed into them longingly.

Snapping his fingers, Rolland took one last look at Jackson before bringing both of his palms together with a loud smack, closing his eyes and waiting for the inevitable.

Time corrected itself, and suddenly battle raged once more.

Rolland, however could not see it, for he had closed his eyes out of fear. No sane person, he reasoned, would do what he was about to do, and therefore he wanted to pretend it was all a dream. An insane, adventurous, gone on too long dream, and when he awoke he would be healed, good as new. Or dead. Either way, he wouldn't have to watch as other people made decisions for him. He was sick of watching, sick of the lack of control, sick of being lied to. Purgatory or not, it was time to take control.

Jackson's face was a mixture of confusion and gratification as he looked at the impaled teenager who had been ruining his campaign for days, watching the boy come to terms with his last remaining moments on this Earth. The General got to his feet, dropped his bow, and ran back into the forest, leaving behind more carnage in one hour than he had inflicted upon Florida that entire year.

Sephanie was again blinded, this time not by sand but by a thick, warm liquid - the blood of the boy suddenly standing in front of her, Rolland Wright.

Chapter 19:
Time's Arrow

The red splatter that filled the air washed over Sephanie like a tidal wave. At first, Sephanie didn't understand why she couldn't see out of her left eye. Stumbling forward, Sephanie stretched out both of her hands to get her bearings. Out of the corner of her good eye, she could see a dark figure standing over her, sheltering her from harm.

Her hand instinctively found its way to her eye, eagerly and she tried desperately to eliminate the obstruction and survey the scene around her. The noise was intensifying all around her, but whoever was standing in front of her was blocking everything, giving her a much needed moment to compose herself.

Sephanie's eyes, once cleared, left her free to thank the man guarding her. Because he had always been the one in the right place at the right time in the past, she expected to see Turtledove, and her first inclination was to thank her mentor.

"Thank you, Turtledo..." Sephanie said, but stopped short as she felt the fine point of the arrow protruding from the man's back. Her heart sank as her vision began to focus and she saw the hairline of her savior.

"Oh, no," Sephanie whispered, as Rolland fell to his knees in the sand.

Rolling Rolland onto his left side, Sephanie moved closer to him to assess the damage. The wooden arrow had pushed cleanly through his lower abdomen, a mere centimeters to the right of his kidney.

As she made her way out from under the pile of pirate bodies, Blaisey saw Sephanie crouched over him and rushed to her friend's side.

"Wha – what happened?" Sephanie heard Blaisey's voice from over her shoulder.

"You've got to help me get him out of here!" Sephanie pleaded, but Blaisey just stood there, shell-shocked, staring as Rolland spilled his lifeblood into the sand.

"What, what happened?" Blaisey again asked, unable to pull herself from the moment.

"Hey!" Sephanie yelled, snapping her fingers at the Seminole girl, freeing her from her panicked daze. "I need you here, ok?"

"Yeah," Blaisey said, kneeling down to look Sephanie in the eye.

Together they dragged Rolland roughly fifty feet off to the side of the beach, desperately trying not to move the arrow still lodged in his abdomen, managing to move him underneath a small, three-walled rock shelter. A trail of blood followed them.

"Hold his arms apart," Sephanie said, running her hands along the shaft of the arrow on either side of Rolland, trying to decide where to make the break. "It's really important you don't let his hands touch, alright?"

Not able to face Rolland, Sephanie broke off the tip of the arrow first. Even unconscious, the sharp movement sent him into a fit of agony, and Blaisey had to struggle to keep his hands apart.

"He's strong," Blaisey said, using the full weight of her body to hold Rolland's arms apart. "How did you know he would try to move his hands?"

"Because that's how he controls time," Sephanie said, picking loose splinters off of the arrow where the barbed tip had been. She grasped it tightly to keep it from causing more damage as she set to work on the other side. "That's how he brought us here."

"I thought he said that a machine, a dream something, brought you all here?" Blaisey asked, still struggling against Rolland's arms.

"The Dream Phoenix. Yes, but it could only take us so far. He's the one who directed it, navigating the way safely," Sephanie said, slightly jiggling the front of the arrow a bit to get a feel for its give. This action elicited another painful groan from the semi-conscious Rolland as she broke each of the arrow's two fletchings off of the end which was sticking out from Rolland's back. This action left the arrow as nothing more than a wooden stick attached to a flint head

A cry rang out from nearby as Joan fought anything with two legs in an attempt to find her husband. Sephanie felt an obligation to help her best friend, but she couldn't leave Rolland here to die.

Then a thought popped into Sephanie's head. A dangerous, possibly deadly idea that could get her into a world of trouble. On the other hand, if it worked she would be able to save the last remaining member of the Wright family.

Slipping her hand into the knapsack, Sephanie removed the shiny silver flask that Judah had used to collect a sample of the healing water from the cave and handed it to Blaisey. "Here, take it. I have to go."

Blaisey accepted the flask, but was at a loss as to what to do. "What do I do first, I..." she asked, but Sephanie was already gone, leaving them alone to fend for themselves.

She turned around to access the damage to Rolland's wounds, but what Blaisey found was not the half-dead young man she had left lying there comatose only moments before. It seemed that Rolland had not only woken up, but was on his feet, actively pacing back and forth looking for a solution to the large chunk of wood sticking out of his stomach.

"Help me," Rolland pleaded, holding onto a nearby tree for balance. "Please!"

Late to the scene of the beach front battle was the caravan of horses carrying Turtledove, Joan, Tina, Nahoy, and Charlton of the Nabawoo tribe. Approaching a precipice overlooking the beach, the group stopped long enough to look over the cliff and see the carnage that had preceded them.

"Oh, no," Tina spoke first, bringing her hand to her mouth as she bent down to retrieve the silver lining of what looked like Lucky Strike cigarettes in the sand.

"Turtledove, how could this have happened?" Joan asked, her horse twisting wildly beneath her.

"Do not fear Joan, I'm sure your husband is fine," Turtledove said, extending his free hand to her.

His gesture fell short; it was not comfort that Joan sought, but answers. Dismounting, Joan walked the short distance to Tina and grabbed the girl roughly by the top of her shirt, dragging her off her horse.

"Where is he?" Joan demanded of Tina, who was still half on her horse, in a sideways, nearly upside down position, similar to someone mid-cartwheel.

"Hey, what's your...?" Tina began, but the taller blonde woman cut her off, hell-bent on getting the information she needed.

"I know you can hear people!" Joan yelled, grabbing Tina's hair forcefully and dragging her back to eye level. "Now where is my husband!?"

"Joan Rothouse Raines!" Turtledove said, shocked and overcome by Joan's sudden violent outburst.

The dozen or so Nabawoo spectators didn't move a muscle, recalling Joan's formidable display of superiority in the ring the evening before.

"There, that way – toward the ocean!" Tina screamed as Joan shook her violently.

Apparently satisfied, Joan released Tina and hopped back up on her horse, taking off down the path that led down to the beach, leaving the safety of the group behind.

"She had the right idea, Turtledove," Nahoy said, pulling slightly on his horse's reins. "We should split into two groups. We can find them faster that way."

Realizing that he had very little choice in the matter, Turtledove reluctantly agreed, on the condition that Nahoy take Tina and a sizeable force with him. Turtledove commanded the left side of the beach while Nahoy took the right.

Minutes passed as Turtledove and his borrowed Nabawoo archers patrolled the coastline to no avail. It was not until nearly half an hour later, after the two groups had reunited back at the over-look, that Tina saw the ships set sail further down the coast.

"That's them!" Tina nearly screamed as she ran to the edge of the rocky cliff. Without the slightest trepidation she ran down the path to the sandy shore, searching for something only her heart could define.

Without another viable option, Turtledove went after her, leaving his company of men as well as his weapons behind.

"It has to come out," Blaisey said with one hand resting firmly upon Rolland's shoulder.

Rolland was filled with rage and regret, but he could not bring himself to look at his abdominal wound. Using his fingers, he slumped down next to a tall oak tree and cautiously felt around the arrow jutting out of the front of him. A quick inspection of his lower back revealed the other end of the arrow, breaking his otherwise smooth skin into a painful starburst of flesh. His eyes were wet, and filled to the brim with an unspeakable hatred for Jackson, Vilthe, and the entire state of Florida.

"Seph, where's Sephanie?" Rolland asked, breathing as hard as he could with the foreign object in his body. The panic was so intense that he fell over onto his side, getting sand in his already parched mouth.

"She's alive," Blaisey said, hoping that he would pass out again before...

"Where, where is?" Rolland said, writhing in agony on the ground. The explosion of American cannon fire attempting to stop the pirates from fleeing back to their ship drowned out the soft words of the mortally wounded boy.

"She left," Blaisey said, believing that even in his final moments Rolland deserved to hear the truth. "You saved her, and she left."

The sand was like a plague in its unforgiving treatment of the wounded who had the misfortune to find themselves in Rolland's position mid-battle. Its fine grains tore like small insults in every bit of exposed flesh as he twisted wildly in an attempt to find comfort. He could feel the vibrations from cannon fire and galloping horses pulsing through ground beneath him, but for Rolland, the battle was over. He had lost; Jackson had won. The news of Sephanie's abandonment, so like his parents, was the straw that broke the proverbial camel's back. He had just enough energy to see one last thing thorough.

"Owwww," Rolland bellowed, stretching his right arm outward onto the sand and bringing his legs in front of him to a kneel that quickly turned into the fetal position.

Blaisey's attention was focused on searching for a way past Jackson and his American soldiers - to get Rolland to safety so he could die in peace. When she turned around, however, she was quite surprised to find Rolland gone. If it were not for the trail of blood, she would not have known how to find him.

"Rolland!" Blaisey said, finding him standing nearby, swaying a little as he stared dead on into the large, solid tree.

Rolland turned slightly and found Blaisey's gaze with his own red, bloodshot eyes. His face was pale and expressionless. The fury, the hurt, the lies, the abandonment, it was all in the past. For him, life now centered around one goal, getting the arrow the hell out of his stomach.

Taking off as unexpectedly as he had arrived in Florida, Rolland started into a light jog that quickly became an all-out run.

It took several moments for Blaisey to realize what Rolland was doing. Perhaps it was because he desired a running start, or maybe he thought his body's natural momentum would expedite the process. Either way, after running full pace for about twenty yards Rolland Wright threw both of his arms to his side and made full, head on impact with the large tree that stood before him, forcing the arrow straight through his chest, and popping out behind his back enough for him to pull the rest of the way.

"Ooowww…" Rolland managed to say, before allowing himself to fall over, dropping the arrow beside him, and closing his eyes for what he truly believed to be the last time.

When driven by the proper motivation, the human body can accomplish incredible things. For Joan, the determination to find her husband sped her through a marathon sprinting session along every nook, plateau, and marshland that Western Florida had to offer. With the ease and training of a master scout, she was able to avoid every danger that crossed her path - from artillery fire, to a band of five stray hypnotized soldiers. As she passed, Joan kept her eyes locked on the bunch, each of which was stepping in time with the man before him.

For the rest of Joan's life, she would be unsure as to how she should feel about what transpired next. As she ran by the huddled mass of soldiers on her right, each of the heads turned to watch her go, almost as if by command, at once. Normally this sort of attention would warrant a sincere 'at-a-boy' in regard to personal grooming and fitness, but not this day, and not for Joan Raines.

Dodging the suddenly transfixed bunch of soldiers, Joan turned the corner leading to the final plateau distracted, crashing head first into a group of American cavalry men led by General Jackson himself. The General's large, wooden stick conveniently found its way to Joan's gut as she rounded the bend, sending her to the ground in anguish.

"What have we here?" Jackson asked, dismounting from his horse and approaching Joan, whose only concern was her lungs, as they screamed to survive. He approached her cautiously at first, as one would a dangerous wild animal in the final throws of death.

Jackson bent down onto one knee and found Joan's gaze.

"My dear, what say you?" Jackson asked, extending his hand to the blonde second in command of the Knights of Time.

Joan fought to inhale once again before reaching up, accepting Jackson's hand, and using his weight to raise herself off of the ground.

"Go to hell," Joan managed to say before gasping again and delivering an upper cut to Jackson's chin.

Joan fought with all of her might, her mastery of the ballet of warfare evident to even the most casual observer. With a round-house kick to the temple of the soldier on her right, and a clothes-line delivered with relative ease to the one on her left, she practiced her art with a grace possessed by few warriors throughout history.

Yet, as it is with so many conflicts, their numbers finally caught up with her and Joan was subdued. She soon found herself in bondage, one hand shackled behind her back and the American soldiers fighting to get the other to join it. While this hindered the commander, it worked to someone else's advantage.

Without warning or provocation, three American privates standing guard around the area drew their sabers and walked toward Jackson with an increasing veracity. One by one they began unbuttoning their shirts and casting them aside, revealing their tattooed native skin to the hypnotized onlookers. If only Jackson's trust in his men has been stronger, they could have warned him of the infiltrator's assassination attempt before it was too late.

The first assassin went after the four soldiers who held Joan, stabbing two of them before falling to their comrades and being beaten to death. A similar fate befell the second, who made it within ten feet of Jackson before three arrows from an unseen bow appeared in the man's chest.

Only the third assassin reached Jackson; only the blade on his dagger would know the taste of Jackson's blood, the true measure of his character in battle. Making his way past the fallen, he was able to engage the still mounted Jackson enough to disarm the General by sheer strength alone before subduing him and going to work. He stabbed Jackson in the side twice, puncturing his kidney, before starting on his scalp. His blade was rusty, and had seen many buffalo hunts without being washed. Still, his mission was to kill, the claim of taking Jackson's life was about to be his - a great victory in the world of violent warfare.

A nearby Joan watched this in horror as the historical ramifications came into perspective. With one hand still free, Joan held four fingers out and tightened them before using the hand gesture as one would a punch aimed at her remaining guard's throat. As he fell, she raced to Jackson's side, the nearly three-foot-long chain shackled to her left hand dragging behind her. With a great force, she body-checked the unsuspecting assassin away from Jackson, knocking the weapon out of his hand, and directly into the arms of six American troops, all of which were suddenly back in command of their own faculties.

The dying Jackson lay sprawled out on the dusty ground, blood pouring from his mouth, head, and side. He pointed toward the bag that lay a mere ten feet away from him, the one he had taken into the cave.

Joan saw this, and after shaking loose the cavalryman grasping at her, ran over to the satchel and picked it up, one hand still shackled behind her back.

Arriving at Jackson's side, Joan tossed open the bag to reveal its contents - books, a journal, and a flask. With no bible, and no explicit instructions, Joan could not figure out what it was the dying Jackson was yearning for with the precious few moments he had left on Earth.

Joan picked up the flask, unscrewed the lid, and handed it to the dying soldier in hopes that he found some comfort in its contents before he passed on to the next world.

Turning the flask over, Jackson poured its entire contents on his scalp, in his mouth, and over his wounds before throwing it to aside and resting his head in the dirt. A hissing noise filled the air as every one of the holes on Jackson's flesh mended themselves within a matter of seconds.

For all the glorious things she had witnessed within her lifetime, nothing compared to the instantaneous healing that took place before Joan's eyes.

Two of Jackson's men stepped forward to assist him to his feet before escorting him out of sight.

In shock, Joan was taken to the side of a large cart and placed alongside several men and women also in chains. They stood there for hours as Jackson's fate was decided. The afternoon sun and the humid Florida air beat down on them with a merciless force that demanded their respect as entities in their own right, as if they, too, had been taken captive by Jackson's oppressive regime.

Finally, Andrew Jackson emerged from a newly erected medical tent, his left arm was in a sling, but his stab wounds were completely healed, as if they had never been there at all. His scalp was also intact, miraculously repaired and good as new. Though he appeared to be walking with a slight limp, there was no indication that he wouldn't be posing for the twenty dollar bill any time soon. With a simple nod to a nearby awaiting officer, the General was handed a ceremonial sword before walking calmly back to his attacker, who was being pinned down by eight different servicemen, all back under Jackson's hypnosis.

"Nah cheap, hie awatu Nahoy," the native assassin said, just before Jackson plunged the tip of his sword into the man's neck.

Standing over the man, the future President of the United States used his free palm to break past the last ounce of force separating the tip of his blade and the ground below. Looking deep into the man's eyes, General Andrew Jackson relished every second as the dark brown panic in the assassin's eyes became a dull haze of white.

"Any more savages that need to be dealt with?" a bloodthirsty Jackson asked, still brandishing the blade he had just used to kill the man who had scalped him.

"Yes, general, three more," said one of Jackson's lieutenants, followed by a small processional complete with nearly a dozen more armed soldiers, all of their weapons drawn and aimed at their captives, Nahoy and Charlton of the Nabawoo tribe and the British officer who had helped Victor escape, Ambrister, who was not lucky enough to be assisted in his escape attempts by the mysterious men in black bodysuits.

"Kill us now, then," Charlton said, almost as a demand to be executed before suffering further indignation.

"Oh no. No, no, no," Jackson said, shaking his head and holding his left side where he had been stabbed a few hours before. "It's a public execution for you. For all of you."

Hearing this, and knowing full well how serious he was, Joan decided to speak up and remind Jackson of the miracle that had just saved his life.

"Do you know what we have in common, General?" Joan asked, looking up at the rogue who had handed her husband off to pirates and now held her and her Seminole allies captive. Her attempt to draw his vengeful eye off of Nahoy was predicated on his inability to resist beautiful women.

"What would that be, my dear?" Jackson asked, stroking Joan's blonde hair as one would a cat, but in a creepy, possessive manner.

"Orleans," Joan said with a smug smile.

"My lady — I had no idea," Jackson said, dropping Joan's hair, stepping away, and bowing deeply to her. "I had my suspicions about you people before, but once I learned who you all were, well..."

"So you will let me go then?" Joan asked, biting her lower lip in a half-nervous, half-flirtatious gesture toward her moderately attractive but completely overbearing captor. "Out of respect?"

"Oh, dear me, no, of course not," Jackson said laughing a bit. "No, no, you will be a slave. Maybe one of mine, eh?"

With that chauvinist comment, Jackson walked off toward his horse, leaving Joan to be dragged roughly by her handcuffs like an ox or cow. She was placed in the back of a cart next to multiple other individuals, mostly captured runaway slaves and captive native women. All was not lost though, as fate delivered a small gift. Sitting beside her, in a state very similar, stood her friend and teammate, Sephanie Kelly.

"They got you too, huh?" Joan said to her gagged friend, who merely nodded her head in agreement. As the cart took them to their ultimate destination, Sephanie's thoughts could not help but wander back to Rolland and how he was probably dead.

"To the compound," Jackson ordered his lieutenants, all of whom stood at rigid attention, eyes glossed over and mouths hanging open. "Take the women with us."

Blaisey refused to leave Rolland to die. Although there was nothing she could physically do since the wound was too deep to heal, the Seminole Princess could not accept that her great grandson had traveled so far, only to end up dead.

Suddenly, figures like the outlines of silhouettes started to appear around the enclave as if from nowhere. Blaisey at once recognized them as the individuals who had freed her from her restraints at the American camp the night before. Their presence was welcome last night, but now they looked rather spooky, covered head to toe in pure black cloth.

They all stopped moving and joined shoulders in what appeared to be a military formation. One of the men dressed in black emerged from behind the others and stepped toward Blaisey. He was large, larger than the others by at least a foot, making his body suit appear on the very edge of comical with about six inches of his ankle exposed. He had brown skin.

Removing his mask, the hooded vigilante crouched down beside the two of them and looked Blaisey directly in the eyes. Smiling, he said, "Hello. My name is Victor. That little guy is a friend of mine."

Chapter 20: Request Denied

When she arrived at the bottom of the narrow hill leading to the beach, Tina noticed that there wasn't as much activity going on. In fact, there was no longer any activity going on at all. Where just an hour before Rolland had taken an arrow to the gut for Sephanie, the beach lay empty of life, but cluttered with junk.

"We're too late," Tina said, her eyes watering as she stepped over yet another corpse - a man missing all of his teeth. This one, at least, had been wearing all of his clothes at the time of death.

"Not for our people," Turtledove said, crouching down and picking up a large handful of sand. It slipped through his fingers as he closed his eyes and concentrated on it. He could feel the turmoil and surprise that the souls who were here an hour ago were saturated in shortly before their deaths. Yet all of their signatures were foreign to him, meaning that none who died were Travelers of Light. This bit of good news elevated his spirits slightly as he opened his eyes and looked at his youngest protégé.

"Where did they go then?" Tina asked, her big, blue eyes tearing up under the pressure of the moment. She knew Turtledove's empathic abilities allowed him to sense the emotions of others, but she wasn't sure if it applied in their particular situation. Her cheeks grew wet as she looked around fervently.

"Judah went to the sea, like you said," Turtledove told her, scooping up another handful of the sand and looking in the direction that Judah was dragged off in. "I'm guessing against his will. I'm sure Joan will already be on that though, so we need not worry."

"I don't care about Judah!" Tina said bluntly, causing Turtledove to turn back to her. "Where is Rolland?!"

Rolling the tiny particles of sand between his thumb and forefinger, Marcus Turtledove found the answer he was looking for, though he wished he hadn't. He stood up and walked toward the section of beach, where a dark crimson trail of blood belonging to the youngest Wright stained the Florida shore for seven feet before disappearing.

"Oh no…" said Tina, burying her face in her hands. "That's Rolland's isn't it?"

"Yes," Turtledove said, bending over to examine it. "Shot with an arrow, it appears. There is enough blood here to be fatal."

Hearing the word 'fatal' seemed to bring Tina to the brink of hysteria. Her panic would be short-lived, however, as high on the hillside above them the last Nabawoo soldier from Nahoy's forces came wobbling into view, his leg sporting a large bullet wound. The tale he told them was full of death and heartache, ending with the capture of both Nahoy and Charlton. The Nabawoo were now leaderless.

The hooded man who had identified himself as Victor took another step toward Blaisey as she huddled over Rolland. The fact that Rolland had not been able to find closure for the wounds of his past lay heavy on her heart - a worry that quickly morphed into something else upon further contemplation.

"Can you read my thoughts?" Blaisey asked, realizing how foolish she must have sounded to this strange man. "Like your older friend, the one who can become a spirit when he wants to?"

"Oh, Turtledove?" Victor asked with surprise. "No, I'm not like him. I'm no empath."

Not content with his answer, Blaisey crowded closer to Rolland's lifeless body, irrationally trying to shield him from any danger the man in the hood might pose.

"Please," Victor continued, taking another cautious step toward them. "I'm a friend of his. Let me help."

"If you're a friend of his, then where is your ring?" Blaisey asked, one hand shielding Rolland's head in a maternal attempt to protect.

"My what?" Victor asked, the circle of hooded figures still slowly closing in around them.

"Your time travelling ring!" Blaisey balked at him, but was met with a genuinely blank stare. "Never mind."

"Wait, do you mean the silver ring that the kid was wearing?" Victor asked, tilting his head to one side and raising an eyebrow.

"Yeah," Blaisey stammered, feeling quite foolish and superstitious. It was obvious by the look on the man's face that she had made a wild assumption and either Sephanie or Judah had lied to her.

"You think that's what let him time travel?" Victor asked, not able to suppress a small laugh as he spoke.

"It's not?" Blaisey asked him in genuine curiosity. She decided to forgive the stranger's rudeness. She was a princess of the Nabawoo tribe, but it occurred to her that in that moment she probably looked less than regal. Although her experience with Africans had been limited, she had never seen them as nearly as large a threat as the white men. An odd thought indeed, considering her current state of duress was inspired by concern for one of them.

"No, no, Princess, that isn't what allowed him to bring us all here." Victor replied, his smile fading as he walked closer and sat down beside Rolland's nearly lifeless form.

"Then what did?" Blaisey asked, confused as to what it was that Jackson and Vilthe were after if it hadn't been the ring that Rolland was wearing. She looked at Victor, studying the lines on his face and searching for any sign of dishonesty or malice.

"A need for revenge," Victor said, placing his hand on Rolland's, and looking at the young man's deathly pale face. "Natural talent, and an instinct to survive."

Given Judah and Sephanie's obvious desire for secrecy, Blaisey had not expected such a level of honesty from Victor. It was both refreshing and terribly depressing all at once.

"I don't think we've officially met," Blaisey said, holding out her hand to her new favorite of Rolland's friends. "I'm Blaisey, Princess of the Nabawoo tribe."

Victor smiled and took her hand with his free one, never letting go of Rolland's with the other. "I'm Victor."

The two shook hands and stared at one another and their surroundings as the hours passed, turning afternoon into night, both wishing that they had met under more ideal circumstances, and both suffering the same heartache for the injured boy who had risked his life time and again to save both of theirs in the short time he had been in their lives.

The night was uneventful.

Jackson awoke the next day with a renewed sense of purpose. The morning air felt cool in his lungs and gave him a renewed sense of strength and tranquility. This was his destiny. By cleansing the Earth of the savage filth known as the Seminole people, Jackson would be scoring yet another victory for the American cause.

There is a general consensus among historians that the importance of Andrew Jackson in American history is undeniable. He remains the only president who has an entire era named after him.

This day, however, would go overlooked by all modern historians and remain untold. Such is the way that the Master of Evil does business.

"A fine mess this is," Joan said, beating the dirt off of a blanket. Both she and Sephanie had been imprisoned in a turn of the nineteenth century version of a tacky miniature mansion, formally known as Jackson's personal plantation, modified to his specific tastes. Chief among these modifications from the previous owner was the transformation of one of the back rooms from a guest suite to a dungeon, complete with barred windows, reverse locking doors, and an armed guard standing outside.

"He's not going to kill us," Sephanie said, looking out the cell window at the preparations for the about to take executions about to take place in the field below. "Jackson, I mean."

Ambrister, Nahoy, and Charleston stood on the platform, blindfolded, with their hands tied behind their backs and shackles paralyzing their ankles.

"Well, he is going to kill them," Joan said, sticking her arm out of the barred window as far as it would reach. "For sure."

Sephanie stood next to her and watched as all three men had nooses placed around their necks. "I just wish there was something I could do."

"We'll think of something. We always do," Joan said, attempting to get comfortable on the bed of hay that sat in the corner of the room.

"You know, you could always just sleep on it...?" Sephanie asked her blonde friend, hoping to steer the conversation to Joan's abilities.

"Way ahead of you," said Joan, fluffing up a stack of hay in to a makeshift pillow.

"Oh thank you, thank you so much Joan. I really think it's our best move," Sephanie replied, her face the very definition of the word gratitude.

"Yeah, well, hopefully I'll find some answers," Joan replied, getting as cozy as one can while lying on hay.

"Good luck," Sephanie said, sitting down next to the window. "We could use it."

No sooner had Joan closed her eyes than the clanking of iron announced a guard opening their cell door. He was a plain, skinny fellow with eyes as milky and blank as the day is long.

"You, the brunette," the guard said, pointing at Sephanie. "General Jackson wants to see you."

Joan and Sephanie glanced at each other in astonishment.

"Ask, and ye shall receive," Joan said, raising her eyebrows and pouting her lips in a satisfied smirk.

The guard escorted Sephanie out of the cell, locking the door behind him. Joan was left alone for the first time since arriving in

Florida. This strange thought kept her from sleeping, and for some reason drew her toward the window, toward people.

Though the iron bars that separated Joan from freedom were thick, there was plenty of room to see through them. The window itself was no bigger than the size of a large microwave oven or wall safe, and sat roughly five and a half feet off the ground.

Joan watched as the executioner pulled a long wooden lever, releasing only the trap door beneath the British man, Ambrister. He died immediately, his neck snapping from the sudden shift in gravity. His body hung limp, suddenly deprived of the spark of life. Never again would he see the man he had so desperately pined for.

Nahoy and Charlton jumped at the sound of the trap door, and Joan could only imagine how they felt hearing the sickening snap of Ambrister's neck.

"Ponce, hit the second switch," Jackson said motioning again to the large man in the black mask, who pulled another wooden lever to release the door beneath Charlton, leaving him dangling and choking to death before Joan's eyes.

"Please," Nahoy begged, fighting against his bonds. "Please take me instead."

"Old man…" Jackson whispered threateningly. He leaned in close to Nahoy and waved a hand carelessly over the crowd of people watching. At once, all of their eyes turned milky white under Jackson's hypnosis. After ripping the blindfold off of Nahoy he threw it aside before making it abundantly clear that he didn't wish to force Nahoy like the others, but to break him of his will instead. "You will surrender your land to me. Now."

Nahoy turned sharply to face Jackson, their eyes meeting for the first time since the fog covered battlefield days before. The odd dichotomy of Nahoy's deep brown against Jackson's gray and silver were like two sides of the same soldier's coin.

"I… very well," said Nahoy, breaking their stare and bowing his head in defeat. The fear of losing Charlton was too great a threat for Nahoy to face. He knew that regardless of what happened to him, Charlton was the best hope to lead the Nabawoo people into the future.

Cut free and returned to the pen from where he came, Charlton found himself being pushed and shoved by many hands at once as another convoy of hypnotized soldiers led him away from Jackson. Although he wasn't sure why his life had been spared, he knew a deal must have been struck and was not happy with the possible repercussions for his people. He did not want any more blood on his hands.

It is said that the key to success exists as two parts: half timing and half opportunity. For the roughnecks of the pirating vessel known as *The Dewberry*, they unknowingly found themselves with a large supply of both, for deep within the ship's hull sat the smartest man who had ever lived, shackled to the ship's cargo hold by wrought iron restraints.

Though he was unconscious, Dr. J.J. Raines would soon awake to find the salty taste of sea water on his lips and the chill of cold iron on his wrists. The predicament he was about to wake up to find himself in was unlike any challenge he had ever faced, one of servitude, bondage, and death.

"You know the more I think about it, the more it makes sense," Blaisey said, sitting on both of her legs beside Rolland. "You being my descendent, I mean. Your bravery, chivalry, and complete lack of common sense reminds me of – well, me."

No sooner had the words left her mouth than Blaisey thought of how foolish she must look talking to a nearly dead man. Casting aside such thoughts, Blaisey continued, determined to say her piece before he passed on - an important tradition for her people.

"I just wish you would have told me HOW you were like me." Blaisey said, brushing a tuft of Rolland's wavy, blonde hair away from his eyes. "I have so many questions about my, our, family."

Silence sat between them, hanging in the air like a strobe light reminding Blaisey over and over again that she was the reason Rolland was lying on death's doorstep. If she had just listened to her father and stayed away from that battlefield days ago...

"Grrrrgggghhhhhhhhhhhhhaaaaaaaaaaaaaaaaarrrrr," came one of Victor's ground-trembling snores. He sat propped upright against a large tree, his head slumped over his left shoulder and his mouth wide open. A wet spot had formed on his sleeve where a bit of drool had collected.

Blaisey smiled to herself as she looked at Victor "standing guard". Admitting to herself that she was wrong about him was one thing, but telling him so would be quite another. His loyalty to his friend was unquestionable, and for that he deserved her respect.

"Grrrrgggghhhhhhhhhhhhhaaaaaaaaaaaaaaaaarrrrr," came another snore from the large African man protecting them from harm.

A sudden thought popped into Blaisey's head. A wonderful, life-altering thought so simple and obvious that she was shocked she hadn't thought of it until now: the flask of healing water Sephanie had given her from the cave.

Taking Rolland's head off of her lap and placing it gently onto the dirt floor, Blaisey scooted sideways into a crawling position. From there she made her way to the knapsack on the far side of the wall.

Rummaging inside, Blaisey found the compartment that held the two flasks. She was surprised to find only one flask there, but she was grateful to have found the key to rescuing her great grand-son. She grabbed the remaining flask and opened it with great vigor.

"What are you doing?" Victor asked from behind her, startling Blaisey as she crawled back to Rolland.

"Healing him. Come, watch me," Blaisey said, arriving at Rolland's side. The water inside the flask glistened as it made its way out over the top and onto Rolland's open wound below.

Victor was up and over to where Blaisey sat in three steps. This particular occasion warranted more than just his presence, it demanded his attention.

The clear elixir washed over a gaping hole the size of a golf ball six inches above Rolland's belly button, and the wound immediately began to steam. Hissing, bubbling noises could be heard from the wound. Neither Blaisey nor Victor were paying much attention to that though, for before their very eyes the skin around the gash repaired itself, tying tissue to tissue and replacing the bloody rip with smooth, pale skin.

Victor looked at Blaisey in disbelief. In a matter of seconds she had managed to heal Rolland completely, bringing him back from the edge of death. "Can I get some of that water?"

"We must elect a new leader!" shouted the nearly unanimous Nabawoo warriors over Tina's voice as she explained her plan for retrieving both the Dream Phoenix and their lost knights to Turtle-dove yet again.

For his part, Turtledove was having difficulty concentrating. It wasn't that the girl had bad ideas, just that she was so young and opinionated. Though he had to admit that age had brought as much wisdom as it had a lack of energy, and the thought of teaching Tina all that she needed to know was about as appealing as leading the lost Nabawoo following their leader's abduction. The years had worn on the man that they all knew as Marcus Turtledove, and even the Protector of Eden could not change that fact. Tina would need to find someone else to teach her, someone else to channel her spunk and energy, two traits he had not seen since...

'Not unlike her predecessor,' Turtledove thought to himself, though he would never say such a thing out loud. Not anymore. There seemed to be a changing of the guard among his Knights of Time once again.

"You, my-damn," said Enapay, the Nabawoo warrior making the proclamations, as he pointed to where Tina and Turtledove sat.

In a moment of confusion, Tina smiled bashfully. The color drained from her face as she realized that Enapay and with the other Nabawoo were serious, and addressing her directly. She looked to Turtledove for clarification, but found no reassurance.

"I think he's talking to you," Turtledove said to Tina, grinning at the considerable difference in culture between the two, and the Nabawoo's mispronunciation of the English word 'madam'.

"You for leader," Enapay declared, turning to face the crowd. "Who will vote for this?"

A unanimous groaning and shaking of Seminole sticks told Tina that she had won their version of an election, becoming the defacto leader of the Native American tribe.

"Me?" Tina asked, holding her palm to her chest and tensing her legs: two of the classic signs humans display when about to lose consciousness. Going over the other, more suitable candidates in her mind, she began to realize that they had all been taken hostage, or were feared dead.

"Yes," came the staggered reply from what was left of the Nabawoo Warrior Alliance. The roughly three dozen warriors left all looked toward her with the same apprehensive expressions they had worn when she first spoke to them.

Tina looked back at them and to Turtledove behind her, who was smiling like a proud parent, chasing the thought that this might be some sort of a trick from her mind.

Tina straightened her back, taking a deep breath before she did, and said, "You don't want me. You wouldn't follow me where I'm going."

"Where are you going?" Enapay asked, genuinely interested in Tina's plans.

Marcus Turtledove watched his young intern attempt to dissuade the persistent warriors and smiled to himself. She was a clever one, far more clever than he had given her credit for. He made a vow then and there never to underestimate Tina Leigh Holmes again.

"I think Jackson is just a puppet, working for a much more evil man named Edward Vilthe," Tina said, her cool demeanor and matter-of-fact tone were textbook motivational tactics for would-be leaders - an Academy of Light basic course taught in the first week.

The name Vilthe seemed to illicit a hushed terror from the remaining Nabawoo warriors, who began shuffling and gossiping amongst themselves at the mention of the name.

"As I was saying," Tina said coldly, continuing without reserve. "Vilthe is that tall, skinny man with the bad fashion sense. He controls the Elemenos; the green creatures that captured Nahoy and Charlton. Does everyone follow me so far?"

Heads nodded all around her, and Tina realized she had them hanging on her every word. Her heart was beating a mile a minute as she turned to look at Turtledove, her mentor and guide. The smile he gave her said it all: Tina was now flying by the seat of her pants, and it was either time to reel it in, or let the fish go.

"I say we follow the Elemenos to their master, kill Vilthe, wait for Jackson, and then deal with him ourselves," Tina said, motioning to the machete Enapay was held up to emphasize her point.

"A sneak attack," Enapay said under his breath. "It's brilliant!"

Chapter 21: Hickory

The one-eyed, first generation African American man that Sephanie knew as George led her down a dark and twisted hallway adorned with portraits of famous individuals from the early days of the republic. Though it was too dark for Sephanie to see their faces, she guessed all the better known founding fathers were represented. Jackson was, after all, the last of the presidents to fight in the Revolution, serving at age 17.

Arriving at the end, George made a series of strange movements in the lock before the door inched open. He looked at Sephanie sharply before opening the door for her and gesturing for her to enter. This pleasantry was lost on Sephanie however, her eyes temporarily blinded by the room's light.

"He be rai' wit chu, Miss," George said politely, speaking for the first time.

This prompted an immediate reaction, and Sephanie looked over at him in blind confusion. Though she could only see a bright purple spot where his head was, she was grateful he had finally spoken. What she couldn't see was the downward gaze of the old, blind man as he made his way along, arm extended in front of him.

"Thank you, Geor-," Sephanie said, but it was too late. The kindly slave was gone, and Sephanie felt less human by simply having crossed his path. It made her sick to think a man like Jackson could exist.

Her eyes back in focus and finding herself alone, Sephanie finally had a chance to observe her surroundings. The room wasn't especially large, for an officer of Jackson's caliber: roughly half the size of a basketball court. There was a fire crackling in the corner closest to her. It was an odd choice for Florida, but Jackson struck her as a man who did many things simply for the sake of appearances.

Then something caught Sephanie's eye. A large book sat atop a wooden podium directly opposite a large wooden desk stacked haphazardly with poorly placed papers, maps, and other various tools. From the looks of it, it was a single, brown, leather bound volume with metal clasps and worn out edges.

Sephanie crossed the small distance between her and the book before picking it up. The urge to open it ran through her like a shot of adrenaline, and before Sephanie realized what she was doing, the clasps had been unhinged and the cover opened. By the first page she could already tell that she had guessed correctly – it was Jackson's personal journal.

Hesitant to proceed further into the mind of one of history's greatest monsters, Sephanie stopped for a moment and breathed, filling her lungs and exhaling a cathartic medley of tension, fear, and apprehension. Her fingers traced the edges of the neatly banded pages, hoping to catch the first one.

In a moment of luck, or perhaps well-placed adhesion, Sephanie's finger caught the first page, bringing her to the moment of truth that separates innocent wondering and purposeful snooping. Though true to her nature, her decision had already been made by her actions– she was going for it.

March 8, 1785– Charleston, South Carolina - Morning

Today is my eighteenth birthday. Though it has been nearly four years since Mother's death, the pain has not eased in my heart one bit. I fear it never will.

To commemorate the event, I have left the rough teachings of the wilderness and returned to my Aunt Meridith's estate in Charleston. My reception, while warm, was treated with mild annoyance.

While at the time I hoped our initial awkwardness would subside, I fear to report it has been nearly two weeks now since my arrival and we have made absolutely no progress toward familial bonding. I do not blame my aunt for her resentment of me. Her choice to place the blame for the deaths of my mother, her sister, and my brother Robert on my shoulders is well-founded. They did not die by my own hand mind you, but such is the burden of war, leaving beloved patriots to die in your stead.

I cannot claim that Aunt Meridith has been a rude or inhospitable host. On the contrary, my presence was greeted with a gift – this journal I am writing in now. Truthfully, I am only putting my pen to paper to appease my aunt as she watches me from afar. It is rather difficult to keep a pensive look about oneself through an entire afternoon, but I've managed to do so.

Because I believe I've written enough nonsense, and because I intend to burn this log should I have the opportunity, I will write the true account of something that happened to me this morning that left me nervous and filled with angst.

This morning I awoke early and decided to head down to the barn to take a horse, an activity I had previously declined. Upon entering the barn I noticed that there were about half a dozen horse stalls. Most of the doors were open and only the farthest two held horses.

Walking toward them, I must have been blind to her presence. Such is the way of angels, I suppose.

"Do you ride, sir?" I heard a heavenly voice ask from somewhere behind me.

Turning around, I saw what appeared to be a slave girl, beautiful and chesty, sitting on the ground in the first stall caring for a dying horse. Her slender arms were busy as she groomed the beast with the steady rhythm only earned through years of practice. This seemed to soothe the poor animal as it lay there, subject to the slave girl's gentle attentions.

"Often," I told her, before moving to a position that supplied me with an ample view of her breasts. I guessed her to be somewhere between fourteen and sixteen years of age, but not a day over.

"Then master would be wise to skip riding today," she said to me, her voice full of concern. It was comforting to know that someone cared for my well-being, even if it was only a slave girl.

"I've ridden in strong winds before," I told her, walking closer to her, to the warmth that emanated from her grace. She was pure and humble, everything that my mother attempted to instill in me, everything I had lost since her death. I admired her and desired her all at once.

"Not that," she told me calmly, so as not to startle the dying horse she continued to care for. "Natives are out today, it is a special day in their culture."

In the briefest of moments there came a great change inside of me, one that had me considering dropping not only my gentlemanly guard but also my breeches. Unaccustomed to slaves talking back or giving their opinion on matters, I was tempted to strike her down for her insolent insinuation that I, a proud white man in his peak, could not defend myself against a savage or two. Instead I decided to teach her a different type of lesson, one that would please me much more than raising my hand against her.

"Meet me back here just after night fall," I told her, twisting my face with anger to intimidate her into obeying. "Come alone, understood?"

The slave girl looked shocked and afraid, but had grown up with enough knowledge of the way of things to know better than to offer any objection to my will. She gave me a weak "Yes master," before I turned and walked back to the main house.

While I know it is not generally in the nature of men to dwell on such trivial pursuits, my mind, and therefore this first journal entry, swirls with lustful thoughts of the slave girl who will be waiting for me in the barn this evening.

March 8, 1785 – Evening

Today I am a man.

Her embrace was a question of when, not if.

Bending the slave girl over, I grabbed the ends of her dress and yanked them up over her head.

I was rough, as every man is expected to be, taking her without permission or consent. In a world of triviality and Southern courting, this exchange of animal lust was a welcome change, a break from tradition that gave new definition for the master/ slave relationship.

She was as beautiful as she was forbidden. Her long coarse hair felt soft to the touch of my callous-ridden hands as I ran my fingers through it again and again.

Social norms be damned, I'll be returning to her barn again tomorrow night. Perhaps then I shall learn the maiden's name. Perhaps

One thought remains - She was mine tonight... and she will be again.

October 30, 1785

It has been some time since I recorded my thoughts on paper. Though I have very little time to write with the harvest approaching, I shall do my best.

An update on my living arrangements – I have decided to stay the winter at Aunt Meridith's plantation outside of Charleston, my invitation having been extended as a sign of family unity in these uncertain times.

Most days, my time is spent preparing the field hands and managing the affairs of the estate. My Uncle Bartholomew (Lord rest his soul) passed away this past February without his affairs in order.

Rewards for my service to Aunt Meridith are plentiful and include room, board, and her discretion in regard to my continued relationship with her slave girl, Miss Fi. Though we have not discussed the matter, my aunt has given me certain looks when I am around Fi, not dissimilar to the ones my mother used to give me when I was younger.

To complicate matters, Aunt Meridith caught me addressing Fi as an equal instead of the slave she is. For this, I offered no apology or explanation.

Fi and I have grown quite close in our seven months together. I thought of her once as merely another hand; now, I place her on the highest of pedestals alongside Helen of Troy and Saint Joan of Arc. Comparable icons, as her beauty and humble nature are unlike any I've come in contact with, slave or freeman. We spend most evenings together in her barn or walking the grounds of the estate.

The only issue we have had so far was a particularly nasty argument over the fate of her father, an older slave named George. He had lost his eye defending a section of corn crop from natives, and the general consensus was to put him down. After all, a field slave with one eye is of very little use on an active plantation.

Fi was opposed to this, and wanted to keep her father alive and useful elsewhere on the estate. Our ideological differences and worlds were as nailed to our foreheads as our hearts were to each other. My argument, comparing her kind to dogs or horses, did not go over as well as I had hoped, causing a larger rift between us.

My feelings for Fi, and by extension her father, George, transcended both the color of our skin and our stations in life, however, and for that reason alone I spoke to Aunt Meridith. George has been moved inside the house and now tends to the laundry. I expressed my gratitude with promises of bringing in the harvest and keeping the estate running through the winter, tasks I am happy to perform for my only living relative, who also happens to own the woman to which my heart belongs.

For the first time since the death of my mother and my brother Robert, I am content in life.

January 4, 1786 – Charleston, SC

Finally the day all males of the human species biologically strive for has come. Though the circumstances may not be ideal, Fi has informed me this morning that she is with child.

These winter months have rung in the New Year with tidings of joy for the two of us.

Though on occasion I still fear that her love for me is merely an expression of her obligation of a slave, I believe her to be true to her word when she says she loves me. I love her, and I will love our child regardless of what color it may be.

March 1, 1786 – Charleston, SC

I woke this morning to a tapping at the door to my chambers. Opening it, I was greeted with the presence of Constable Miller. It seems that a tribe of Cherokee had moved into the area and were sending scouts regularly to my Aunt's estate. He suggested that we equip ourselves and follow them back to their main camp, burn it, and kill them before they can raid our land.

I agreed with the Constable, of course, pledging my services and promising to meet him in one hour at the westernmost edge of my Aunt's land. After dressing and preparing for the expedition, I went to tell Aunt Meridith about the journey. She agreed in principle, but insisted that I take George with me as he had been doing a poor job as a house slave and her patience with him was running thin.

With supplies, food, and ammunition all loaded upon George's back, we set off for the slave's quarters where I said goodbye to Fi and kissed her stomach for the first time. With a tear in her eye, Fi bid us both farewell.

We met Constable Miller at the edge of the property and the three of us set out on horseback to wait for a Cherokee scout to appear. Our wait was not long, and within an hour a savage on his own horse (without a saddle) came blazing into view, stopping near the border of Aunt Meridith's property. He remained for several long minutes as he prepared his rifle.

We waited until dark before sacking their camp. I collected nearly a dozen scalps this night, as well as a fine meal of buffalo killed, cooked, and heated for us by the savages we killed. Having eaten, I now record my thoughts. Though Fi is always with me, I cannot help but wonder at how far I've come.

Looking back on the past year, I can scarcely believe the transformation my life has undergone since my return to Charleston. I've found trust in my aunt, love in Fi, and kinship in good neighbors like Constable Miller.

Grief still grips me when I think of mother or Robert, but not as painfully as before. Perhaps time does heal all wounds. Regardless of the reason, I must now protect what I now have: a family… and a child on the way…

March 2, 1786 – Aunt Meridith's Plantation

Madness and utter destruction greeted me upon my return. Words do not describe this atrocity…

March 4, 1786 – Meridith Plantation

My apologies for not documenting my thoughts earlier; it is my hope that this entry will explain the reasoning behind my actions with due course and fairness to my character.

Two days ago, I was dispatched into the native lands to locate and kill any intruders who might be conspiring with British soldiers to take my Aunt Meridith's land. Constable Miller and I set a trap, and we, accompanied by my faithful slave George, followed a Cherokee scout back to his camp a few miles due west of our location.

The next morning, confident in our assumption that we had discovered the savages before they had time to act, the Constable and I stopped for breakfast. Shortly thereafter we came upon three savages, produced our weapons, and shot them where they stood. Two of them died before we could get within ten feet.

The third savage had been shot once through his shoulder and once through his belly. It was only a matter of time before he died as well, so I asked him in plain English why he and his companions had been snooping around. To my disbelief, the dying savage began to laugh. With blood painting his teeth a gossamer shade, he died.

Unsettled by the altercation, I was all too happy to return to the plantation. The Constable and I rode onto Aunt Meridith's property around mid-morning, only to find the entire place burned to the ground. Tossing the reins aside, I slipped off my horse and ran to the pile of rubble where my aunt's home had stood only the day before.

The house, barn, and land had been completely razed. Outside lay six bodies, all scalped and set on fire to make them indistinguishable. One of them though, was Fi's height and nearby I found a piece of the dress she had been wearing when I left. There is no doubt in my mind that that charred corpse is all that is left of her earthly vessel, and my unborn child. They are at peace now, spared from bearing witness to the carnage I shall bring in the wake their deaths.

Another of the bodies that was recognizable was Aunt Meridith. Gunshot wounds had left her torso a bloody ruin, but her lovely face was still mostly intact. Even in death, she still looked like my mother. Her eyes had melted away in the fire, but I could still see them gazing at me with the same impatient, arrogant, and maternal look that burned a disappointed shame into my soul.

George knelt down beside what was left of Fi, clutching the remains in his old, weathered arms. His tears flowed freely, yet he made not a sound. Quiet as a church, I believe he shared the solitude and failure that I felt at that moment. We eventually walked back to the Constable at the edge of the property.

Where I'll go next, I have no idea. The Constable reckons that the savages that did this are the same ones who are helping the British prolong the war. Maybe I'll reenlist. All I know is that somehow, some day, I'm going to kill every last one of those savage bastards.

March 5, 1817 -Washington D.C

It has been decades since my pen has last spilt its ink upon these pages. A lifetime has passed since I catalogued my thoughts and memories here for posterity. Since then I have returned to the life of a military man. This has been quite effective, as I seek the dignity my name so rightly deserves.

By accepting the rank of Colonel in the United States Armed Forces, I took upon myself the responsibility of protecting Tennessee from any savages that might enter her without the proper discourse befitting a lady of her caliber.

In addition to my rank and military honors, I've also experienced a different kind of change…one within myself. Two years ago this month, I was in the middle of a Cherokee hunt with a few fellow officers, friends of mine, when we were ambushed by a large savage force outnumbering us ten to one.

One by one, my fellow officers fell to the savages' hands, each scalped and left to die slowly as they bled out. All the while, I fought valiantly in hand-to-hand combat with every enemy that crossed my path, ending their lives one by one as they approached me both on horseback and on foot.

I remember clearly that it was after I had killed the sixth savage that I thought how much easier it would be if they were to simply kill each other instead. No sooner had I formed this thought that it came to pass before my very eyes. Then again, and again. Each time, all I had to do was imagine it happening, focus, and they would do it.

After roughly the ten or eleventh time I did this, all of the savages lay dead at my feet and I stood supreme over all of them, conqueror of the American landscape.

Removing my nine-inch, serrated hunting knife from my side, I grabbed the long, matted hair of the closest corpse and pulled it close. Then, using the tip of my knife, I pierced its scalp and began to cut in an circle until the hairy flesh came off in one solid piece. I proceeded to do it again and again with every dead savage I found, creating a pile of scalps numbering perhaps twenty eight. I finally nailed them to a long piece of hickory log I had stripped from a nearby tree.

Fire seemed to be the only fitting burial for both the savages and my fellow officers. After setting the entire area ablaze, I returned to headquarters some ten miles away, twenty-eight scalps bobbing up and down on the long slice of hickory slung over my shoulder.

When I arrived, I presented the grizzly prize to my commanding officer as a gesture of my continued support and loyalty to my country, even in the face of death. His astonishment and respect were my reward, the piece of hickory, my legacy.

My talent includes, but is not limited to, making others kill. At first it was only savages, but after clashing with Lt. General Clinton over the post in Florida, it soon spread to rivalries in every facet of my life. Still, I attempted to use it for good, whether eradicating pockets of natives, or assisting Protestant settlers needing Thy will done.

Since then, I've come to peace with my new powers of manipulation. It seems that I can place ideas into people's minds, forcing them to do my bidding whenever I desire. While I am aware of the grave consequences that such a feat could bring, I am also well aware of the potential this power possesses. I've read books on training my mind, and have found solace especially in Sun Tzu's 'The Art of War'; a piece of literature that serves as both my Bible's companion and a guiding light in my life when I am without hope.

Under the direct orders of President James Monroe, I have been commissioned to lead a company of men into the former Spanish territory known as Florida to root out any resistance to a colonization by American settlers in the near future.

December 4, 1817 - Spanish Florida

In regard to my attempt to quell the savage fever gripping the Florida landscape, a strange event occurred this morning. Just as I was about to take the head of Nahoy, local chieftain of the Nabawoo Seminole tribe, an odd disturbance right out of a children's fable appeared before my very eyes.

Without warning, the very heavens opened and spat out a multitude of objects at once. It was if a Midwestern twister had fallen sideways and ejected more than half a dozen people and numerous items of indeterminable material.

While we only fought them briefly, none of the sky people seem to be of the traditional military rank and file. We engaged one old man, three females, and one slave, leaving four or so unaccounted for. Even so, an army of four or five against the might of the American forces led by the immortal General Andrew Jackson stands no chance.

My men have since collected a large amount of the items that accompanied them, even if most of the sky people escaped. We now have in our possession a fair amount of supplies, strange machinery, and even their slave. Could they be angels? British intelligence? Only time, and a healthy dose of the switch, will tell.

December 5, 1817 - Spanish Florida

If the sky people, those from Eden, are indeed angels, than I am now in league with the devil.

This morning I came face to face with death himself. Oddly, he looks nothing like the artists portray him. Instead he is an older, skinny man with bushy eyebrows and a pensive demeanor. What really set him apart from mortal men were his eyes – black with copper rings.

"What, what shall I do?" I asked Death meekly, with my head lowered and eyes cast downward in a show of subservience. I wanted to offer my sword, my heart, and my very soul; he had other ideas in mind.

"Go forth and kill all who stand against my will," Death said to me, his eyes never blinking. "Kill the ones you call sky people."

"Yes, yes, I shall do as you say," I recall saying to him, backing away slowly with my head still down. Turning around, I had the feeling that should we meet again without me holding up my end of the agreement, he would not allow me to walk away at all.

The silence of the doorknob behind Sephanie offered her little warning that she was no longer alone.

"I like to think of my life as an open book," Jackson said, crossing the threshold into his office and approaching Sephanie with a brisk confidence to his steps. Acquaintances had always told Jackson that his walk seemed like more of a strut, though he pled ignorance on the matter. "But this is taking the phrase a bit literally, don't you think?"

Sephanie, not accustomed to being caught off guard, closed the book quickly before placing it back on the pedestal where she had found it.

"Sorry," Sephanie said meekly, backing away and casting her eyes downward like a guilty child. This act had won Sephanie the favor of many males before, and by the look of Jackson, she was willing to bet it would work again.

"Think nothing of it, my dear," Jackson said, stepping behind her and wrapping his arms around her waist. "It's best you know the real me instead of the version your friends made up."

Meanwhile, a mere five hundred feet from Jackson's office, the slumbering form of Joan Rothouse Raines began to stir. A slow, steady sweat beaded on her brow and formed a damp puddle on her pillow. Her lip twitched as her face contorted with small, piercing spasms.

Beneath the surface, Joan was experiencing a painful, but somewhat normal occurrence in her life. Her extra sense of perception was both a blessing and a curse, as her gift came in the form of incredibly vivid dreams foretelling the future.

While some might think this neat, or admire Joan's gift for knowing what lies ahead, they would fail to consider the great amount of mental anguish this would cause the person who intercepted such unnatural messages from beyond. Flashes of Elemenos, Vilthe, arrows, a raft, and the ocean kept coming back to her, but she believed she knew why.

As it is for all people in love, the main protagonist and most frequent player in Joan's visions was her husband, Judah. His fate was the most threatened in all the scenarios she foresaw for the duration of the Knights of Time's stay in 19th century Florida. Joan saw a veritable cornucopia of possibilities and outcomes, none of which resulted in Judah's return to her, or even his survival.

Then, plucked directly from her wildest dreams, a clear path leading to Judah's safe return emerged, hinging on her direct intervention. Though sound asleep, she began to speak in a low, respectful manner.

"Please, just let me see him again."

With another violent convulsion Joan awoke from her slumber, her mind racing and sweat running down her face. It didn't take her long to assess the situation and form a plan of escape.

"Hey, want to fool around?" Joan asked the guard, an older man whose greasy, black hair hung limply on either side of his face. His crooked yellow teeth formed a grin at the prospect of laying his hands on Joan's beautiful body.

The foolish guard sauntered over to Joan's cell and unlocked the door, standing directly behind the iron door. Joan applied a bit of force, sending the side of the door straight into the man's skull, knocking him out cold.

Slipping past the unconscious guard, she made her way through the two story complex and out the front pasture. Sneaking past the perimeter guards, Joan ran as fast as she could toward the beach, the last place she knew her husband to be.

Historian's Message: Part II

Thank you, kind reader, for travelling with me this far on our adventure through mankind's long and sordid history.

As you become familiar with the Wright family, and more specifically Rolland, it is understandable to have various conflicting opinions about his actions. Deciding to help the Seminole girl evade capture, angering Andrew Jackson, and plotting revenge on his parent's murderer are all the actions of a wayward teenage boy finding himself on the threshold of deciding which path in life to follow. This has landed Rolland in a bit of a mess. He appears to be lost, both physically and spiritually.

It might be a good time to take a break from our tale to reaffirm our shared history, as I realize that most of you have found a couple of inconsistencies with what you were taught and what you have read in my account thus far.

Despite his rough demeanor, Andrew Jackson was a man of great passion. His lust for life extended well beyond the battlefield (as was written in his journal), and his unbridled enthusiasm for love and violence took a toll on both America and the world at large that extended well beyond his lifetime.

This fact brings me to my next and final point: history is made by those who survive to tell it. Most accounts are biased, one-sided tales, told only by the victor. While it is not my place to decide who is right or wrong, it IS my responsibility to document the finer details in an attempt to present the story from all sides.

In chronicling every human event, I have borne witness to some amazing moments over the course of the millennia. From great men of prestige and title, to the lowest serf and peasant staking their claim to infamy, I can personally attest that the fates know no prejudice when weighing one's heart.

It is for this reason that I interject myself into our tale of triumph and tribulation involving the last member of the Wright family -- not as I am now, but as I was as a young man, for this all took place many years ago.

Remember, I am very old and have been a Historian for nearly a millennia. Though I was a young man when I first met Rolland, I knew him to be special when he entered our realm. Because of this, I took a great risk and approached him.

I now share with you pages from my own log of our fateful meeting. It is my hope that in sharing them, my conscience shall be cleansed of any guilt my presence might have caused. Illumination is never as simple as black and white. We live, dear reader, in a galaxy of gray matter.

Chapter 22: Enter the Historian

Before Rolland opened his eyes, he somehow already knew that he was dead. The cold, clammy feeling in his arms and legs and the knot in his stomach told him that if he reached down and did not feel the arrow there, his suspicions would be confirmed. Using his tingling right hand, he felt the smooth, hairy skin covering his stomach and chest. The arrow was gone and he was dead.

Deciding that this was a good enough excuse to finally open his eyes, Rolland sat up, his head swimming from the mixture of fast movements and the bright sunlight pouring through the windows above him. The term 'skylight' eluded him in that moment, as a flood of other thoughts poured through his head, the least of which was his surroundings.

The large and impressive room reminded Rolland of a cross between a museum and a holy site. Rows of books lined the shelves as far as the eye could see, and each volume had a distinctive spine with its own unique color and shape. No two of them matched exactly.

Spotting a large, brightly colored volume, Rolland reached out to pick it up. A strange silver print flashed across its cover before vanishing as quickly as it had appeared. Though his eyes only caught the word 'Wright' before it was too late. The book's spine was thick with at least five or six hundred pages.

"I really shouldn't let you be looking through that," said a voice from the large reading area in the center of the room. "Though I doubt you can understand it, so no harm done."

Spinning on his heels, Rolland came face to face with a younger, fresh faced version of the intensely methodical keeper of records. Rolland guessed the man to be no more than thirty to thirty-five years old.

"Are you...?" Rolland wondered aloud, tilting his head slightly and attempting to find the right words to describe the creator of, well, everything.

"The Grand Architect of the Universe?" the young Historian asked, bringing one hand to his chest and bowing slightly. "Good heavens, no. I'm merely a simple Historian, a keeper of records."

"There doesn't seem to be anything simple about this place," Rolland said, spinning around to take in his surroundings. "Nice to meet you though, Mr. Historian. My name is..."

"Rolland Alan Wright," the Historian said with a smile. "Son of Taylor and Scott Wright. One of only five human beings in the history of his species to possess the ability of naturally conceived time travel."

"One of five?" Rolland asked, shocked at the low number.

"And the most powerful," the Historian added, his lips curving into a half smile before he turned away and walked to a nearby shelf.

Taking his last statement into consideration, Rolland asked bluntly, "So is that why Vilthe gave me his best recruitment speech and sent Jackson to kill me?"

"You have within you the ability to control time and space. You simply must understand the magnitude of that," the Historian said, growing slightly exasperated at Rolland's ambivalence toward his abilities. The few whiskers on his face were black, matching the sleekly combed hair that graced the top of his head.

"Do I have the ability to find the door out of here?" Rolland asked himself aloud, making light of the confusing situation he found himself in. Though the Historian seemed like a nice guy, it was obvious there was much to be desired in the way of his social skills.

"You are in a place outside of time and space that is usually reserved only for those individuals crossing between life and death," the Historian said with a brisk certainty.

"So, I'm dead then?" Rolland asked, his voice notably softer.

"Close, you're very close," the Historian said with a slight smirk as he continued his speech.

"So, I'm alive?" Rolland asked, his hand reaching up to find the spot where the arrow had hit him.

"You are in a place outside of time and space..." the Historian began again, raising his arms high above his head.

"Yeah, I've heard that one before," Rolland interrupted "Sort of how I got here."

"As I was saying," the Historian continued, his good temper becoming obvious as he spoke. "This is a place usually reserved for those crossing over. You, however, are just visiting."

"Alright," Rolland pressed, biting his tongue in frustration at being abducted yet again. "Why am I visiting?"

"Because you are being careless, Mr. Wright," the Historian said, arranging a large stack of volumes on a nearby shelf. "You're allowing your emotions to cloud your judgment. You must rely on your instincts when facing the world's problems."

"Uh-huh..." Rolland said, looking past the obviously insane gentleman to a group of golden embossed books that seemed to be glowing on the shelf behind him. "The world's problems aren't my problems though, so, there's that."

"They are, Mr. Wright," the Historian said, sitting down on a well-placed wheelie cart and folding his forearms on his legs so that his hands dangled over his knees. "You are all planet Earth has in the way of a hero."

"What about Turtledove, and Sephanie, and Victor? They're all heroes, what about them?" Rolland asked, raising his voice steadily as he listed off names of people he felt better qualified to be recruited to a higher purpose.

"They all have their parts to play, yes," the Historian said, his steady calm never faltering as he attempted to put Rolland's teen-age mind at ease. "But ultimately what these people have is you."

"No, not me. It's got to be someone else," Rolland said, sucking both of his cheeks in slowly as he fought back the urge to cry or punch someone. He wasn't sure which option would feel better at that moment. "I'm...flawed."

"You cannot allow the perfect to be the enemy of the necessary," the Historian said, his eyes gazing into the distance away from Rolland.

"Voltaire," Rolland responded immediately, recognizing the great philosopher's words. They had brought him great comfort one night during the early days of his life without a home. He remembered it like it was yesterday. It had been raining, a rare enough occurrence for Southern California, especially in the fall months. The night was cold, and he was lonely. The only comforting thought that night was the promise of a better tomorrow.

"You are unique, Rolland Wright. Like it or not, great and unfortunate things lie ahead," the strange man who called himself the Historian said to Rolland, clasping his shoulder tightly. His thumb and pointer figure found their way to either side of the muscle and gave it a squeeze.

This startled Rolland, who turned around to protest, only he could not. The Historian was gone, along with his library. Nothing but a white, dull haze remained around Rolland. Looking down, even the carpeted floor was gone, replaced by a vacuum of nothingness that Rolland freefell into.

Elsewhere, in the land of the living, Judah sat cross-legged inside the Captain's quarters, shackles around his ankles. Believing that the long, narrow hallway that went from the ship's deck to the room where he sat would give adequate notice of someone approaching, Judah began to snoop around the tiny room for clues to his captors' identity.

The inside of the Captain's quarters was littered with trinkets, maps, and food parcels of all sizes. Most casual observers would consider these the surroundings of a man who lived in squalor, but not Judah Jacob Raines. No – he recognized the careful placing of the maps (both on the wall and on the floor) and the trail of food remains that led to carefully placed (not to mention hidden) rat traps around the back. Perhaps the most telling sign that this mess was intentional sat in the middle of the room.

The Captain's desk was not large by any means. Judah guessed it was around 50 inches long and made out of a dark wood, perhaps walnut. It was also auspiciously clean and organized. The bottle that held its contents of ink was full and free of scuff marks: markers more indicative of a business man than of a 19th century pirate. At the far end stood a silver tray with a half-eaten loaf of bread, some fruit, and a copper knife, which was enticing enough to make Judah instinctively move in its direction.

With a loud creak to the ship's floorboards, in walked a brisk and unusually well-dressed man with a trimmed black mustache and beard. His hazel eyes found Judah's immediately as he entered the room and walked over to the desk.

"You're British, no?" the Captain asked, sitting at the desk and picking up the knife and apple. "So you speak English?"

"I am," Judah shuffled his feet a bit, causing the shackles around his ankles to rattle against the wooden floor.

"You will have a proper death at sea, then," the Captain said to him, as if it were nothing more complicated than hoisting the ship's sails.

"Come again?" Judah asked, raising one eyebrow and attempting to stand. He was not successful, and within moments Judah had buckled under his own weight and fallen painfully to his knees on the cold steel of the shackles.

"I know what you are," the Captain said, standing up and walking the length of the small quarters before turning back to meet Judah's stare. "You Traveler of Light, you gypsy, vagabond, freak."

There are times in life when laughing is completely inappropriate, such as in the restroom, while being questioned by security at the airport, and when being held prisoner by a group of 19th century Barbary pirates. Yet for Dr. Judah Jacob Raines the idea of being called a gypsy was so preposterous that he could not help himself.

"Good looking? Well endowed? Come on, keep the descriptions coming..." Judah said, really getting into the joke. "How about just plain ole' smarter than you?"

In the blink of an eye the Captain had the razor's edge of a knife close enough to Judah's jugular to draw blood. The Captain of the Dewberry then walked behind his captive to address his audience more intimately. Kneeling down until his lips were pressed against Judah's ear, the Captain spoke with a soft conviction.

"Most people don't think you are real. That you are like mermaids and sunken treasure, a myth, based on a fable, based on a drunken lie," the Captain said, releasing his pressure on the knife, and waving it around in the air as he spoke. "But not me, I know what's real. I know about you, and Eden. And that if I kill you, I'll be rewarded."

It was the mention of Eden caught Judah's attention, and made him suspect outside interference. "How do you know about Eden?"

"Death came to me in my dreams," the Captain said, standing up and walking toward the door slowly, each step lasting an eternity as he thought about how crazy he sounded. "Told me you would come – a blonde British man with a smart mouth."

Judah could smell Vilthe's craftsmanship all over this, meaning that he had been behind the attack on the beach, a trap to split up the Knights to create confusion. Simple divide and conquer.

The Captain opened the door to the hallway and this time two of his crewman stood there, waiting for their orders. They marched in and picked Judah up off the ground, dragging him away.

"Enjoy your last night on Earth!" The Captain called as he shut the door behind them.

The Sun was beginning its daily ritual when a sharply silhouetted figure appeared on the sandy shore. With a most un-lady like grunt and a leap, Joan Rothouse Raines landed with a tuck and roll on the beach.

Joan had been running from a squadron of Elemenos since dawn and had lost all but two. With them still hot on her tail she was presented with few options, none of which pertained to her true goal of helping her husband.

In her vision Joan had seen this beach. She had stood in this exact spot and stared at that same rock resembling the planet Saturn without its rings, right before seeing an oddly shaped tree, and then, well, the rest was kind of fuzzy.

"The tree…" Joan said to herself, putting her palm to her forehead as she walked. The warm coastal water of the Gulf felt gentle against her toes as it came in waves. It was a pleasant distraction from her current predicament. Joan often wondered why she never had visions of those things: the simple, happy things.

Images of sharp, jagged branches shot through Joan's mind like lightning bolts, giving her the next clue to finding the treasure she sought. As she set out further down the beach there seemed to be very little vegetation, much less the uniquely shaped tree from her visions. Doubt crawled further into her mind with each step.

Then Joan saw it - about twenty feet inland and roughly the same distance high. The branches were as jagged and sharp as they were twisted. In this oddity, there was a beautiful sort of perfection. A sort of basket crowned its top, formed from the mangled tree limbs, and there inside of the crown sat the yellow emergency raft Joan had placed in Judah's lab a few days prior.

Running to it, Joan got within three feet before something a few hundred yards away caught her attention instead. Out of the corner of her eye little green dots began to appear against the contrasting white sand of the beach. One by one they walked from the cover of the marsh to the edge of the sea and began turned their attention to their surroundings, to Joan.

It came as little surprise when the entire pride of Elemenos came clamoring down the hill and toward the beach where Joan stood. Knowing she had two choices, she decided quickly and grabbed onto the lowest of the trees branches, propelling herself upward, grabbing each limb as if it were her last resort and using her wrapped legs for leverage.

Joan was able to quickly and successfully climb her way to the top of the tree with only a few cuts and scrapes to her arms. Her legs, while sore, seemed to handle the task with relative ease as she climbed to the top and reached into the crown of twigs and leaves. Grabbing the yellow, boxed raft, Joan brought it close to her chest, securing it tightly between her fingers before looking down at the predicament she was in.

Beneath her were nearly two dozen Elemenos, all baring their claws and scratching against the tree. She thought it humorous that it was her and not the humanoid felines stuck up a twenty foot tall tree. But it didn't matter - the previously intangible was now within her hands, and with it was a chance for Judah's return to her.

Joan began to form a plan to get out of the tree and back to the ocean where she knew the Elemenos would not follow her. Her wandering thoughts caused Joan to miss the rock that hurled toward her head, finding its mark and causing the commander of the Knights of Time to lose her balance and free fall to the sandy beach below.

Claws tore into her back, stomach, and right arm before Joan rolled away from the concentration of their attack. While her jump had subdued three of the Elemenos, roughly twenty remained with ravenous appetites and orders to bring Joan back to Jackson dead or alive.

Leaping into the air as two Elemenos advanced on her, Joan flipped sideways in mid-air, landing on the shoulders of another. Wrapping her legs around its neck, Joan used him like a puppet, directing him to slash and stab the oncoming Elemenos with squeezes of her legs. It took the death of five or so of its friends before the Elemeno between Joan's legs wised up and dropped his weapon.

This did not deter Joan, however, and she chose instead to jerk her legs to one side, snapping the Elemeno's neck before doing a cartwheel onto her feet and kicking another Elemeno in the face. Only six remained now as Joan reached for the knife her puppet Elemeno had dropped. Picking the raft up off of the ground, Joan thrust the knife out in warning to the six remaining Elemenos who were attempting to form a circle around her.

Carrying the inflatable raft she had retrieved from the mangrove tree, Joan made a mad dash for the water. With a wild disregard for her own safety, she approached the water head on, gathering the momentum necessary for the great jolt of strength, and threw the raft as far as she could into the open ocean.

Watching as it floated out to sea, Joan prayed silently that somehow, someway, it would find her husband safely and bring him back to her. A prayer she knew might not be answered.

The price of living in a post-Industrial Revolution society is lost on those born in the 20th and 21st centuries.

For those like Marcus Turtledove, old enough to remember a world without man made smog and pollution, it was good to be back. Not since coming to Eden had he seen the night sky in such a vibrant display of spectacular elegance.

The Sun began to emerge at his back, shining a light onto the only path where Turtledove saw any kind of happy resolution for the Nabawoo people, an alliance with the Creek. Remembering the reluctance of the Creek to get involved, Turtledove knew the only option was to go to their leader Blackfoot and plead his case personally.

"You're up early," Tina observed, appearing in between Turtle-dove and his knapsack. "Where are you going?"

"I am going to negotiate a peace with the Creek people. At this point they're our only hope," Turtledove said, leaning around the teenage girl and back into his tent to retrieve his things.

"Please don't leave, Turtledove," Tina pleaded, balling her fists in an attempt to suppress her emotions. "Not you, too."

"Tina, dear child, have faith that things happen for a reason," Turtledove said with a smile, throwing his knapsack over his shoulder.

"Rolland and his parents died for a reason?" Tina asked him, her eyes watering at the thought of the blood stained beach.

"That is precisely what I am saying," Turtledove told her, taking a few steps down the dirt path that led towards the dark woodlands. "I'll be on my way now."

"Wait, let me come with you!" Tina said, but Turtledove wrapped his arm around her and placed her in a tight hug.

"You are needed here, my child," Turtledove said, releasing his grasp on her and looking down to see tears in her sparkling, clear blue eyes.

Tina knew he was right. Turtledove's youngest prospective protégé was chest deep in her new responsibilities as leader of the Nabawoo Warrior Alliance. The demands of maintaining a secure perimeter and dispatching men on scouting missions left only a little more than two dozen remaining for an army, hardly an intimidating force by anyone's standards.

The thirty or so warriors left under Tina's command remained so under a very uneasy truce based on a mixture of their word and a hereditary game of chicken their fathers and grandfathers had passed down to them. It seems the volatile male ego knows no limitations when it comes to culture.

Wiping the tears from her eyes, Tina never expected Turtledove to take the opportunity to slip away, but when she turned back, he was gone.

Not knowing if she should cry or be filled with confidence, Tina merely stood there and stared straight ahead. Hoping, wishing, praying for nature or some other divine to take hold and pull her in a direction so she did not have to choose one herself.

For Tina Leigh Holmes the prospect of executing the wrong plan was more intimidating than thinking of her own impending death at the hands of Jackson's forces.

"Madam Holmes!" Enapay shouted much to Tina's chagrin as he came jogging out of the brush toward her accompanied by another Nabawoo warrior.

"Please don't call me that, Enapay," Tina said, closing her eyes momentarily out of frustration. While she felt slightly bad for being so rude to the native man, the thought of Judah or Rolland hearing her being called something a prostitute might adopt as a moniker was more horrifying.

"The Elemeno spies. They keep hiding in the bush and attacking our scouts," Enapay said, pointing to a location on the map sitting on nearby.

"And that's stopping us from advancing?" Tina asked, a million options running though her mind. The right strategy would come to her, she was certain. The question was not a matter of if, but when.

"Undetected, yes," Enapay replied, shouldering his newly acquired knapsack once again.

"Then we follow them," Tina said, a new sense of vitality in her voice as she turned to face her warriors full on.

"Teena?" Enapay asked, obviously confused by her declaration. "Follow who?"

"The Elemeno spies," Tina said resolutely, clasping her hands with a sense of satisfaction. "They're going somewhere, right? Relaying our position back to someone?"

"We have been chasing them west of here," said an older Nabawoo veteran. "But wherever they're going, it is not north. It is not toward Jackson."

"Could you track them?" Tina asked the older Nabawoo, the fire glimmering in her blue eyes.

"Should we not go after Jackson? Nahoy?!" came a loud protest from another Nabawoo warrior.

"In order to defeat the enemy," Tina began, raising her voice so that the entire campsite could hear her small, soprano voice. "We must first eliminate their forces."

"There are hundreds of those little green men," said the Nabawoo tracker, clutching his bow with one hand and gesturing wildly with the other.

It was clear to Tina that the stakes had risen in this game of cat and mouse. She knew that if the American aim was to destroy the Nabawoo Warrior Alliance and bring an end to the Florida Seminole forces, then they would need to be supplied, which meant a hoard of goods. A hoard they would not expect to be attacked.

"Let's see where they're going..." Tina said with a knowing smile.

The hour was late – or early depending on who you asked. Blaisey had fallen asleep in the same spot she had been sitting in for nearly eighteen hours. Although this was an impressive feat in and of itself, it was worrying Victor, who hoped that the Seminole girl was resting in preparation for the day ahead. If things went well then she would be needed by Rolland in his recovery; if they went poorly, he would need her help in digging a grave.

Victor sat, musket in his hand, ready to defend his friend from any harm that might befall him. With his back pressed firmly against the door, it was easy to succumb to the temptation to drift off again, but he knew his snoring would wake Blaisey, and maybe even Rolland.

Then Rolland's eyes opened, and he sat up with a great deal of gusto. Oxygen filled his lungs, bringing him rapidly to awareness.

Words could not begin to describe the amazement that graced the faces of both Victor, and a very groggy Blaisey.

"How do you feel?" Blaisey asked Rolland, hurrying to his side.

Pulling his pearl snap shirt back on around his shoulders and adjusting the collar, Rolland saw the scar on his stomach left by the arrow and poked at it a bit, saying, "We have to go east."

Chapter 23: Still Waters

The picturesque Florida coast with its crisp, blue water and its white sandy beaches is a hoax perpetrated by those who wish to attract tourists. In reality, the majority of the flat, inhospitable land is covered with swamps, mud, and lots of rocks.

For Joan, her surroundings were less than an afterthought to keeping her life past the next several minutes. After cutting the raft loose and sending it out to sea, a group of Vilthe's Elemeno guards had spotted her and had been pursuing her inland for nearly an hour.

It was unfair, Joan thought to herself, that she should be pitted against creatures that were capable of running faster using all four of their limbs when she was limited to just two.

But then, almost as if she had willed it herself, the Elemenos behind her began to fall one by one under the heavy barrage of arrows that rained down from above them.

Without stopping, Joan used her forearms to shield herself as she turned slightly to find that the number of Elemenos chasing her had dropped significantly. Spotting a clearing ahead, Joan decided it would be a good place to make her stand. Drawing her weapon, Joan ran into the open, expecting to see the three remaining green devils close behind.

To Joan's great surprise, it was not a clearing that awaited her just past the tree line, but the entire Elemeno encampment. More than two hundred pairs of catlike ears fell backward in an overt sign of aggression as they saw her.

Hundreds of piercing red eyes fell upon Joan as she stood paralyzed. All around her the heartbeats of the green, cat-like beasts pulsated loudly, assaulting her ears like the drums that Tina claimed to have heard coming from her husband's direction a few nights before.

"Merde…" Joan said under her breath, backing away slowly before turning and sprinting back the way she came. Behind her, she could hear the clamoring of the Elemenos as they stood up and filed out of their camp toward her. Joan leaped over the corpses of the Elemenos that had pursued her into the camp, arrows piercing each fallen form.

Exiting the grassland, Joan ran back to the area where the arrows had come from, hoping for some more of that oddly placed friendly fire.

Fate is a matter of character, and for Joan Raines, her character included having forgiving friends in high places. Literally. High above her, hidden in the brush that covered the hillside was Tina and nearly a dozen Nabawoo archers.

"Fire on two!" Tina ordered her Nabawoo Warriors as she looked through the binoculars she had recovered during their scouting mission the first night. She watched her blonde bait herd the Elemenos into a single pride before exterminating them. At her command, a single archer to her left fired his arrow. She watched it fly through the air for a few moments through her binoculars before it found the chest of the Elemeno gaining ground on Joan a few thousand feet away.

This went on for some time. Their positioning gave Tina and the Nabawoo archers an excellent view of the tiny fleshly dot she considered her friend. She watched as it ran from the hundreds of green dots, many of which fought with one another as the pride of moved along without them.

"There are too many of them, my-damn," Enapay said, eyeing the Elemenos as they began to organize and gain ground on Joan.

"It's Madam, Enapay," Tina said, her eyes distracted by something unusual on the horizon.

A wave of blackness fell over the clearing, though it was not the one Tina expected. Not Vilthe making an appearance on the battlefield, but Victor's newly befriended runaway slaves. They met the Elemenos head on in their black body suits, passing Joan by completely and engaging her pursuers in hand to hand combat.

"What are they..?" Tina heard several of the Nabawoo ask each other. The fair-haired beauty had no interest in the fate of the Elemenos, only Joan, who had run back towards the Elemeno camp. Tina aimed her binoculars toward the area, only to receive the greatest shock of her seventeen years.

Another fleshy dot had appeared from in front of the tree line, a wavy-blonde-haired dot wearing a faded blue jeans and gray pearl-snap shirt.

"He's alive!" Tina said under her breath in complete surprise. Without thinking, she handed the binoculars to Enapay and cupped her hand to her right ear, turning to listen carefully to the battle. She strained to listen for Rolland's noise, for his trumpets, but they weren't there. "But...he's quiet."

"Madam?" Enapay asked, only half-paying attention as he continued to call targets forthe archers.

The breath that she had been holding escaped without the slightest indication that it might ever return. Receiving the news of Rolland's death was a foregone conclusion in Tina's mind, a conclusion that encouraged her to accept the position as leader of the Nabawoo Warrior Alliance. This bit of information threw a huge cog into the metaphorical machine that was Tina's brain.

It was dark. A cold, wet splattering of liquid hit Judah's left cheek. Then another, and another, until Judah was forced to open his eyes and witness the harsh truth the new day brought reminders of. The dripping was sea water, and Judah was on a ship. A ship filled with what appeared to be genuine pirates. Another wave brought fresh turbulence to the ship and a new wave of salt water to his face, lips, and inside of his dry mouth.

Hours passed with nothing for Judah to do but take in his surroundings. He spied on every guard, every crewman, and every deck hand, trying to get a feel for their role, their behavior, and most especially their names. An interesting lot they were too, many of which were missing limbs, were barely audible, or simply had the common sense of a lemming. Escape would be possible, he concluded, but only with a certain amount of assistance.

In taking stock of his fellow captives, Judah found himself one of only a few who spoke English, leaving his options limited to the three men who responded to his call of "Who wants to get the bloody hell out of here?"

There was Grimes, a former member of the crew who had disobeyed orders; Bernie, a stowaway drunkard from a previous port the Dewberry had visited, and finally Arbuthnot, a Captain in the British navy. Judah felt that their best plan was to create a distraction, and allow the other men the privilege of physically rushing any pirates that stood between them and their freedom. Only one question was left; once free, where would he go, how would he get back to land?

The thought haunted Judah as time passed and he began counting the wooden planks that comprised the ship's hull. In this simplicity, a plan formed within the mind of the world's smartest man, one that would require careful execution, and more importantly, a gifted showman.

On the deck above, the crew members swapped positions, as if a shift change was taking place. Each man found himself greeted with a shove toward their next assignment as their replacement took over unscathed.

Judah pitied them, really. Through the rusted, iron bars that caged him he watched as the men scurried about on the deck above, going in and out of the makeshift enclosure that led to the hallway where the ship's wheel was housed. At the helm stood an older, balding man who appeared to be one with the wheel, their kindred relationship the linchpin that kept the entire ship afloat.

"In you go, pond scum!" shouted a middle-aged pirate with blackened teeth standing below the prisoners and holding a large pointed stick that he used to annoy Judah mercilessly.

The little ball of pity that sat in Judah's stomach moments before morphed into an annoyed glob of rage, picking up bits of suppressed marital squabbles as it went along. Straightening his shoulders and standing upright like a true British gentleman, Judah Jacob Raines finally opened his mouth and said, "Piss off!"

The march toward the end of the wooden plank was not what worried Judah. He had faced dilemmas much deadlier than this one with no problem. It wasn't the mid-80-degree temperature of the Gulf water or the many hidden dangers that could conceivably lie within its murky abyss. In the forefront of the smartest man in the world's mind was a childhood fear he could never quite conquer. The one weakness he had hoped would never be exploited. Judah Jacob Raines could not swim. At least, not well.

"Time to go, boy," a voice said from out of Judah's line of vision as the other pirates caused a commotion, their bloodlust demanding a fresh exercising. Taking this as his cue, he immediately set his plan into motion. In doing so, Judah first turned to face the majority of the pirates, captivating their attention as he was pushed toward the plank. Then, without warning, he began to convulse.

What started in Judah's hips spread northward to his chest, causing him to perform a sort of pop-and-lock motion (much to the pirates amusement). He rounded off his performance with an eye twitch, an overly dramatic fall to the deck below, and, just for good measure, a healthy dose of drool.

The distraction was just enough for the two other captives, Arbuthnot and Grimes, to cut their bonds free without being observed. Grimes went first, having jumped the gun by a full five seconds, leaving at least half of his cloth wrappings cut by the time Judah's fake seizure had begun. The pirates' lack of attention to detail would go down in history as their greatest downfall, especially in the area of personal hygiene.

Having counted to thirty-five 'her majesties'[4] while convulsing wildly for the crew of Barbary corsair pirates, Judah opened his eyes to view his audience for the first time. This moment, like no other in his thirty-four years of life, defined his strategic genius. Every eye on the ship was locked on him, completely oblivious to the rebellion being staged directly behind them.

---

4   Her Majesties are the British version of 'Mississippi's; Ex: One Her Majesty (Mississippi), Two Her Majesty

Spotting the thumbs up from Arbuthnot, Judah stopped hollering, stood up, and proceeded to pop his shoulder back into place.
All the while, the pirates, including the captain, stared gaping at the
blonde genius as his show came to a close and he prepared to take
his final bow.

"You've been a lovely audience," Judah said before bowing low
and righting himself.

Unbeknownst to the confused pirates, Judah's bow was a signal
to Arbuthnot and the others to run full tilt toward the pirates. As Judah ran to the end of the plank, he hopped in the air once for luck,
a habit he had picked up taking swimming lessons in Liverpool as a
child. Then, with a jubilant exuberance, Judah dove into the ocean
taking the gazes and rapt attention of nearly every pirate with him.

Though Judah only got to see the initial impact, it was enough
to satisfy his immediate need for revenge against his abductors. He
hit the water with a noisy splash that would have been met with a
series of hoots and hollers had it not been for the mutiny going on
above deck.

During the initial run at the Barbary hostiles, only Grimes
was successful at getting through to the plank and following Judah overboard. Their two comrades, however, were having a much
tougher time.

Arbuthnot, being the largest of all the men on the ship, naturally attracted a certain amount of dangerous attention over the other
slaves, who only had one pirate engaged at a time. For Arbuthnot,
it was not uncommon for three to four men to surround him at all
times. In dodging an attack from his right, he left himself open to a
knife that nearly reached his arm. In response, he tossed the knife's
owner across the ship, straight into two more pirates that Bernie
was engaged in fisticuffs with.

Unfortunately, as with all violent group altercations, firearms
soon entered the equation, something Judah had warned them

about if they wanted to get off of the ship alive. Sensing this, Arbuthnot grabbed the pirate closest to him, a short and skinny man who was missing an eye but had no patch to cover it with, and held him up in front of himself. Using the man as a human shield, Arbuthnot grabbed the back of Bernie's shirt and dragged him the ten or so treacherous feet to the plank before dropping the nearly unconscious pirate and jumping into the water himself.

"What shall we do, my-damn?" Enapay asked Tina, careful to keep an eye on the tiny flesh colored dot in the sea of green dots.

"I —" Tina began, but stopped, not knowing what to say.

"Should we assist further?" Enapay asked, holding the binoculars to his eyes.

"We'll follow her lead," Tina decided, taking charge before one of her many male subordinates could add their two cents. "Follow her closely."

As the Nabawoo archers gathered their materials and ran down the rock formation to follow the Elemeno's pursuit of Joan, help in the form of the newly resurrected Rolland arrived.

From the clearing beyond the rocks, Rolland watched as Joan came hurtling toward him, a weapon in each hand. Rolland also saw something worryingly familiar: a glowing white orb hovering in Joan's direction. A mixture of alarm and impending doom washed over him, but he dismissed both the feeling and the orb as figments of his imagination brought on by nerves.

Nearby, the situation was becoming tense.

Alora suddenly appeared between the two Travelers of Light, catching Joan off guard. She cracked her whip at the commander of the Knights of Time, tightening the coarse, electric-blue leather around Joan's neck like a boa constructor. The ginger-haired woman cackled, assaulting Joan's ears as she struggled to breathe.

"Hey!" Rolland shouted at Alora, who merely turned her head and laughed as she raised Joan high up into the air and with a quick flick of her wrist, spinning the blonde woman around half a dozen times in mid-air before shooting her like a helicopter propeller into the air.

Running toward Alora head first, Rolland stood little chance as she teleported away, causing him to skid to a stop in the soppy, muddy ground. He had but a second to turn before Alora made herself known again, appearing within arms' length next to him before launching a fresh barrage of punches that Rolland was only partially able to defend against. The two exchanged blows to the stomach, midsection, and legs before Alora gained the upper hand by knocking Rolland onto his back. Though she was trained in martial arts, and he was clearly not, there lacked a measure of sympathy on her part, evident by the attacks she launched while he was still down. It wasn't until her fifth punch to Rolland's gut when she crouched over him, noticing that his shirt had ridden up past his navel, revealing the spot where Jackson had shot him the day before.

"Is that where the good General got cha' then? Pity..." Alora teased Rolland, reaching for the scar on his stomach. Using this distraction, Rolland was able to kick her chest, sending her rolling over and away from him.

Getting to his feet, Rolland quickly realized why as Alora looked beyond Rolland to something, or someone behind him.

There stood Alora's brother, Rudolph Hess, with a gun pressed against Blaisey's temple, and one arm wrapped firmly around her neck. The former SS Officer snarled vindictively.

"You gave it your best shot, but it's over now," Hess shouted, moving closer and circling Rolland like a predatory dog, Blaisey dragging behind him, nearly unconscious from the manhandling. "Accept defeat."

The white orb flew behind Hess before hovering near the hillside on their right. A small opening at its limestone base told Rolland where the orb wanted him to go.

"Do it!" said Hess, interrupting Rolland's train of thought. "Accept defeat!"

Rolland found Hess's demand amusing as he moved to match the Nazi's movements so that they were circling each other.

"Alright," Rolland said, dropping his father's knife at his feet before walking another five feet closer - too close for Hess' comfort.

Sensing a trick, Hess countered Rolland's approach with the same apprehension he had displayed previously, moving five feet away from Rolland and within inches of an Elemeno corpse.

"But there's something I've always wanted to say to you, Rudolph..." Rolland said, putting both hands up in the air in a sign of surrender.

"Oh? And what is that?" Hess asked with a stone cold expression and dead stare into Rolland's eyes.

Hess was too quick for Rolland, who was unsuccessful in his attempt to slow down time.

With a right hook, Hess clocked Rolland across the cheek, sending him sideways off of his feet and sending the teenager flying into a limestone outcropping. Rolland landed hard, and slid to the ground.

Lucky for Blaisey, Tina had regained her senses enough to re-enter the fight, drawing Alora temporarily away while Rolland was down for the count.

Joan, too, had recovered, engaging Hess in hand to hand combat. Once again, as it had been so many times throughout history, the French and the Germans came to blows.

The white orb buzzed longingly around Rolland's head, clearing the cobwebs that come from physical altercations. It roused him to his feet, encouraging him to follow it into the small opening.

For Rolland, the prospect of following another imaginary ball of light was less than appealing, but he knew he had no choice.

The opening was wider than it looked from the outside. Whereas the cave gave Rolland a foreboding feeling, the added presence of the white orb gave this 'crawl space' a more determined, temporary nuance, as if it would be over as soon as he did what he was supposed to do there.

Looking ahead into the darkness, Rolland saw the orb stop near a sheathed object roughly ten yards in front of him. No sooner had he crawled to it than the orb vanished, leaving him completely in the dark.

Using his hands for guidance, Rolland felt the ground around him, finally grasping the object with one hand, and tracing its edges with the other. It took but a moment for him to realize what it was. His father's old knife.

Meanwhile, outside, the unarmed Joan and Blaisey were fighting Hess, Alora, and the legion of Elemeno warriors at their disposal. With Tina busy calling the Nabawoo archer's shots from above, her focus became split as she constantly checked on the status of the battle below, not seeing the dot she knew to be Rolland for some time.

On the ground, Hess swiped at Blaisey with his sword, missing her by a wide margin but getting close enough to grab her hair and force her close to him. She squealed with surprise and struggled to free herself to no avail.

"Hey!" Rolland yelled in a low, intimidating voice, attracting Hess' attention. In Rolland's hand was Scott Wright's knife, the one companion that had made him feel safe and protected all those lonely months.

"So you have a new toy," Hess said, backing away and pulling Blaisey back to her feet. "I still have her."

With bravery he had never known before, Rolland Wright charged at Hess, meeting the former SS officer's blade with his own as they crossed, turned around, and repositioned for another clash. It came almost instantaneously.

A master swordsman, Hess easily bested Rolland's skill with a blade, only falling short to the boy in weight, but being skinny was not a great advantage. The two men reached a stalemate, disarming each other and creating a momentary break in the action.

Hess stopped fighting, and using the smallest bit of slack, Blaisey slipped out from beneath his grasp and lunged for a pile of leaves a couple of feet away. Hess quickly bent down and pulled her back up by the back of her vest, only to get slashed across the chest with Scott Wright's knife, clutched tightly between her fingers.

Hess stepped backward clumsily, taking his eyes off of Rolland for a few moments - a dangerous mistake when fighting a time traveler.

"Burn in hell," Rolland said with a clenched jaw from behind the Nazi, Hess.

Within a millisecond a great inferno surrounded Hess, trapping him within a circle of fire, leaving him a proverbial fish in a barrel.

"You think can trap me?!" Hess shouted, stifling a laugh. "I've sent thousands, millions of shits like you to their deaths. What makes you so special that you think to stand against the great Hess?"

Without a word, Rolland smiled, and watched as a single arrow shot out from the hills above, made its way through the fire surrounding Hess, as it lodged itself in the former Nazi's shoulder, setting the cocky villain on fire. Within seconds the chaos surrounding the battle was concentrated to the ring of fire, and the shocked, burning bit of living flesh standing within. The howls and cries were poetic justice to all who had fallen victim to Hess's savagery, including the distant archer, the smiling, and once again empowered, Tina Holmes.

Seeing their commanding officer aflame, many of the Elemenos began to lay down their arms or flee outright. The battlefield was clearing of all but the arrows and the bodies of the fallen.

"Oh my..." Joan said, walking over and taking stock of the scene. Leaves and dirt matted her blonde hair and fresh bruises graced her arms and legs, but aside from minor scuffs she was alright.

Hess on the other hand was not.

A crowd of Knights, freedmen in black, and curious Elemenos gathered to watch as Hess was burned within an inch of his life. Not a single soul offered to help him, and growing increasingly uncomfortable, Blaisey decided to appeal to Rolland's better nature by saying "I think it's time to put him out."

"You do know that this is the man who was ordered to kidnap your brother and sisters, right? The same man who helped Jackson and Vilthe kidnap your father," Rolland said to her, a bit surprised at Blaisey's sudden humanitarian turn.

"But that's what makes us different from them. Better," Blaisey said, her smile illuminated by the firelight. It reminded Rolland so much of his mother's, there was no way he could say no.

Walking over to the screaming, burning man, Rolland picked up one of the large buckets of water that the Elemenos had on hand for drinking and approached the immobilized Hess. Perhaps it was the clanking of the water buckets, but something kept him from hearing what everyone else did: the sharp crack that signaled the return of Alora Hess and her electric-blue whip as she appeared onto the scene.

Alora teleported in next to her brother and with one crack of her whip that cleared a ten-foot radius around them. This caught everyone off guard, especially Rolland, who stood up, ready for another fight. But with another crack of her whip, Alora Hess and her badly burned brother were gone.

The battle was finally over.

Delving deep into the ocean water, Judah squinted to see something, anything of value. But nothing clarified. The warm, murky water of the Gulf of Mexico drank him in and pulled him under in hopes of claiming him as part of its vast collection of hidden treasures.

Reaching his arms out as wide as they would go, Judah felt around in a mad attempt to find the side of the ship. Finally, the smooth roughness of the wood met his fingertips and he dove beneath it and up underneath to the hollow compartment directly beneath the slave quarters. There was enough give between waves to accommodate his plans of sneaking off once the pirates stopped paying attention to their surrounding waters, but he would need a bit of luck to pull it off completely.

Judah took a few moments to savor each deep lungful of air. The faint light from a candle above gave him some company as he waited for his companions, praying that his plan worked. Then without warning, Grimes poked his head out of the water next to him, followed a few minutes later by Arbuthnot and Bernie.

"What took you so long?" Judah asked Arbuthnot, grabbing a few of the holes in the ship's floor above them.

"That would be me, sire," Bernie said, smiling and lifting his left hand out of the water for the first time. A trail of crimson blood was leaking from the man's chest as he chuckled, his belly jiggling up and down.

"Oh Bernie…" Arbuthnot said before reaching for his comrade's wound. But before he could, Bernie was gone, sunken back beneath the water.

"Where did he go?" Grimes asked between gulps of air.

"My best guess, a shark," Arbuthnot said, coughing up a bit of water.

Sticking his head beneath the water, Judah could see very little if anything, though a very faint outline of a large, long, menacing figure was visible as it swam away from their group, slowed down by its struggling prey.

"Foolish sod, I'll be right back," said Judah before taking a few deep breaths.

"Where are you going?" Grimes asked Judah, ducking beneath the water for a moment as the ship went over a particularly high wave.

"Gonna get me some courage," Judah said, diving beneath the water and disappearing from their sight.

Swimming toward the strange figure, Judah kicked off the hull of the ship to give himself some momentum as he shot through the water like a missile. It didn't take long for him to realize two things. The first being that the object was indeed a shark, which held a still struggling Bernie, locked in his jaws as it swam deeper into the water's depths.

The second thing that Judah realized was that coming face to face with a shark when smelling like blood was not a wise choice. He watched as the shark's excitement reached a pinnacle, tearing Bernie in half as a cloud of blood surrounded the creature, obscuring him from view.

Thinking quickly, Judah swam directly to the creature's tail, grabbing it tightly before opening his mouth, and biting it enough to get a full taste of salt and blood. The result was a swift send off by the creatures extreme velocity as it swung around, coming face to face with its attacker, its prey still clenched, now dead, within its jaws.

Using its nose like a battering ram, the shark swam straight towards the blonde genius as its camouflage floated away. Prepared for this, Judah remembered his physics and performed a front flip as the shark made its move, leaving him straddling the shark's back.

Knowing that he had only seconds before the shark overpowered him, Judah scooted as close to the bucking animal's head as he could before beginning a merciless barrage of punches straight to the shark's nose.

Remembering his aquamarine training from the Academy of Light, Judah knew that the most effective defense during a shark attack was to focus your assault on its most vulnerable area, the nose. After the tenth blow, Judah began to lose count of how many he was getting in. The animal rocked and swam violently, but not nearly as badly as Judah had anticipated it would.

Finally drawing the shark's blood, Judah decided to let go and began to float back towards the surface, away from the retreating shark, and away from the two halves of Bernie.

The heavy burden of winning the day lifted, Rolland found refuge on a nearby log. There, he believed, he would have a few moments to collect his thoughts before…

"So what now?" said a voice from behind him.

Rolland knew at once that the voice belonged to Victor, and only now thought about how he had not talked to or thanked the man for standing guard at his bedside as Blaisey had claimed.

Walking into the clearing where the Elemeno encampment had been just hours before, Victor looked around to see more familiar faces than he anticipated. To his left sat Joan, looking hot, sweaty, and armed to the hilt with two rifles and enough ammunition to take out a brigade all by herself.

"That's a good look." Victor said to Joan, hoping to illicit a smile from the obviously stressed out commander of the Knights of Time.

"Hey, man," Rolland said tentatively.

"Hey," said Victor, an obvious weirdness lingering in the air.

"I, uh, just wanted to say thank you," Rolland offered, looking Victor straight in the eyes with the most sincere look he could conjure. "For having my back, I mean. And I'm sorry for leaving you with those dudes in black body suits."

While he said nothing, the broad, toothy smile that plastered itself to Victor's face and the rougher punch he delivered to Rolland's arm were evidence that the two were 'cool' again.

"Hey, it's okay. And you shouldn't be sorry. Without them I never would have saved you two," Victor said in his deep, booming voice, still smiling and trying to land playful jabs to Rolland's midsection. Despite his muscular, rock-like arms Victor was incredibly graceful and could masterfully fake-box with the best of them.

"So, what's their story?" Rolland asked, looking over Victor's shoulder at a group of the African American gentlemen in the black body suits who had taken over the Elemeno campsite, making it their own.

"Runaway slaves mostly," Victor said in a low, reserved voice. "Good men though, the hearts of warriors beat within their chests."

The topic was obviously a sore subject for Victor, so Rolland decided to change the conversation to something more optimistic. "Did you see the way Hess tried to crawl away with his hair on fire? Fucking hilarious."

The two shared a good, honest laugh together as Blaisey watched from a safe distance. She could not believe that a few hours ago Rolland, her great-grandson, had been knocking at death's door. Blaisey had heard stories growing up of mythical creatures and larger than life characters visiting her ancestors and explaining the ways of the world to them. These fables seemed more real than now than ever.

"We'll wait for Turtledove, and, in the mean time, you two behave. My husband is out there, and Sephanie, too," Joan said, looking out toward the ocean. She followed a wave from one hundred yards out as it crashed into the rocks on the shore in a matter of seconds. "The real question is, what do we do now?"

The swamplands and barren valleys that make up Western Florida are unique in the fact that they offer an abundance of absolutely nothing, but somewhere between the humid air and hard soil that his horse galloped across, Marcus Turtledove found himself wondering why. Why had fate chosen to place him in this time at this place? Upon further consideration, he realized that a simple explanation would seem almost moot at this point.

A slight northern wind blew past Turtledove as he re-entered the Creek territory, this time as an uninvited guest. He heard a rustling in the trees to his left. A scout, no doubt – one who would surely alert the others as to Turtledove's presence in their land.

He rode on at a gallop, careful to watch out for traps laid by the Creek people. It was not unheard of for them to act every bit the 'savage' their white counterparts made them out to be. Indeed, one of the Creek warriors favorite pastimes was capturing white settlers and scalping them for sport. The very notion made Turtledove's stomach turn.

As he reached the small, wooded path at the bottom of the hill, Turtledove began hearing noises. Sensing danger, anxiety, and fear, Turtledove drew his sword from its scabbard and tossed it to the ground.

"I am unarmed!" Turtledove shouted, dismounting from his horse.

The hairs on Turtledove's arms began to stand and contort as the Creek warriors circled in on the leader of the Knights of Time, yet he did nothing.

In a matter of seconds, Turtledove was surrounded by over a dozen Creek assassins, all armed with bows aimed at his jugular.

"Bad move, white man," said the Creek warrior known as Arvi as he stepped forward to pick up Turtledove's sword.

"Please, take me to Blackfoot," Turtledove urged the Creek warrior with pleading eyes. His empathic instincts told him that the man, whom he recognized as Blackfoot's chief security officer, was riddled with the same angst and fear as the rest of them. He also had something else though… rage.

"You were warned," the Creek warrior known as Arvi said, before jamming the handle of Turtledove's sword into the old man's temple.

Like a misbehaving dog, Arvi continued to beat Turtledove with a reckless abandonment. He reminded himself that he was a soldier: a warrior for his people, who would not submit to the white man's will.

"Pick him up," Arvi ordered to the other Creek warriors, taking the hilt of Turtledoves sword and examining it closely. The embossed handle glowed against the late afternoon sun.

"Your leader, I must see-" Turtledove said, gasping for air and doubled over in pain.

"You can see our leader. Take him to Levi," Arvi said to the two Creek guards behind him,

Levi was the last person Turtledove wanted to see at that moment, but surrounded and unarmed, there was little he could do about it. Arvi had bested him, and changed the game while Turtledove was away. Now he must deal with Levi, who had threatened Turtledove with death on his last incursion into their land.

"You should NOT have come back, old man," Arvi said before spitting on Turtledove and stomping away like an overgrown child.

Turtledove had expected this sort of reaction upon his return, but saw no other way to gain the trust and support of the Creek people. No, he had been around long enough to recognize a change in leadership. If the Creek and Nabawoo peoples were to unite, it would be with Levi as the leader, not Blackfoot.

Chapter 24: Nothing Further

On the Pensacola coast, roughly ten miles inland, sat a large trading ship that had been marooned when a flood in the latter half of the 18th century washed her onto her side. The rickety wood and rusting nails of the hull creaked and groaned with age.

From the bowels of the marooned ship came a long, slow, pitiful sound. The pitter-patter of footsteps echoed in bursts, mixing with sobs for mercy and sharp intakes of breath.

Two distinct shadows could be seen on the flat wooden doors that once led to the upper deck. They were as different as they were secure in their two roles, master and groveling subject.

"I've been waiting for you, Puck," hissed a voice from the large figure cloaked in shadow.

"Forgive me, my liege," Puck said, his curly, ginger hair bobbing back and forth as he quivered. "I meant no dis- disrespect, sir."

The dark figure rose from where he had been leaning against the wall and walked to the edge of the shadows before beckoning Puck to meet him there. The skinny, ginger man responded, hesitantly walking to the edge of the darkness with more than a mild apprehension.

"Since you felt the need," the shadowy figure said, drawing Puck's left arm in closer and turning its head to capture the dangling morsels that were trapped there. A crunching noise, followed closely by another identical crunch filled the air, leaving a perverse silence in its wake.

Puck's face was a stark white mask of shock when the darkness released his arm. Stepping backward, he looked down to see his pinky and ring finger missing, cleanly snapped off by his master. He didn't say a word for fear of further punishment: the line had been crossed and he dare not push further.

"Thank you, master," Puck said, his voice cracking. A chill fell over him as his body went into shock, his mind numb with the desire to escape his master's presence. "For allowing me to live."

Puck longed for the days when he only dealt with the man in the sweater vest.

A faint scream broke the concentration of the classically beautiful teenage girl with the responsibility of an entire people on her shoulders. Tina Holmes sat alone at a small writing desk in the middle of a large tent. With a pen in her left hand, she scribbled out the plan of attack for the following day with a ferocity inherited from her father.

Tina's mind and heart played a game of chess for her attentions, as thoughts of Rolland kept creeping into her head. She had been so sure he was dead, but her eyes didn't lie to her. If he was alive, then it was possible that the two of them might somehow find one another.

"Madam, I thought you could use a break." Enapay said, entering the tent with a beverage and placing it near her hand on the desk.

With only the purest of intentions, Enapay wanted to offer physical comfort as well as refreshment, but he wasn't sure how to approach his commanding officer.

"I appreciate you thinking of me, Enapay," Tina said, blushing slightly at the rather forward gesture of drinks and wondering how anthropologically this custom had managed to continue through the centuries.

"Yes, I think of you often," Enapay replied, moving closer to her as one hand found its way to her back and the other to her face. Their eyes met, and a quiet understanding washed over them, quelling the spark between them forever.

"It's just that there's someone else," Tina said, every fiber of her teenage body wishing this moment had taken place a week earlier, before she had met Rolland.

"The white man who distracted you this afternoon. It's him, is it not?" Enapay asked, displaying a unique insight into the mind of a near stranger.

"Yes, actually," Tina said, abandoning all sense of professional dignity and opening up for the first time since joining the Nabawoo. "I thought he was dead, but seeing him…"

"Say no more," Enapay offered, holding a finger to Tina's lips and stroking her left cheek softly. "A leader does not owe her soldiers any explanation."

"You are my friend, Enapay," Tina said, holding his hand and looking him in the eye. "Thank you for having confidence in me, even when I don't."

Enapay, though not thrilled with this rejection and subsequent emotional outburst, understood the pressures her job was placing on her and believed it to be his duty to alleviate these in any way possible.

"You are the only one smart enough to lead us to victory," said Enapay, backing out of the tent and leaving Tina to her thoughts.

Deciding that a gathering was in order to discuss their next course of action, The Knights of Time, Nabawoo, and freed men met in the clearing where Hess had fallen just hours before.

"Turtledove is gone," Joan said flatly, not allowing any semblance of doubt in her wake. "And I'm taking the lead on this mission."

Silence filled the clearing as the motley group of warriors watched their new leader give the first of what promised to be many rousing speeches.

"Where did he go?" Rolland asked, sitting between Victor and Blaisey.

"I'm guessing that Turtledove gave himself up to the Creek as a sacrifice and token of friendship," Joan replied, looking at Blaisey for confirmation.

"Yes, that seems likely," Blaisey nodded in agreement, this new method of making decisions by council piquing her curiosity.

"Meaning that as a prisoner of war he should be relatively safe, right?" Joan asked, directing her question at Blaisey but not making eye contact.

"They'll scalp him," Blaisey said flatly. She looked to Rolland, who shot her a look of concern.

"Great," Joan said as she sat back down and grabbed a nearby bottle of what Rolland assumed to be alcohol, taking a long swig and staring off into space. "Just great."

"So what's the plan?" Victor asked Joan, a chorus of 'yeah' from the runaway slaves accompanying him.

None of them had any answers. Not Rolland with his supernatural orbs of light, or Joan with her battle experience. For once, neither the Nabawoo warriors nor the freedmen offered to lead the battle against the American forces, fearing utter destruction and certain death. All were quiet, all were terrified.

With the group coming to nothing even close to a unanimous decision, the only reasonable course of action was to adjourn and reconvene in the morning. This left many restless spirits still eager for action. Joan, Blaisey, and Rolland were left alone as the uneasy alliance broke into its separate factions.

The free men dressed in black body suits gathered around Victor, who told them tales of their futures as inspiration for fighting, after offering up two or three guards to keep watch while the rest slept.

"Barack a what?" asked a confused Mansa as he forced another strip of alligator meat onto his skewer and rested it on a rock to roast over the fire.

"Barack Obama. He'll be the first black president of the United States." Victor said with a grin. It was childish, but he could not help himself. Being the first person to regale these men with stories of such great African American leaders as Fredrick Douglas, Malcolm X, and Dr. Martin Luther King, Jr. was intoxicating.

"An African as leader of America?" another one of the men asked, causing a fresh chorus of skeptical laughter.

"It will happen, and we will all be equal in the eyes of man and maker." Victor said, his voice ringing with patriotism for a place he had never claimed citizenship to or spent any significant amount of time in.

"Are these good men?" one of the younger teenagers asked Victor. He appeared to be Latin in origin, perhaps from South America.

Looking down at him, Victor saw youth in the man's eyes, hope and the possibility of what the young man's future could bring – provided he was free.

"They are the best of men," Victor said solemnly, a flood of historical knowledge swimming through his head. He knew in his heart it would still be another fifty years before these people would be free from the bondage of slavery, and longer still before they gained any semblance of equality, but his Knightly oath held him to silence, and his sense of obligation kept him to his word. He would follow the example of these great men as he led these men into battle against insurmountable odds. "Just like all of you."

Luxury had taken on a new meaning since Sephanie had read Jackson's journal, and she couldn't be happier about it. Never in her wildest dreams had she imagined that the man she had caught stalking them to the fountain and beating his slaves like dogs could bestow such kindness on anyone, let alone her.

Still, Sephanie could not forget that she was nothing more to Jackson that a glorified pet, collared and kept for his amusement. That knowledge tore at her psyche all morning and into the afternoon, weighing her down and making her want to abandon her quest.

Wandering the hallways by herself was a big deal for Sephanie at first. Like a child with its first real responsibility, the guard outside her door attempted to stop Sephanie from exploring the place unsupervised on her first day at Jackson's compound, and finally insisted on accompanying her.

While most of the rooms were being used as storage for rations, ammunition, and various other supplies, some were being used as barracks, and others were completely empty.

Another odd thing Sephanie noticed was that though all of the doors had the capability, none of them were locked. After exploring the basement, and three out of the four wings of the compound, she hoped that the Dream Phoenix lay in wait for her behind door number four.

Jackson was a sexist. Although he seemed like a hollow man, taking Sephanie for a typical nineteenth century girl and not the strong-willed woman she was, he appreciated her in his own ways. He enjoyed her company, her companionship, and her unique physical attributes, the likes of which he had not enjoyed in years. Because of his male weaknesses, Sephanie was able to convince Jackson to let her go on her walk unaccompanied the next morning.

Sephanie walked down yet another corridor with another four knobs to turn and rooms to explore before she would have to turn around and start rechecking places she'd already been. The first room was empty, and the second was full of guns, but the third knob she tried did not jiggle. She had found a locked door.

With a renewed sense of purpose, Sephanie cupped her hands against the frosted glass and was barely able to make out the shape of the half-bed, half-chair that belonged to the Dream Phoenix. Jackson's words echoed in her head as she began plotting and picking at the door's lock.

"You are my guest, not my captive."

Solitude is a constant when you live on the streets. If you aren't dealing with the crippling realization that you are in your current situation because of your solitude, you are haunted by the lingering memories of what you once had.

Thinking on this, the brooding, blonde teenager walked along a well-beaten path to a clearing beside two small trees before sitting down and closing his eyes.

It was not long before he was interrupted.

"Your weapon," said Turtledove's voice from the path. "Has already proven quite useful. Tell me, where did you find it?"

"Oh, you know," Rolland replied, not opening his eyes "Just lying around."

Without looking, Rolland could tell that the apparition of Marcus Turtledove was giving him a scowl worthy of his late mother.

"Thought that I might have had a moment to myself but I realized they're totally overrated," Rolland said sarcastically, placing both of his hands behind his head and resting them there, half-leaning against a dead tree.

"Your brevity in stressful situations will serve you well, provided you don't lose it," Turtledove's apparition said, examining Rolland closely.

"Oh, you mean because I died and all?" Rolland asked bluntly.

"I would prefer to think of it as a near-death experience, but yes," Turtledove stated, his apparition walking around the dimly lit tree line to Rolland's right.

"He says hi, by the way," Rolland said, looking right through the smoke of Turtledove's likeness. "The Historian, I mean. Says you've done a great job as Protector of Eden. He's glad he chose you."

What followed was the first known case of a ghost blushing. Truly, it put Casper to shame as the friendliest ghost.

"So you met him, and he said all that, did he?" Turtledove said in one of those statements that's phrased like a question but is really a reiteration of fact.

"I don't want to talk to you," Rolland said, turning away from Turtledove and closing his eyes. "You left."

"I did leave, but that's no reason not to talk to me, especially if you're thinking of leaving, too," Turtledove's apparition said, scratching his nose and adjusting his glasses.

"Why did you just abandon us?" Rolland screamed, knowing full well that his anger and blame was misplaced by a generation.

"It's called strategy, Rolland. And this is a good one. By enlisting the Creek to our cause we might just be able to stop Jackson and Vilthe," Turtledove's apparition said, his smoky chin bobbing up and down as he spoke.

"Whatever," Rolland retorted smartly before storming off down the beach, only to be followed by Turtledove's apparition.

"Please just listen to me. Vilthe is here," Turtledove's apparition said urgently.

"I know," Rolland replied, staring straight through the ghost's eyes.

Disappointed and hurt, Turtledove's apparition nodded once before vanishing, leaving Rolland to stare beyond to the native girl standing close by.

"I was looking for you," Blaisey said, walking to Rolland and sitting down next to him. "We need to talk."

"Ok, let's talk," Rolland replied, watching Blaisey eye their surroundings suspiciously.

"Are we alone?" Blaisey asked him with the utmost seriousness. "No ghosts around?"

Wanting so much to laugh at her, he decided to keep his mouth shut and simply go with the flow of the conversation. "No, no we are completely alone. What's up?"

"The group doesn't seem to be deciding on anything, and well... I just..." Blaisey offered, trailing off. She did not know exactly how to phrase her thoughts without sounding selfish.

"You want to find your father, don't you?" Rolland ventured a guess, knowing full well where Blaisey's priorities lay. "And your brother, and sisters?"

"I am very grateful that you are alive. Very happy. I just think that for the good of my people, their leader should be..." Blaisey said, before being interrupted.

"No it's alright, I understand. I'm in, let's do it," Rolland said, his mouth forming the words as if he was being compelled to say them.

This chivalrous act brought a happy response from the Nabawoo Princess as leaned over to hug her great-grandson.

Maybe it wasn't chivalry that compelled Rolland to do it. After all, he had only known the girl for two days. No...it was something else. Something deep down inside his soul that called out and told him not to allow Blaisey to pass into the night like some forgotten memory.

Rolland's decision was quick, but confident. "It's time we take a stand."

"No more bull's shit?" Blaisey asked, a smile appearing for the first time since she pulled him from the battlefield bleeding.

"No bull's shit," Rolland said, smiling back at her.

And with that, the two of them gathered the necessary supplies before making their way out of what had been Elemeno territory and traveled on toward the American-occupied Creek lands. On toward Jackson, on toward Nahoy, on toward Sephanie, and on toward the answers Rolland sought after his near-death experience.

The Creek native known as Yatia was always the first to wake up in the morning. If he had been born in the 20th century, he would have been right at home as a military drill instructor. Despite his short, stout frame, he possessed a certain air of authority. As it was, he had been tasked with the unappealing task of skinning the kill that the hunters brought in every morning. In this role, Yatia had excelled for many years, always dependable and never falling behind or failing to hand the animal carcasses off to the cook.

This morning was different. Today, Yatia had not woken up on his own, but had been startled awake during the night by Levi, the head of Creek perimeter security.

"Can you handle it or not?" Levi demanded of Yatia, mere moments after pulling the man from his pallet.

"Yes," Yatia replied in his soft-spoken voice, looking up at Levi and seeing the zealous smile of a seasoned warrior staring back at him.

"Good. Be there in an hour," Levi commanded, walking away from Yatia's tent.

After eating his breakfast of oats and honey, Yatia gathered his tools and set out for the place Levi had arranged for their meeting: the farthest reaches of the Creek land and the place of their greatest tragedy, the Valley of the Blood-Stained Earth.

Arriving at the grassy field on foot, Yatia half expected to find Levi and a group of Creek warriors gathering for a day's campaign, or preparing for a hunt. What he found instead was one old, white male prisoner. Although one of his eyes was swollen shut, his importance was obvious from the fact that he still wore his scalp.

"Do it," Levi said to Yatia, walking past him and joining Arvi.

"Please – you don't," Turtledove said, coughing up blood as he plead his case. "You don't have to do this."

Yatia sat down calmly beside Turtledove, opened the turquoise bag he had brought with him, and began pulling out the small fish hooks that he used to torture enemy captives. He placed one of the small hooks beneath Turtledove's right middle fingernail, and pushed until it was clearly visible halfway down the nail bed. Applying force, Yatia bent Turtledove's nail back until it ripped and twisted.

"Where are the Americans attacking from?" Levi asked Turtledove.

"I am not American, I wish you no harm, I just – "Turtledove screamed.

The motion was swift and did its job, severing the fragile bit of tissue that lay between Turtledove's fingernail and the flesh beneath. Surprise mixed with pain caused him to fall over in agony.

"Wish you no harm…" Turtledove mumbled weakly, offering no resistance as Yatia and Arvi hoisted him up by his shoulders and placed him back into position.

As Yatia pressed the piercing steel into pink flesh, he could not help but wonder what the poor man had done to anger Levi so. Stories had been told of Levi's temper, but surely nothing could justify this degree of human suffering. Better to scalp and kill the man, clean and quick.

Marcus Turtledove withstood the agony of four severed finger tips before passing out from the pain. Not once did he relent, not once did he betray any of his companions.

Growing frustrated with this, Levi abandoned his questioning and demanded a private audience with the prisoner instead.

Yatia, all too happy to be dismissed after a particularly grueling morning, walked away a richer man for his troubles, but a lesser man in his soul. He turned one last time to see Levi cutting the prisoner from his bonds and arming him for combat: an event Yatia did not want to stick around to see. The last time he had seen Levi fight, it was over in seven seconds but had enough intestines and entrails to last him a lifetime.

A slap to Turtledove's left cheek roused him back to consciousness, and back to the situation at hand.

"Please," Turtledove said, spitting blood onto the ground in front of him. "What can I do to convince you that I'm telling the truth? What can I say!?"

"Nothing further," Levi said, sharpening his knife in preparation for Turtledove's slaughter. This drew the eyes of his would be prey, who was surprised to see Levi finish sharpening the blade and throw it to the ground near Turtledove's hands before removing another blade from his side.

"It is to be like this, then, is it?" Turtledove asked, leaning over to pick up the knife stuck in the dirt. "Very well."

Turtledove stood up carefully, cracking his knuckles, neck, and back before readying himself for what might be a fight to the death. He eyed his opponent wearily, not exactly sure what to expect from the Creek native with the bad temper and short attention span. Reflecting on this, one thing became clear to Turtledove; in order to win he would have to make the first move.

What Levi did not expect was for the older man to literally take flight. Using his well-maintained sense of agility, Turtledove evaded Levi by running along the side of the wall parkour style, rounding about and landing a swift kick to the back to Levi's head, sending the Creek warrior to the ground.

Composing himself, Levi jumped back up and caught one of Turtledove's ankles as he attempted to kick him in the chest. Flipping the old man over turned out to be a mistake however, as he quickly adapted, putting all of his weight on his arms and balancing upside down on top of Levi.

The two men fought on, Turtledove mastering the skies with his agility and Levi gaining the ground as his youthful legs landed easy blows to Turtledove whenever he got close. Both too stubborn and too proud to give an inch, fearing it might come with a hidden mile attached, their contest went on, eventually ending in a stalemate.

Chapter 25:
View from the Lowlands

Finding their way back to the healing fountain was easy enough. With Blaisey's tracking expertise, it took them less than an hour to get there from the Elemeno camp. They gave no notice to Joan or Victor of their departure, something Rolland regretted almost immediately.

It was with a considerable amount of surprise that Rolland and Blaisey arrived back at the cave to discover that a new resident had taken up quarters there. Surrounded by nearly fifty Elemenos and his usual gang of miscreants, Vilthe sat upon a makeshift throne as they moved around him.

"When did this happen?" Blaisey asked out loud as she and Rolland avoided the Elemeno guards' attention by hiding behind a large boulder on the hillside above the cave.

"Just as good a place as any, I suppose," Rolland answered Blaisey in a whisper. "Do you think he knows about the fountains?"

"He knows everything," said a female voice from the brush behind them.

"Who's there?" Blaisey asked, raising her bow and aiming into the darkness.

Rolland armed himself as well, pulling Scott's knife from his belt. Staring into the darkness, he expected to be confronted with another beast or something equally grotesque. To his pleasant surprise, however, it was not a green critter, but two blue eyes staring back at him from the bushes.

They were the same blue eyes that Rolland had seen staring back at him after their long kiss in the foyer of the Halls of Time, the eyes that had looked up at him from the banister the night he snuck out of his room and sent them all there. They were Tina's eyes, the seeds of his salvation and currently, the answer to a majority of Rolland's problems.

"Am I glad to see you!" Rolland said, a little louder than the occasion called for. His enthusiastic response was met with another of Blaisey's more-powerful-than-she-believed punches to Rolland's arm, making it tingly and numb in places.

"Good to see you, too. Hi!" Tina whispered loudly to Rolland and Blaisey. The nearly fifteen-foot distance between them was difficult to hold a conversation over.

"That's Tina," Rolland said to Blaisey, pointing at the teenage girl making her way across the divide.

"You don't say," Blaisey muttered, moving her bow slightly to get a better view of the goings-on below them.

Vilthe had convened a meeting with the Elemenos wearing vests, who formed a tight circle around their leader as he spoke secretively to their huddled, green mass.

"Do you see this?" Blaisey asked Rolland, scooting over a red package with the end of her bow. He recognized it immediately as some of the dynamite that Judah had stored in the corner of his laboratory what felt like a lifetime ago. Though he had seen something that looked like it in the cave before encountering the fountains, he had written it off as an oddly shaped rock. "There was some of this in the cave as well. Know what it is?"

"Is that..?" Rolland asked, leaning in closer to get a better look.

"That's dynamite," Tina said, taking a large step backward, playing chicken again with the ledge, raging teenage hormones getting the better of her logic.

"Oh, yeah, there was some of this in the cave," Rolland said, touching the outer casing of the brick of dynamite with his knife. Each was roughly the size of a shoebox and wrapped in a plastic sleeve.

"There's more of it over here. It must be from Judah's lab," Tina offered, picking up an armful of the red, Saran-wrapped explosive.

"What didn't fall out of the sky that day?" Blaisey griped under her breath.

Below them, Vilthe sat impatiently upon his throne. After giving instruction to General Hess, he had yet to hear back from him. The lack of communication was making Vilthe listless and unresolved. A bored monster is a dangerous monster.

"The Wright boy, he's alive," Vilthe said, raising his head higher and sniffing the air around him. "And he's here with someone."

At these words, several of the stout Elemeno guards standing behind Vilthe began to do the same, prodding the air with their whiskered muzzles for any trace of intruders.

"You better get out of here," Tina said, grabbing Rolland's arm subconsciously and giving it a squeeze. To her pleasant surprise, there was no give to Rolland's arm, only muscle.

"The native girl, Blasé, I believe is her name," Vilthe said, his voice somehow amplified as it rang out through the rocky green-belt above the cave. "Keeping your friends close, are you boy?"

An odd chill washed over Rolland as he crouched a little lower behind the rock. The thought of running was quickly pushed aside as his brain came to the conclusion that if this near omnipotent caricature of death knew of his presence just by being near, surely he could chase and catch him. Surely he would, surely... but what if that was the point?

With a renewed sense of purpose, Rolland turned to face Blaisey and Tina, both wearing grimaces of terror. A mischievous smile crept across his face before he said, "I've got a plan, but we've got to move fast."

Immediately moving past the discussion phase, the three broke apart and went about executing the finer details needed to accomplish their goal of getting Vilthe away from the cave.

Running around the far side of the hill, Blaisey placed a pack of dynamite in a small crevice, turning it sideways. This angle directed the explosion upward, creating a much-needed distraction for whoever was unlucky enough to detonate the mass of dynamite, a job she was not eager to volunteer herself for. She hoped Rolland was not too attached to the blue-eyed girl.

"I can smell you..." Vilthe taunted from his throne, drawing the attention of Blaisey and Tina, but not Rolland.

While Rolland and Tina were occupied laying more dynamite in other parts of the rocky incline above the cave, Vilthe sat still, guarding the cave like a junkyard dog in a sweater vest. Though his heightened senses could detect Rolland was in the area, he dare not send any Elemenos after the boy. Not before he knew how many he was up against.

It was Tina's direction that determined where the dynamite would be placed, being the most adept with architectural principles.

None of it made a lot of sense to Rolland, but the thought of Vilthe flying fifty feet in the air was too good to pass up. Even if it didn't kill him, it would be one hell of a show.

"We need to get more dynamite into the cave, I -" Rolland began, but stopped mid sentence as an urgent feeling snuck up on him. The need came out of nowhere, bringing with it an onslaught of itchiness and burning of his sinus passages. Without warning Rolland sneezed, a quick, loud expression that immediately gave away not only his position, but Tina's as well.

Laughter filled the air all around them as Vilthe realized what Rolland had done.

"Bless you," Tina whispered over to Rolland, a quiet, graceful kindness in her eyes. Though it was obvious that she was nervous from the multiple quick glances she shot over the edge, she was still smitten.

Vilthe brushed a leaf from his sweater vest as the sun began to set above them, signaling the end of the traveler's third full day in Florida. Though none of these people, save Blaisey, belonged in this time and place, all of them were imposing their will, forging ahead and creating history in their wake.

"The two of you should come out now," bellowed Vilthe, growing tired of placating the Wright boy. "There is no sense in trying to deceive me. I know all, I see all. Right now, I see two children who need to come out and allow the grown-ups to finish their work."

Tina, Rolland, and Blaisey all eyed each other, presumably with the same thought. It didn't matter, not when they were so close to executing their plan.

"Look, I have to detonate the dynamite. He already knows I'm here, what point is there in risking your lives too?" Rolland said, refusing to make eye contact with the fair-haired beauty that had found a soft spot in his heart.

"He's right," Blaisey said, placing her hand on the Tina's shoulder. "We should leave, and find your friends. Bring help."

"Listen to me," Tina shot back, grabbing Rolland's hands, holding them in her own. "Vilthe smells you, both of you, but not me for some reason…"

"You're not suggesting that you –" Rolland began, but much like when he called her by the wrong name in the Halls of Time, he immediately wished he hadn't.

"And why not me?" Tina said furrowing her brow and placing her hands on her hips.

Rolland smiled at Tina and nodded his head in agreement.

"Good luck," Rolland said, running into the open space between themselves and the pride of Elemenos below.

"Thanks…?" Tina said, watching Rolland foolishly draw the attention of nearly fifty green brutes.

When Rolland stood, he became visible to everyone in the valley, including Vilthe and his legion of Elemeno guards.

"Hey Vilthy!" Rolland shouted, flailing his arms around until he saw the eyes of his parents murderer fall upon him. "You look like Mr. Rogers' hillbilly cousin!"

Perhaps it was the vast cultural differences between them, or the crude manner in which Rolland addressed him, but Vilthe didn't move. Instead, he continued to smell the air between the two of them.

"Been making friends with supernatural storytellers, have you boy?" Vilthe shouted, somehow aware of Rolland's run in with the Historian. "Well, I've met him too. Told me I'd be an astronaut, whatever the hell that is. Point is, he's a fraud."

"You're still ugly, though," Rolland shouted, hoping to entice Vilthe into unleashing his forces. "How come you don't take people's looks too?"

The last comment did the trick, offending Vilthe's sense of vanity and causing the sweater-vest-wearing psychopath to send his Elemeno guards after Rolland. Not wasting time, Rolland took off, running away from the girls and back into the cover of the woods.

"What is he talking about?" Tina asked Blaisey in a hushed voice behind the boulder's safety.

"Best saved for another time," Blaisey said to her, grabbing her bag and chasing after Rolland, following him closely in to the brush line. "Come on!"

Motioning to Tina wildly with his hands, Rolland moved eastward toward the final pack of dynamite. Though it lay only a yard away from her on the overhang, Tina was hesitant to pick it up for fear of being seen by the Elemenos in the valley heading toward them.

Sensing her hesitation, Rolland walked out from behind the boulder's camouflage and eyed the group of green mercenaries with a cocky impudence reminiscent of his father, Scott.

"What are you doing?" Blaisey asked, grabbing Rolland's arm as he moved past her.

"I'm taking Vilthe out of the equation," Rolland said to her, placing his hand on hers and squeezing. This small gesture took only a moment, but would last a lifetime within the Seminole girl's heart.

"Just be careful." Blaisey said, her maternal instincts kicking into hyper drive.

"Yes, Rolland, do be careful," Vilthe said in a sing-song voice that evolved into an eerie laugh Rolland quickly grew tired of listening to.

"Give me your hand," Rolland called to Tina over the short distance between them.

"They're gonna see me and shoot and I'm gonna die, I'm gonna die!" Tina hollered as her face grew red with panic and body grew rigid with anxiety.

"They're not -" Rolland managed to say back to her before finding her hand in his. "Now jump."

Harnessing the confidence in his voice, Tina jumped across the divide, landing so close to Rolland that their previous kiss in the library would make them strangers. She had little choice but to wrap her arms around Rolland's waist, a welcome surprise for the both of them that perhaps led to Rolland's proclamation of "Here goes nothing," before snapping the fingers on both of his hands, and smacking his right fist against his left palm, effectively slowing down time to 1/100ths of its original speed.

"Wow, are we...?" Tina asked, looking around and seeing things as if it were her first time. Blaisey, the Elemenos, Vilthe, even the wind stirring up the dirt was moving in slow motion around them. Though none seemed to be doing anything particularly interesting, the speed at which they did so amazed her so much.

"Yeah," Rolland said to her, helping Tina up onto the ledge to get a better view by guiding her hips with his hands; she still had not unclasped her arms from around his waist. A familiar, and overly comfortable sensation gripped the hearts and hormones of both teenagers as their hands found each other.

"Rolland..." Tina said, her eyes searching his.

"Yeah...?" Rolland asked, leaning in for a bit for a more successful encore of their first kiss.

"I think I..." Tina said softly, drawing closer to Rolland before placing her free hand to his, and handing him something cold, long, and metal. "I found the detonator."

"Oh," Rolland said, taken aback by Tina's charm. Always the gentleman, Rolland stuttered a bit before attempting to shift his body slightly, and give Tina more room. She, however, had other plans, and in encroaching on his space further, ended up tripping him instead.

"Sorry," Tina said, looking down at Rolland as she knelt close.

"Don't mention it," said Rolland, as Tina scooted off of him and stood up to see Vilthe still on his throne. "Anything good?"

"Nope, everything is going as planned," Tina said, giving Rolland the thumbs up. "This is beautiful though. Can you do this any time you want?"

"I don't know, really," Rolland willfully admitted before he could stop himself. "Haven't figured that part out yet. Pretty much a crap shoot every time I try."

"This is…" Tina said, looking around again before finding Rolland's eyes. "Great."

Though he had never thought of it as 'beautiful', the more Rolland thought about it the more he realized that there were worse superpowers he could have, and maybe there was a certain charm to the world once it was slowed down. For all of his thoughts and feelings on the subject, his inarticulate lips could only muster a simple "I guess," before returning time to normal and changing the subject.

Blaisey came running around the corner to find them still caught in a moment of romantic possibility. The Nabawoo Princess cleared her throat, drawing their attention and reminding the pair that time stood still for no one.

"Here, take this," Rolland said to Tina, returning the detonator and breaking her train of thought.

Looking flustered, Tina accepted the device with an expression of mild embarrassment. "Thanks. I just wanted to say that I'm really glad you're not dead, and…"

"If we survive this, do you want to go out some time?" Rolland blurted without realizing what he was saying.

The two females stared at Rolland, one with indignation and one with unbridled enthusiasm.

"I'd love to," Tina said, her face turning bright red as she realized just how long she had been staring at him.

"Someone is mad at you…" taunted Vilthe from below them as the rest of the Elemenos closed in.

Rolland nodded his head and turned to leave, but Tina stopped him again.

"Sorry, but here take these," Tina said to Rolland pulling a small plastic box that sounded like it contained small pieces.

"Thumb tacks?" Rolland asked curiously, taking the small clear plastic box from Tina.

"Elemenos hate them, makes each one jump like ten feet in the air," Tina said smiling and rolling her eyes.

"See you later then," Rolland said to Tina as Blaisey pushed him out of sight, stealing a quick glance as they walked away.

"Bye," Tina mouthed silently. The smile was still on her face as she crouched behind the boulder before sliding down the hillside, and coming to a rest behind another large rock formation. A few moments passed before she stuck one arm out from behind the stone and made a peace sign with two of her fingers, then sticking her thumb through the peace sign to indicate the detonator.

Tina waited for a long moment before she saw the shine from the mirror she had given Enapay dance across the flat rock behind her. Her men were in place. All that was left to do now was make her move.

Sprinkling the box of thumbtacks at the bottom of the hill, Rolland and Blaisey jogged a few hundred yards before turning around to admire their handiwork.

"Well, that went well," Rolland said, breathing heavily but smiling.

"Yes," Blaisey said curtly, walking with her hands balled into fists.

"What?" Rolland asked her, attempting to balance his weight as they made their way down another hill.

"It's nothing," said Blaisey, skidding across the dirt to the bottom of the hill. She seemed to somehow almost walk above it, the very definition of grace. Blaisey reached the bottom with a smooth, satisfying landing, before turning to watch Rolland attempt the same.

Rolland was smack dab in the middle of an epic failure worthy of America's Funniest Videos. While the hill wasn't terribly steep, it was enough of an incline to give someone as large and clumsy as Rolland a hard time as he attempted justify his actions with Tina to his slightly older great-grandmother.

The absurdity of the situation was not lost on either of them.

"I just didn't know that you liked her, is all," Blaisey stated bluntly, a coy smile stretched from one of her ears to the other.

"She likes me," Rolland said matter-of-factly.

This newfound confidence was both surprising and perplexing to Blaisey, as until this point Rolland had been a fairly straight forward and modest individual. He was not being pretentious about it, simply accepting it as a fact of life.

"Uh-huh — and will she be bearing my great,-great-grandchildren?" Blaisey asked him, hoping to quash any thoughts he might have of fulfilling any of his teenage fantasies any time soon.

"Why?" Rolland asked, sputtering and cringing at the very thought of 'passing go' and not collecting the metaphorical two hundred dollars.

"Let's get moving," Blaisey said, softly punching Rolland square in the chest.

Not wanting to look weak in front of any female, Rolland was unsure how to respond, other than to comply with her demand to follow her. Half keeled over, his mind wandered toward the idea of growing up some day and having children with someone, anyone. Maybe Tina, maybe Sephanie, maybe someone else.

"So, what's the plan?" Rolland asked, changing the subject and shaking off the weight in his stomach.

"Head northeast, find my father, and take out Jackson," Blaisey said to him, settling her pack comfortably on her shoulders.

"Sounds great," Rolland said to her, feeling a sense of accomplishment for the first time in a while.

After fifteen hours on a raft with two other men, Judah Jacob Raines was ready to go back to the shark. Although grateful to find the bit of 20th century life floating in the Gulf, he was in no mood to be thankful for small miracles.

"Oy, where's that bag we nicked?" Judah asked his companions without opening his eyes. "With the rations I mean."

"Bernie had it, so it's the shark's now," Arbuthnot said, having given up mincing words when his friend was eaten.

"Bloody hell," said Judah, turning over onto his side for what felt like the 500th time that afternoon.

Grimes lay motionless, asleep from the looks of it. So Judah hoped. Grimes was an odd bird, content with not moving for long periods of time. They had been in the water maybe an hour or two before Judah began to worry that Grimes might be dead due to his unusual habit. Upon closer inspection, Judah found that he was better than alive; he was leaning on a long, yellow device that kept him afloat.

The hot Florida sun beat down mercilessly on the three wandering companions as their little yellow raft floated back to the Florida coast at a snail's pace. With no food, water, or shelter to protect them from the sun's fury, each man had taken to wearing his shirt as a headband and/or dunked it in water to keep cool.

"If we ever get back to land," Judah said, turning over again to face Arbuthnot. "I'm going to kill that son of a bitch Jackson."

"Get in line, mate," said Arbuthnot, the prospect of escaping the sun's death seeming less and less likely to him. It was nice to dream though, a pleasure that the insanity of heat stroke and severe dehydration could not stomp out of him. Not yet, anyway.

There was very little hope of reaching shore, a fact that all three men accepted. Not once did any of them mention their plight, for when circumstances look bad, it is the foolish man who points it out. The wise man sustains.

Without food, water, or sunscreen, the only nourishment any of the men could offer one another was the peace of mind of their communal resolve to survive.

With the planned invasion of the Seminole lands quickly approaching, reinforcements from Georgia began to arrive in Jackson's camp. One of these men, a Colonel Nicholas Donaldson, showed up as Jackson was finishing the evening scouting trip. When he arrived back at camp, the General immediately took notice of his batch of new recruits.

"Are the prisoners ready?" Jackson asked, dismounting with the assistance of a Spanish slave boy.

"They have been prepared for transport, General." Colonel Donaldson stated, his voice full of fear and respect. The oddity that was the camp of mindless drones with glossed over white eyes terrified him so much that he considered asking the General, but thought he might sound crazy.

"Good, Colonel..." Jackson asked, checking the man's uniform rank and folding the correspondence handed to him by another soldier.

"Donaldson, sir." the Colonel said, not yet fearful of his commanding officer like the other soldiers.

"Well, very good work Colonel Donaldson," said Jackson, bending down and plucking one of the daisies growing near the man's feet. He plucked half a dozen before realizing that the Colonel was unintentionally standing on a few. Righting himself, Jackson took a long smell of the flowers before gathering them all in one hand.

"You should be more careful of delicate things, Colonel," Jackson said, waving his free hand in Colonel Donaldson's direction.

Donaldson's corneas faded from his eyes, and along with them, the man's free will.

Like countless others before him, the Colonel was left but a helpless, pliable mass of human flesh.

Jackson walked back to his quarters, daisies in hand, thinking happier thoughts. Thoughts not only of what awaited him inside, but of the prospect of securing the fountain for Vilthe and fulfilling his promised destiny. He whistled a tune as he walked casually through the barracks, greeting each soldier he saw. Some still possessed their corneas, others were completely white-eyed.

"Keep up the good work, men," Jackson bellowed sarcastically, shaking hands and patting backs. This was his favorite part of the job. In rallying the troops he assured that they would love him enough to lay down their lives for him, their cause, and their country.

Chapter 26:
A Chance Encounter

The morning brought with it the promise of more than just enough privacy to use the restroom in peace. For Judah, the past twenty-four hours at sea had been marked by heat exhaustion, irritability, and thirst, but his chief concern was not for his own well-being, but that of his two companions. He feared they both might meet their untimely ends by his own hand should they not find land soon.

"It's land," Judah said with extreme trepidation. He rubbed his eyes and looked again. The Florida coastline that he had been forced away from days before was still there.

Paddling faster against the ocean current, all three men summoned what little energy they still had left in their fight to the shore.

"Look, people!" Grimes managed to yell through a bone dry throat.

"I see um, I see um!" Arbuthnot said, attempting to angle the raft by shifting his considerable weight to the left.

"Smart. I like it, ButtNot," Judah said, a hint of humor reappearing in his voice for the first time in nearly a day.

Perhaps it was because Judah and the others were so happy to see land, but they did not notice the green, almost leopard-spotted skin and pointed, feline ears donning the heads of the inhabitants of the camp until it was too late.

"Excuse me, I.... oh....." Arbuthnot said, the first of the three men to remove himself from the raft and approach the Elemenos.

"What the hell...?" Grimes asked, close behind Arbuthnot and noticing the red, beady eyes peeking out from beneath the thick tufts of dark green fur.

Several of the Elemenos hissed and began chanting. One or two of them held rifles, while the others appeared to be the straggling survivors of the attack on the beach a few days prior.

"Just do as they say," Judah said to the others, doubting very much that any the Elemenos spoke enough English to make sense of what he was saying.

"J.J., what are these things?" Arbuthnot asked as they were marched away.

They marched for only a few minutes before they came upon a much larger line of prisoners. Most of them were still dressed in their red uniforms, complete with all the trimmings of his majesty's armed services.

"They think we're British," Judah said, a smile finding its way to his face.

"We are British, mate," Arbuthnot replied from behind him.

"No, no, I mean they think we're just British. They have no idea who we are," Judah clarified.

"And who are we exactly?" Grimes asked, tilting his head back so Judah could hear him as the line of captives trudged further into the swamplands.

"We're the guys who are going to wreck their world," Judah said, holding his head a little bit higher than before. "Now let's get back to our loved ones before tea."

Though he appeared to be a confident leader, inside Judah's mind lay his true nature, that of skeptic and pessimist.

Sauntering through the woods with his hands tied behind his back, Judah found little comfort in the fact that he was not alone. A man he knew to be a mutinous pirate walked in front of him, hell bent on killing and pillaging everything he came across – not a total loss of life if he were to die today. At his back was a British officer who had the misfortune of being born a homosexual in the 19th century navy. All three of them were outcasts in their respective societies.

Truly believing himself and the others to be walking toward their deaths, Judah cast caution to the wind and began whistling a tune similar to 'Blitzkrieg Bop' to the confusion and amazement of everyone around him.

A quiet isolation between man and his own genius is always favorable over an existence of pandering to another while his intellect cries for nourishment.

There was nothing Blaisey would not do for her father. Even if she had to cheat, steal, and murder, Nahoy would be returning to his people before the day was out, she was sure of it; the only question was how.

As Blaisey and Rolland approached the large but poorly defended American encampment, two guards were clearly visible just inside the wooden gate.

"How are we going to get in?" Rolland asked, already ready to offer his time stopping services and show off to Blaisey what Tina had already seen earlier that day.

"I will take care of it," Blaisey said, her eyes already fixed on something just past Rolland's face.

A nearby grey pigeon was trilling happily as it searched for remnants of anything edible on the ground nearby. Blaisey walked over to it and began speaking in a throaty, incoherent pattern of coughs and face twitches. The bird immediately took flight, circled above their heads for a moment, and then jettisoned off in the direction of the two guards.

"Um, Blaisey?" Rolland asked curiously.

"Just wait a few moments. She knows what to do," Blaisey said, confident in the pigeon.

The bird flew above the heads of both guards for several minutes before either of them even noticed it. What they did notice, however, was the large amount of bird droppings it bombarded them with on each pass.

"What in the blue hell...?" one of the guards asked the other, reaching above his head to find a palm full of the white, gooey distraction.

Rolland watched this with absolute delight. His good humor was only broken when Blaisey grabbed him by the arm and pulled him in the opposite direction.

"Come on, while they are both distracted," Blaisey said, jogging to a small hole in the base of the wooden fence and squeezing herself through it.

While Rolland followed her through the fence and inside the camp, he could not help but be impressed at Blaisey's ingenuity and dedication. Though a bit disappointed that he couldn't show off for her, he was pleased with the result just the same.

Upon entering the American's vast military complex set up just outside of the native lands, it quickly became obvious that both Rolland and Blaisey would have to be sneaky to avoid getting caught by one of the hundreds of American troops stationed there.

The primary building had only one story and seemed to form a large letter 'H', with two front doors on the south end of the complex standing before them. The question was, which one would lead them to Nahoy and Sephanie?

"I'll go left, you go right," Blaisey said to Rolland, pointing to a hand drawn map that had been posted near the entrance for the benefit of new recruits.

"Hmmm? Oh yeah, sure," Rolland said, a bit distracted by the details, both the great and small, of being inside an actual American military complex in the early 19th century. Politics aside, it was a cool place to be for anyone who has ever picked up a history book.

Blaisey merely shook her head and ran to the door to the left, disappearing behind its wooden frame and leaving Rolland to his thoughts. Deciding to follow suit, Rolland jogged to a similar door on the right and walked inside. There was nothing on the other side but a long, dark corridor with several locked doors along the wall. For a few minutes he wandered, not seeing anything or anyone, until he saw Sephanie.

Upon entering the door, Blaisey found herself in nearly absolute darkness with nothing to guide her but a soft, far off light. Having no other choice, she followed it, and as she approached, she found herself face to face with George, Jackson's half-blind personal assistant. Though loyal to Jackson, his intentions were true on a higher level, one that spoke to the fiber of his character more than the color of his skin. Before Blaisey could raise her bow, George raised a finger toward a dimly lit hallway that led further into darkness.

"Dem kids, dem little kids is down there a that-a way," George stammered through the few teeth he had left.

Blaisey could not believe her ears. Although she understood him with the universal translator in her ear, she knew that saying anything would be pointless, for he could not understand her. Guilt wracked her heart as Blaisey's mind worked, quickly searching for a way she could convey her gratitude.

Raising her right arm, Blaisey balled her hand into a fist before pounding it softly against her heart twice, and holding it up at eye level. Her suspicions were confirmed, the man was blind.

Still, George smiled at Blaisey, hearing the beats against her chest. Though he knew, deep down, that he was betraying Jackson; he had seen the kind of man his late daughter's love had become. He could not support the sort of man who stole children. George was better than that.

They stared at one another, slave and Nabawoo, grateful for the opportunity to have met, glad for the chance encounter that brought them together that day. After a few moments, Blaisey smiled, turned, and walked in the direction the old man pointed. There, at the end of the long, dimly lit corridor was a single room lined with iron bars and a thick wooden door. Blaisey could see even without light that three small figures sat inside the cell. They were barely moving, but they were there.

Rushing to the door, Blaisey eyed the door, an old, rusty-looking lock hanging against the bars as the final barrier between the Nabawoo Princess and her family. With a zealous downward kick the lock popped off, allowing her to pull the remaining piece of metal from the door, and open the cell.

"Blaisey?" a boy no older than ten asked, sleep still weighing on his eyes as he moved slowly toward her. His wrists were thin and his face sunken with malnourishment. Still, he was alive.

"Yes." Blaisey said softly between wiping tears from her eyes.

"We knew you would come," the boy said, shaking his two sisters awake.

Together, Nahoy's four children left the dark confines of the cell and made their way back through the dim passages leading back to the entrance, and out past the gate to the freedom beyond. There, Blaisey sent her three siblings away toward the Creek lands, toward safety. Though reluctant to leave their older sister's side, her insistence on finding their father convinced them that her attention was needed elsewhere.

There she was - the girl who completed his strange and twisted fairy tale adventure, standing inside of what looked like a private quarters, next to a bed, vanity, and large mirror which reflected her beauty back to him. Rolland had not seen Sephanie since she and Jackson had left him for dead the day before. The jagged scars in Rolland's stomach could still attest to his shame on the subject, something he was not eager to bring up. With a silent apprehension, he approached the doorway before hesitating slightly, and finally taking a step inside.

Sephanie's philosophy of acting the same in great moments of joy and great moments of despair served her well in the poker game of life, but left those who cared for her approval wanting. Looking up brushing her hair, she looked into the mirror to see Rolland standing there behind her, walking into the room slowly. She turned around slowly, half expecting him to disappear.

"You look good," Sephanie said, taking special notice of Rolland's small, yet toned abdominal muscles. The classic six pack was common enough, but objectifying men when possible was a personal pastime Sephanie happened to be fond of.

Unbuttoning all of the snaps on the front of Rolland's pearl snap in one, fluid motion Sephanie flung it open and off of his shoulders before casting her eyes downward and crouched low to get a better look.

"Looking real good," Sephanie remarked as if she were underneath the chassis of a classic automobile. "Fountain water?"

"Yeah," Rolland said bashfully, hits hand immediately grabbing the two sides of his pearl snap and proceeding to re-snap the corresponding buttons.

"So, what are you doing here, kiddo?" Sephanie asked Rolland, hoping for some sort of insight.

"I'm here to rescue you," Rolland said, puffing his chest out a bit in his best action hero impersonation.

In what Rolland would remember as the most emasculating moment of his entire life, Sephanie burst out laughing, wreaking havoc on Rolland's composure and personal feelings.

"Are you serious?" Sephanie asked, wiping a tear from her eye with the back of her hand.

"Yeah, but I – well what I mean to say is…" Rolland stuttered, seeking the right words as his mouth dried and he began to sweat in other places.

"Look, I don't need to be rescued, but thanks for thinking about me. I know your father would be proud," Sephanie said as she wrapped her arms around Rolland's neck, further confusing his impressionable seventeen-year-old mind.

"First of all..." Rolland said, grabbing Sephanie's hands and pushing her away with a gentle but firm body check to her side. Despite Blaisey's opinion, Rolland was still determined to have his say. "You're like what, a year older than me? And calling me kid? Not classy."

"Shut up!" Sephanie said, a bit taken aback by the sudden appearance of Rolland's spine in her presence.

"You'd like that, wouldn't you?" Rolland asked, throwing one of his arms up in the air in mock indignation. "But only so you could sexually harass me."

The jingling of keys and the clanking of metal on metal told Sephanie that Jackson was back, probably outside the door and on his way inside.

"He's coming, you have to get out of here!" Sephanie said, grabbing Rolland by the back of his collar and walking him out of the room to a door he had not previously seen. Before he could get a word out, he found himself on the opposite side of the old wooden door, frustrated and anxious. Dignity is a funny thing. It seems important in theory, existing in the fine line between self-loathing and egotism. Yet what good would we be as a society without a good stroke of the ego every now and then?

Turning around, Rolland pressed his eye to the small fogged glass window and realized that someone had entered the room immediately behind him from its intended entrance, though it was immediately impossible to tell who. The figure was taller, and more importantly had much wider shoulders than Sephanie. It was probably a male. It was probably Jackson.

Sephanie's figure pulled Jackson's closer as he moved his hands from her shoulders to her hips.

Rolland immediately began a frantic search for a hole or a crack in the door that would give him a better view. Within seconds he had found it, though once his eyes confirmed what he had feared, he immediately wished that he hadn't.

Jackson's eyes never left Sephanie's body as she drew him into her web and rewarded him with a long, passionate kiss. They stood there for several moments, lost in a moment of passion. Forced or not, the moment between them was as odd as it was real.

When the two finally did break apart, Sephanie's eyes remained closed while Jackson's focused on her face, no doubt in an attempt to hypnotize her into further exploring their chemistry. Both men knew then that up until that point Sephanie had not been under the influence of Jackson's supernatural charms.

No, Rolland knew better. He knew that she was doing this of her own volition, and in front of him, no less. This was a display, a message, clear and direct. Sephanie wasn't interested in him, and just wanted to make as big of a fool out of him as possible. Probably so she could go back and tell Judah so the two of them could have a good laugh at his expense.

"I've been thinking about your offer," Sephanie said to Jackson, resting her hands on either of his face before they drifted down to his neck. The crook of her arm rested there, acting like a doorstop to maintain the distance between them.

Sephanie had perfected this technique as a means of driving men wild on previous missions - sort of a Weapon X, or ace in the hole for whatever side she was playing for at the moment; and right now Sephanie felt loyal to herself and no one else. "I'll do it."

"Splendid!" Jackson said, leaning into Sephanie once again and kissing her on the forehead. "We'll get started right away."

Rolland could not help but watch through the crack in the door that his entrance had made. Pain and jealousy tore at his heart like savage vultures circling his newly crushed heart in the afternoon sun. With a heavy heart he rose to his feet and began to walk back down the dark hallway, this time without a mission.

The hallways of the American compound seemed almost like a maze to Blaisey as she maneuvered her way down the path she knew would lead her to her father. With very little resistance, it took Blaisey barely half an hour to discover the cells where her father was supposedly held.

There were four of them, all of which were empty save for a few leftover possessions from inhabitants who had, until an hour ago, called them home.

Finding the first one covered in risqué drawings of women, Blaisey moved on to the second cell only to find similar clues that it did not belong to her father.

It was the dream catcher that sat on the makeshift bed in the third cell that caught Blaisey's eye. She picked it up and thought of the last time she had seen her father, right before Rolland and his people had arrived.

The memory seemed so long ago, far longer than the four days that had actually passed. An odd thought when rationalized against how long Blaisey had known Rolland. For those few days felt like a lifetime due to their numerous adventures.

A nagging notion in her mind and a crippling fear of losing her father in her gut told Blaisey to hold true to her family, first and foremost. As she had done in freeing her siblings, so she would do in finding her father.

With Rolland's divided interests in other females, Blaisey feared that this time she would have to attempt a rescue alone. Grabbing the dagger she had brought with her off of the bed, Blaisey walked briskly out the door and back down the hall. There was no one who would stop her from finding her father. No one.

Turtledove was barely hanging on. The man with the grey beard and mystical eyes lay on the floor of the Creek teepee, helpless and beaten. Both of his hands were bandaged from the torture that Levi had ordered the day before. Though he had resisted the pain and refused to give the Creek second any useful information, it had cost him dearly.

Drifting in and out of consciousness, he was only half aware of the man sitting nearby and offering him water from a crudely made cup. The moment it touched his lips though, the old man came alive.

The coughing was first, followed by a realization that Blackfoot, leader of the Creek people, was crouched there by his side. Levi was nowhere to be seen.

"You have pledged not to do us any harm," Blackfoot said to Turtledove, his moist breath falling down on the protector of Eden with a complete disregard for its impression. "You have allowed us to harm you. Allowed us to disfigure you. Torture you. Yet you still keep your pledge."

The limitations imposed on Turtledove's hands provided him with a constant, if not mundane, activity to keep his mind sharp while his nerves cried out with pain and anguish.

"It's not too late to help Nahoy," Turtledove spoke softly between gulps of air and water.

"A humble man to the last," Blackfoot said, a smile crossing his lips as he poured a cup of water for his captive turned ally. Offering both the cup and his assistance, Blackfoot added, "My army is yours."

Back at the cave, Tina watched as the morning sun brought renewed vigor to the Elemenos surrounding Vilthe. A parade had marched into the camp, headed by two people that she recognized: Alora, and her half-healed, half-burned brother, Rudolph Hess.

"I wish I had better news, my liege," Hess said to Vilthe as he slithered away from the man in the sweater vest.

"Rudolph..." Vilthe patted the battered man on the chest delicately. With each pat, Vilthe's eyes grew redder with his mounting fury. The rage inside of him was building, multiplying within the empty core of his soul.

"If I wanted an excuse I would have asked Puck to bring the boy back. Instead I asked you," Vilthe continued, extending his hand and patting his inferior counterpart on the head in a comforting, accepting way. "But that isn't what I asked for, is it Rudolph?"

"No. No, my master," Hess said, tears of fear forming in his eyes.

Alora stood close by, tears streaming down her face as she watched her helpless brother bear his punishment for failing their master in battle. Her red hair was matted with dirt, and hung lazily over her face, mixing with her fresh tears and making it impossible to see her face. Still, she made no sound for fear of joining Rudolph in their master's bad graces.

"You do realize, Rudolph, that without at least one of the Travelers of Light I cannot open the cave, and therefore cannot claim the prizes within," Vilthe said, pacing purposefully across the makeshift throne area the Elemeno slaves had hastily prepared before his arrival.

"Yes, my master," Hess said, shaking slightly from both nerves and his badly beaten body. "Please do not tell-"

Vilthe stopped his pacing and turned to face Hess. Walking over to the nervous man, Vilthe bent down so that he was only slightly taller than his servant, intimately close.

"You shall bring me the head of... oh, two Knights should do it," Vilthe said, placing his fingers underneath Hess' chin and raising his face slowly. "Then, and only then, shall you be back in my good graces."

The jubilant look on Hess' face must have disgusted Vilthe, for he raised his hand and knocked Hess back to the ground, where he landed with a thud. He smiled and motioned for Alora to collect the unconscious man.

"Take your brother," Vilthe said to the mass of hair that was Alora. "And be sure that one of those heads belongs to the boy."

With each curve of the path the Elemenos led them down, Judah recognized more and more of where they were being marched to. The familiar sloping of the path, the odd shape of the vines as they grew in a spiral formation... all signs that meant the green cat beasts were taking them to the cave that housed the fountain and gateway to Eden.

Because of this, Judah made a calculated decision about which one of his fellow Brits he liked more. The choice was very easy. Leaning in close to Arbuthnot, Judah got as close as permissible by the guard whose attention had lapsed for a rare moment.

"Listen quick, Buttnot, I think I know where we're going. If I tell you to get down, you be ready to hit the deck. Right? " Judah said in a tone slightly above a whisper.

"What? How? Where?" Arbuthnot asked Judah, making enough of a commotion that he attracted the attention of many of the Elemeno guards, three of which moved in on their position after stopping the processional.

Judah immediately threw both of his hands in the air in a sign of submission before proclaiming loudly, "Easy boss, I don't want no trouble."

"That's a shame, because it looks like you're in a lot of it, Doctor," said a low, scratchy voice from behind Judah that he immediately recognized as the bastard Vilthe. Judah turned around slowly, hesitant to come into physical contact with death incarnate… and the man who cost Judah two years of his life.

But to his surprise, it was not the dark, ominous figure Judah had expected. Instead, there was a slender man standing before him with both hands stuffed neatly into his tweed pockets.

"Who are you, then?" Judah asked, looking Vilthe in the eyes. The deep chasm of black nothingness that awaited him there fell on Judah's shoulders and heart all at once, stealing the breath from his lungs.

The Elemenos all cowered and lowered their heads in fear of their master's retaliation. Though not believed to be incredibly intelligent beasts, the wisdom of proper respect shown to Vilthe was evident, even to their tiny minds.

"You may call me, General Vilthe," he said as he looked down his nose at the blonde man. With his arms still bound behind him, there was little chance of the prisoner retaliating against Vilthe, no matter what he did. Still, there was something to the blonde man's scent. Something foreign, something that smelled like Eden…

"I think I shall make an example out of you," Vilthe said, rising to his feet and approaching his prey with the speed of a much younger man.

"You're not Vilthe." Judah said with an obnoxious smile that he had mastered over the years when pointing out the mistakes of others.

At this statement, every head in the camp, human and Elemeno alike, turned to stare at the two men; Judah was lifted effortlessly in to the air by a mere flick of Vilthe's left hand, where he hovered for several long moments as the scoundrel studied him intently. With another, almost cavalier flick of his opposite hand, the force holding Judah broke, releasing him to gravity's will.

Dropping like a large sack of potatoes, Judah coughed furiously trying to catch his breath as his would-be murderer lorded over him demanding answers. Confusion setting in even deeper, Judah composed himself before answering with a curt, "I've met Vilthe, I've fought Vilthe. Hell, I've even had a drink or two with the old bastard and believe me when I say boy-o, you are not Edward Vilthe."

Not a sound was made throughout the entire camp, possibly even the entire forest; all eyes were glued to Judah and the man who had called himself Vilthe for hundreds of years.

"I am Vilthe. At least I am for the time being, and I'll be damned if I'm going to let some sniveling little bag of meat like you stop me from getting into that cave. Now, open it or die!" Vilthe demanded, kicking Judah hard in the stomach and sending him sideways into the dirt below.

"Go back to hell," Judah said, coughing up blood as the pain in his side began to ease.

"Oh, you first." Vilthe said, placing his hands behind his back and smiling at Judah. "Shall we proceed with the execution then?"

At his words the Elemenos sprang into action like ants on a hill, each lost in their respective role amid the sea of green leopard print and poorly made togas as they prepared to rip and claw at the cave entrance in the event that whatever it was Vilthe was hoping Judah would do did not work.

Roughly five hundred yards away sat the graceful sleeping form of Tina Holmes, who had been waiting for Vilthe to make a move toward the cave for over twelve hours. She awoke to see a mass exodus of Elemenos as they moved away from their lines in front of Vilthe and toward the cave and outlining rock formation where the dynamite was placed.

Removing the pocket mirror from her side, Tina flashed it against the flat side of the rock, catching the sun's rays and making a light visible for a few moments. The signal was returned a mere seconds later, probably by Enapay, who had most likely been up all night worrying about Tina's safety.

Peeking out from around the boulder's edge, Tina saw for the first time who exactly it was that was drawing Vilthe's venomous hate. Though she had never connected in any meaningful way with Doctor Raines, Tina respected him as the smartest and perhaps most capable of all her colleagues. Besides, saving his life would look great in a recommendation letter. The pressure to make or break the situation was now squarely on Tina's shoulders.

In the hustle of the Elemenos and the preparation of the firing squad, Judah and the other British servicemen were left unattended for a moment, just long enough for the smartest of the bunch to begin thinking of escape plans.

"What are these things?" Arbuthnot asked; sweat mounting an offensive on the cusp on his brow with each passing moment.

"They're sodding Elemenos, and you need to relax, alright?" Judah said, a resolute confidence filling his voice as they faced what appeared to the other to be certain death.

Looking around for a sign that his prayers were to be answered, the self-proclaimed smartest man on Earth was at his wit's end.

Luckily for Judah he, much like his wife, had friends in high places, as Tina slowly breathed in and out in an attempt to overcome her anxiety and act decisively, like a true knight would.

Like a silent but deadly blossoming of razor wire from smooth asphalt, the copper tips to over two dozen arrows hid beneath the darkness that the tree line provided behind Vilthe's firing squad. The sun rose just above the tree line, causing many of them, including Judah, to avert his eyes for a moment.

Noticing this strange emergence in a sea of hopelessness, Judah craned his neck around, and squinted his eyes to get a better view of the hooded figure standing front and center among the deadly barrage about to rain down on them. At first, the figure was indistinguishable, only coming into focus once his eyes adjusted to the light.

Tina Holmes' blue eyes were already a universally sweet sight for anyone lucky enough to find them, but in this moment, they were the saving grace Judah had been praying silently for.

"Well, baby blue..." Judah Jacob Raines said, smiling wholeheartedly.

One of the skinny Elemenos wearing a vest gave a small hand gesture using two of his fingers, prompting one of the others to approach Judah and beat him with the end of his rifle.

"When did they start arming you beasts?" Judah asked, pull slightly at his bonds, but to no avail.

"Last chance, boy," Vilthe hissed, leaning forward on his throne. "Open the cave now."

"No," Judah responded, his chest stuck out and his head held high. "Not for you."

Expecting an immediate reaction, Tina, Judah, Arbuthnot, and every Elemeno waited with bated breath as Vilthe leaned back into his seat and readied himself. "Very well, if you will not do as I have asked, then you will die. Have you any final words?"

"I believe in peaceful resistance and cool catch phrases," Judah said, in an attempt to not only draw the conversation out longer in hopes of Tina performing a miracle, but to also add a bit of levity to a literally life or death situation. In all of his years in the field, humor was the one variable that Judah believed could make a bad situation better, no matter the circumstances.

"Neither of which you can display here," Vilthe said from atop his throne. With his left hand he held up two fingers, causing two of the British soldiers in the firing squad to step forward and fire their weapons at Grimes. The first bullet missed him by a mile, but the second one hit him square in the heart. He died on his feet.

"Bastard!" Judah screamed, taking a step forward and drawing the attention of nearly the entire firing squad as they raised their weapons against him. The one standing closest to him approached, turned his rifle sideways, and rammed the butt of it into Judah's stomach before walking back to his original place in formation.

"Are you in such a hurry to die, Doctor?" Vilthe asked, laughing a bit under his scowl. "Am I not showing you more mercy than your so-called friends have? Is it 'not cool', as you say, to not even attempt to look for you?"

Silence filled the air as the metaphorical question resonated through both Judah and Tina's minds. It was the proverbial 'straw that broke the camel's back', and Tina stepped out from behind the boulder, revealing herself to every soul in and around the cave below.

"You're wrong, Vilthe," Tina said, lighting the match she had been holding for the past several minutes. "I am cool."

Rounding the corner, Rolland was in a world of his own. He no longer stuck to the side of the hall in hopes of not being caught. He no longer saw the point. Worst case, they caught him and he would get to take his frustrations out on someone else. Maybe it was something he was even beginning to hope for - thus are the inner workings of an angst-filled teenage mind.

They say that an animal in the wild knows its own scent above all others in order to mark and maintain its territory. Although this principle does not apply to human beings, something within Rolland encouraged him to go the extra one hundred feet to the door at the end of the walkway, something bright and inviting, like a lighthouse in a sea of time.

It was the cords that connected to the needle that caught Rolland's eye. Some genius had left the disposable tubes plugged in, obviously confused by 21st century technology in a 19th century setting. He could make out his own dried blood still filling the bottom of the tubes attached to the Dream Phoenix. The whole thing was horrific when viewed from Rolland's perspective. Still, the teenager couldn't be happier at the chance encounter that had brought him there.

Sitting within the confines of the cramped little room was the contraption that he had the misguided misfortune to tangle with back in the Halls of Time.

Rolland had found the Dream Phoenix, and with it, a clear path back to Eden.

Chapter 27:
Tragedy, Strategy

There is something to be said for those individuals existing on this Earth while truly believing it revolves around them, people who are so set on their specific wavelength, bypassing all other intensions and forsaking all others to meet their own ends. General Andrew Jackson fit this mold perfectly.

After vowing to change the mind of the harpy still waiting within his office, Jackson returned to the business at hand - eliminating the Seminole threat. Leaving the dim light of his office for the bright Florida afternoon, General Jackson mounted his waiting horse and made his way to join the line of officers standing at the top of the adjacent hill.

"Are they ready to move, Colonel?" Jackson asked, pulling on the reins of his horse to emphasize his own anxiousness. The horse reared on its hind legs and turned wildly.

"Yes General, sir," came the nervous reply from Jackson's new second in command.

Since Jackson had yet to learn the man's name, he referred to the man by his rank only, in case he met the same end as his predecessor, Colonel Frost.

"And the prisoners, where are they?" Jackson asked him slowly, freezing his already intimidating presence.

"In front, sir," the Colonel said, hoping to be free of his commanding officer's company.

"Good man. Well then, let's get to it. March!" Jackson hollered to his company, kicking the horse's side with his boot and galloping on to inspect the line of soldiers before they went into battle.

The Colonel turned and reiterated his superior's order to the other officers, who in turn rode to their respective regiments. Soon Andrew Jackson's four thousand men were scrambling into battle positions, their muskets at the ready.

It wasn't that Jackson disapproved of the job his army was doing, it was just easier to win a battle when he was the only one making the decisions… for all of the troops. By tapping in to their collective sub consciousness. Jackson rationalized his actions by maintaining that the President himself had seen fit to appoint no other man but the hero of New Orleans to oversee this invasion of Spanish controlled Florida. Eradicating the natives was step one.

Once in position, the order was given to move out and the line began to move. Guns ready, boots laced, and cannons armed, every American soldier marched mindlessly head-first into certain death. At the forefront of this processional was not General Jackson or one of his officers. Instead, it was the two Nabawoo leaders, Nahoy and Charlton, both of whom were bound and gagged as they were marched toward their deaths.

From a safe distance away, Jackson watched as the two Nabawoo men he had been fighting for the better part of a year were at last taken away to meet their fate. Though the hour was still early, barely six o'clock in the morning, past experience had taught the General to always be on the lookout for possible rescue attempts from the savage natives that lived in these woods. The sound of twigs breaking below his horse's feet only fueled Jackson's paranoia.

The General's eyes dashed back and forth from the Seminole leader to the surrounding brush and tree line, scanning every square inch for a last ditch attempt to save the old man. If an attack were to come, surely it would be from the sides. But none came.

Jackson's supposed plan of marching the Nabawoo leaders head on into battle with their people, allowing the Seminoles to unknowingly kill their own leaders, was coming to fruition perfectly. If his secondary strategy, that of luring the British regulars into a concurrent fight from the north, trapping the Nabawoo between them and obliterating their chance for retreat, could also come to pass then he would win the day, adding yet another chapter to his legacy of greatness: a thought that sent a chill down his spine.

The sun's arrival overhead brought smoke and the sound of drums being played far off in the distance. The Colonel saw and heard these warnings first, knowing full well that natives wouldn't employ either of these tactics, nor direct combat. His suspicions were confirmed as the troops came into closer view, their individual red coats as distinctive as the stars and bars themselves.

"General! General, those aren't savages, those are the…" the Colonel was interrupted as Jackson raised his hand, depriving the officer of his free will and returning him to a more malleable state.

"Thank you, Colonel. You may return to your post now," Jackson said, lowering his arm.

"Yes, General," the Colonel said before rounding about on his horse and riding back to join his fellow soldiers.

The sight was all too sweet for Jackson as he watched one of the last remaining servicemen on either the American or British side who was not under his hypnosis be overtaken by it so quickly.

A feeling of elation washed over the General as he knew that soon he would have a high Seminole body count, an American victory, and a permanent role as a national hero.

Rolland looked high and low for Blaisey, but to no avail. The cell that had held Nahoy was bare, the hallway was clear, and he was officially out of places to look for the Nabawoo princess. He knew that without her help there would be no way he would be able to move the Dream Phoenix, but leaving it there unattended would be folly.

As he ran down the H-shaped hallways of the American compound, the burdens of the past week began closing in on Rolland again. All of the regret and misfortune that the Historian, if he was even real, had told him to forget, not harbor inside like some secret agony.

Nervous habits took over, goading Rolland's knuckles to crack, neck to pop, and hands to wander inside his pockets. These were annoying under usual circumstances, but when sneaking around armed guards they became liabilities that he had to purposefully remind himself not to do.

Then, like divine intervention, he saw it. There it was, and there it always had been. The answer came to Rolland in the form of a slick, heavy piece of metal that had been weighing him down since Rick's locker. Inspecting it, he spotted a bit of Jackson's dried blood from his first night there. Giving the combination lock a quick spin, Rolland decided to take the risk and slammed it shut on the hinges of the door leading to the Dream Phoenix.

Believing his ticket home to be secured, Rolland turned toward the exit and ran for all his worth, barreling out of the wooden door and past a couple of armed guards who stood in disbelief. He no longer cared about being caught or shot at, he only hoped that it was not too late to prevent Blaisey's foretold death. Though he had prevented the original events predicted by Judah's Cause/Effect machine, he knew it didn't necessarily mean that she, or any of them, would survive their misadventure.

A thought crossed his mind that made Rolland smile and mutter to himself as he ran. "Blaisey AND Tina would have thought of that combination lock quicker."

Little did Rolland know that another woman who had recently dominated his thoughts was hiding in the shadows of Jackson's compound and watching his every move.

The green eyes Rolland had pined for, yearned for, even took an arrow to the gut for, followed him every step of the way. Sephanie watched as Rolland pulled the lock from his pocket, secured it, and sprinted from the room.

Frustrated beyond belief that had Rolland found in a matter of minutes what she had spent the better part of three days looking for, Sephanie leaned against the padlocked door and sunk to the floor into a heap of brunette hair and melancholy.

"Why couldn't I have ended up with some dynamite?" Sephanie moaned.

Victor had barely slept since arriving in Florida. Though he had been averaging roughly three and a half hours a night, last night he had gotten absolutely zero rest, a growing uneasiness of what the next day would bring gnawing at his thoughts. The little rest he did receive came with an odd recollection of how he came to join the freedmen in black.

The night the men in black had freed him from Jackson's camp, they had been led by another man, an older individual known simply as J. While rescuing Victor, Mansa, and nearly a dozen others, J had taken a saber to the stomach. As he lay dying, he pointed to Victor, saying "You... I knew you would come back."

The shock of the unexpected proclamation, mixed with the already impressive display of his abilities back at Jackson's camp, made it easy for the leaderless Freedmen to elect Victor as their leader in J's place. He still had no idea who the old man was.

Awaking with a start, Victor cast aside memories for more immediate concerns. With the fresh batch of new recruits Victor had gotten from Hess and the Elemenos, came fresh legs and good men to fight for their collective freedom. After some light training and arming, Victor gathered his remaining forces and took stock of what he had to work with.

Nearly three hundred men, all of which would be otherwise helpless under the white imperialist powers that ruled them, now banded together to create a fighting force that could change all of their fates. Deciding to exercise their only option, Victor gave the order to move out, heading southeast towards the Spanish port.

Though the trip took his small army most of the night, they arrived just before dawn, securing a tactical advantage. Victor left Mansa and the majority of his soldiers behind, using only a fraction of his troops to seize the ships.

Leading the way, Victor took his rag-tag group within fifty yards of the dock before sending his scouts into the surrounding area. Squinting his eyes a bit, Victor could see the outlines of figures as they walked the hull of the ship, muskets by their sides. He planned on starting a fire onboard the ship to cause a panic and round up all of the Spanish sailors, but that relied on whatever intelligence that his scouts could provide him with. They had been gone for almost five minutes.

Without warning, gunshots rang out over their heads, forcing every one of the men in black to duck and cover. Trees, rock, and bits of Earth scattered like shrapnel in all directions as bullets pelted the ground around them.

Believing the fire to be coming from the trees, Victor motioned for his two right hand men before a fresh spray of bullets found their way to their location. The resulting barrage killed one of the men Victor was attempting to speak to, but the other managed to cover himself enough to avoid harm. Fearing that he had led hundreds of men into an ambush, Victor cautiously looked up to confirm his suspicions of where the fire was coming from before returning to his flat as possible state on the ground alongside his men.

As he settled back to the ground, another volley of bullets flew through the air, this time from the docks. It seems the Spanish had now taken an interest the goings-on only fifty feet away. With shots now coming at them from both sides, Victor and his one hundred and fifty men were caught in the middle of a gun fight with nowhere to go. Fearing that Mansa and the others he had left inland were dead, he knew that acting too carelessly now would surely cost him all of their lives.

Screams rang out in warning before cannon fire filled the air on both sides, sending everyone who had attempted to rise back to their hands and knees for cover. The explosions rocked the ground where Victor lay, causing large amounts of rock and dirt to rain down on him. One particularly large rock hit the back of his head, leaving a large gash and nearly knocking him out.

Cornered, defenseless, and nearly unconscious – Victor felt like he could only breathe in and not out. The sounds of the Spanish troops regrouping a mere five feet away gave him enough reason to stay awake, if only to witness his own destruction. Shuffling feet, kicked rocks, and moving leaves told Victor, even in his stupor, that he was still awake, if only barely.

Though the ringing in his ears was constant, the sounds of gunfire had ceased, giving him a small, comforting hope that perhaps he wouldn't die in this century - perhaps things would be alright after all. But then, as is the burden with all responsibility, his biggest concern was not his own welfare, but that of over three hundred other men.

"You there," came a low, Spanish voice from above where Victor lay, fading in and out of consciousness in a dull haze of ambiguous awareness.

Opening his eyes, Victor saw a tall, lanky Spanish man with shoulder-length, black hair pointing the end of his bayonet directly at Victor's chest.

"Victor Aquasi III?" the Spaniard asked.

"Yeah…?" Victor said to the man, a fresh layer of confusion laying itself onto his brain as Victor raised his head to examine the man closer.

"Took you long enough," the low voice said, changing pitch in the middle of the sentence and confusing the surrounding men in black body suits who had never seen someone change their physical appearance before.

Shaking his head to negate the first rays of the morning sun overhead, Victor again focused his eyes on the face of the Spanish man to get a better idea of who he was.

"Geoffrey?" Victor asked, his mind refusing to believe what his eyes told him.

"In the flesh!" Geoffrey said, smiling broadly and offering his fellow Knight of Time a hand.

"How long have you been here?" Victor asked, climbing to his feet with Geoffrey's assistance. It was not easy assisting the nearly 270 pound Victor, but together they managed to get him up and over to a safer part of the harbor.

"Since we all fell out of the sky," Geoffrey said, acting as if this should have been common sense. "I landed way over by some cave. Saw you guys land where the fighting was. Everyone else still alive?"

"As far as I know," Victor said, his mind still reeling from the realization that Geoffrey was not only here in Florida with the rest of the team, but that he had infiltrated the Spanish fleet. "Um, Geoff, do you think you could get the Spaniards to stop firing at us?"

"Oh, they're not firing at you," Geoffrey said, taking a small whittling knife out of his pocket and using the sharpened tip to carve something into the wooden railing they leaned on.

"They're not?" Victor asked, looking over at the docked ships, their Spanish occupants running around the decks. "Then who are they firing at?"

"Them," Geoffrey replied, pointing toward the dense vegetation that Victor and his men in black had appeared from just before dawn.

A line of bodies lay at their feet. A mixture of soldiers and Elemenos, dead as can be. Still, even among this gruesome carnage, the indomitable spirit Jackson's manipulation instilled in his troops persisted on, forcing the American line to continue their advance on the Spanish ships docked in the harbor.

"Fall back..." Victor whispered as the American troops approached, their dead, zombie-like eyes chilling him to the very core of his soul.

"So the little girl is going to take me hostage, is she?" Vilthe asked with a low, sadistic chuckle.

"Actually," Tina began in the most annoyingly cheerful tone she could muster, "I pressed the button five seconds ago. It takes ten to kick in. Just thought you should know."

The confusion brought by Tina's statement was briefly replaced by panic before the initial detonation, which not only took out the left side of the cave entrance, but everyone within ten feet of the opening itself as well. Vilthe's makeshift throne was destroyed, broken into scattered pieces of wood in a haze of dirt and smoke.

Panicked Elemenos met with resistance as Enapay and the other Nabawoo warriors displayed their amazing archery skills once again, giving faces to the arrows that had been haunting the green creatures all morning.

Ignited by the line of gunpowder spread out and around the campground in a giant circle, more and more Elemeno guards were catapulted through the air in explosions of mud and rock. Dust filled the air, and Tina lost sight of her target as Vilthe scurried away in the confusion.

Looking for refuge, Vilthe did not run away from the cave, but further into it. Dodging the battered and broken Elemeno guards buried in rubble and debris, Vilthe squeezed his slender frame through the half of the entrance that was still clear. Finding it to be dark, he removed a box of matches from his vest pocket and lit one, observing the challenge that lay before him for the first time. Though he was a skinny man compared to most, his bulbous head made maneuvering within the cave's confines difficult and painful for the epitome of death.

Crawling through the first chamber was much like Vilthe predicted it would be. The cool, dead air of the cave reminded Vilthe of home. Once he was about thirty yards in, a strange package blocked his path from entering the birth canal passage that led to the second chamber. It was rectangular, and wrapped in translucent red tape.

It was then that Vilthe recognized the familiar smell of the gunpowder that was spread all along the space where he crawled. Sensing the potential for danger, Vilthe immediately extinguished his match, leaving him measurably safer, but completely blind.

Flanked by her brave and skillful Nabawoo archers, Tina followed closely behind Judah and Arbuthnot as they fought their way through the dozens of Elemenos who had not yet fled. As they approached the cave, a group of four Nabawoo warriors began pouring more gunpowder around the half of the entrance that still stood.

"Vilthe is in there!" Judah screamed at Tina over the noise of falling rocks and explosions.

"I know," Tina said, igniting the end of a trail of gunpowder beside her feet that led through the hillside into the cave. "Let's keep it that way."

Both Knights watched as the fire raced along the predetermined line, causing a small chaos in its wake. Almost half a dozen men, Elemeno and Nabawoo alike, caught some part of themselves on fire. Several of the archers lowered their weapons and ran to their friends to extinguish the flames. Most were successful.

With a loud boom, the cave entrance collapsed with a concussive force, killing or trapping anyone inside. Already enveloped in darkness, Vilthe was knocked unconscious for the first time in centuries as the vibrations from the blast sent him bouncing between the dirt floor and the rocky ceiling of the cave. Though quite handy in other situations, none of his stolen abilities could help him now.

As the battle died down and all the Nabawoo were accounted for, Rolland, Tina, and Arbuthnot stood side by side, waiting for any signs of life emerging from the cave. After a few minutes passed in silence and none came, someone finally spoke.

"Shame, really," Arbuthnot said, gazing at the cave. "That a such a beautiful geological structure had to be destroyed."

"Yeah, real tragedy," said Judah, wishing for nothing more than his wife's embrace, or at the very least, a cigarette.

"I'd say it's more strategy," Tina stated, a satisfied smile sneaking across her face.

"Well done, Baby Blue," Judah agreed, extending his hand in congratulations. "Just one thing though."

"Yeah?" Tina asked, completely overcome with joy at being accepted by one of her colleagues, and a pioneer as well.

"'I am cool? Really?" Judah asked, patting Tina on the back as they led their group of survivors back to the Nabawoo camp, to where this adventure began four days ago.

"No good?" Tina stopped for a minute to pout and ponder her word usage, wondering why no one thought she was funny.

Chapter 28:
Death March

Marching mindlessly in straight, rigid lines, the British redcoats strode across the battlefield toward their well-armed enemy. Their eyes were glossed over, and their faces expressionless; death was all but a foregone conclusion. Fear gripped their hearts to a man, and they felt themselves to be prisoners within their own bodies as they lined up to be presented with the standard issue bayonets before falling back into formation and moving out toward their ultimate collective fate.

A modern observer might have pitied their complete lack of free will in this forced suicide march. Their minds remained, stripped of all ability to resist their fate, and unlike their American counterparts, they were unarmed. The silent screams of thousands of England's finest drifted through their minds. With one motion Jackson had forever stifled their cries for mercy. It was just as well, for he had none to give.

Marching at gunpoint straight into the heart of the oncoming battle, Nahoy, leader of the Nabawoo people, found himself in a similar state.

The sound of battle drums drifted across the last hours of night; morning was coming, and with it the promise of spilt blood.

Nahoy assumed this would be where he met his end. He bore the weight of this feeling not with anger or fear, but with a serene acceptance that some things were beyond his control. As a boy his father had taught him the to respect the natural progression of events, the order of all living things, and the common threads that connected them all to one another.

"Good land though. Not too far from where I was born and learned to hunt. I might have even camped here once, hard to say, it being so long ago," Nahoy thought to himself as he walked forward, hands still tied behind his back. With each step he took, any lingering angst or worry fell from his shoulders like melting snow.

"I just love parties, don't you?" Jackson said, childishly mocking Nahoy but failing to ruffle the feathers of the Nabawoo leader. "Off you go now."

Charlton took major offense to Jackson's words, however, and began struggling anew against his bonds. His thoughts raced with images of his wife, his children, and what grizzly death these white devils had planned for both him and his father-in-law, Nahoy.

"As for you..." Jackson said, removing the blindfold from Charlton's eyes, "I think you should see what happens to naughty savages who refuse to negotiate."

Remembering Joan and her reckless defiance, Charlton spat directly in the face of Andrew Jackson, hitting the General square in the forehead.

Though he did not react with immediate violence, Jackson knew that comeuppance would find this savage, and every other that dared to cross his path today. He turned and walked back toward his horse, leaping upon its back and wiping the spittle from his brow.

Time is a fickle mistress, captivating her prey with the promise of a first breath and offering them a world, a blank canvas of opportunity to build dreams upon - Dreams carved brick by brick from hope, courage, and love.

For Andrew Jackson, all but one of these were dead in his heart. Propelled by a morbidly decaying sense of courage, he had begun building his dream with the blood of men he considered savages.

The thought of absolute adulation from his countrymen was too much for the General to resist any longer; Vilthe had shown him that. The comparisons to General Washington were too compelling to not take notice of now. Both men had come from humble origins: aristocratic in their own unique way, yet still possessed a forceful, commanding presence on the battlefield. The one thing, the only thing, he felt missing from his legacy was a singular ultimate victory, a real knockout blow to the British; one with a high body count. By controlling all of the pieces on the board, he knew how to win while making himself look brilliant in the process.

With this thought dancing through his mind, Jackson gave the order to fire on Nahoy, any mercy he may have had washed away by the tide of his own ambition.

The faint sound of Nahoy's ancestral chanting filled the air as the tall chief walked directly, proudly, into the American line of fire. It broke the morning twilight as the American rifles fired into the open valley that held the elderly Seminole leader. Another flash, then another and another. The smoke from their guns filled the air around them. Seven shots, then ten, then six more: three more uneven volleys rained down upon Nahoy thirty yards away.

Vision limited by the clouds of gunpowder smoke, it was a foregone conclusion that at least one shot had felled the Nabawoo chieftain, though none of the spectators could see clearly until the smoke wafted away into the morning sun.

The ringing still fresh in Jackson's ears from the gun blasts, he could not believe his eyes as the smoke lifted to reveal Nahoy, unharmed and walking slowly and confidently towards the hypnotized British front lines.

"Bullshit!" Jackson screamed furiously, spooking his horse into a nervous dance beneath him. "Again, do it again! All of you this time, fire!"

Once again, the American line raised their rifles. Nearly fifty men stood at the ready this time, releasing a succession of shots that rang out through the chilly morning air, peppering the air with miniature explosions as their payloads released. The smoke blanketed the countryside, forcing Jackson to ride ahead of his guns to confirm that Nahoy had finally fallen under the second barrage.

To Jackson's astonished horror, Nahoy stood untouched by their second attempt to execute him, waddling slowly further from his would-be murderers.

"I don't believe…" Jackson mumbled to himself, trailing off as his eyes struggled to make sense of Nahoy as he continued to make his way across the open field.

Arriving just in time to hear the second volley, Princess Blaisey of the Nabawoo climbed up the small, grassy hill overlooking the open field where Jackson and his men were still attempting to execute her father without success. Though she had been told stories as a child of their family's special connection to the heavens and the Earth, nothing could have prepared her for the sight of her father walking untouched through the deadly rain of American fire. Like the wind, she ran down the hill toward him, toward some hope of respite from the torturous world her people had been thrust into in the space of a generation.

Without warning, a small, black shape, no bigger than the size of a softball, appeared in front of Blaisey and preceded her down the hill. The black orb began to swell, roughly ten times its original size by the time it caught the attention of the Seminole Princess, who stopped and eyed it suspiciously for a only a moment before continuing her flight to her father in the valley below.

Nahoy smiled broadly as he felt the familiar touch of his daughter's hand upon his arm. "Yazhi... my little one."

"Hello, Papa," Blaisey replied, prying away at the bonds that held his hands behind his back.

"It is not safe here, my child, you must leave before..." Nahoy said, turning to his daughter before his expression morphed from empathy to concern. "You are not alone, my child."

About four minutes behind Blaisey, Rolland reached the clearing only to be taken aback by the sheer numbers Jackson had collected under his command. On either side of the field Rolland saw what must have been thousands of American and British servicemen marching toward one another, Blaisey, Nahoy, and the black orb directly between them.

"Orbs are black now?" Rolland said to himself, gaining a footing on the hill and rushing down towards the two Nabawoo. He watched as the strange black orb rammed into Blaisey's face, legs, and head, completely incapacitating her. Rolland snapped his fingers wildly, but nothing happened, stress stealing his focus. "Damn it all!"

The orb grew larger with every step Rolland took, gaining features as well as size. A single, scaly tentacle with jagged spikes running down both sides emerged from the orb's otherwise flawless circle, followed by another, and another, until there were six of the long, angry-looking feelers, each developing its own unique feature, such as claws, nails, eyes, or a mouth. Though Nahoy was blind to the beast taking shape before him, Rolland could see clear as day the now too familiar characteristics of the beast the Elemenos had called Ballua.

Reaching the bottom of the hill, Rolland decided to proceed with caution. Thinking back to the creature's strategy of using its size to impose its will, he believed that he could outsmart it and outmaneuver it, like the bald goliath had done on the beach. Except, Rolland hoped, with a different outcome.

To Rolland's surprise, the creature did not immediately attack Nahoy. Instead of advancing on the Seminole leader, Ballua moved back a couple of feet and bent its massive flattened head down to peer closely at Nahoy, as if it was attempting to stare the man down through his blindfold.

"You are late. Our hour of destiny draws near," Nahoy spoke to the horror only inches away from him, his face expressionless. The chieftain then turned in Rolland's direction and said simply "Remove my daughter from the field of combat, if you please."

The monstrous beast whipped its tail high into the air, the deadly foot-long spike at the end aimed directly at the elderly Nabawoo chieftain's heart, bringing it down on him in a blur of speed.

Yet, it did not hit him.

Nahoy listened for the sound of the great scorpion's tail as it fell on him. When it was near enough, the aged Seminole sidestepped the tail completely, angering both the beast and General Jackson, who watched them from atop his horse nearby.

The unconscious Blaisey bounced nearly six inches in the air along with everything else not planted firmly to the ground as the impact of Ballua's tail rippled through the battlefield like a earthquake.

Again Ballua brought its mighty tail around. Like two magnets drawn to each other, it once again met the Earth instead of its intended target.

"You can do better," the Nabawoo Chieftain taunted the beast, not sparing a single thought for cutting the bonds that tied his hands or the blindfold that robbed him of his sight. Nahoy ran on adrenaline and prophecy, the world narrowing down to the destiny he must fulfill for the sake of his people: the aspiration of all great leaders.

Ballua beat its large tail on the ground again, this time landing on bone fragments embedded in the soft clay below. The red, muddled clay formed a tidal wave of Earth that traveled a few feet before spending itself.

Rolland, determined to honor Nahoy's wishes, fought desperately to remain standing and push on towards Blaisey, finally reaching her legs. He grasped both of her ankles, dragging her back towards the hill with as much speed as he could muster. She wasn't awake, but at least her pulse and her breathing were both normal.

Nahoy was a picture of composure as he listened to the great monster before him breathe heavily, panting for air. Ballua let out a great wail before pawing at Nahoy, its great claws flashing in the morning light. In a sudden blur, Nahoy spun around, bringing the bonds stretched between his hands up into the path of one of Ballua's claws.

Free from bondage, Nahoy pulled off the blindfold and eyed the beast for the first time. In renewed fury, Ballua launched a fresh round of attacks. Fire poured from its mouth as Nahoy attempted to outmaneuver the hideous monster, but he was eventually knocked onto his back, the beast looming over him once again.

Charlton watched in horror as Nahoy engaged the massive creature. Though he admired his commander's resolve and natural talent for evasion, he failed to see why Nahoy delayed the inevitable. With the Creek all but wiped out and the Nabawoo Warrior Alliance dead, Charlton saw little reason left to go on fighting. Even the white people who fell from the sky had abandoned their cause, leaving them with nothing but a humiliating death at the hands of the American scoundrels.

"Papa…" Blaisey stirred, opening her eyes to find Rolland. "What, what happened?"

"Your father is still fighting that thing," Rolland said to her, pointing back toward the field. "He told me to get you out of there."

"What? But he can't! He's…" Blaisey stopped as her eyes found her worst fears a reality.

A few hundred yards away, Nahoy stood up and straightened his garments, ready for the final confrontation. Within seconds, Ballua struck. The spiked tail pushed straight through the Seminole warrior's back, emerging in several places across his stomach as the creature finally hit its mark. Ballua dragged its tail along the ground and whipped it around wildly, flinging Nahoy through the air like a paper doll before dropping him unceremoniously on the ground below.

"No!" Blaisey screamed as Rolland shot past her toward to where Nahoy lay broken on the ground. She feared it was already too late for Rolland to do anything but get himself killed.

Removing his father's knife, Rolland lunged at Ballua just as the beast was readying for the final blow. Jumping onto the creature's leg, Rolland jammed the blade as far as it would go in the first soft spot he found between scales, finding a grip with his free hand and using it for leverage to climb onto the beast.

Perhaps Ballua did not realize what was happening, but it was smart enough to realize that something was very wrong. It began to squawk, shifting its weight from foot to foot as Rolland continued to stab it and climb up its side until he was firmly planted atop the creature's back.

It was then that Rolland noticed something he had not anticipated. In front of both of his legs were two flattened but obvious gray and brown wings. As they sprang to life, Rolland had enough time to cling feebly to the scaly backside of the beast before they took flight, leaving Jackson's battlefield far behind.

Satisfied, Jackson rode forward a few yards and watched as Blaisey ran to her father's side. A normal man would have felt some compassion for the pair, if only because they were living creatures with feelings. But for these two, Andrew Jackson felt nothing but disdain. Whistling loudly, Jackson signaled for the hundred green feline creatures Vilthe had lent him to finish the job their larger comrade couldn't.

Before moving in on the two Nabawoo, the Elemenos spooked at something coming from the forest behind them. The tall, dead-looking trees fell as something large approached.

Jackson could see the unusual disturbance, and decided to fall back behind his American lines just in case. He was glad he did.

Beyond the dark cloud of suffering hanging in the early morning air came a light of hope - horses carrying Creek warriors, armed to the teeth and burdened with as much ammunition as they could carry.

Turtledove led the charge, riding proudly upon one of the finest white stallions ever bred. At his side rode Blackfoot, Arvi, and Levi, heads held high. They spread out in the middle of the battlefield, facing both sides of the coming onslaught and forming a protective circle around Blaisey and the fallen Nahoy.

The Elemenos climbed over each other in their panic to get away from the Creek warriors. They fell one by one, arrows, tomahawks, and stampeding horses mercilessly removing them from the battle just as suddenly as they'd appeared.

The white stallion Turtledove rode came to an abrupt halt next to Blaisey as he dismounted and hurried to them. Dismissing pleasantries, the leader of the Knights of Time ignored the princess and went straight for the Nabawoo leader.

"Nahoy, my friend," Turtledove said, placing his hand on Nahoy's face despite Blaisey's protests.

"Marcus," Nahoy said, pushing his daughter's hands away to view his brother in arms. "The Creek, did you get the Creek to join us?"

"Yes, yes I did," Turtledove said sullenly, taking the Seminole chieftain's hand. "They're here protecting us, protecting your daughter, just like you hoped."

"Good. Marcus," Nahoy fought to say, his breath shallower and more forced with every word. "Your boy. It left with him."

"What?" Turtledove asked.

"Rolland and the beast went up in the air right before you got here," Blaisey said, pointing into the cloudy blue sky.

"Where are they now?" Turtledove asked, panic filling his eyes

"They haven't come back," Blaisey said, her expression devoid of all emotion beyond guilt and sorrow.

Turtledove knew her suffering, but now was not the time for grief counseling; that would come later. "He'll be fine."

"It takes them up, but they don't come back down Marcus," Nahoy said, the whites of his eyes increasingly cloudy

"He will be fine my friend. All of the children are accounted for," Turtledove said, holding Nahoy's hand as he closed his eyes and coughed weakly.

"Yazhi...my little one," Nahoy said. His breath rattled in his chest once more and then fell silent as his grip on his daughter's hand fell slack.

Lying across her father's body, Blaisey fought back tears. She would not leave her father behind again. Dead or not, he was still the only parent she had. She would not abandon him.

This presented a problem for Turtledove. No sooner had he said goodbye to Nahoy than he heard a chorus of squawks above him, signaling the return of Ballua and Rolland.

Landing near the American front line, Ballua threw Rolland off of its back, sending the teenager flying through the air, knife in hand, to land with a skid in front of Andrew Jackson's horse.

"Perhaps it is I that am fortune's fool," Jackson said, pulling his double-barrel flintlock pistol from its holster and firing at Rolland, less than five feet away.

With little time to compose himself, Rolland focused his concentration on each individual explosion that the trigger of the gun created. Watching their paths carefully, Rolland snapped his fingers, and clasped his palm to his fist, dodging five of the six shots as they zoomed by his head and upper body, embedding themselves instead directly in the scaly hide of Ballua.

The last shot found its way directly past his eyebrow, leaving a sort of burn there on the side of Rolland's face. Though it stung, he had no time to nurse it, and a low growl followed by a shaking of ground brought back the elephant on the battlefield.

Angered by the attack, Ballua turned its attention from the Creeks and fell upon the American front line. Rolland was caught in the crossfire, flat on his back and rolling out of the great beast's way with every step it took.

If he was surprised by this turn of events, Jackson did not betray any signs of it, instead brandishing Nahoy's tomahawk as he watched Rolland struggle to get up.

"Take your time, my boy," Jackson said as he dismounted, shouldering the tomahawk like a championship belt. "I'll wait for you to compose yourself."

"If I never see your face again, it will still be too soon, Andrew," Rolland said, resisting the urge to attack Jackson and instead forcing himself to concentrate on the task at hand. "I don't think I'll ever be able to use a twenty dollar bill ever again."

"Don't worry, boy," Jackson said smugly. "Today is your last day on Earth. I hope you made the most of it."

Before Rolland could prepare a clever retort, a bright, overwhelming light behind the teenager blinded Jackson, temporarily stopping the British march on the other side of the field mere feet from the Creek defenses. One by one, they moved out of the way of the blinding light within their circle as it gained a clear path to the beast that ravaged the American lines.

Marcus L. Turtledove, the sworn Protector of Eden, had been entrusted with the responsibility of carrying a weapon as mighty as the name that came with it – the Golden Sword of Eden.

Forged by the founders of Eden and passed down through the generations, it had never left Turtledove's side for the decades he had spent defending his adopted homeland. Though he had been given specific instructions not to use it unless under great duress, today was a day unlike any he had experienced in nearly sixty years of life.

"You have taken a friend from me this day," Turtledove shouted, brandishing the gleaming golden sword high above his head for the beast to see. "For that, I shall end your time upon this Earth!"

Raising the golden sword a few inches higher, Turtledove's sword caught the morning light, reflecting the rays of light and blinding the beast that stood before him. It reared on its back legs, but Rolland had left one lame and unable to hold its weight, forcing the beast to wobble. This distraction allowed Turtledove enough time to cross the distance between them and leap into the air without a moment's hesitation.

As Marcus Turtledove plunged the golden sword deep into the heart of the beast, a shock of electricity surged through Ballua's body, shutting down every organ in its path. It fell over, writhing in pain for a moment before shrinking down to less than a quarter of its original size.

Odd features began to take shape. A nose, a mouth, two human eyes, legs…

As the crowd watched the beast morph, General Andrew Jackson saw an opportunity to flee, backing away slowly through the sea of hypnotized American soldiers. Flicking his wrist to the right, the line of British redcoats resumed their charge toward the Creek natives. Satisfied, General Jackson made for the rocky hillside where he would ride out the battle in safety.

Though still shaken from his joyride on the back of the great beast, Rolland had not taken his eyes off of Jackson since he had felt solid ground. He knew the moment that the General turned and fled that he had a choice to make: stay for Blaisey, or pursue revenge on Jackson. As if they had decided for him, Rolland's legs were already propelling him forward, his father's knife clutched in his left hand.

"Turtledove, they're moving!" Blackfoot screamed over the confusion. Sure enough, both the British and American lines had begun to move again, putting the Creek directly in the middle of their soon to be mindless clash.

"Man your positions!" Blackfoot shouted over the clamor of his Creek warriors arming themselves for the coming clash. Taking stock of the situation, Turtledove decided that his first attempt would be one of unification, which meant finding his generals. He climbed back onto his horse before mulling over what to do next.

"Archers at the ready!" Arvi screamed over the heads of a dozen Creek surrounding him.

"The girl," Turtledove said before riding over to where Blaisey still sat beside Nahoy's body. "Where is Judah?"

"Taken by pirates," Blaisey said through a great deal of tears, "Days ago."

"Oh," Turtledove responded at a loss for words. "We must leave now, Blaisey. Gather Rolland and the others before we are all killed."

"No. I won't leave him," Blaisey said, her eyes filling with a fresh round of tears. "And Rolland is already gone."

Eyeing her for a moment, Turtledove realized that the boy's lack of involvement in the slaying of the beast was indeed suspect. Needing answers but knowing how fragile the girl was, he decided to tread lightly. "Where did Rolland go, Blaisey?"

"After Jackson," Blaisey said, wiping her nose on her sleeve and pointing toward the overlook at the top of the hillside.

"Very well," Turtledove sighed, sliding his golden sword back into is scabbard and taking off towards the rocky cliff where Rolland and Jackson had disappeared. He hoped that he was not too late.

The loud banging that filled the makeshift compound made it easier to sneak up on Sephanie.

With her back turned and her attention consumed by the finer art of theft, Sephanie was completely taken by surprise when a hand tightened around her right shoulder. Sephanie turned to meet her attacker with a brisk whack of the wrench she concealed, only to have it knocked away easily.

The look of shock on Sephanie's face was well worth the long chase the Elemenos and stray American forces had given.

"Busted!" a female voice said, throwing Sephanie for a loop and forcing her to take several moments to register who it was.

Sephanie's mind scrolled through names like one would a rolodex exactly as she had been trained to do by her father, a skill she had later learned to warp into a manipulative way of categorizing people according to their potential usefulness.

With her head hung low, the nineteen-year-old smiled coyly before meeting the eyes of her best friend, Joan Rothouse Raines.

"Joan!" Sephanie exclaimed, throwing her arms around her best friend for the first time in days. "What are you doing here?"

"Same as you I suspect," Joan said dismissively, hoping to pry a bit of information from her closest, best source of gossip. "Find anything good?"

Chapter 29:
One Clean Shot

"Imagine running into you here," Joan said, a knowing smile creeping its way across her pale face. "How ya been?"

"Words wouldn't do it justice," said Sephanie, relaxing for the first time in days.

"I hear you," Joan replied, looking her friend up and down and taking stock of the oddly lavish dress Jackson had given her. "I'm not even sure if my husband is alive. What's your malfunction?"

"I, uh…" Sephanie began, choking a bit on her own words. "I've been staying here… with Jackson."

The look exchanged between the two women carried a unique mixture of amusement and understanding that two men would never have shared.

"As your commander, I should tell you that it is against protocol to involve yourself with a person of interest like Jackson," Joan said, while raising one of her eyebrows higher than the other. "But as your friend, way to tap that silver fox, babe."

Sephanie laughed uncomfortably and attempted to change the subject, returning to her efforts to pick the lock Rolland had placed on the door separating her from the Dream Phoenix.

"Whatcha doing?" Joan asked, walking around to see Sephanie with her hands in the proverbial cookie jar.

"Trying to break in," Sephanie said, knowing better than to lie to a pre-cog.[5]

Joan looked through the small, frosted window and instantly recognized the shape of the Dream Phoenix, sitting like a prize just out of their reach. "Well, damn, girl, you're just full of surprises today!"

Moving past Sephanie, Joan removed a slender, pointed safety pin from her long, blonde hair and began to tinker with the padlock. Within seconds, a click broke the silence, and the combination lock was no longer an issue.

"That's one," Joan said, turning her attention to the door's original lock. "Well damn."

"So you're happy, right?" Sephanie asked her friend hopefully.

"I'd be happier if I could get this damn thing open," Joan said, using her pick to jimmy the lock. "Thing must be from the days of colonial rebellion, late 18th century. Well past my time."

"I mean in life…with your husband?" Sephanie asked, pacing around the hallway.

"Yeah. I mean, I love Judah, and we're happy together," Joan stated with a smile, a flood of memories of the two of them on the couch, in the park, and on their wedding day coming to her mind.

---

5   Pre-Cog/ Precognition - One who sees future events/timelines before they happen.

The reverie seemed to center Joan, renewing her focus in the task at hand, and the lock finally turned over. "Voila!"

Though impressed, Sephanie was still troubled and didn't want to waste her time alone with Joan while she still had it. She sat down next to her and asked "How did you feel when you first met him? Judah, I mean."

"What do you mean?" Joan asked, fiddling furiously with the 18th century door and pulling it open to reveal the Dream Phoenix sitting idly within. Though it wouldn't open much due to the swelling of the door's wood from age, splinters breaking at the bottom, there was barely enough room for her to squeeze through and find something larger to use for leverage.

"I know you're just being supportive, Joanie. It's just that you and I have a lot in common. So I figured that you would be able to tell me how you felt the first time you met the guy that you know… you settled down with," Sephanie said with an increasing degree of apprehension to each word.

Joan stopped attempting to squeeze through the door and grabbed Sephanie's hand, staring fiercely at her friend.

"Are you in love with Jackson?" Joan demanded.

"What? No! Of course not!" Sephanie balked in indignation and disgust.

"Good," Joan said, releasing Sephanie and slipping beyond the door. "So who is it then?"

There it was, the question Sephanie had feared answering before she even decided to bring the topic up. No sense in beating around the bush, Sephanie took a deep breath and said the name she had tried not to think about for days now. "Rolland."

A silence fell between them before Joan's head popped back out. "The Wright kid?"

"Yeah..." Sephanie said bashfully, the knot in the pit of her stomach tensing up at the double meaning of the boy's last name.

"Awww, that's freakin' adorable!" Joan exclaimed happily, her enthusiasm catching Sephanie off guard.

"Okay, you don't have to be THAT excited about it," Sephanie grumbled, attempting to drop the subject and show a little more interest in helping Joan pry open the door.

"I just think it's cute," Joan said, pushing the door completely open and freeing them up to move the Dream Phoenix out. "Does he know yet?"

"No," Sephanie replied, sitting back down next to the open door. "He was here earlier though. Said he had come to rescue me."

"Are you serious?" Joan asked, clasping both of her hands over her mouth. "That's the most precious thing I've heard all day. So what did you do?"

"What could I do?" Sephanie asked earnestly, tossing her hands in the air. "I told him to get lost."

Joan smacked her brunette friend upside the head. "What'd you do that for?"

Not having an answer she was comfortable with, Sephanie sat quietly, lost deep in thought. Her heart knew, but her brain and mouth could not form the words necessary to explain why she kept everyone at an arm's length, why she protected herself and so, why she was all alone.

Making their way through the Florida swamps at a breakneck speed, Judah and Tina led their small band of Nabawoo warriors with weapons in hand. Flanking them was a group of seven Naba-woo archers, all ready to fight back any advancing Elemenos or hypnotized American troops. Though they were making progress inland, the numerous sinkholes and high brush made it easy for would-be attackers to catch their convoy before it reached safer trails.

Though she was growing into her role of de facto leader quite naturally, the bloodshed that surrounded Tina Holmes was troubling. Be it Elemeno, American, native, or British blood being spilt, the thought both horrified and disgusted the teenager beyond words, and the reality was devastating. As they passed a dry creek bed Tina saw a large patch of solid land in the distance, but before she could speak, an Elemeno dove out of the brush to their left and met with the business end of an arrow that flew past Tina's ear and into the creature's chest.

"Don't kill the soldiers!" Tina shouted, looking back as she ran. Her inability to see any obstacles in front of her combined with her natural clumsiness and she stumbled. Luckily, Judah caught on in time to turn her around before she stepped in a sinkhole. He couldn't understand why his wife had never taken a shine to this girl.

"If you can!" Judah screamed to the archers guarding their back as they all moved in one great processional. Then they stopped.

Standing in their path was what looked like a large band of men in black body suits. Tina recognized them as the ones who had assisted in battling the Elemenos when she set Hess on fire, but beyond that knew nothing of their intent or loyalties. One of them, the tallest and broadest by far, stepped forward and took off his mask off, revealing a welcome ally.

"Good to see you two," Victor said, motioning for his fellow Knights to join him on drier land.

Without warning, the man to Victor's right blurred for a moment before his features rearranged themselves into those of their fellow Knight, Geoffrey. While this drew a shocked gasp among the Nabawoo, it was a more than welcome sight to Tina and Judah, who were relieved to see their most wayward companion not only safe, but able to join their forces.

"Well, I'll be…" Judah grinned toothily, nodding his head in approval. "Say, you got anyone else I know hiding underneath them masks ?"

Before another word could be spoken between them, the harsh reality of their situation came crashing back. Suddenly, death struck the little clearing where the friends had only just reunited.

The long, shimmering electric whip came out of nowhere, wrapping itself around Arbuthnot's neck nearly six times before any of the Knights or Nabawoo had time to move. The electric current coursing through the whip surged, impossibly bright, and shot through the man's flesh, pulling his head from his shoulders in one clean, cauterizing tug.

As Arbuthnot's decapitated body fell to the ground, everyone in the clearing scrambled to make sense of the seemingly flawless sneak attack. Not a sound could be heard, except for the rustle of leaves, as the head of Judah's companion rolled away into the brush.

For Tina, who had never before seen a human being die first hand, went into a kind of shock, standing eerily still, the blood draining from her face, and a clenched expression crossed her entire body from her face to her very stance. Inside of her mind, Tina knew what was happening, knew that the reality of death was something she had not yet been trained to accept and move beyond. Still, she decided to get past it, turning her bodily process in dealing with the murder as a means to an end, and not a permanent state. With this in mind, Tina's insides churned as the acids of her stomach propelled what little contents it had up, outward, and into the nearby swamp.

Judah threw caution to the wind and ran to his fallen friend's side, hoping to do something, anything to help him. But it was too late. Arbuthnot was gone.

Holding the lifeless body in his arms, Judah cradled it like one would a small child. In that moment, the self-proclaimed smartest man on Earth was grateful he did not have to look into Arbuthnot's dead eyes; the overwhelming guilt of being the only man to survive their Dewberry escape would be too much. His only hope was that wherever Arbuthnot was now he had found his partner, Ambrister.

With a single crack of his neck, the tall grass that lay between Rudolph Hess and the group of Knights, Nabawoo, and freemen was scorched down to blackened Earth and barren soil, drawing the attention of the convoy, all of which turned from Judah's grief to meet Hess' gaze. His wounds healed, Rudolph was ready to exact revenge for the loss of his skin, his time, and his master's approval.

The distraction would have worked well if Tina had not been prepared for it. Though Hess was the one drawing the attention, Tina recognized the trademark blue whip as belonging to his sister Alora, who stepped out from the remaining brush to approach the grieving Judah.

Raising her arm high into the air, Alora held the electric blue bullwhip with a master hand, so focused on her task that she failed to see Tina charge shoulder first into her stomach with such force that the red headed woman was knocked off her feet and back into the brush.

As if in a trance, Judah stood up and screamed, "Victor – go!"

Confused, Victor backed up a few feet before asking, "What?"

"You heard me, Flint," Judah said, drawing the sword he had taken from Vilthe's camp from his belt and walking toward Hess. "Go. Find Turtledove and the others. We got this, right Baby Blue?"

A muffled "Yeah," came from the brush as Tina continued to wrestle with the much larger Alora, neither woman having gained the upper hand.

With a simple hand gesture, Victor, Geoffrey, and Enapay led their Freemen and Nabawoo away from the clearing. Though his inclination was to stay and help, Victor had learned long ago that there was no use in arguing with the good Doctor.

As both Hess and Judah watched the group disappear down the trail, both knew something between them had changed. The stakes in their cat and mouse game had been raised; one man would lose this round today, and quite possibly his life as well.

"That little weasel!" Rolland exclaimed as the sun caught his eye. He knew there wasn't much time before Jackson shook him.

Thinking of his mother and the hole in his chest, Rolland had gathered his things and raced after America's most celebrated monster. Rolland's tune quickly changed when he saw the near dead end of the overhang; he had Jackson cornered like an animal.

With the energy and agility of someone half his age, Marcus Turtledove climbed the hillside one rock at a time.

Farther and farther up the hill, Turtledove climbed toward what he assumed would be a difficult situation between a mass murdering racist and a troubled teenage boy with abandonment issues.

"Ain't life grand?" Turtledove muttered to himself, stepping over a rock the size of a small automobile. The chase was on.

Entering the battle from the west, Victor led the band of Freemen and Nabawoo behind him, allowing the Creek to see clearly that they were no longer alone.

Upon his arrival, Enapay saw the tied up form of someone he cared for greatly, Charlton. Rushing over to the man's side with blade in hand, Enapay breezed by the American servicemen, all still under Jackson's trance, before cutting the ropes that bound his brother.

"Enapay?" Charlton said, a bit surprised to find his kid brother doubling as his savior.

"Yes, my brother. The battle is about to begin," Enapay said, reaching to the soldier standing next to them and removing a set of keys from his belt loop. With a single motion, the shackles around his ankles fell to the ground.

Scanning the Creek, Nabawoo, and Freemen warriors standing ready to fight for their homeland, Charlton was taken aback for a moment before more personal thoughts crowded his mind. "Where is Blaisey? Where is my wife?"

Pointing towards the overhang, Enapay knew his brother would look for his wife first. A sense of normalcy filled his heart as the two exchanged a warm embrace and went their separate ways again, the natural order of their family restored.

"Enapay, we could use your help over here!" Victor called out as the British army moved in, weapons ready to make contact with whoever stood in their path.

Passion alone will only get you so far. Without the right conditions, the odds of victory can quickly fall from slim to none. Knowing this, Blackfoot still had faith that Turtledove had not been sent to him by the powers that be without reason. For his two generals, on the other hand, the glory of battle meant forging a name for themselves in the history of their people.

Any moment the British line would walk into the American soldiers standing there, bayonets at the ready.

Victor's men moved in from the west. The Freedmen knew that their very appearance struck a note of intimidation in the hearts of those they faced in combat. Though uneasy about them at first, both the Creek and Nabawoo people found solace in the fact that the men in black chose not to cower behind them, but form a circle in front of the tribesmen, shielding them as they all stood in defiance of Jackson's campaign of terror and destruction.

The clash began with Geoffrey, removing his mask and catching a British bayonet with his own, forcing them both to the ground before he punched the soldier in the face, rendering him unconscious. His sense of victory was short lived, however, as no sooner had the first one fallen before five more redcoats took his place, all aiming to kill.

Jackson's influence of carnage and madness was only amplified by his complete lack of compassion. Line by line, the British advanced into the Freedmen, Nabawoo, and Creek volunteers, their textbook lunges, stabs, and shots taken almost mirrored across the field by their similarly hypnotized American counterparts. At the head of the American army, however, was the madman driving both sides.

"What is happening?" Levi asked Turtledove, whose response was cut short by a frenzied refocusing of American fury.

Grunts broke out amongst the American soldiers; low, gruff, primitive noises that grew louder with each repetition, eventually climaxing in a battle cry across the hypnotized force, propelling them forward, bayonets at the ready.

The strange phenomenon had a disastrously unequal effect on the British. For just as the Americans began lunging forward with a renewed vigor, the men representing the King's army began dropping their weapons to the ground, thrusting their defenseless chests forward, frozen in place and awaiting their own doom.

It took the overly stretched resistance forces led by Turtledove and Victor a few minutes and a few dozen senseless British deaths, to realize the full extent of what had transpired. What had been a two sided battle their forces were sandwiched between had suddenly handed them the much more dangerous task of subduing the Americans, and protecting the British.

The Americans fought with extreme valor and bravery – against defenseless opponents. Like puppets the British soldiers walked emotionless into the American front lines, only to fall to the ground in death and dismemberment. Gone were the repetitive motions of simple training tactics, replaced with the advanced military training a 19th century man could be taught at West Point. Somehow, Jackson was not only controlling these men's actions, but he also directly dictating what they individually did.

Turtledove watched as a young British regular, no older than seventeen, stood with a single tear trailing down his cheek as an old American man plunged the blade of his weapon deep into the boys sternum, twisting it sideways, and pulling it out quickly. He moved on to the next Brit, and the next, before Victor was able to disarm him and send him head first into the back of a nearby horse's behind. While he hoped that the animal would kick the old man for his misdeeds, he had no time to watch, as a fresh round of attacks came from three American soldiers on his left.

This was all being done for the amusement of one man, General Andrew Jackson. Though physically absent from the conflict, his will remained the overriding force in the heat of battle. A true scoundrel, he cared not for the repercussions of his actions, merely the benefits that would spring from them.

From all sides they came; bodies and weapons, cannons, arrows, and bravery were on full display. Though the immediate problem of numbers had been averted with the routing of the

Elemenos by Creek and Freeman reinforcements, the larger issue of stopping the hypnotic advancement of the American forces still remained.

For Victor and his free men, facing their opponents head on instead of with guerilla style attacks was a learning experience. Between the guilt of killing mindless human beings and the long minutes spent dodging cannon fire, time was running out for the free forces of Florida.

Standing at six feet, five inches, Victor looked every bit the hero that the Knights of Time attempted to be. Though it was not for a lack of trying, none of them, not even Victor, had been strong enough to prevent their current situation. None of them could raise the dead, or break into Jackson's mind and force him to stop the chaos.

A cannon ball went whizzing past Victor's ear like a very large, very angry honey bee. The inertia would have knocked any normal man off of his feet. Victor, however, merely wobbled drunkenly as the ringing in his ears turned to deafening silence.

"This is madness," Victor said plainly to Geoffrey as another one of the British soldiers fell dead a few feet away. Fear gripped the heart of the large African man before another emotion reared its ugly head in his psyche – pity.

Tina had assumed that outwitting Alora would not be a problem, and she was correct for the most part. The bane of Tina's existence instead became putting up with the physical abuse that came from Alora's constant hit and run strategy.

"Come out and face me, you, you inbred!" Tina screamed, surprised to hear her own voice form such an insult.

Alora, whip in hand, continued slicing through the air, unaffected by the other woman's taunts. Strands of blue flame whipped and slashed around Tina, restricting her movement and making it impossible to fight back.

"Dance, little girl, dance!" Alora cackled madly.

Matching him blow for blow, Judah advanced on Hess, clashing in midair as Tina finally freed herself from Alora's whip at the same moment. Slipping underneath the two men, Tina crawled to safety, drawing Alora in between their blades, cutting the long red ponytail from Alora's head, leaving her nearly scalped.

"You bitch!" Alora screamed, clamoring to her feet to run after Tina. With one hand atop her head to feel the damage done to her scalp, Alora's movements were awkward and full of rage.

Seeing the red-faced giantess racing toward her, Tina looked left, right, and behind her for a place to dodge the coming attack. Then her eye caught the blue whip that lay discarded in the dirt just out of her reach. With seconds to make a decision, Tina decided to risk it all.

Hess was the better swordsman after all, it seemed, as he pushed Judah aside, stealing the Brit's weapon in the process. Laughing heartily, Rudolph took a sadistic pride in seeing his enemy on his back. Even more satisfying was seeing Tina crawl on hands and knees toward Alora's whip as his sister went charging after her. With a careless thought, Rudolph kicked the whip hard out of Tina's reach, sending it flying through the air into the swamp water nearby.

Looking down at the teenager, however, Hess was not greeted with the sad look of the condemned he had come to relish over the years. Instead, Tina smiled at him, raised her brow and contorted into an almost crab like position, before bracing herself for Alora's furious wrath.

Using Alora's own momentum against her, Tina tripped the redhead as they collided, flipping the woman over her completely before launching her with both legs through the air and into the swamp, landing face first in the water right alongside her electric whip.

The results of the whip, the water, and Alora interacting with one another were instantaneous. The electric shock that traveled through her body was so supercharged that it made her limbs swell and expand before the life within her was extinguished and she stopped convulsing altogether just as the whip shorted out.

"Mein Schwester!" Hess screamed, dropping his saber and running to his sister's body. Grabbing both of her arms, he dragged her from the swamp and back onto dry land. But there he saw not the familiar freckled face of the child he had helped raise, only the burned, blackened remains of the woman he had just unintentionally helped kill.

Both impressed and surprised by the turn of events, Judah wasted no time, grabbing Tina by the hand and insisting that they head after the others. With a final look behind them, both Knights of Time watched Hess cradle his sister much the same way that Judah had done with Arbuthnot minutes before and found a pity for the man that neither had known was within them.

Hot on the trail of the American General, Rolland climbed against the steep incline that led to the rocky overhang beside the open field where the battled raged on. Though Rolland had not physically seen Jackson since he had fled, somehow he knew that Jackson was close by. Arriving at the top of the incline, Rolland looked around to find nothing more than a large, circular boulder and more brush.

Taking refuge behind the large boulder nearby, Jackson decided that it would be best to lay low and wait for the adamant teenager to pass him by before heading back down to the battlefield. Though he wasn't exactly worried about his chances against the boy, the simple fact that he had lived through their last encounter gave the lad something to fight for, revenge.

Inhaling a slow, deep breath, Rolland pushed every emotion out of his mind and centered himself before snapping both thumbs to his index fingers, and clasping his hands together, slowing down time around him to a crawl. Though this gave Rolland enough time to find Jackson, which he did in a matter of seconds, it unfortunately also gave him time to stand out on the overhang and see the carnage below.

There was not a part of the field that wasn't engrossed in some sort of deadly engagement. It somewhat resembled a child's toy box, the way that the American, British, Creek, Nabawoo, Freemen, and Elemenos clashed with one another.

This hodgepodge was alarming in that it made Rolland feel even more responsible for its existence. Though he knew it wasn't *him* using mass hypnosis to incite violence, it felt like he had been the one who pissed Jackson off enough to use it. Even though he wasn't the one that killed Nahoy, he still felt responsible.

Determined, youthful, and angry beyond words, Rolland decided in that moment to correct his mistakes. He stood close to Jackson, pushing him up against the boulder, before removing his father's knife, and holding it to the General's throat.

Then he did something he had not yet done before and would not be able to do again for quite some time: Rolland corrected the flow of time to its natural state without using his hands, only his mind.

At first he wasn't sure, save for the return of the noise of the cannons and gunfire nearby.

Jackson blinked before trying to move, finding immediate resistance from Rolland's blade. An ordinary person would meet this kind of threat with panic, but Andrew merely smiled and sat stock still.

"Nice trick you've got there," Jackson said, swallowing hard to see how much give Rolland's grip had on the weapon. The skin along his throat scratched along the steel surface, leaving it red and inflamed. "But we both know you're not going to kill me."

"Oh no?" Rolland asked, sliding his knife upward towards Jackson's jugular. "On your feet."

Begrudgingly, Jackson complied and stood before Rolland, his back straight and head held high. Silence filled the air between the two men as Rolland contemplated his next move.

"That's a nice blade," Jackson said, his eyes fixed downward on Rolland's knife. "Know how to use it?"

That question was the last insult Rolland would stand from the man who tried to take his life but days before.

"Well enough," Rolland whispered through gritted teeth.

What happened next Rolland would never be able to explain, for few can explain the independent actions of one's conscience. But from out of nowhere, Rolland remembered the words that the maybe real, maybe fictional Historian gave to Rolland about his emotions controlling his actions.

All at once, the absurdity of the situation came into sharp focus. The time travel, the fight with Andrew Jackson, the giant beast, each of which was a one in a million shot to happen to anyone, especially the same person; especially to a homeless kid from Southern California.

The realization of his predicament led more words of wisdom to rise to the forefront of Rolland's teenage mind: a banner he had seen hanging in the dining room hall at the Halls of Time. On it was laid out a creed by which all Knights of Time live, their purpose, and how they are to conduct themselves.

When Rolland first read it, the entire thing seemed lofty, maybe even a bit corny. But now, after living the life and experiencing the impossible decisions that came with being a time traveler armed with the knowledge of the future, it made perfect sense.

Rolland backed away from Jackson slowly as he began to speak.

"I am a Knight of Time. I pledge to uphold the standards, practices, and fraternity that come from holding my title, and defend the time stream from all those who wish to do her harm. I swear to lay down my life in the defense of Eden, her citizens, and any whose heart strives for the betterment of humanity." Rolland spoke slowly as he put four feet of distance between himself and Jackson.

The General, confused by what he perceived to be cowardice, was already planning his next move. The saber he had dropped when he hid lay near his left foot beckoning to him.

"You are truly a fool."

Tina could not have described what war was like before that day. Sure, she had an idea based on historical study and mandatory schooling, but she had never experienced it with her senses. She had never smelled the freshly lit gunpowder or heard the cries of men as they succumbed to the mindless violence. Nor had she seen so many people dressed in black body suits, but that was beside the point.

Still, these sights waited for her and Judah as they found their way onto the field. Worry gripped Judah as he thought of sending

Victor and the rest of their groups before them. Maybe it was the lingering guilt of Grimes and Arbuthnot's deaths, but he could not help but think of how many had already fallen.

It was easy to distinguish their allies in the center of the field based their fervent fighting styles. While all around them men on both sides of the American and British lines were mindlessly shooting to kill, the Creek, Nabawoo, and Freemen were disarming and disabling the soldiers they came across, though a few of the more renegade Nabawoo and Creek natives were making sport of the easy pickings with their well-placed arrow shots.

Spotting Enapay fighting alongside his brother Charlton, Tina approached with a friendly caution before gaining the attention of her Nabawoo confidant. Though happy to see her, Enapay looked rather preoccupied, attempting to subdue three British soldiers.

Instead, it was Charlton who spoke directly to Judah, recognizing in him a kindred spirit. "Are you with the old man, Turtledove?"

"Yeah, we are," Judah said, tripping an American soldier in an officer's uniform who came charging at them. The saber in his hand went skidding across the dirt as the soldier fell onto his face. "Know where he is?"

"Yes, he went after the boy and the General – up that ledge," Charlton said, pointing to the rocky overhang where it was obvious that two figures were quarrelling above them.

"Oh, bloody hell!" Judah said to himself before looking over at Tina. "Excuse me, love."

Dr. J.J. Raines took off toward the overhang himself without delay, leaving Tina no option. Her only choice was to join the fighting alongside her fellow Knights. Though she wanted nothing more than to find Rolland, her sense of duty kept her there, close to Victor and Geoffrey. Close to the group she felt like a true part of.

With things getting quieter behind him, Judah knew that he must be getting farther away from the battle, leaving his teammates more vulnerable. He rationalized his actions by deciding that catching Jackson would stop the violence down below; the fact that he believed Jackson was also in possession of his wife was another matter.

"Bloody hell!" Judah exclaimed, seeing the scenario playing itself out on the hillside above him.

There upon the overhang stood Rolland, bow and arrow in firing position, high and aimed directly at Jackson's chest.

Jackson, saber in hand, appeared to have only briefly bested the teenager, but still refused to yield. In his mind, honor would only be won by the survivor.

"I'll just be stopping this right now!" Judah bellowed, entering the fray.

"This doesn't concern you, Lion," Rolland shouted over his shoulder, refusing to take his eyes off of Jackson.

"As your commanding officer I DO think it concerns me," Judah said, careful not to get too close to the already unstable teenager.

Usually pulling rank on a subordinate is met with an immediate cease and desist, though Rolland knew he held no obligation to comply with Judah's wishes. "You don't give me orders, Dr. Raines."

Swallowing hard, Judah took a step back, standing a mere seven feet from what had the potential to be a disastrous, history altering event. The silence was deafening.

"Tell me why!" Rolland finally managed to say though gritted teeth. "Why should I let you live?"

The silence filling the air was broken not by menacing words or cries for mercy; but by the large, rather Cheshire looking grin that appeared on Andrew Jackson's face.

"My boy," Jackson said, rubbing metaphorical salt into the wound he had already inflicted upon the young man who would momentarily decide his fate. "I am the voice of the American people. Preordained by…"

"Shut the hell up!" Rolland shot off, pulling his bow's string ever-so-slightly closer to the firing position.

Another couple of tension-filled moments passed. Rolland wanted to clear his head, but knew that backing down now would be a major sign of weakness. No two ways about it, he was just as trapped as the mindless zombies Jackson had created for battle.

Taking a step back, Rolland blinked before looking at Jackson anew. He saw the wrinkle lines that had already begun forming under his eyes. It gave him that distinguished, yet still unhealthy look that Rolland remembered seeing on every twenty dollar bill he had ever used. That seemed like a lifetime ago.

"This is it you know," Rolland began in a calm, paced voice. "No more magic healing water. No more cave. Either of us dies now, we die for real, for good."

"It would appear that way, yes," Jackson said, his fingers moving slightly as if he were popping his knuckles.

"Cut that shit out," Rolland said, pulling back on the bow's string a considerable amount. "You're the monster here, not me."

"Yes, because I'm the one holding a United States General at the tip of an arrow," Jackson said sarcastically, careful not to move anything but his lips. While he had not pegged the boy for a killer, Jackson had drawn the boy's blood during battle; that sort of experience usually creates a vengeful spirit.

"I said shut up!" Rolland yelled, his steady, even hands much different from the ones Jackson recalled seeing days before on the battlefield.

Things were not going according to plan at all.

Behind the overhang was a steep, limestone hillside where Sephanie leaned on a nearby branch to support her weight. Having run most of the three miles from Jackson's compound, she was exhausted and found no joy in continuing her lower body workout by climbing more hills. Although she was intrigued, the scene before her surprised the teenager; she would have assumed that if anything, Rolland and Jackson's roles would be reversed.

"Do it then," Judah said with a steady voice from just out of Sephanie's eyesight. "Shoot the little bastard, alter history. Go ahead. I've always wondered what would happen me self."

The goading words were as worrisome as they were damning to whoever Judah was speaking to, but Sephanie already had a pretty good idea of who it was. The cocky one liners and half-sarcastic begging sounded like her recent host, a confirmation that awaited her as she snuck up the opposite side from where Judah and Rolland were. She remained hidden, a strategic advantage should she need it.

"If you're going to kill me, then go ahead and make a name for yourself, *boy*," Jackson stated bluntly. "Otherwise I have an army to command."

"Shut it you blubbering pile of excrement," Judah snapped towards Jackson.

"I believe he just called you shit, Andrew," Turtledove said, once again making a dramatic entrance. "Rolland, you do remember what the Historian told you, yes?"

"Yes," said Rolland, unsure where the old man was going with his line of logic, but generally not caring.

With a kindly, almost gentle motion, Turtledove drew Rolland's eyes away from Jackson for the first time since picking up the bow.

"Then trust in yourself, and all will be illuminated," Turtledove said with an understanding smile.

For better or worse, with those words Rolland allowed his instincts to kick in. His eyes closed and his fingers relaxed, releasing the tension in the bow's string and launching an eight-inch-long wooden splinter toward the century's most blood thirsty man.

The spectators, including Rolland, at first could not fathom what he had done. The arrow tore through the air toward its target, the defenseless General Andrew Jackson. The distance between Rolland and Jackson seemed to disappear, uniting them in ways not conceivable to any human mind.

Then, a miracle happened.

Suddenly and without warning, a mangled form, half man and half beast, began to take shape between Rolland's arrow and Jackson. Though Rolland couldn't tell exactly what it was, he could clearly see bright red hair peeking out from the otherwise scaly patches of fur and tatters hanging from the naked form.

An old, rusty dagger was clenched in its one human hand as the monstrosity known as both Puck and Ballua raised its weapon high, intending to stab the General through the heart before anyone else could react. It might have succeeded, too, if not for Rolland's itchy trigger finger.

The red-headed figure materialized fully, twisting its neck around to see the arrow as it barreled towards him. The arrow made contact not with Jackson, but instead cut through the tender flesh of the monstrous ginger-haired creature that had been Puck, as he appeared unexpectedly between them.

Only once the arrow had stopped, lodged deep in the throat of the man, could Rolland see the look of disbelief that filled every inch of his mangled face. They stared at one another for a long moment, neither one daring to move for fear of what must inevitably come next, the harsh waking from this nightmare, and the real world consequences that their actions wrought.

Dropping the dagger in his raised right hand, Puck stood motionless, in mid-lunge toward Jackson, within mere centimeters of making contact. He had failed.

For those who dared not blink throughout the ordeal, it was a spectacle of timing as Rolland's arrow raced Puck's dagger – both aiming to take the prize of General Andrew Jackson's life.

With one last gasp for air, the creature turned and fell to the Earth below, eyes open, never to rise again. The glimmer of caged enthusiasm for life was gone, replaced by a chasm of emptiness.

Chapter 30:
The Ties That Bind

Silence filled the air as shock and awe reigned over the moment.

Rolland looked straight ahead, consumed by an eerie, dead calm. The gravity of the situation hit him slowly as his eyes followed the arrow straight through Puck's throat, stop, and fall to the Earth below. The sudden, wet thump of the arrow hitting its mark punctuated the spectacle of murder that Rolland alone bore the burden of responsibility for. The weight of the act was immense. Rolland Alan Wright had taken his first human life.

Serendipity holds no prejudice. It was as if all of creation, the laws of probability, chance, good fortune, and nature had come to an agreement to allow these players to continue past this stage in life's game.

Though Rolland and Jackson's contest continued, the state of their affairs had changed drastically in the thirty seconds prior to the renewing of hostilities. This was a new world. A world in which Rolland, not Jackson, held the power of persuasion.

Sephanie was first to realize that Rolland had murdered someone, though not the person he had intended to. Having seen this particular series of events play out before for lesser men and women, she expected the youngest Wright to either launch into a fit of panic, or declare a mulligan and have a go at another attempt on Jackson's life. What she did not expect, however, was sound judgment and the use of tactical leverage.

With a hollow, resonant breath Rolland lowered the bow, breathed deeply, and walked the distance to Jackson's side, his eyes wide.

Perhaps Jackson had not expected Rolland's composure, or was just possessed by the great shock of proceeding events; either way, the American General dared not move, and he was taken completely off guard by the knife that Rolland again produced and pointed at the fleshy part of his neck.

"This ends now, General," Rolland said, allowing his blade to find the sweet spot where Jackson's pulse beat. The steely chill of the weapon perfectly mirrored Rolland's demeanor to all who watched him make his demand.

For Jackson, Rolland had gone from an enemy to a lifesaver within moments. He now faced the challenge of showing gratitude to the boy who had been wreaking havoc on his life for the past four days, a prospect that seemed insurmountably worse than meeting the end of the arrow he knew deep down must have been intended for him.

Without warning, Rolland punched Jackson square in the nose and stood over the General with his left hand still brandishing his knife. Lowering it again to Jackson's throat, he coaxed a few droplets of blood from the General's neck as he let it dance across the man's skin — back and forth.

A quick nod toward Puck's lifeless body drove the point home as Rolland finished his demand, firm and commanding. "Or I will finish what he started."

Jackson looked up into the deep brown eyes of the teenage boy who had bested him for a long moment. What had been an impossible thought only a minute before had turned into a reality before his very eyes. Despite his powers of persuasion, the so called 'Hero of New Orleans' had been outfoxed by someone less than half his age. The only comfort he could take from the situation was that the majority of his forces were intact: enough to bring him a victory for the newspapers.

"Do not make me demonstrate my powers again, Andrew," Rolland said, pinning Jackson to the ground.

With a look of quiet discontent, General Andrew Jackson nodded once, closed his eyes, and brought peace to the minds of every living being within a ten mile radius. Like flowers of tranquility blossoming from the imagination of a child in spring, every soul was freed from their hypnotic servitude instantaneously.

As confusion set in along the battlefield, many of the men had much the same reaction. Laying down their weapons, soldier after soldier meandered away from the field in various, scattered directions. Afraid and unsure of who to accuse for their state, most of the men dared not speak a word of their circumstances, only thankful to be free of them.

British soldiers cast off their oppressive red coats and walked arm in arm with American troops, in many cases helping each other's sick and wounded. The level of cooperation was unprecedented for the time, but then again, so was waking up from a nearly week long hypnotic trance.

The Creek natives led by Blackfoot, Arvi, and Levi stood in the center of the field, nearly all unscathed save for a few cuts and bruises. Though a few of their warriors had died, they had done so side by side with their Nabawoo brethren, forging a bond that would prove to be beneficial for both parties in their fight for the preservation of their people's shared heritage.

Enapay, sensing an opportunity, approached the three Creek warriors in the proud, yet humble manner befitting a chieftain, though he knew that should his brother live, he would claim that title. Still, he greeted them warmly before introducing himself and his remaining archers with great pride.

As the wounded were carted off and the battlefield was stripped for supplies, all that remained were the hundreds of bodies carelessly strewn about the ground, completely indifferent to the energy it took for them to arrive there.

For those away from the battle, the experience was much like sleepwalking, a mild inconvenience at worst. For the unfortunate lot whose consciousness had returned to their body in the heat of battle, conditions had been much more perilous.

For Victor and what remained of his legion of freedmen, victory meant living to flee, and fight for freedom another day, a mantra that many of them would remember, along with Victor's other inspirational words, in the turbulent decades ahead.

When Tina, still flush with endorphins and adrenaline, finally had cause to put down her weapons, it became clear that in protecting the Nabawoo people and stopping Jackson, much blood had been shed. The term 'battle' seemed inappropriate in her mind as the crimson stained hillside and ghostly faces of the dead highlighted the scene all around her. This was war. A sentiment that Enapay, who gazed longingly at Tina as he tended to wounded soldiers nearby, shared in earnest.

Meanwhile, the souls gathered at the overhang who watched Jackson release his hold on so many, waited with bated breath as the General returned the world to normal.

"It is done," Jackson said solemnly, swallowing what saliva he had remaining and slinking ever further into the ground where he sat.

From his vantage point, Judah could see the bandage that covered the left side of Puck's head begin to slip, revealing a large hole where his eye should have been. Not having seen the events surrounding Nahoy's murder, he had no idea that both Puck and Ballua were one in the same.

"The bloody hell happened to the ginger kid?" Judah asked, turning to Rolland for clarification, finding none. This set a trend, as everyone surrounding Puck's body followed suit, apparently thinking that Rolland's intuition carried never-ending answers to the unknown.

All eyes fell to Rolland, from the bemused look of General Jackson, to the teary, sorrow-filled eyes of the Nabawoo Princess Blaisey, who emerged from the steep hill behind Sephanie. Their gazes burned into him, piercing his soul with their accusatory stares and silent accusations.

Just like when he arrived in Eden.

With the fighting ceased, the immediate threat to the Knights of Time was no more, though it did nothing for their more long term problems, the most obvious of which was that Rolland had just committed murder. When no one felt the need to point this out and instead began to leave, Judah took it upon himself, once again, to play devil's advocate.

"Excuse the hell out of me, but he just murdered someone!" Judah argued to no one in particular, pointing in Rolland's direction. "Not to mention how many codes he broke in using his powers without proper training, trying to kill a historical figure, alter the damn time stream... Honestly, this boy is good for nothing."

Hearing this, Rolland could not help but remember what the Historian had told him about readying himself for unexpected emotions. In that moment he wanted nothing more than to oppose Judah, fighting back and pointing out how he personally saved all of their lives. Instead, he kept his thoughts to himself in exchange for a much simpler, "I found the Dream Phoenix."

"Snooping around I bet. Looking for a good time, were you?" Judah asked quickly, still not impressed with Rolland's prowess.

"No, he's right," Sephanie chimed in, surprised at her own voice. "It's sitting in Jackson's compound. I left it with Joan."

"Joannie? My Joan is where now?" Judah asked, allowing himself to be distracted briefly. He shook his head. "That's beside the point. Look, if we're not careful then there's gonna be hell to pay when we get back."

With jaws clenched and brows furrowed, Rolland and Judah stared at one another as Sephanie glared at them both, her arms crossed defiantly. The tense stares between the four Knights of Time finally broke when Turtledove burst into a large, infectious grin.

"I think we can make an exception to the rules just this once, Doctor Raines," Turtledove said with a wink and a smile. He was careful to include the 'Doctor' to butter Judah up so that he would allow the matter to be swept under the rug.

"Are you fucking with the lion?!" Judah exclaimed, nearly beside himself with indignation. "Because I don't think you want to be doing that. Not now."

Then his argument was gone, for at that moment the love of Judah Jacob Raines' life graced his eyes for the first time in days. His saint had arrived.

Judah could almost swear that her blonde hair glowed in the early morning sunlight. He had forgotten how beautifully round and symmetrical her face was, and how kissable her lips looked. A cold hearted man knows nothing of matters pertaining to the soul and its mate. For Judah, his beloved Joan was the Sun, all of her warmth consuming him with a never-ending peace and tranquility no matter what era they found themselves in.

Words escaped him.

Joan walked toward her husband, smiling in gratitude that she was lucky enough to set eyes on him once again. His hair was matted, his clothes were dirty, and he looked like something that washed up on to the shore, but he was hers, and hers alone.

"If I could capture the stars in the sky, I..." Judah said, drawing Joan's finger to his lips as she stopped him from babbling on.

"Kiss me," Joan demanded, pulling her husband into a warm, loving embrace.

Their lips met with a comforting togetherness that only time, patience, and the sheer will of true love can claim as its champion. Then again, soul mates never need words of encouragement, only the touch of one another through life's ups and downs.

As Blaisey watched the grouchy white man with blonde hair reunite with his mate, she could not help but pine for her own.

"Princess...?" came Charlton's voice from behind Blaisey, causing her to spin around.

There, balanced on the rocky incline, was the one person on Earth she allowed to call her princess, the one man who treated her as such and always had, the father of her children and other half to her soul, Charlton of the Nabawoo.

Meeting near the large boulder, the two came together, Charlton lifting his Princess Blaisey high into the air before holding her to eye level and kissing her deeply for the first time in nearly a week.

"I am so happy to see you," Charlton said, his eyes watering with joy.

"As am I," said Blaisey, kissing her warrior once again.

Rolland, Turtledove, and Sephanie watched these reunions with both a pinch of jealousy and an overriding sense of accomplishment.

"So what happens to them?" Rolland asked Turtledove, staring at his great-grandparents as they made out in front of him.

Turtledove looked somewhat apprehensive as he answered, knowing exactly what it was the teen meant with his question.

"Your grandparents go on to have three more children of their own. Charlton becomes a diplomatic leader, securing land grants in Oklahoma for his people. Unfortunately, neither he nor his wife, Blaisey, live to see it. They both perish during relocation," Turtledove stated solemnly.

Sephanie looked from Turtledove to Rolland, and back again before saying the words "Trail of Tears."

Numb to the fact that Jackson still got them in the end, Rolland watched the two Nabawoo as they hugged and held one another, completely oblivious to the rest of the world. "At least they were together. Old, and together."

All three time travelers were smiling when Jackson, filled with a fresh sense of courage, decided to stand up and retreat from the scene.

"We aren't done yet," Rolland said, taking a step in the General's direction.

"Oh, yes, you are," Sephanie interrupted, scooping up Rolland's hand. "Come on, I want to talk to you anyway."

Hormones besting teenage rage, Rolland followed Sephanie as she led him away from Jackson and into the woods.

This left Turtledove and Jackson alone for the first time.

"Hello," Turtledove said, extending his right hand to Jackson, who offered his own in return. "My name is Marcus L. Turtledove, leader of the Knights of Time and proud Traveler of Light. I believe you've seen the cave, met Vilthe, and understand that we are not from this era, so I will be brief. For failing to kill us, your life is now in grave danger from your former master. I, along with the other Knights, can protect you, as long as you agree to our terms."

Taken aback by such direct negotiation in the savage jungles of Florida, Jackson inspected Turtledove's face for any hint of deception before righting himself and deciding to play along.

"What are your terms, sir?" Jackson asked briskly.

Turtledove smiled at the American, nodding his head slightly and saying, "No need to call me sir, Andrew. You are in good company. I, myself, am a military man. As such, you must be keenly aware of the importance of good, reliable intelligence contacts."

"I am," Jackson said, his voice flat.

"Then how would you feel about being our contact in this era?" Turtledove asked bluntly, deciding to get the point right away.

Caught between a rock and a weird place, Jackson fidgeted uncharacteristically, scared for both his life and his reputation. "Why me? What would I have to do?"

Much to Jackson's distaste, Turtledove smiled again before explaining himself. "You are a powerful and capable man, Andrew Jackson. Someday you might find yourself in a high office, maybe even the presidency, and it would be a shame for such an office to change the character or fabric of a man's being."

Confused by this train of logic, Jackson squinted and followed Turtledove further down the metaphorical rabbit hole. "What, what do you mean, change me?"

"Look at Caesar, Alexander, or even Napoleon, now. Each man failed because they refused to listen to their children, to their people," Turtledove said, his demeanor going from soft to serious before Jackson's eyes. "You have been given a special talent, Andrew. You understand the people and what they want. Each of them wants a vote, a say in how things should be run."

"And I could offer that to them? How?" Jackson asked, his curiosity piqued by Turtledove's proposal

"Offer them a popular vote," Turtledove suggested with a sly grin and a twinkle in his eyes.

"A popular vote?" Jackson asked with an inquisitive look on his face as he looked into those gray, merciful eyes.

"Yes, you will lead a country of people who vote, who give their opinion on WHO should lead the country," Turtledove said plainly. "And if you ever see Vilthe or his people again, you go back to that cave, use the fountain, and tell us. Do you hear me?"

"Give all of them an equal vote? Slaves, even?" asked Jackson, ignoring contact responsibilities in favor of the prospect of real power. He now thought the old man in front of him crazy. Capable with a sword, yes, but sane? To think that simple country folk like his father would be allowed to decide who would represent them and sit side by side with the kings of England and Spain…Preposterous.

"Everyone," Turtledove continued. "And you, General, you will be the first man they choose to lead them."

These words seem to have the intended effect, as for the first time since their initial meeting Jackson stopped moving. All was still now as Jackson sat down and thought for a long moment.

"No. No, I won't do it," Jackson said with surprising conviction for a man his age. "I won't give a voice to no slave; no savage either."

Turtledove continued on with a steely, wolf-like resolve. "Like it or not, sir, we all have our parts to play in this life. Your burden is larger than most, I'll admit, but immortality is your reward, and your glory will never fade."

This combination of words seemed to work on the general. As it was, Turtledove would have sworn that he saw Old Hickory's face slacken. The lines around his eyes gave him a character that was recognizable to Marcus now. He had seen it hundreds of times from hundreds of men, women, and children who he had revealed their fate to.

"Deal," Jackson said, standing up and shaking Turtledove's hand in partnership. Proving once and for all that within every man lies at least a glimmer of humanity.

A short distance away, Sephanie and Rolland walked hand in hand as the minutes lingered innocently around them. In fact, the two walked for what seemed like a mile without saying a word to one another.

"That was…" Sephanie began, her eyes squinting as she thought of a polite yet honest way to finish her sentence.

"I know," Rolland said, the weight of the still-young day weighing upon him with a sense of guilt for taking a life. "It was dumb."

"No," Sephanie said, lifting her free hand and placing it on Rolland's shoulder. "It was brave and instinctual."

Rolland's senses were reawakened by her touch, as he raised his eyes to meet hers. The green sparkle in the windows to her soul shined upon him like a beacon to a better future.

"You've got good instincts, kid," Sephanie said, taking another step closer to Rolland.

"Thanks, I guess," Rolland said, his eyes not meeting hers. Mentally diving into another pool of self-doubt and repeating her 'kid' comment again and again, Rolland was slowly losing hope of ever being of any romantic interest to Sephanie.

In fact, Rolland was so deep into his own thoughts that he did not notice Sephanie move in for the kiss that she planted on his pleasantly surprised lips.

Closing his eyes in sheer passion, the teenager who could control time itself wished for nothing else other than to stop the metaphorical hands of time and make this moment last forever. Like all good things, their lip-lock was broken, but not before some of the most passionate and electric moments in either of their young lives.

Sephanie pulled away, staring longingly at the dumbstruck look on Rolland's face.

Standing there, his eyes still closed from the kiss, Rolland's world felt complete. The adventure, the rivalry, the friendships, and now the girl, were all his. For the first time in his entire life, Rolland Alan Wright felt like he was living the kind of life he had always meant to.

"Not bad for a guy living in his car a week ago," Rolland thought to himself, finally deciding to open his eyes. To his delight, Sephanie was still there.

She turned away from him and sat down on the ground.

"We won't be seeing each other for a while," Sephanie said, playing with a loose stick from the mound of dirt that sat between them.

"Why?" Rolland asked her, sounding like a child on Christmas Eve who had just been informed Santa would be a day late. He crouched down beside her, and she stood up again.

"You'll be going to the Academy to train," Sephanie said, attempting to avoid staring into Rolland's big brown eyes. She worried the sight of them, so like his father's, would change her mind and break her will, so she decided to power through to the end and leave as quickly as possible. "And I have to go away, as well."

"You do? Where? I'll go with you," Rolland said, as if he were already ready for another adventure.

"You can't," Sephanie said, turning to Rolland and resting her hands on top of his. "I have to go alone. It's mandatory for my, uh, power level."

The once bliss-filled expression on Rolland's face turned sour with fresh disappointment. Not knowing what a corny but impressive term like 'power level' might indicate, he decided not to ask and merely nodded his head with somber disappointment.

"Will I see you again when you get back?" Rolland asked, hope shining through his face and finding its mark.

"You know it," Sephanie said before winking at him, turning around, and walking away.

With the day won and all of the various individuals coupling up, Geoffrey decided to go for once last stroll before the Knights' return to Eden. Given his penchant for exploring new places and shifting into new people he met along the way, it was not unheard of for Geoffrey to go wandering off by himself: a habit that Turtledove had been attempting to squash for years.

Knowing this, Geoffrey still decided to take the long way back to the former cave where all the Nabawoo, Freedmen, and Knights were convening: a path filled with shadows and thorns. Though mostly wooded, there was a smell of something foreign in the air, something tempting and intoxicating.

Following it, Geoffrey crossed the barrier that separated the sunlit morning from the overgrown path he embarked upon. It narrowed as he walked, and shadow and vegetation blocked out any remaining sunlight around him. The darkness surrounded Geoffrey.

Calmly, Geoffrey slowed his footsteps, keeping to the dirt path leading to a clearing some hundred yards ahead.

"Geoffrey..." said a voice from the pitch-black darkness before him, spooking the Knight to the very core of his being. In his panic, Geoffrey shifted forms wildly, from a fully-shelled Victor to a somewhat scarier miniature Ballua and back again; the frightened and confused man panicked.

"Be at ease my child," said the voice that didn't seem to be coming from his ears, but from inside of his head. "I mean you no harm."

The darkness formed a figure with a long, black cloak covering a face of white bone and rotting flesh.

"Say nothing, for I have much to tell you of the world," the voice continued, picking up momentum as it hovered closer to the shape shifter. "Then you may go on your way."

Making his way back to the forum where the Knights of Time and Nabawoo met, Rolland couldn't help but let his mind drift. He thought about his parents, his school, and his car. Oh, how he had loved that car.

The mid-morning wind carried a pleasant sense of renewal and promise for the future.

Rolland in particular was nervous with anticipation, especially given that his role in the ordeal was that of navigator. He arrived to find the Dream Phoenix set up, and every one of the Knights' new allies gathered to see them off.

"Just do what comes naturally," Turtledove kept reminding Rolland as the minutes streamed onward until it was time.

Approaching the Dream Phoenix, Rolland concentrated, blocking every thought out of his mind save for opening the time stream. With the snap of his left, then right thumbs against his hands, he raised them together, and smacked the bottom of his left hand against his right palm, all the while pointing his index finger at the Dream Phoenix and focusing his energy directly into it.

The effect was as immediate as it was powerful.

Within milliseconds a gateway identical to the one that brought them there in the first place opened behind the Dream Phoenix, expanding into a ten by ten foot portal filled with the familiar swirling white light.

Rolland recognized it as an entrance into the time stream, and more specifically, Eden. It felt so powerful, reminding him somewhat of another El Dorado that he had held the keys to not too long before. This thought brought a smile to his face, one that Blaisey noticed as she hugged her great-grandson and wished him farewell. Following the long embrace, the two silently looked into each other's eyes, parting ways better people for having met.

"Thank you for all you've done," Blaisey said to Rolland as they broke apart. "I will remember you always."

"And I, you," Rolland replied somberly.

Standing behind his newest protégé, the oldest Knight leaned in to shake Blaisey and Charlton's hands before directing Rolland's attention back to the gateway. "Now lead us to Eden, you must think of Eden."

"Oh, is that all?" Rolland asked sarcastically, rolling his eyes comically for the others to see.

"No, actually," Turtledove said, shoving Rolland into the portal. "You must also go first. Good luck to you all!"

With those words, Turtledove climbed in after Rolland and disappeared from Florida forever.

Tugging on her husband's arm gently, Joan led him down the procession of Nabawoo tribesmen to say their final farewells. Then, with the assistance of the rock formation, they, too, leapt into the rift and vanished.

Next was Victor, who was followed by two of the Freedmen. None of them still wore their hoods. Sorrow for losing their leader filled their faces once again, leaving them in a state not unlike the one Victor had met them in days before. Instead of pointing this out and picking a successor, he decided instead to leave them with a message of hope for the future.

"A long line of great men are coming," Victor said, placing his baseball glove sized hand on Mansa's shoulder. "But they need your help. Get the rest of your people to Haiti. Be free."

After a few handshakes, Victor, too, went through the portal, followed by a somewhat dazed Geoffrey, leaving Tina alone with the Nabawoo.

"Thank you, madam," Enapay said to Tina, carefully pronouncing each syllable as he watched her push the Dream Phoenix to the ledge of the portal before hopping onto it, and falling in.

Her last sight was that of Enapay, Blaisey, and Charlton standing side by side with the remaining Freedmen, and her Nabawoo soldiers. Though Tina knew what history said would befall them, she couldn't help but hope against hope that somehow, someway, they might band together to stop Jackson from taking their homes, and their lives.

Eden - Sunrise

For the good people of Eden, time had gone on unimpeded. All three hours of it.

Crowning itself upon the crimson sunrise as it fell upon Eden's rolling hills, was a pure white beacon that carried the Dream Phoenix and the Knights of Time home. The seven travelers appeared on top of the hillside situated between the Halls of Time and the Blackard Family Orchard.

"Well, that was… fun," Turtledove said, walking briskly in front of the others toward the large front doors that led into the Halls of Time. Behind him walked Joan and Judah, hand in hand, followed by Victor, Geoffrey, Tina, and finally Rolland.

"Yeah, you three strapping lads wouldn't mind fetching the Dream Phoenix from the hill and bringing her to my lab, would you?" Judah said in a matter-of-fact tone to Victor, Geoffrey, and Rolland.

"Actually," Tina said softly. "Can I talk to Rolland for a minute please? Alone?"

Smiling his pearly whites, Victor laughed slightly, motioning toward Geoffrey before heading back outside.

"I think we're heading for bed," Joan said to the others, her eyes never veering from her husband's. They left the room, arms around each other's waists. At least at first.

With a knowing smile Turtledove beamed over at his two remaining pupils, Rolland and Tina, before clasping his hands together and bidding them adieu. This left the two teenagers alone, a fact that took both adolescents a moment to realize.

"Would you maybe like to… talk?" Tina asked Rolland, phrasing the question more like a suggestion.

"Sure," Rolland said, putting his bag down beside him and walking further into the dining hall.

"I just wanted to tell you, back there in the forest. That was…" Tina struggled, her feet shuffling nervously beneath her as she attempted to find the right words.

"Brave?" Rolland interrupted with a raised eyebrow. Based on the look that fell upon Tina's face he immediately wished that he hadn't.

"Dumb," Tina said, turning away from him. "You could have gotten someone hurt, not to mention what would have happened if you had been wrong and had actually killed Jackson."

With all of the bluster that had fallen on Rolland over the past few hours, savoring this piece of humble pie from Tina was almost comforting in its familiarity.

He looked at her fondly. There Tina stood, lecturing Rolland about the merits of his actions, casually letting her hands slide from her waist to her hips. He had seen her do this before, when she was attempting to concentrate on her words.

Finding the gesture too adorable for words, Rolland turned Tina around and pulled her into a close embrace.

Their eyes met. His intense stare, her soft, inviting glance - it was nature in motion.

Deciding to continue her recent streak of seizing the moment, Tina stood on her toes and kissed him. Her hand made its way behind his head, bringing them closer together as he wrapped his arms around her waist and lifted her.

It felt natural, almost effortless, in its simplicity.

The moment was highlighted by the ease in which the two seemed to fit together. Tina melted into Rolland's arms as her lips continued to show him the affection she had felt since first laying eyes on him.

For Rolland, this kiss was special in that it was much different than the one he had shared with Sephanie hours before. This seemed easy and light, happier almost, like a spring day or a cool glass of water.

It was then, with both of them lost in each other's world, that the final player entered the scene.

No sooner had Rolland found himself existing in tandem with another human being for the first time than the front door of the Halls of Time opened with a loud thud.

Tina looked at Rolland with a quizzical expression as they were interrupted by the presence of a man dressed in a strange navy blue uniform Rolland did not recognize. He was older, probably in his mid-fifties from the looks of his sparse but boyish haircut and neatly groomed graying beard.

"Who the hell are you?" the ornately dressed man asked Rolland as he walked further into the room.

"Rolland. And you are?" Rolland asked with obvious indignation to in voice. Tina squeezed his hand tightly.

"Major General Varejao – Council of Eden dictate. I'm here to serve sentencing on whoever caused your little trip back to the 19th century," the man said, taking another step toward Rolland and Tina. His belly jiggled a bit as he walked.

"How do you know about that already?" Tina asked, speaking before she had time to think.

Rolland felt as though he could almost see the look of worry on Tina's face out of the corner of his eye. 'Tina gives away too much,' he thought to himself. She was obviously scared, and he wanted nothing more at the moment than to alleviate that fear.

"Doesn't matter. Look, with Scott Wright dead, there's only one man who could pull that kind of trick off, and he'd have to use Wright's plasma. Where is Doctor Raines?" Varejao demanded, his tone turning downright nasty toward the teenagers.

A smile spread across Rolland's face, and a new spirit filled his soul. If he could vanquish monsters, the grim reaper, and presidents-to-be, he could certainly make this cute girl feel better by taking the blame for something he did anyway. He squeezed Tina's hands not once, not twice, but three times.

Tina gave his hand a squeeze back and smiled at him, blushing slightly. It was the first time a boy had held her hand in public, and the first time she had fallen in love: two moments that would remain with both of them for the rest of their lives.

"Yeah, I'm the one you want," Rolland said with great conviction.

"Rolland!" said Tina, genuinely surprised with Rolland's honesty, and after a moment of thought, horrified at its implications.

"You?" the man known as Varejao asked him cautiously. "How?"

Letting go of Tina's hand, Rolland stood up and crossed the few remaining steps between them until he and Varejao were face to face.

"Easy," Rolland said, looking the man up and down for weapons. "I'm Scott Wright's son."

For a long moment, or maybe even several minutes, Anthony Varejao looked directly into the shining brown eyes of Rolland Wright, perhaps searching for a bluff. When none was to be found, Varejao broke the stare and took a step backward.

"So you have both of their...?" Varejao asked Rolland apprehensively, almost afraid of finishing his own sentence.

"Yep," piped Rolland proudly.

"And your name, again?" Varejao asked, now moving slowly around in a large circle on the far right side of the room.

"Rolland Wright," Rolland said, his confidence boosting him like an adrenaline shot. "Nice to meet you."

Turning his back to them, Varejao stopped his pacing and stood terribly still mere feet from the door. Clicking his heels together, Varejao turned to face them again, a very pleased look upon his face.

"Then that's all I need to hear," said Varejao, his right hand gesturing as it peeked out from beneath his cloak to hit the 'open' button on the wall behind him.

Within seconds the doors opened to reveal both the blinding sunlight of Eden and two dozen shock troops dressed in full battle gear.

Rolland's first instinct was to protect Tina at all costs, but even throwing himself in front of her seemed futile as the troops surrounded them.

Tina, for her part, remained mostly calm as row after row of soldiers poured into the dining hall and elbowed their way into every available free space around her. Throughout it all, she never let go of Rolland's hand.

Varejao looked at them with pity. He realized they were only a couple of kids – but he was determined to bring them in anyway.

Although his vision was obscured by the guards, Rolland saw Turtledove and Joan arrive, elbowing their way past the troops and into the fray at the head of the table.

"What is the meaning of this, Anthony?" Turtledove spat the words at Varejao as three soldiers apprehensively approached him from behind.

"Just following orders, Marcus," Varejao stated callously as he watched his troops circle Rolland and prepare for his capture. "You didn't know anything about this, did you?"

The two men stared at one another for a long moment, neither breathing nor blinking for fear of exposing a weakness the other might exploit. Strategy played out in both of their heads like a chess board, each attempted to prepare for the next three moves that might benefit them and cripple their opponent.

It was Turtledove who spoke first.

"Yes, as a matter of fact. I went with him," Turtledove said confidently. "You should probably arrest me too. But we acted alone, Mr. Wright, and I."

Nearby, six of the shock troops advanced on Rolland and began manhandling him with great force. Although he was willing to go quietly, Rolland took exception to be treated in such a manner and decided to fight back.

Landing a punch to the head of the trooper in front of him, Rolland began to feel a sense of momentum. Smiling broadly, he looked to Turtledove for support only to be bitterly disappointed by the passive old man with his hands being bound behind his back.

"What are you doing?!" Rolland hollered with indignation.

Turtledove merely looked at him, his eyes sad, before saying simply, "Do not resist, Rolland. I assure you that we will soon be free of them again."

Rolland opened his mouth to argue, but the thought seemed silly without Turtledove's support. They had no choice but to comply with Varejao and his troopers. Calculate, and comply.

Tina watched as her new man was cuffed, beaten, and led off with Turtledove out the front door into the harsh light of a day.

"Don't worry," Joan said, wrapping her arm around Tina as she cried. "We'll get them back."

1817 Florida

While her fellow Travelers of Light were making their way to the Dream Phoenix, Sephanie headed back up the hills to the overhang where Puck had fallen an hour previous.

There she waited, while one by one the other Knights of Time made their way through the Dream Phoenix and back to Eden. A gentle wind caressed her cheek as she watched Joan take Judah's hand and walk with him into the chaotic and unpredictable time stream, then Victor and Geoffrey after them, until only Tina was left.

Sephanie thought it a bit off-putting that Tina was lingering around after her goodbyes with the Nabawoo people. Pangs of jealousy and regret filled her as she breathed in and out at a purposeful pace. This anxiety-reducing trick worked for her on occasion, but rarely when it came to other people.

The realization that her feelings for the youngest Wright may be genuine filled Sephanie with a fresh wave of remorse for her actions as she replayed them again in her head.

In the bookstore five days ago, Sephanie had been on strict orders to make visual contact with the boy without being seen. She had failed miserably. She justified it by channeling her loss and sadness for Scott and Taylor to their previously unknown son.

That morning had begun without a hitch, as Sephanie prepared herself by scouting a good, out of the way location with a clear view of the Books Half Price entrance. Assembling her weapon, she took special care to firmly attach the scope to her rifle. Scott had died with some kid's picture in his hand, and if this guy was an imposter or one of the Traveler's spies...

But then the unthinkable happened within the heart of Sephanie Ann Kelly.

As she laid her eyes on Rolland, she was struck by how much he resembled his parents. Having worked alongside them for the better part of five years, she had come to recognize certain features and ticks that they both possessed. There, within the scope of her lens, lay Scott's furrowed brow beneath a widow's peak, and Taylor's brown eyes and wavy blonde hair.

Sephanie sat there a moment, not moving a muscle. She had been so sure, so prepared to take the life of an imposter, that she hadn't given the slightest credence to the thought that perhaps her friends, the people she had spent years getting to know....

'Another lie,' Sephanie thought to herself, as she watched Tina step through the portal.

There was something strange about Rolland Wright, but for the life of Sephanie she could not yet figure out what. He was cute, no doubt about that, but his attraction lay not in any physical distinction. It was the acknowledgement and respect the Nabawoo had given him, as if he actually meant something to them, as if this wasn't just another mission, one of hundreds. Then she realized, for Rolland it wasn't.

It wasn't because it was his first, or even because he wasn't yet properly trained. It was special for him, because he genuinely cared about more than just the mission, or the bottom line. He cared about the people, the circumstances, and the climate that he left behind.

Genuinely bothered by this, Sephanie watched as the Nabawoo and Freemen went their separate ways, waited nearly an hour, and then proceeded down toward the cave where she went to work.

Detonator in hand, Sephanie clicked the tiny silver button on the side of the small bomb before laying it next to the cave's blocked off entrance and stepping back.

The blast was small, but enough for Sephanie to remove the remaining rubble with nothing more than her hands. After a few minutes, she heard a familiar coughing that she knew belonged to the 19th century version of Vilthe.

"Help, help me!" Vilthe shouted to her through the rocks.

Sephanie was unfazed, focusing her mind instead on the Wright boy and the confusing feeling she had developed for him as she kept digging an opening for Vilthe to escape.

Finally, when the last stone was clear and Vilthe had wiggled his way out and into the mid afternoon sun, Sephanie acknowledged him directly.

"You are free now," Sephanie said, bowing low in front of the tattered man in the sweater vest before straightening up and walking away.

"But, but why?" Vilthe asked, a mixture of confusion and limestone dust overwhelming him.

"You know why," Sephanie stated in a cold, emotionless voice without stopping. "We all have our orders. See to it that you carry out your own."

The ominous warning from the brunette teenager seemed to be a clear enough message, as when Sephanie turned around, Vilthe was gone.

She smiled; everything was going according to plan.

511

Sephanie walked back to the cave, crouched down, and entered it like she had days before. Onward she crawled, squirming and sucking in her stomach at every turn until she was finally face to face with the fountains again.

As she suspected, the fountain that had previously contained the healing water was half destroyed, the spring itself no longer flowing.

The other fountain however, functioned perfectly, though not in the way that Rolland and Judah had suspected when they were here days ago.

"Kid was wrong about that," Sephanie said aloud to herself, the echo of her voice reverberating throughout the chamber as she sat on the fountain's ledge and examined at its crude design. Running her hand along the fountains edge, Sephanie found a triangle engraved into the stone. Brushing off the dirt, she then placed her index finger into the center of the triangle, causing the entire rim of the fountain to glow and vibrate.

Sephanie stood up, took a step back, and watched as the fountain sunk into the ground, opening a gateway into another world, another land, that was not at all like Eden.

Instead of a white, jettisoning portal, before her stood a dark blue and purple vortex of terror.

With a deep breath, Sephanie closed her eyes and jumped in.

Tartarus (Underworld)

In much the same manner that the gateways of light illuminate the path toward Eden, a similar system of passages work for a darker, more sinister world below. Known by many names throughout recorded civilization, the dark underbelly of the Earth is simply called Tartarus to those who are unfortunate enough to call her home.

Opening her eyes, Sephanie found herself in a familiar, dimly lit hallway. The stone floors echoed under her feet as she walked into the main corridor of the welcome building.

Piles of corpses and bags of refuge lined the outer banks of what passed for streets and greeted Sephanie with the smells of rotting flesh and neglected society. She ignored it and went about her way. Headed due south, she knew the consequences of being late.

As she went further along, the atmosphere around her grew thicker, dimmer, increasingly different to the world above. The darkness brought Sephanie the familiarity of childhood. Each time she returned to this place she was reminded of the days when she went without love, without hope, without anyone at all to comfort her. Then, he came...

Entering the castle gate with a shaking hand, Sephanie made her way up the cobblestone steps leading to the front door and the man waiting for her. His voice greeted her long before his eerie presence could made itself known.

"Persephone..." the horrifically deformed figure hissed, the tip of his half frostbitten nose peeking out from the long, black cowl. The figure took a few measured steps forward, extending its arms outward toward Sephanie in a paternal manner.

Without flinching, Sephanie took the left hand and wrapped it around her hips before gripping the cold, vacant frame of the barely corporeal figure.

As they embraced, the translucent, rotting flesh covering the brittle, boney fingers caressing the teenager's face found their way to her lips, parting them slightly.

For Sephanie, the ties that bound her to the man some knew as Ed Vilthe and others knew as the Grim Reaper or The Devil, went beyond mere familial bonds. He was her trainer, her mentor, her friend. Until Scott found her as a child, Vilthe was all that Sephanie had known. She had been helpless.

Sephanie no longer felt the same helplessness, for she had given those feelings up nearly a decade ago. Long was she past grieving for things that would never be, not when in the presence of an immortal being like Vilthe.

"It's good to see you, husband," Sephanie said, her eyes watering.

"And you, my wife," the walking remains that were Vilthe hissed to his teenage bride, never once taking notice of the tears that ran down her cheeks.

The End

Historians Message Part III

As you can see, young Rolland Wright's first steps on his journey to becoming Father Time did not happen without incident. In saving the life of General Andrew Jackson, Rolland set into motion a series of events that would lead to a period of American culture and democracy known as the 'Jacksonian Era'.

But please, don't let an old Historian like me bore you with such details. Not when there are much more relevant and juicier topics to cover.

Sephanie's treachery knows no bounds, it seems, as she plays both sides to perfection. Will she slip up, revealing her true nature to someone close to her? Or will her schemes come full circle, winning the eternal war between Eden and Vilthe for one side or the other? What of Tina? Or Victor, Judah, or Joan?

It is, alas, time to bring Volume One of the Tale of Time to a close.

Fear not though, faithful reader, as Rolland and the rest of the Knights of Time will return in Volume Two of our story.

The action continues as Rolland Wright and Marcus Turtledove are placed on trial, charged with attempting to manipulate the time stream to their own gain. Will Rolland be exonerated in time to pursue his education at The Academy of Light? Or will Council of Light member Anthony Varejao make good on his promise to have them both hanged for their crimes?

The Knights of Time avoided disaster in Volume One, but like all good things, their luck will come to an end and one of our beloved Knights will lose their life at the hands of an assassin. Yet not all is grim, as a new Knight will rise up and accept the call to become one of history's greatest heroes.

But can even the bravest souls survive the betrayal of one of their own? Find out where Sephanie's sympathies TRULY lie in our next adventure...

Time is Relative for Wavering Loyalties

Made in the USA
Charleston, SC
25 October 2012